Tabikat

Harriet Redfern

Published by Ambessa Publishing

First Edition 2016
Second Edition 2018

A CIP catalogue record for this title is available from the British Library.

By the same author
Katseye, 2018

ISBN-13: 978-1-9996348-0-3

Prologue

0800
Cheltenian News Radio, Traffic News

There are major delays following the closure of the Gloucester-bound carriageway of the A40 on the west side of Cheltenham, opposite GCHQ. Traffic is queuing back into the Lansdown Road and Princess Elizabeth Way.

Traffic coming into Cheltenham is also affected and both the Benhall Roundabout and the Arle Court Roundabout are gridlocked.

Traffic is already heavy in the area following the end of the Cheltenham Festival yesterday.

There is no information on when the road will re-open. Avoid the area if you can.

0830
Cheltenian News Radio, News

We are getting reports of a body discovered alongside the A40 outside GCHQ. Police have closed off the westbound carriageway, causing major traffic delays in the area.

There is no information yet on the identity of the dead person. It is understood that the body was discovered by members of the public who were waiting for the 94 bus to Gloucester. A witness, who did not wish to be named, told our reporter at the scene, "The body was hidden in the bushes. We thought it was a pile of old clothes someone had dumped there. A woman walked by us with a dog and the dog started barking at it and then we saw what it was. It was awful."

The police have said that they will be releasing a statement within the next half hour.

0835
BBC Breakfast

Natalie Holmes, Presenter

We have some breaking news. Reports are coming in of the discovery of a body on the road outside government listening station GCHQ in Cheltenham. Max Bennett of BBC West is at the scene. Max, what can you tell us?

Max Bennett, Reporter

Hello, Natalie. Well, we have very little information at the moment. As you can see, the road behind me is closed off and police are keeping everyone well away from the scene. The location is on a very busy road, the A40, right outside the headquarters of GCHQ.

Traffic would normally be lighter on a Saturday with fewer people travelling to work than during the week. But today is the day after Gold Cup day, the final event of the Cheltenham Festival at Cheltenham racecourse. So, there are a lot of people on their way home after staying in Cheltenham overnight.

Those people who are arriving for work at GCHQ have had difficulty getting access to the car park, as the two roundabouts at either end of this stretch of road are completely at a standstill. People going in and out of Cheltenham itself are also being subject to severe delays.

What we know so far is that the body was discovered by people who were waiting for the bus here earlier this morning. The bus stop is over there, in a layby alongside the dual carriageway. The body seems to have been hidden in the bushes alongside the footpath. It is not clear how long the body has been there.

The local radio station reported that a woman walking by with a dog had noticed it first. Up until then, it had looked like a pile of old clothes.

Natalie

Do we know anything at all about the identity of the body, Max? Is it a man or a woman, for instance? And is there a connection with GCHQ?

Max

As I said, Natalie, there is little to go on at the moment. We don't even know whether it is a man or a woman. Given the location of the body, we have to ask the question as to whether it has any connection with GCHQ. There are about five and a half thousand people employed there, all civil servants, of course. There has been no statement from GCHQ as to whether anyone has unexpectedly failed to turn up for work. But, given the traffic chaos here, there are probably lots of people who have been unable to reach their workplace this morning.

Natalie

But could it be someone trying to enter GCHQ who should not be there?

Max

Natalie, we just don't know at the moment.

We understand that the body was discovered well off the road, so it does not look like a hit and run accident.

We have been told that the police are going to release a statement sometime in the next half an hour. So we should know more then.

Natalie

Thanks for that, Max. We'll come back to you later.

That was Max Bennett, in Cheltenham, outside GCHQ.

0910
Gloucestershire Constabulary Official Statement

A body has been recovered this morning from undergrowth beside a layby on the A40 close to the Benhall roundabout on the west side of Cheltenham. It was discovered by a member of the public at about 0700 this morning.

The body is of a male aged between 30 and 50 years. Forensic tests are currently being carried out. At this stage, the death is being treated as unexplained.

Anyone with information, or who knows of someone fitting this description who is missing from home, please contact Gloucestershire Police in Cheltenham or any local police station.

0912
BBC Breakfast

Natalie

We have just heard that very brief statement from the police in Gloucestershire. Max, can you tell us any more?

Max

Well, the statement was issued in writing, Natalie, and the police are not saying any more at the moment. We are waiting to hear whether they intend to hold a press conference later this morning.

Natalie

Does that mean they think the death is suspicious, Max?

Max

As the statement says, Natalie, they are just treating the death is unexplained at the moment. But a body lying by the road in undergrowth does sound suspicious, especially near to such an important facility as GCHQ. So I think we will be hearing more, even if it is just to allay the concerns this event has created.

Natalie

Thanks Max.

BBC Breakfast will be off air shortly, but you can keep in touch with this story on the BBC news website or on BBC News.

1000
BBC News

Newsreader

Police are carrying out a fingertip search of undergrowth close to a bus stop on the A40 close to GCHQ in Cheltenham, where the body of an unidentified man was found by a member of the public earlier this morning.

Gloucestershire Constabulary has issued a statement, describing the death as unexplained. The results of forensic tests are awaited.

Given the proximity of the location to GCHQ, there are inevitably questions as to whether the incident is connected to the work of the government listening post. A spokeswoman for GCHQ has confirmed that all their staff are accounted for but declined to make any further comment.

We understand that a further police statement is due to be made at midday, and we will bring that to you – and indeed any other information – as soon as we have it.

1030
Cheltenian News Radio, News

We are still waiting for more information about the body discovered by a member of the public along the A40 near GCHQ this morning. In a statement released earlier, police have said that the body is that of a man aged between 30 and 50, and that they are treating the death as unexplained. They are asking for any information about people in the local area who may have gone missing.

A local garage owner, who did not want to be named, told our reporters that drug dealers sometimes operate in the area. A resident on the nearby Benhall estate said they had heard screaming the previous evening, but had assumed that it was just teenagers messing about.

1100
Cheltenian News Radio, Traffic News

Traffic on the A40 to the west of Cheltenham is starting to return to normal now, following a road closure earlier today.

A layby on the westbound carriageway remains cordoned off by the police and the bus stop there has been suspended.

1200
Gloucestershire Constabulary Official Statement

An initial forensic examination has been completed on a body discovered this morning. The body was found in undergrowth by a bus stop on the westbound carriageway of the A40 close to the Benhall roundabout in Cheltenham. A fingertip search of the area has also been completed.

We can confirm that the body is of a male aged between 30 and 40 years. The cause of death was a blunt force trauma to the head and there is evidence of attempted strangulation. The body had also suffered injury from being dragged, possibly under a vehicle. It is not clear at present whether these injuries happened before or after death occurred. Further forensic tests should establish this.

The findings of the fingertip search include some drug related items and a handgun. The fingerprints on the handgun match those of the body. There is no evidence that the gun has been fired nor has the body sustained any gunshot injuries.

The case is being treated as murder. Identification of the deceased man is now a priority.

The officer in charge of the case is Inspector Christopher Briggs of Gloucestershire Constabulary. Any information received will be treated in the strictest confidence.

Six Months Earlier

1

On an early October Sunday, James Sampfield Peveril, racehorse trainer and member of the rural establishment, stood impatiently outside the yard office door. He was looking at a still mass of opaque grey cloud.

Thick dampness hung dull in the surrounding air. The lane leading into the yard appeared to have been stuffed with a mass of wet cobwebs. The smart wooden posts, which marked the end of the short approach leading from the road beyond, emerged occasionally through the murk, only to disappear as the clinging moisture submerged them once again.

The lost sounds of sheep could be heard from the paddock behind the dense screen. The thorny hedge separating them from the yard was adorned with the ghostly skeins of their white wool, each one heavily draped with individually crafted liquid droplets of shivering dew. It was as if some unseen elves were planning a Halloween party.

The silence was complete and impenetrable. The laden air pressed down, heavy against the ground, a sodden cloud of fog. It was warm for the time of year but everything was, and felt, deathly still.

Six horses were waiting, tacked up and with their riders beside them, within twenty feet of where James Sampfield Peveril was standing. A further eight remained in the loose boxes which surrounded the neat L shaped yard built of a warm yellow stone, now made dull by the grey light. He could hear the horses snuffling and shifting behind the cloying screen which engulfed the buildings.

The horses and riders were ready to go out for their morning training. But, until the mist lifted, they were held in the yard. The track at the back of the stable block led up to higher ground, but someone needed to tell the trainer whether that ground was clear enough to take the horses out without fear of injury in the dim conditions. So, someone was out there now, checking up.

Then they would go out, following the unvarying routine of the training day, sending the horses up the hill above the yard and the extensive estate, their breath merging with the foggy air, their limbs working the ground beneath their hooves, their riders pushing them upwards towards the summit. From the top there would usually be glorious views of the sea.

James Sampfield Peveril felt both oppressed and exhilarated by the atmosphere around him. It seemed like a shell which was about to break. The sun was hovering above the gloom, there was a blue sky waiting to appear, and he knew that there were red, gold and copper leaves on the trees lining the gallops, all of which would soon emerge in faultless and shining glory once the mist began to disperse.

The mist, though, was not yet dispersing, and it was getting late. The sun had been up for two hours and was making no impression on the wet world below.

A grey horse suddenly loomed out of the gloom on his left side. He had hardly heard its footfall, so dense and thick was the air. Its rider, bundled up in an aged waxed jacket, signalled to him as she brought the horse to a halt.

"It's clear on top, Mr Sampfield," she said.

"Good news, Sadie," he responded, "Can we get the ride out now?"

"I should say so, Mr Sampfield," the rider replied.

As if by magic, the six riders and horses began to emerge from the ghostly atmosphere of the yard, all ready to ride out, once the signal to move was given.

James Sampfield Peveril was about to give the signal when something unexpected happened.

Sadie Shinkins' dappled horse shifted suddenly beneath her and emitted an alarmed whinny. The other horses, following suit, clattered about in the gloom of the yard, whilst their grooms and riders soothed and held them, wondering what had caused the sudden commotion.

The muffled throb of a car engine could be heard floating somewhere in the mist. The horses had heard and felt it first.

Sadie briskly assembled the string behind her as the engine sound came gradually closer. Aside from her grey mount, there were now an additional six horses, strong bay and brown hunters, smartly presented in well-polished leather tack, topped by skinny teenaged riders. They clustered together in the centre of the yard, waiting for the head groom's directions.

Sadie brought her grey mount around as if on a small turntable on the yard floor.

"Get behind me, Curlew and Ranger first, Rooker at the back," she shouted, and the creatures fell obediently into line behind the grey horse's rump.

"We're ready to go, Mr Sampfield," called Sadie.

Just then, the car engine sound rose to a crescendo, and a dark green four wheel drive vehicle emerged from between the gateposts. It stopped suddenly in the yard entrance.

The horses did not like the unexpected appearance of the noisy machine. They skirted sideways and glared at it from the corners of their wide brown eyes.

James Sampfield Peveril had been about to get onto his own horse, which was tacked up and waiting for him, to join the back of the ride. There had been no reason to expect anyone or anything to arrive in the yard.

As James Sampfield Peveril stepped forward towards the vehicle, whilst his staff and horses waited impatiently in the mist for the word to get the ride moving, the driver's door opened. A tall man got out and stood facing them all.

"Hello, Sam," the stranger said, "Sorry to burst in on you like this, old man. It's been a long time."

Sadie and the stable staff were taken by surprise. People who called their employer Sam were few and far between. They waited to see what he would do, the horses shifting impatiently beneath them.

James Sampfield Peveril did nothing. He stared at the newcomer in silence for several seconds.

"Sam," repeated the visitor, "I really would appreciate a talk. If you can spare the time, that is," he added, suddenly appearing to acknowledge the significance of the assembled horses.

"Mr Sampfield," intervened Sadie, as her grey horse rattled and pulled at its bit crossly, "What do you want us to do? Are you coming out?"

"I'm afraid I will have to deal with this," responded James Sampfield Peveril, "Please take the ride, Sadie. Nothing special, just the usual routine. Put Curlew at the front when you get up to the top gallop. Don't let any of the others pass him. Kye can untack Caladesi, don't worry. I'll take him out later."

Sadie was surprised, but the sudden responsibility she had been assigned was an opportunity not to be wasted.

"Walk on!" she called, without hesitation, and the string moved quickly out of the back exit of the yard and was swallowed up within seconds by the fog, the sound of the hooves cut off suddenly as if covered by a thick blanket.

James Sampfield Peveril had still said not a word to the new arrival, who continued to wait by his car, expectantly.

A wiry young man in well worn riding gear emerged from the yard office. He had followed every word of the exchange and had watched the ride depart up the hill behind.

"I can take Caladesi up, if you like, Mr Sampfield," he offered.

"No, thank you, Kye," his employer replied, "I'd like to ride out myself later. Would you be so kind as to untack him for now and give him his feed?"

"Yes, Mr Sampfield," responded Kye. He disappeared into the gloom which still surrounded the boxes and could be heard speaking soothingly to the invisible horse, as though he feared it would be upset not to be joining its stablemates on the now departed ride.

James Sampfield Peveril turned to the man by the car.

"You had better come up to the house, Frank," he said, tonelessly.

Kye watched the two men disappear towards the big house. The fog was at last beginning to disperse a little, and he could see their backs as they followed the path from the open end of the yard towards the old building which was slowly emerging in all its warm grandeur from its grey shroud. They walked in single file, saying nothing, James Sampfield Peveril at the front, the stranger walking silently behind.

"This is a piece of shit, Cal," said Kye to the horse, which ignored him, shaking its head disapprovingly as its bridle was removed and the bit dropped away from its mouth.

James Sampfield Peveril, or Sam as he had now become, was thinking much the same thing. He had not seen Frank Stanley more than a few times since they had both left school more than thirty years ago. What the hell was he doing turning up like this unannounced? Especially, he added savagely to himself, after all the problems there had been.

The path from the yard led to the boot room, which was temporarily empty of its usual array of boots and jackets, all of which were being worn by the work riders now making their way up to the top gallops.

Through the boot room was the kitchen door, a heavy wooden affair with metalled studs and a paned window made up of coloured glass. Sam pushed it open.

A young woman with brown hair scraped back into a pony tail turned towards him as he entered, her face expressing surprise.

"Mr Sampfield?" she said, "I thought you were out with first lot. Is something wrong?"

Sam began to remove his jacket and the woman stepped forward to take it from him, looking questioningly at the unfamiliar figure which followed Sam into the kitchen.

"No, there's nothing wrong, Kelly," Sam reassured her, "This is an old friend of mine, Mr Stanley. He will be joining me for coffee."

"Me and Lewis hasn't sorted the breakfast things," Kelly sounded slightly panic stricken.

"That's not a problem, Kelly," Sam reassured her, "We can go into the Music Room. Lewis can bring the coffee in there."

"There's no fire in there yet," Kelly told him.

"We don't need a fire, thank you, Kelly," Sam told her, "Coffee on its own will be all that is required."

With that, Sam walked round the large square pine table in the centre of the kitchen and crossed the empty hall beyond the door.

Kelly offered to take Mr Stanley's coat and the brown trilby hat which he had removed on entering the house, but he held up a hand in a gesture of decline.

"I'll not be staying long," he told her.

The two men entered a door further down the hall, and it shut with a dull thump behind them.

Kelly's husband, Lewis, emerged from the scullery beside the kitchen, carrying a tray laden with crockery.

"What's going on then?" he asked, "I heard Mr Sampfield's voice. Shouldn't he be out with Sadie?"

"He's gone in the Music Room," replied Kelly, "He's got someone with him. They want coffee taken in."

"Fine," said Lewis, depositing the tray onto the kitchen table, "I'll go in with it. Who's with him, then?"

"I dunno," Kelly responded, "Never seen him before. Mr Sampfield said he was an old friend."

"Must be a very old and out of date friend if we haven't seen him before," commented Lewis.

"Well, Mr Sampfield might usually see him somewhere else," ventured Kelly, "Like his place, maybe."

"Bet your mum would know," suggested Lewis.

Kelly's mum, who was also, as it happened, Sadie's mum, had been the housekeeper at Sampfield Grange until her retirement three years earlier. Lewis's grandfather had once been the butler, in the days when the Grange had employed someone in such a position. Lewis's father had been head gardener. Staff who worked for the Sampfields kept the jobs in the family. The ancestry of the servants was almost as consistent and well documented as that of their employer.

Nowadays, there were only two staff employed full time at the Grange. The family had once been served by a team of fifteen individuals, including two gardeners, and four full time stable staff. But now that only Mr Sampfield lived at the Grange, Kelly and Lewis looked after the big house, whilst Sadie and the recently employed Kye looked after the horses. Gardeners and work riders came in from the local area, operating under the directions of Lewis,

Kelly and Sadie. With the exception of the running of Sam's office and related financial administration, for which specialist knowledge was required, there was not a part of the operation of the house and stables in which these three individuals did not have a hand. Their control was absolute and they intended to keep it that way.

Lewis and Kelly lived in the old house, whilst Sadie and Kye occupied a cottage beyond the stable yard. A chauffeur's flat above the garage was also available, but had remained unoccupied since Mr Sampfield had decided, in the face of some opposition from Lewis, who thought his brother might make a good chauffeur, that he preferred to drive himself. A smart green Range Rover and a black Audi sports car occupied the garage, but the flat above them remained shut and unused.

Kelly pulled out a mobile phone and selected Mum from the contacts list. Lewis busied himself making the coffee, listening as Kelly told her mother about Mr Stanley and received a stream of information in reply.

"Well, then?" he asked as Kelly cut off the call with a final, "Thanks, Mum. See you later."

Kelly was pleased with what she had found out.

"Mr Stanley was at school with Mr Sampfield," she said, "Mr Stanley – Frank his name is – used to come here during the school holidays and Mr Sampfield used sometimes to go and stay with him. Mr Stanley's family took him to America with them once, Mum said. This was before old Mr Sampfield died and our Mr Sampfield left school and came home to be here at the Grange and take charge of the horses. Mum didn't see much of Mr Stanley after that. She thinks Mr Stanley went to be an officer in the Army, you know, at Sandhurst."

Kelly stopped for breath.

"Hmm," grunted Lewis, "Weird he should turn up again after all these years."

"Mum said that," agreed Kelly, "She said something happened, and old Mrs Sampfield took against Mr Stanley. So he didn't come here again, although she thinks Mr Sampfield sometimes met him in London when he went there."

That seemed to be as much information as was likely to be immediately available, so Lewis re-laid the tray and carried the coffee jug and associated items towards the Music Room door. He knocked and, at the sound of Mr Sampfield's answering voice, went into the room.

The Music Room was so called because it housed an impressive grand piano, a Bechstein, which nobody except the piano tuner, on his six monthly visits, ever played. Rumour had it that the ancient Mrs Evelyne Peveril, who represented the one fault in the Sampfield male line, had acquired it along with the Peveril name. The family had been simply Sampfield until that time, but Miss Evelyne Sampfield, the eldest of three unexpected Sampfield daughters, had been obliged to add a Peveril into the family name in order to preserve the Sampfield designation. The Peveril family were not keen to have their own name suppressed, particularly given that they were contributing to the continuation of the Sampfield line. So the two names were henceforth used together. Except by the servants, that was, who insisted on continuing to use the name Sampfield alone, as if nothing had changed.

All this history was, of course, water long passed under the bridge, and the Sampfield line had continued unbroken until it reached the present Mr Sampfield. And stopped.

The present Mr Sampfield, Lewis saw, was standing looking out of the window, from which little of the usual view was visible owing to the continuing presence of the fog. The mysterious Mr Stanley was sitting in an armchair by the woodburner in the chimney, which, as Kelly had pointed out, remained unlit. They were not conversing and were silent as Lewis brought the tray into the room.

"I'll put the coffee on the table, Mr Sampfield," Lewis said, "Do you want me to pour it?" he added hopefully, thinking this might prolong his stay and provide him with some clues as to what Mr Stanley's business might be.

"We'll deal with it, thank you, Lewis," replied James Sampfield Peveril.

So Lewis had no choice but to leave the tray and return to the kitchen, where Kelly remained in a state of scarcely contained excitement.

"Nothing," said Lewis, in response to her questioning look, "They never said a word."

"I'll do some phoning round," said Kelly.

2

James Sampfield Peveril was, for the present at least, the last of the Sampfield bloodline. Forty five years old, he remained unmarried and lived alone in the ancestral home, Sampfield Grange, attended only by his staff, and giving his attention almost exclusively to his horses.

Most of the horses were his own, but a few were sent to him by their owners for training. In one sense, James Sampfield Peveril was an unambitious trainer, having little need to earn a name and a living for himself, but a highly ambitious one in wanting to get the best possible results out of the horses in his charge. Most of his string were pointers, an area of competition in which he felt totally at home, but he had not infrequently trained horses which competed in Listed and even Graded hurdle and steeplechase races at more prestigious racecourses.

James Sampfield Peveril tended to confine his activity to the South West of the country, so his horses had been seen at the racecourses of Wincanton, Exeter, Taunton and Newton Abbott, but rarely further afield. Cheltenham he considered a bit of a stretch, in terms of status rather than distance, although he often attended the meetings there at the invitation of those other trainers who had valued his freely given input to the training of the horses for which they had responsibility.

Fellow trainers referred to him by the nickname Sam, as he had told them to do, saying this his full name was far too long to bother with. He was generous with his time and advice, as did not regard himself as in competition with any of these men and women, whom he saw as colleagues engaged in a similar line of work to himself, pursuing excellence and success in the animals whose development they oversaw.

Sam had worked with horses ever since he could walk. The early months of his life in his mother's womb had been spent mostly on the back of a horse until his presence had become sufficiently noticeable that the expectant parent had been obliged to continue her association with her horses solely from the ground. Old Mrs Sampfield had been a well known event rider in her youth, and was not going to allow pregnancy to get in the way of her eventing career nor that of her horses.

Sam's father had appeared to be set on the traditional family path, on the way along which he would marry someone of suitable status from the local county community and, with her, produce the next Sampfield heir. Richard Sampfield would have done just that, had he not been introduced, at a prestigious three day event meeting, to an attractive Australian rider. The introduction had progressed, much to the chagrin of the various eligible brides who had been lined up for Richard, into a quick romance which had ended in an equally quick marriage, partly provoked by the need to prevent Geraldine Elliot returning with her horses to her native Queensland.

The opprobrium felt initially towards the new Mrs Sampfield had been dissipated to some extent by the revelation that her family was extremely wealthy. Indeed, they appeared to own half of Queensland. Geraldine herself, who for some reason was normally known as Raldi, had been brought up on a vast cattle station along with her two sisters and the large gang of children who were the offspring of the many employees of her father. It was only the most disaffected of Richard's potential brides who was heard to observe that nevertheless the new Mrs Sampfield's ancestors must have made their first journey to Australia with a ball and chain around their ankles.

Once established at Sampfield Grange with her horses, Raldi continued her eventing career uninterrupted other than by the arrival of her first and only child. Her husband too continued with his occupation of training pointers, and Sam grew up in a contented and comfortable household where horses were the centre of all the attention. By the age of seven, he knew more about horses and their training, both for eventing and for racing, than most adults in the business.

There had been, however, one fly in the ointment. Raldi had seen no need to educate her son in anything other than the way she herself had been educated, and assumed that it would be satisfactory to employ a schoolteacher to tutor her son for a few hours a week at home, after which the family could be out working with the horses together. But on this, she and her husband disagreed. So, at the age of seven, Sam was sent away to boarding school.

The school was not far away from the Sampfield estate and Sam was assured that he would be able to come home each weekend to see the horses and to ride out with his mother or to accompany her to events.

It was strange, then, to Sam to find himself one unwelcome morning in a pleasant classroom with twelve other boys. They were overseen by a kindly young teacher who had asked each of them to write their names on the front cover of the new exercise books which had been given to them.

Sam had grasped his pencil with a feeling of trepidation. His name was very long and writing it down represented a major challenge. In fact, writing anything at all was something he found difficult. The letters seemed to dance and shift before his eyes, and he could not see their patterns and work them into the sounds which his home tutor had told him could be found from the symbols before him.

He started carefully, writing J A and M, the three letters of his given name. Fortunately, James was his only given name, his Australian mother having insisted that having two surnames meant that a second given name was unnecessary. But, as he looked at the paper before him, he was not sure that he had actually written J A and M. The J looked strange, like something out of the next part of his name, perhaps the S. He felt flummoxed, looking at what he had written, and a feeling of panic rose in his chest.

The helpful teacher seemed to have noticed his confusion and came over to stand by him.

"Now, young man," she said, "How are you getting on? Do you know how to spell your name? Shall I help you?"

"My name is James Sampfield Peveril," Sam told her.

"That is a very long name," said the teacher, "What letters have you written so far?"

As Sam struggled to decipher the shifting symbols before his eyes, another boy sitting at the next desk, suddenly spoke up.

"His usual name is Sam, Miss," he said, "His real name is so long that it won't fit on the book, so he always writes Sam instead."

"Is that right, James?" asked the teacher, "I think I can see that you have written Sam here, although the S could be a bit tidier."

"Yes, my name is Sam," James Sampfield Peveril replied, with relief, and, so, from then on, it was.

The teacher moved away and the newly named Sam looked at the boy beside him. He had dark hair and sharp blue eyes set in a pale, oval face. Sam felt his chest contract.

"Hello," said the boy, "I saved your bacon there, didn't I? My name's Francis Stanley. You can call me Frank if you like."

"Frank, that's a good name," said Sam, simply, and at that very moment he fell hopelessly and completely in love with Frank Stanley.

Sam and Frank from that day became inseparable. The teacher was not so gullible as Frank had perhaps thought, and quickly recognised not only that Sam's unconventional education had left him with a level of literacy which was lower than would be expected for a child of his age, but that he might also have a learning disability. She suspected dyslexia, and subsequent tests, administered under the guise of helping Sam catch up, proved that she was right.

Fortunately for Sam, his school was a sensible and caring establishment, and the help he needed to learn to read in a way that his brain could accommodate was quickly provided. His schoolfellows became used to the fact that reading and writing tasks were set in a different way for Sam, an arrangement which was explained as being because Sam learned things in a different way. This was somehow attributed to the fact that his mother was Australian, which, as Frank told everyone, meant that Sam saw things upside down.

Sam, standing in the Sampfield Grange Music Room almost forty years later, felt a twinge of sadness at this memory. It was not a bad description of the problem, although the reasoning left something to be desired.

"Sam," Frank Stanley addressed him for the first time since they entered the room, "I need you to do something for me."

Sam turned around for the first time, and looked at his erstwhile schoolfriend. Before him was a man of six feet in height, smartly dressed, his coat and hat slung over the arm of his chair. His glossy black hair was now streaked with dull grey.

"Frank," he said, simply, "Why did you never get in touch?"

"You know why," Frank responded, firmly, "Your mother thought our relationship would upset your father. You needed to get married and continue the family line."

"I know that, dear God, I certainly do know that," responded Sam, heatedly, "But surely you didn't just have to walk away so finally. And then to refuse to speak to me when we met in London those couple of times – it didn't have to be like that."

"Sam, it did, you know it did," replied Frank, firmly, "It was never going to be accepted. I know your mother didn't do it for herself. But you had responsibilities to your family, your staff, for God's sake. Perhaps now it would be different. But not then."

Sam remembered his mother's words, spoken on the evening of the day when she had found the teenaged Sam and Frank curled up against each other in one of the Grange's bedrooms, their clothes strewn across the floor, the two of them breathing the summer air and sleeping contentedly. The two boys had always looked beautiful together, like a Renaissance painting of youth at its best. Sam, with his shaggy blond hair and deep brown eyes, Frank, with sharp azure eyes and a black mane, were an ideal couple.

Raldi had a relaxed view about physical relationships, especially amongst young people, having seen a lot of unconventional examples during her upbringing on the cattle station. Her argument against the relationship between Sam and Frank had been related solely to their responsibilities and duties to their respective families.

Dragging them both from their contented sleep, she had summoned them to her bedroom, the one place in which the servants were unlikely to overhear their conversation. Her instructions were devastating. The relationship must cease completely and immediately. The two young lovers had been shaken to the core by her words, and Frank had been banished from Sampfield Grange from that day.

No argument from Sam was made or expected to be made. Like the horses, he accepted his mother's directions. On their many rides over the hills together, she explained her reasons, and the need for his father to remain in ignorance of the situation. She told him that she would ensure a supply of suitable female friends and that perhaps one of them would become as special to him as Frank.

Raldi did everything she could to make her son's position bearable. But, he ached to the very depths of his soul, and a hard shell slowly began to form over his heart. Not that he did not make attempts to contact Frank, but these were in vain. Frank went to Sandhurst and was unreachable. Then he went to Iran, Afghanistan and to other even more remote and distant places, and in this way passed beyond Sam's limited horizons. So Sam closed down and focused his love on the horses.

Raldi's plan to bring her son back onto his intended course in life backfired spectacularly, other than in one respect. Richard Sampfield died without ever knowing that his son was a homosexual. But because Sam was destined to be loyal only to his first love, Raldi's action inevitably condemned her son to a lonely life. The many young women who accompanied him to social events around the county and further afield found him polite, attentive, amusing, and aloof. None of them could fault him for courtesy and eligibility.

Many of the young women would have happily settled for these limitations in an otherwise highly suitable husband, but, to Sam, the thought of sharing his bed with any of these respectable girls was unacceptable. He knew it was dishonest and that he could never pretend to regard them as anything other than kind and loving friends.

Frank, for his part, also took Raldi's directions seriously. His own family knew nothing of what had happened, so his progression through Sandhurst and an Army career scarcely deviated from their plans for him, although his two failed marriages and their lack of progeny subsequently became a source of great sadness to his mother.

Over the course of the next quarter century, the two men grew older and more successful on their respective paths in life. Outwardly high achievers, inwardly unfulfilled, they had remained apart. Until now.

The constriction in Sam's throat was so great that he could hardly speak. He was still angry with Frank at what he saw as a betrayal, and the memory of his teenage emotion sprang up raw and acid in his soul. He was conscious that Frank was speaking and forced himself to concentrate on his words.

"There are more important things than you and me," Frank was saying, "I am asking you to help me now with one of those. There is no-one else who can do this for me."

"Please tell me," responded Sam, tonelessly, and sat down in the nearest chair.

Sensing a slight relief in the tension, Frank asked, "Shall I pour us some coffee?"

"Of course, please help yourself," replied Sam.

Frank moved over to the tray which Lewis had left for them. He poured coffee into the two china cups and handed one, on its saucer, to Sam. Then he sat down and started to speak with an authority unfamiliar to Sam.

"I am not longer with the Army," he said, "I work for the security services now. I have to ask you to say nothing of this meeting. If anyone asks, I am an old school friend who called in to see you whilst I was in the area. I have a request to make of you. I want you to give someone a job."

Sam remained silent, his gaze fixed on Frank.

"All you need to know is that she is a friend of my ex-wife," Frank went on, "I believe that your office manager has just asked for a few months off until after her baby is born. That means that her job is available for a temporary period, which is what would suit the person concerned."

Sam was beginning to think that he was in the grip of a bad dream. He put his coffee cup down on the closed lid of the piano. His hand was shaking and the cup rattled angrily, slopping its contents into the saucer.

"How the hell do you know all this, Frank?" he asked, but Frank's blank gaze stopped him from saying anything more.

"I know a lot more about you than you think," replied Frank, "I keep up with what's going on in racing. I've seen you many a time at race meetings."

"Then why the hell didn't you make yourself known?" Sam was becoming more agitated.

"Not possible, Sam, I'm afraid," said Frank firmly, "But please be assured that I have certainly not forgotten you. That wouldn't be possible either, believe me. But we can't discuss this now. Once this is over, then we can talk."

"Once what is over?" asked Sam, feeling rather desperate, "You are talking in riddles, Frank."

"Give it six months," responded Frank, "Then it will be over."

He stood up, drank his remaining coffee in a single gulp.

"This is how you contact me," he said, offering Sam a plain white card. It said simply Col. F E Stanley with a telephone number printed beneath.

"But it is only for use if something goes wrong," Frank added, "For the next six months, anyway."

Frank picked up his coat and hat and headed for the Music Room door.

"Is that it?" asked Sam, incredulously.

"For now," said Frank, "My ex-wife's friend will be in touch. Her name is Isabella Hall, by the way. You can give her the chauffeur's flat. She can drive, too, if you need her to."

At that moment, there was a knock at the door.

"Yes?" called Sam impatiently, in response to which utterance Lewis entered the room, bristling with curiosity, to announce that Sadie and the horses were back and what did he want to do about second lot?

"Tell Kelly to give everyone breakfast," instructed Sam, "And we'll take second lot out late."

"Will Mr Stanley be staying for breakfast?" asked Lewis hopefully. "He will not," said Sam firmly. The need for him to give instructions to his staff had restored to him his usual air of calm authority.

Lewis returned to the kitchen.

"Thank you Sam," said Frank. "Isabella will be in touch."

"And you?" asked Sam.

"Only if there is a problem," stated Frank, "Otherwise, I will see you again in six months – that will be at Cheltenham in March," he added.

"At the Festival?" asked Sam.

"Yes indeed," replied Frank, "Gold Cup day."

3

The Sampfield Grange household had naturally wanted to know more about the reason for Mr Stanley's unannounced visit, but they were destined to be disappointed. Following the departure of the Grange's fleeting visitor, the clinging fog had quickly dispersed under the strengthening sun. After breakfast was finished, Sam had accompanied Sadie and her work riders out onto the gallops and the surrounding hills with the remaining horses. They rode upwards into a shining Autumn day which warmed the riders' backs and filled the horses' lungs with new energy.

The conversation between Sadie and her employer had, as usual, been confined to horse training issues and racing plans. Sadie was bursting with curiosity about the incident which had interrupted their daily routine, but knew better than to ask direct questions of her boss. Mr Sampfield was an excellent and sympathetic employer, but was also old fashioned, and expected to maintain a distance between himself and his house and stable staff.

Kelly's phone calls to her family had produced a little additional information. A number of the retired staff from the Grange remembered Frank Stanley well, and spoke of him as a lively young man, who had been a frequent visitor to the Grange since Squire Sampfield, the courtesy title which the older members of staff still gave the head of the family, met him when he went away to school. Mr Stanley, they said, had been like the brother that Squire Sampfield had never had. The two boys had spent their time riding the Grange's horses alongside the old Squire and Mrs Sampfield, and had often accompanied them to three day events, horse trials, point to point and hunt meetings, and even to racecourses around the country, including Ascot, Cheltenham and Newmarket. The young Squire Sampfield, they said, had also spent time with Mr Stanley's family, who were involved in the military and stationed abroad.

When, at the age of seventeen, Frank Stanley's regular visits had ceased, as Kelly's informants told her, this was because his family had required Mr Stanley to enter Sandhurst so as to follow the family career in the Army. They remembered that old Mrs Sampfield was privately annoyed with him for deserting the Sampfield family, which had done so much for him, not least turning him into an excellent and knowledgeable horseman.

Young Squire Sampfield, they reported, had seemed a bit lost for company at first, but had soon become involved in a social diary full of parties and young ladies and trips to London and further afield, and so acquired new and grown up friends to fill the gap left by his old school friend. Crowds of young people had suddenly started to come to the Grange and it had become a lively and busy place, full of noisy and drunken parties, which some of the household staff had found quite a trial. The horses of that time were frequently ridden by many of these visitors, most of whom were passable, and even competent, riders. They remembered in particular a lively, freckled girl called Helen who had spent a lot of time with young Squire Sampfield. They had all thought that one day she would marry him and join in with the family business of training the horses, especially as her mother was a friend of old Mrs Sampfield. But, as everyone already knew, the present Squire had remained immune to the opportunities for marriage and children and had preferred to continue to train the horses on his own. He and his mother had immersed themselves in every aspect of the equestrian world and had been considered quite a force in their time, with entries at Badminton and horses competing on the racecourse in Listed and Graded races. And Helen had married someone else.

Following the completion of these enquiries by Kelly, a week passed by, and with no further information forthcoming, the gossip and speculation came to a halt, and Frank Stanley's visit ceased to be of immediate interest. Sam's comment to Kelly, who dared to ask whether the visitor would be returning soon, was simply that he was an old family friend who had called in on a whim whilst passing through the area. Sam said it had been good to see him after so many years but that he did not think it likely that he would be in the country for much longer, as he normally lived in Canada. This last embellishment was pure invention on Sam's part, as Frank had said nothing at all as to his current residence or intended whereabouts, but the explanation did as it was intended, which was to shut Kelly up.

The one member of the Sampfield household who continued to harbour an ongoing interest in Mr Stanley was Kye. Kye was not part of the Sampfield staff dynasty and so was able to view household events with rather more impartial eyes than those who had relied on the family for their living over many years. Sadie had met Kye earlier that year at a race meeting in Wincanton, to which she had accompanied one of Sam's horses.

Kye had been brought up on a council estate in Toxteth. His father had disappeared, never to return, when he was two years old. His mother lived a chaotic life during which Kye acquired two half brothers and a half sister, each of them with a different father. His mother was unemployed, illiterate and supported by state benefits, but cared for her children meticulously and had no need of the assistance of any of the transient fathers. And, importantly, she would have lost her entitlement to single parent benefits had any of them moved in with her. So Kye, being the oldest, was required to help look after the others.

Kye did as well as could be expected at his local school and had been lucky enough to get a place on a government funded training scheme and to complete an apprenticeship as a car mechanic. But he had preferred horses to cars, having spent much of his time as a child with his grandfather, who was a farrier. The old man often took the young lad around with him in his van as they travelled from stable yard to stable yard. When a wide-eyed Kye said he wanted to ride the horses, his grandfather persuaded one of the yard owners to give him lessons in return for a few hours shovelling shit in the stable yard, a bargain which Kye was happy to accept.

The yard owner was interested to see that Kye's light, strong frame and fearless attitude made him a natural horseman. Noting that he learned quickly and worked hard, and also knew about maintaining cars, the owner recommended Kye to the manager of a small racing yard in Cheshire as a work rider who could also look after the yard's horse transport. Kye had undertaken this work for a few years, his riding skills improving to the point where it was suggested to him that he might think about becoming a jockey, a proposition which he accepted with enthusiasm.

There was only one problem, or perhaps three versions of the same one. These were Kye's younger siblings, who had been less successful than he at school. His two half brothers were involved with drugs and local gangs and his sister was pregnant at the age of fifteen. His beloved granddad had died several years before and his mother, bereft of both her father and her eldest son, had seemed unable to cope, and now rarely left the flat in which they all lived.

Kye could not deal, either financially or emotionally, with the pressure of all these lives depending on him. His pay at the racing yard was pitiable, and as a conditional jockey, he earned little from his rides. Desperately worried about his sister and mother, he accepted with relief the offer through one of his brothers of an additional job at a garage which supplied and serviced the horse transport lorries, as well as many other goods vehicles.

Unfortunately for Kye, instead of solving his troubles, this additional income came at an unexpected price. And it was a price that had led him to taking a ride on a horsebox which was bringing down two horses from the Cheshire yard to compete at a big fixture at Wincanton racecourse.

When Kye spotted the blonde and wholesome Sadie leading up one of the Sampfield horses, which was being ridden by a Peveril cousin in an amateur riders' event, he knew that she could be his passport out of the murky land into which his money earning activities had begun to lead him. Kye, with his curly black hair and little-boy-lost looks, had had plenty of experience of charming stable girls into his bed and he thought he could do the same with Sadie.

So, he had found an excuse to talk to Sadie whilst Ranger Station was out on the course, asking her opinion about the horses in the race, flattering her on her excellent turn out of the handsome Ranger, and gradually working his way into her easily won confidence. Sadie, for all her ability to exert her will over recalcitrant and awkward horses, was completely unable to recognise devious behaviour in people, and she fell for Kye's smartly worked charms very quickly. A couple of apparently chance meetings at other racecourses soon led to Sadie recommending Kye to Mr Sampfield as an excellent addition to the yard staff.

Kye's current yard manager, knowing nothing of the real reasons which had led Kye to flee, was pleased to provide references and since then Kye had worked very hard to prove to both Sadie and Mr Sampfield that they had made a good decision.

Kye had been intrigued by the visit of Mr Stanley but for a different reason than Sadie and the rest of the staff. Practical experience had taught him to recognise when there was tension between men and he had recognised the presence of tension here at once. He had seen that Mr Stanley, for all his assured manner, was not comfortable, and furthermore that Mr Sampfield was not simply surprised, but completely shocked, to see him. Kye was sure that there was more to this meeting than an old friend simply calling in whilst passing. He said as much to Sadie as they lay curled together in bed under a well worn duvet in the chilly cottage that same night.

"Like what?" had been Sadie's response.

"I dunno," said Kye, "Mr Sampfield didn't look very happy to see him."

"Well, he wouldn't be, would he?" said Sadie, as if stating the obvious, "It stopped him going out with first lot."

Kye had to concede that this was an inconvenience. But that was all it was, he thought, not a reason for Mr Sampfield to be so shocked, and even, he thought, angry. But he knew it was not worth talking to Sadie about his thoughts, as her lack of imagination about humans, as opposed to horses, would only lead to her dismissing his observations as fantasy. Sadie, Kelly and Lewis thought they knew Mr Sampfield well as a respected country gentleman devoted only to the training and development of his and others' horses. But Kye could see too that Mr Sampfield was a man who kept his emotions well hidden beneath a cultured and restrained exterior.

"I 'spect you're right," he told Sadie, and, rolling himself on top of her, said, "Let's do something more interesting than worry about them."

Sam's office manager, Bethany, duly went on maternity leave at the end of the week, as Frank had predicted that she would. The Grange staff had previously asked her questions as to who would take over her role whilst she was away. Bethany had told them that an employment agency in the local town, run by a sharp and businesslike lady called Mrs Purefoy, had been tasked to find a replacement. Bethany knew Mrs Purefoy well, as she had been responsible for obtaining the job for Bethany in the first place.

Sadie, Kelly and Lewis were not pleased at this news, having seen Bethany's temporary absence as an opportunity to move into the one part of the Grange territory in which they were currently uninvolved. Kelly and Lewis were even less pleased now to be told by Mr Sampfield himself that the chauffeur's flat was to be cleaned up and made available to the new staff member, who, unlike Bethany, would be living in.

This revelation overshadowed the posing of any further questions about Mr Stanley, who at least was off the scene, whilst this unknown newcomer was just about to enter it and was therefore of more immediate interest.

Sadie's annoyance was somewhat abated by the fact that Mr Sampfield had agreed to her request to recruit some additional work riders, as the yard was considering taking on more horses. This at least provided the opportunity to do some favours for her family, most of who were competent riders. Word about the jobs had been put about in the local area, if only to provide an illusion that they were open to all suitable riders in the vicinity, whether or not they were related to Sadie.

Sam was now sitting in Bethany's office, rather belatedly realising that there was a lot that he did not know about the work that she did. Although his old school had been successful at improving his literacy skills, he still found reading hard work, and the long ago advent of desktop computing had made things even harder. The technology in Bethany's office at the end of the stable block was not complex, and her instructions to the employment agency in the local town as to the skills required of her replacement described relatively basic IT and record keeping functions, albeit equine related.

Sam felt rather glum as he wondered what to do about Mrs Purefoy's agency. If Frank wanted him to give the job to his ex-wife's friend, then she needed to be quick to present herself at the Grange. He had himself told the agency by telephone that the position was to be filled by a family friend, thereby incurring an annoyed reaction from Mrs Purefoy, who had remained polite only because it was Mr Sampfield himself with whom she was speaking. The trouble was, Sam thought irritably, that the position was not in fact filled, and a puzzled Bethany had now left for her maternity leave with no successor to whom she could hand things over.

"If you need me to come in one day to induct the new person," she had told Sam pointedly, "Just let me know."

As Bethany was one of the few employees who had not been recruited from the families of Sadie, Kelly and Lewis, the information about the position being already filled was not communicated any further, and it was assumed by the remaining staff that Mrs Purefoy was still working on the assignment.

Now that Sam was alone with the office computer and filing systems, the incident with Frank had begun to seem like an imagined dream and he almost wondered if he had misunderstood what Frank had told him. Perhaps he should take up Mrs Purefoy on her offer to find him an employee, should the arrangements he had made prove unsuitable, as she had put it.

The warm, foggy conditions of the previous few days had been superseded by sharp bright weather, as the wind had backed to the north east. The little stone office at the end of the stable block faced south east, so the morning sun was shining brightly through the window and the open door, suggesting, were it not for the chilly temperature, the memory of summer and warmer days. Sam's ears picked up the sounds of the horses as they shifted in their boxes, the moving of barrows and the voices of Sadie, Kye and the stable staff as they swept the yard.

Sam heard Sadie's boots treading their firm way towards the office door. He saw her silhouetted in the doorway and shaded his eyes so he could speak to her.

"I was thinking we could tack up Rooker for the new work riders to try," said Sadie, "Are you happy with that, Mr Sampfield?"

Sam considered. Rooker Sunset was a big animal, a strong chaser with a mind of his own. It might be better to start them off on something less challenging, in case they were not as competent as they made out.

"I think Honey would be a better option for a trial," he suggested, referring to Honeymoon Causeway, the grey mare usually taken out by Sadie in the string, "Rooker might be a bit strong for some of them."

Sadie was slightly nettled at having her suggestion overruled, but accepted his direction, as she always did. Mr Sampfield's decisions were usually sensible, and she rarely disagreed seriously with what he said.

"That's fine, Mr Sampfield," she replied, "I am expecting two girls to come up later this morning."

Sadie did not add that the two girls were her mother's friend's twin daughters, brought up on a local farm and both excellent riders. Neither of them would have had any problem handling Rooker Sunset and his awkward habit of leaning heavily on the bit and trying to drag the rider's arms out of their sockets when he did not feel like working.

Sadie left the office and Sam continued to scroll through the information on the computer, not really sure what he was trying to achieve. Amongst various office software applications, an unusual icon caught his eye. It was a picture of a tabby kitten and was labelled Racing Tips for Smart Girls. Puzzled, he selected the icon and instantly a young woman started talking to him from a box in the centre of the screen. She had long multi-coloured hair and big brown eyes.

"Hey, smart racing girls," the young woman said enthusiastically with a beaming smile, "Today's a great day to get one over on your bloke. I am defo going to find you a winner for the weekend and my good friends Tabby Cat and Jayce are going to help me. Are you hearing me, Jayce?"

From somewhere off the screen, a male voice with an Essex accent could be heard saying, "Yo, Stevie. All ready to go."

"Now you know, girls, how shy Jayce is, so we won't let him show his face. Anyway, this is strictly a girls-only vlog. These blokes think they own the scene when they go racing. But we can beat them at their own game, can't we just? So here to tell us how is the lovely Tabby Cat!"

The woman's image was replaced on the screen by that of a cute tabby kitten which stared out of the screen with big blue eyes.

"Hi Tabby Cat, and how are you today?" said the young woman's voice.

By some stroke of IT wizardry, the little cat's mouth moved and a small and piping voice came through the computer's speaker.

"Hi Stevie," said the kitten, "I'm talking to the girls who are smart enough to choose the horses with the best names."

"Good plan, Tabby Cat," said the woman's voice, "Jayce and I are all ears."

Sam was then both horrified and fascinated to hear a synopsis of the pedigrees of some of the top horses currently competing in National Hunt races, with information as to why their names often represented a very good way of choosing them as winners. The objective seemed to be to equip the listeners with a simple way of selecting good horses whilst appearing to know little or nothing about racing. Sam had to concede that it was clever, and the information, notwithstanding that it was delivered by a kitten, with occasional interventions from the invisible Jayce and the young woman with the multi-coloured hair, was pretty sound stuff.

So wrapped up was he in this weird and unexpected find on the office computer that he did not at first notice a person standing in the office doorway. It was only when the figure moved its head to block out the sunrays falling on the floor that Sam became aware that someone was speaking to him.

Sam looked towards the figure, who, even though the sun had moved further on its daily journey across the sky, still appeared to him as a slender dark silhouette, as Sadie had done a little earlier.

"Mr Sampfield Peveril? I have come about the job," the shape said in a female voice.

Sam noted now that the person appeared to be dressed a lightweight riding jacket and breeches and was holding a riding hat. He remembered Sadie's prospective work riders.

"Sadie is in the yard somewhere," he replied, "She will get things organised for you."

"Thank you," responded the woman in the doorway, and turned away.

Sam went back to the computer screen, but the image of the talking kitten had disappeared and he suddenly realised that he did not have the time to worry about this odd find on Bethany's computer just now. The Master of the local hunt was coming in to talk to him about prospective hunter chase entries later in the season.

Sam closed the computer down, something which Bethany had insisted should always be done when no-one was in the office, and arranged the papers on the desk into a neat pile. But, as he shut the door behind him ready to return to the house, Sadie approached him from across the yard with the recent arrival in tow. Now that he was able to see them properly, Sam realised that the woman was not dressed for riding, but was wearing cycling gear and carrying a cycle helmet.

"Mr Sampfield," announced Sadie, "This lady is Mrs Hall and she is here for the office job, she says."

"Mrs Hall, I do apologise," said Sam, good manners automatically taking over, "I mistook you for one of the work riders. I am just about to go up to the house. Would you care to join me? We can talk there."

Much to Sadie's irritation, the visitor responded promptly,

"Yes, certainly, Mr Sampfield Peveril. May I leave my bicycle here or would you prefer me to put it somewhere else?"

Sam and Sadie turned to the spot she indicated, and saw a smart white racing bike leaning against the end of the office wall.

"Better not," said Sadie, "We don't want the horses taking fright at it."

"You can put it in the garage," suggested Sam, "We can do that on the way."

So, the two of them proceeded towards the house, the new arrival wheeling the bicycle ahead of her with one hand pressed on the tiny black saddle.

Sadie watched them go, her eyes narrowing. Kye came to stand beside her.

"Another piece of shit," he said.

4

If Isabella Hall sensed that she was unwelcome at the Grange, she gave no indication of it.

Isabella's 'interview' in the house with Sam was brief and to the point. Isabella and Sam had passed through the kitchen, Isabella still holding her cycle helmet. Kelly and Lewis were fortunately elsewhere in the house and were unaware for the moment of their presence.

"Frank Stanley told me you were coming," started Sam, as they sat down together in the drawing room, "I understand that you are a friend of his ex-wife."

"That's correct," replied Isabella, "Please let me know where I am to live and what I have to do and I will get on with it. I am very grateful for your assistance. Please be assured that I will do a good job for you."

"Is there nothing more you can tell me about yourself?" asked Sam.

"No, there is nothing more to say," replied Isabella, and then, true to her word, she was silent.

Sam studied the small figure sitting opposite him. No wonder he had mistaken her for a work rider, he thought. She was small and tough-looking with a strangely expressionless face. She spoke mechanically, as if repeating a prepared script. Her hair was a non-descript light colour and was cut short, brushed down across her ears. Her only striking feature was her dark brown eyes, but even they looked dull and expressionless, almost as if she were on drugs. Sam guessed her age as being about forty, but really, he thought, she could have been several years older or younger. He wondered whether she too was an Army officer or even a member of what Frank Stanley had enigmatically described as the security services.

Sam ran a weary hand through his still mostly fair hair.

"Very well," he said, "I'll get Kelly to show you to the flat."

He stood up and Isabella stood too.

"Thank you, Mr Sampfield Peveril," she said, simply, and waited for him to lead her back to the hallway, where a now vigilant Lewis, who had been summoned by a text message from Sadie, was waiting.

Isabella's meagre belongings were sent by taxi from the hotel in the nearby town where she had been staying. The driver was unknown to the Sampfield household, but Lewis managed to obtain from him the information that he had collected the luggage from The Charlton Arms.

Isabella had been awaiting the taxi, and, refusing Lewis's offer of assistance, had taken the three black holdalls up the external staircase to the flat herself. Lewis had informed her that lunch was available in the Grange kitchen at half past twelve. Isabella had nodded and said she would be there.

Over the next few days, Isabella presented herself in the yard office every morning, took meals with the rest of the staff, and returned to her flat in the evening. The pregnant Bethany appeared at Sam's request on the second day and spent three hours showing Isabella the computer system and the paper records kept in the office. These were broadly divided into the records of the horses and their activities, the records of the staff and associated payroll, and the records of the yard and house supplies. Payments for the last were made through an online facility for which Bethany, at Sam's request, supplied Isabella with the passwords,

"You will need to create a new personal file for yourself," Bethany reminded Isabella, who nodded and said she would do so.

Bethany explained to Isabella the need for liaison with Mr Purefoy, the accountant, over such matters as the payroll and the yard accounts and VAT returns, but said that otherwise all bookkeeping, ordering of supplies and consumables was done from the office.

Isabella listened without comment, asking the occasional question, and said she would call Bethany if she needed any further help.

All the staff, including Bethany, agreed that Isabella was a cold fish. Attempts to find out more about her background, both at lunch on the first day, were politely stonewalled. The only useful piece of information which Sadie, Kelly and Lewis managed to extract from her was that she had not been recruited through Mrs Purefoy's agency, and, when pressed, she said that a family friend had recommended her to Mr Sampfield Peveril, as she continued to call him. The staff could believe this, as her reserved and well-spoken manner had more in common with Mr Sampfield himself than with his staff.

Sadie, in particular, remained unhappy with addressing the interloper, as she saw her, as Mrs Hall, a name which she herself had in fact ascribed to the new staff member on the day of her arrival in the stable yard. Whilst she conceded that the office manager was in a rather different position to the rest of the house and yard staff, she objected to the use of a title which implied some kind of superiority over the other employees.

"So what do you want us to call you, then?" she asked Isabella at breakfast on the day after her arrival, "We can't call you Mrs Hall when you work with us."

Isabella turned her expressionless gaze on Sadie.

"I don't mind," she said, "It's up to you. My name is Isabella."

"What does Mr Hall call you?" asked Lewis, and then realised that he had made a bad mistake. She would not be here if Mr Hall was still around.

"Mr Hall doesn't call me anything," responded Isabella, "He's dead. Isabella will do."

And, with that, she had risen from the breakfast table and gone out to her office, leaving the assembled company feeling that they had gone a step too far.

Isabella spent most of her free time out on her bicycle. The days were short in early November, but Isabella appeared to have no concern about cycling in the wet, dark and cold early mornings and evenings, going out obliviously into the nearby lanes wearing a reflective jacket and warm and waterproof clothing. Sadie and the work riders sometimes also caught sight of her running on foot across the tracks on the top of the surrounding hills.

When asked about her gruelling fitness regime, Isabella responded that she was an amateur triathlete and needed to keep up her training whilst undertaking temporary work for Mr Sampfield Peveril. This information gave Lewis the idea of putting her name into a search engine, as a result of which he was rewarded with a list of entries detailing the results of triathlon events around the country. Isabella did not appear to be a member of a club, and was described as an unaffiliated participant. Her age was given in the result sheets as Female Veteran 40-44 years.

After this, the only remaining line of enquiry was The Charlton Arms.

Lewis, with Kye in tow, decided to go drinking one evening at the establishment concerned. Although not far from the Grange, it was not a place frequented by the Grange stable staff, for the simple reason that it was considered rather expensive, being a gastro pub and hotel. The Charlton Arms presented itself as an attractive and atmospheric coaching inn situated in the centre of a medieval market town. Its bowed front windows looked out onto an historic crossroads where stage coach routes had begun and ended and where many working carriage horses had been harnessed, unharnessed, fed, watered and stabled. If Lewis or Kye had read the novels of Austen or Thackeray, they would have been sure that some of their characters had rested at this establishment.

But to Lewis and Kye, the place was just a posh pub which had rooms to let.

"Beer's not bad," said Lewis, as the two young men sat with their drinks in the suitably gloomy and wood panelled bar.

"You worked here long?" he asked the bored looking barmaid who had pulled their pints for them.

"Two weeks," she informed them, "I'm just temp'ry."

"We've got someone temporary at our place," Lewis told her, "She was staying here last week."

"Oh, who's that then?" asked the girl, sounding completely disinterested in the conversation.

"Her name's Isabella Hall," Lewis told her, and went on to describe the appearance of their new colleague.

A flicker of recognition appeared in the barmaid's eyes.

"Yeah, I think I remember someone like that," she said, "Here with her fancy man, she was."

Lewis and Kye leaned forward in their seats, their curiosity almost getting the better of them. Fancy man was not an expression that they had expected to hear in relation to Isabella Hall.

"Yeah," the girl went on, "They used to eat at that table over there. We thought they were police."

"Police?" asked Kye, a cold shiver running up his spine, "Why?"

"Well, the bloke. He was dead tall and formal. Posh too. He spoke to her like she was under orders," was the barmaid's explanation.

"Did you hear what they said?" asked Kye.

The barmaid seemed suddenly to become suspicious.

"Why are you wanting to know, anyway?" she said.

"No reason," said Kye quickly, "Just she doesn't say much."

An older woman who had appeared behind the bar during the conversation, butted in.

"They weren't police," she scoffed, "More like Army, I'd say. Tough types. Sporty. And they were definitely having an affair even though they were in separate rooms."

"How do you know that?" Lewis was agog. He had not expected anything so interesting as this.

"They were in one another's bedrooms all the time," the woman told him, " A lot of noise there was – he was shouting and she was screaming and crying."

Lewis and Kye could hardly believe their ears. The cold and collected Isabella Hall screaming and crying was something they found difficult to credit.

"Are you sure it was the same person?" asked Lewis, "Little woman with short hair, rides a bike?"

"Yeah, that's her," his new informer replied, "We thought maybe he was her coach as well as her lover."

"Why?" asked Kye.

"Well, he was always telling her what to do. You need to be able to cover this distance in this time. Diagrams and charts they had. Looking at it all the time down here in the bar. They made a lot of fuss about the food too. Very choosy, they were."

The woman stopped for breath. The temporary barmaid turned away to serve some other customers who had just entered the bar.

"What was the shouting and screaming about?" asked Lewis.

"Well, that I can't say," the woman replied, "They were as nice as pie to each other down here. It was only upstairs that they started arguing."

"Arguing?" repeated Lewis.

"Well all we heard was her shouting out, "I'm not doing this anymore. You're a bully." And he was shushing her and telling her it would all be all right in the end."

"But that could have been about her training," objected Lewis, "It doesn't mean they were lovers."

"Well she had a packet of condoms by her bed," the woman said, "The room service girl saw it there. And they weren't any left by the end of the time they were here."

"Wow," said Kye and Lewis, simultaneously.

The news that the two of them had just gleaned had exceeded their wildest expectations: Isabella Hall and a mysterious lover who was a bullying cycling coach into the bargain.

"What was his name, do you know?" asked Lewis.

"Well," the woman said, conspiratorially, "His name in the booking sheet was Davies, Hugh Davies. But she called him Frank."

Lewis felt as if he had hit the jackpot.

"Thanks very much for your help," he said, hurriedly, and the two young men left the bar in a rush, anxious to carry their exciting news home with them.

After they had left, a tall man came down the stairs. The helpful female informant turned to him and said, "They seem to have swallowed the story whole, sir. Hook, line and sinker, I'd say."

"Yes, indeed," replied Frank Stanley.

5

Fortunately for all involved, Sam was unaware of the intense interest being taken in Isabella Hall by his employees. Had he been aware, he would have strongly disapproved of their attempts to pry into her personal affairs, and would have taken steps to discourage it.

As far as Sam was concerned, Isabella was an excellent replacement for Bethany. Whilst it was evident that she knew little or nothing about the business of racehorse training, her knowledge of office practice and desktop technology was sound, and she picked up new information very quickly. Sam had every confidence that she would soon understand the business well enough to run the office without his input.

Aside from her excellent performance as an employee, Sam found Isabella Hall a rather unapproachable individual. Her apparent status as a friend of the erstwhile Mrs Stanley continued to intrigue him but he was too well mannered to make further enquiries on the topic. Isabella's conscientious devotion to her cycling and running training was something he could readily admire, but her expressionless face and taut smile deterred him from offering any personal encouragement or asking anything other than the most superficial questions about what she was doing. It had not occurred to Sam to try to use the internet to seek any information about Mrs Hall, as he continued to call her.

Like Sadie, Sam had noticed Isabella out running within sight of the gallops when he was working with the horses. Unlike Sadie, who was concentrating on the horse she was exercising, and whose observational skills were not the sharpest, Sam had noticed Isabella stop to watch the horses appraisingly as the work riders took them over the practice jumps towards the top of the hill behind the house. To Sam, she looked a bit like a punter trying to get inside information on likely winners. But Isabella didn't seem like a racing punter, and, in any case, the events in which Sam's horses were usually entered were hardly at the level where large amounts of money were to be made through getting an inside track on them.

Sadie, Kelly and Lewis had been more than satisfied, indeed gleeful, to accept the obvious, and suitably scurrilous, explanation that Isabella Hall and Mr Stanley were using the Charlton Arms as a secret meeting place, and that Mr Stanley had asked Mr Sampfield to give Isabella a job so that she could remain nearby where he could easily arrange to meet her. The idea of Mr Stanley being a cycling coach was quickly dismissed as a front designed to mislead the nosy staff at the hotel. And Kelly added fuel to the flames of speculation about the couple's duplicity by saying that Mr Stanley had clearly also attempted to deceive Mr Sampfield by telling him that he, Mr Stanley, was going to Canada.

"I bet Mr Hall isn't dead at all," opined Sadie one day, when the work riders had left the breakfast table and the four conspirators were left alone, "Who'd have thought it? She looks so po-faced."

"Those posh, stuck up birds are the worst," said Lewis, rather enviously, "I bet she's a real goer in the sack even if she is over 40. All that sport must make her pretty active."

"Don't be vulgar, Lewis," chided Kelly, although she secretly thought the comment very funny.

"And Mr Sampfield's old school friend being her lover," added Sadie, for the umpteenth time, "Who'd have thought?"

They had been able to indulge in the luxury of this malicious conversation, as Isabella had failed to arrive for breakfast and appeared to be still in her flat. There had been no sign of her that morning running out by the gallops. Admittedly it was a wet and miserable day, but the weather conditions had not previously seemed to deter Isabella from pursuing her usual training routine.

"Must have overslept," said Lewis, "Too much action with Mr Stanley last night."

"What, you think he's been screwing her here?" asked Sadie, theatrically scandalised.

"No, of course not," scoffed Lewis, "Where do you think she goes on those bike rides?"

Their conversation was interrupted by the sight of Isabella Hall herself coming slowly along the path towards the house, her head bowed over her mobile phone. Notwithstanding the cold and rain of the unpleasant November morning, Isabella wore no coat.

"Hey, look out," said Lewis.

Isabella entered the kitchen with her head still bent over her phone. She was not wearing the outdoor running gear which she normally wore in the morning, but was already dressed in her usual office outfit of dark trousers and an equally dark sweater. Her hair was wet and pushed back away from her ears instead of being swept forward rather unattractively across them as it usually did when it was dry. She seemed to be reading and sending text messages.

"Sorry to be late," Isabella said, formally, raising her head towards the group around the table, "If there's nothing left, please don't worry."

"There's some breakfast cereal and fruit," said Sadie, getting up to return to the yard, "Come on Kye, we've got work to do."

Sadie had found heat in Curlew Landings' off foreleg that morning and, now that there was no opportunity to continue the entertaining conversation, was keen to get back to see if her initial treatment with ice and bandaging had improved matters. Sadie was keen for Curlew to be in good shape for a Novice Hurdle race in which the gelding was entered at Newbury on Hennessy Gold Cup day. She had not really enjoyed the miserable and dark morning exercising the other horses whilst Curlew remained in his box.

Lewis and Kelly also got up from the table. As they did so, Isabella's phone emitted a ping to indicate an incoming message. Isabella promptly shut down the incoming message screen, but not before Sadie and Kye, who were passing behind her on their way out of the door, had seen that the incoming message consisted simply of X.

Isabella put the phone in her pocket without comment and went to the sideboard to pour herself a cup of coffee. She ran her left hand through the wet hair behind her ear as she did so.

"Did you see that?" hissed Sadie to Kye as they walked back toward the yard, "Someone is sending her kisses on the phone. It must be Mr Stanley."

Kye privately thought that it was unlikely that Mr Stanley would conduct his affair with Isabella Hall as if they were a pair of dopey teenagers sending soppy text messages to each other. But Kye had seen something much more interesting. Behind Isabella Hall's left ear had been a long red scar which was still in the process of healing. Kye had seen those types of scars before. She's had a face lift, he thought, astonished. And quite recently, too.

Making an excuse to Sadie, he turned back towards the boot room door, hoping to get another look. He could see Isabella through the outside kitchen window, the phone in her hand, staring at the screen. There were tears streaming down her cheeks and she was shaking her head as if in disbelief or despair.

Kye suddenly felt guilty. Whatever she was up to, he thought, she was obviously very unhappy. He turned away again to follow Sadie towards the yard.

"Filth or not, that Frank Stanley must be a right bastard," he said to himself.

So, when, later that morning, Isabella was back in the office, seated in her usual place, Kye stuck his head around the door.

"Are we expecting a feed delivery today?" he asked. He knew perfectly well that a delivery was expected but it was the best excuse he could think of to speak to her.

"Yes, we are," replied Isabella, no trace of her former distress evident in either her face or her voice, "And while you're here, Kye, you need to take the small horsebox in for its MOT. It's due this month. Shall I book it in?"

"Yeah, thanks, Isabella," replied Kye, "If you're not too busy, that is."

He was trying to prolong the conversation with her, he was not really sure why.

"Not at all," replied Isabella, politely, as usual, "I'm expecting Mr Purefoy later, to look at the VAT return with me – though why he's needed, I'm not sure – but there's plenty of time to get the horsebox booked in before then. Is there any day you can't take it down? Is it needed for the horses?"

It was the longest conversation Isabella had ever held with Kye. Christ, she must be lonely here, thought Kye involuntarily.

"No, any day's OK up until the weekend," he replied, and then added, "Don't yez like that Mr Purefoy then?"

"He's getting paid for doing nothing, that's what I don't like," stated Isabella, baldly, and turned back to her computer screen.

Kye grunted and walked away, suddenly realising that Isabella Hall might have been put there to spy on them after all. Though why Mr Stanley would want to spy on the affairs of Sampfield Manor was beyond him. He knew that Sadie, Lewis and Kelly had their ways of helping their family and friends to a share of the Sampfield bounty, but this was hardly stuff of interest to the bizzies - or the Army, for fuck's sake.

Unless it was Kye they were watching. He remembered the lorry and the MOT. He had plans for that lorry once it came back. Surely it's not me, he thought, with a shiver, and resolved to redouble his vigilance.

Sam did not take breakfast with his staff. Lewis usually brought coffee, and some of whatever the work riders were eating, into the breakfast room, a usually sunny retreat which looked across to the lane which led up to the Grange. Today it was dark and gloomy, a penetrating drizzle of rain now filling the air, as dismal clouds hung sullenly in a dead sky. After breakfast, Sam would usually walk down to the yard and speak to Sadie about the horses, reviewing the work they had done that morning. And only then would he call into the yard office to deal with any business or to make any decisions which were required of him.

This morning, the heat in Curlew Landings' leg was the main topic for discussion with Sadie. The icing and wrap treatment seemed to have had little effect, and the leg still felt hot and slightly swollen. Curlew otherwise seemed fine in himself, and shifted about irritably in his box whilst Sam and Sadie discussed what to do about the problem.

"Cold hose the leg down and then keep the compress on," said Sam, "I'll get Mrs Hall to call Rachel and see if she can call in and take a look."

Rachel Horwood was the equine vet who looked after the Sampfield horses, as her father had done before her.

Leaving Sadie to her work, Sam went over to the yard office, to find Isabella looking at a table of figures showing on the screen of the computer.

"Good morning, Mrs Hall," he greeted her.

"Mr Sampfield Peveril, good morning," responded Isabella, with a small smile, "Did the horses work well this morning?"

"I'm happy with all of them, except Curlew," replied Sam, "I think we may need the vet to give an opinion."

"Curlew Landings?" said Isabella, "He's got a race entry on Saturday week, hasn't he?"

Isabella had submitted the entry through Weatherby's under Sam's instruction, and was now familiar with the process to be followed.

54

"Yes, otherwise, I shouldn't bother the vet," replied Sam, "But we need to get some work into him between now and then and we can't do that if he isn't sound."

"I'll call her," said Isabella, making a pencilled note on a memo pad which lay open on the desk, "What shall I say the problem is?"

"Heat in the off fore," responded Sam.

"Heat in the off fore. A tendon, maybe?" said Isabella, absently, as she wrote.

Sam was slightly taken aback.

"Well it could be a number of things," he said, wondering what had led Mrs Hall to suggest a diagnosis of an equine injury.

Isabella showed no sign of having heard his response. Instead she said, "Could I ask you about another matter, Mr Sampfield Peveril?"

"Yes, of course," replied Sam, "What is it?"

"The VAT return," said Isabella, indicating the table of figures on the computer screen.

Sam looked at the screen. The figures were meaningless to him.

"What about it?" he said, "Doesn't Purefoy come up and deal with that for us?"

"Indeed he does," said Isabella, "But the accounting software does it automatically. This is the finished return on the screen. We just have to submit it to the HMRC. We don't need an accountant to deal with it for us. It is already done."

"So what is Purefoy doing then?" asked Sam, not really understanding.

"I have no idea," replied Isabella, tartly, "Charging you a fee just for coming up here, I would say."

Sam felt annoyed.

"Well, he must be doing something," he said, "Bethany always seemed to need to consult him."

Isabella remained silent.

"Well," Sam added slowly, "I will leave it with you, Mrs Hall. If you can manage without him, that's fine by me."

"Very well, Mr Sampfield Peveril," said Isabella.

As she spoke she handed him a smart looking cream envelope, addressed to James Sampford Peveril Esquire and marked Personal.

Very little mail arrived at the Grange, as, even in such a rural backwater, most business was now conducted online. The majority of incoming material was never even seen by Sam, as it was dealt with or disposed of by Bethany and now by Isabella.

Sam took the envelope and looked around for a letter opener. Isabella took one from the drawer and handed it to him, turning her attention back to the computer.

The envelope contained, as Sam knew it would, a personal invitation to join Lady Helen Garratt at Newbury races on Hennessy Gold Cup day. The invitation was also extended to any partner or guest whom Sam wished to bring with him.

Lady Helen Garratt, or plain Helen Smith as she had used to be, was one of Sam's oldest friends. Their mothers had frequently ridden in horse trials together, often sharing horse transport to events, so Sam and Helen, when not at school, had met each other frequently throughout their childhood and teenage years. It had been widely assumed that the two of them might marry. But the two young people had shown little interest in each other beyond their shared passion for horses, although they were, and still remained, good friends. Helen had surprised everyone, except Sam, by marrying a talented musician whose work and performances had subsequently not only made him rich and famous, but had recently earned him a knighthood for services to music.

Sir John Garratt had originally known little or nothing about horses, but his wife had soon changed that, encouraging him to invest in young horses and to take an interest in their racing career. As a result of Helen's careful choices of horses and trainers, Sir John now had a runner in the Hennessy Gold Cup, a beautiful grey gelding of eight years old, called Alto Clef.

Sam thought he might enjoy seeing Alto Clef run in the Hennessy Gold Cup. The horse was trained in Lambourn, but Sam had had some input to the decision by the Garratts to buy the gelding and had been following his progress with interest. On the other hand, Sam knew that, in a group of John and Helen's friends, he could easily become a source of free information and expertise to everyone around the lunch table.

Sam put the invitation down onto Isabella's desk.

"I'll make a decision on this once we know whether Curlew is running that day or not," he said, firmly, "Let me know when Rachel gets here, please."

Once Sam had gone back up to the house, Isabella called the vet, the garage, and Mr Purefoy's office. The receptionist at the equine practice said that Rachel was already out on another call but that she would get a message to her. Graham Colvin, the garage owner, said that he was able to take the lorry for its MOT that same afternoon. Mr Purefoy's secretary noted the cancellation of the appointment and offered to reschedule, an offer which Isabella politely declined.

Isabella went out into the yard to look for Kye. The persistent rain had dried away and a weak, pallid sun was attempting to push its way through the slowly thinning clouds. A light breeze had sprung up, sweeping over the yard surfaces and ruffling the manes of the horses as they watched Isabella cross the yard.

Kye was in the feed store with Sadie, measuring out and filling up the horses' feed buckets ready for later in the day.

"Colvin's can take the horsebox in for its MOT this afternoon," she told them, "Does that suit you, Kye, or shall I ask for another day?"

"No, that's just great, Isabella," said Kye, "I can take it down now."

"When's Rachel coming to see Curlew?" asked Sadie, and looked annoyed when Isabella told her that she was awaiting a call back from the equine practice.

"In that case, I may as well come with you, Kye," she snapped, glaring at Isabella, "Looks like we can be there and back before Rachel even gets here. We can do the rest of the feeds later. Gray will give us a lift back from the garage up to the bottom of the lane."

This suggestion did not suit Kye at all.

"I wanted to speak to Gray about some mods to the chassis while the lorry's there," he said, "It might take a while. And anyway, we've got a delivery due."

"OK, then," Sadie shrugged, "Just felt like getting out for a bit. I'll finish up here on my own."

Sadie turned away and dug a scoop viciously into a sack of pellets. Nothing was going right today, she thought. Perhaps she would go up and have a chat with Kelly and Lewis, if Kye did not want her company. She turned round to vent her bad mood on Isabella, but Isabella had gone.

6

Kye drove the smaller of the yard's two horseboxes quickly out of its parking space behind the barn and into the lane. He was anxious to get away from Sampfield Grange before Sadie changed her mind.

Kye's story about modifications being made to the chassis of the lorry was true. Fortunately, Sadie's knowledge of motor mechanics was not sufficiently extensive for it to occur to her to ask him why such a modification was needed.

The HGV service centre in which Kye had worked in Cheshire did rather more with its vehicles than it was supposed to do. In particular, it did a brisk trade in creative welding work on the underside of some of the trucks and vans which passed through its premises. The welding work involved the installation of a cradle with hooks designed to hold a good sized metal box securely in place on the bottom of the vehicle. So clever was the work that, to the casual, or even not so casual, eye, it was invisible, looking just like a normal part of the structure of the chassis. To see that there was anything unusual, someone would have had to have the lorry over an inspection pit with a strong light shone in exactly the right place. Even then, the modification itself would not have looked out of place. It was only if the metal box had been secured to it that there would have been something to find.

The box to be attached to what Kye had called the chassis mod was an airtight and lead lined container into which a decent amount of neatly packed cocaine could easily be carried. Some of the lorries were capable of carrying more than one container at a time. The structure of the boxes meant that drug sniffer dogs were unable to detect their contents, especially when confused by fumes and diesel smells emanating from beneath the vehicle.

The quantities of cocaine which could be carried by each vehicle were limited, but the large number of vehicles which were involved meant that the trade was good enough for the purposes of the gangs in which Kye's brothers were involved. Their mechanic brother had been just the right person to join the garage where the modifications were made and also to ensure that the containers were emptied by someone they could trust.

Kye had been well paid for his role in this drug trafficking racket which mainly involved lorries arriving from Ireland. But something had gone wrong. The police had suddenly become interested in the activities at the HGV centre, and whilst only a small cog in a much bigger and nastier machine, Kye had found himself close to a dangerous firing line. So, he had decided to look elsewhere for a job, preferably some distance away. He would just have to hope that his brothers could look after his mother and sister until he was able to return.

The racing yard for which he worked knew nothing of his involvement in this racket, so when asked by Bethany for a reference, the owner had been able to give one honestly and without reservation. The staff knew Kye only as a good horseman who had the potential to be a jockey and a reliable stable yard worker and horsebox driver.

Whilst Kye had been glad to escape from involvement in such a high risk activity, it had given him the idea of using the horse lorries at Sampfield Grange for a similar purpose. Class A drugs were somewhat out of his league financially and in terms of an accessible customer base, but weed and Es were more within his reach. There were plenty of young stable staff at the race and point to point courses he attended who would pay some of their hard earned wages for these less expensive highs.

So, Kye was about to go into business on his own account and needed Graham Colvin to help him do the modifications required. Gray, as he was known, had been cautious at first, but, on being assured that free party drugs would be coming his way as part of the deal, eventually agreed to get the work done at his workshop. The need for the MOT on one of the lorries turned out to be a good opportunity for the two young men to make a start on their illicit project.

Kye did not regard himself as a criminal and neither did Gray. To them, low level drug dealing was jus a way of providing a service to their friends and earning themselves a bit of cash into the bargain. They weren't forcing the shit on anyone, so where was the harm? And no-one at a racecourse was looking for recreational drugs destined to be used away from the course by non-racing human bystanders. The racing authorities' concern was with any dope the horses or their jockeys might have in their systems, so that was where their testing and checking was focused.

Whilst Kye was plotting his way down to Gray Colvin's garage, Sam was sitting in his study in the Grange feeling unexpectedly dejected. Sam was an even tempered man with a controlled imagination and a total focus on his horses. So it took something unusual to shake him out of his customary equilibrium. Sam was well aware that people found him boring. His only activities, apart from training and exercising his resident horses, revolved around the local Hunt, and overseeing his estate and private investments.

Sampfield Grange was the least of the family's wealth, in the face of which the local small time backhanding by the Purefoy and the Shinkins families was of little significance. The Peveril estates were located in another county and no doubt had their local leeches too. But the majority of the family wealth was in Australia, not just as a result of Raldi's marriage into the family but also from canny investments by the advisors of past generations of Sampfields and, later, Peverils too. Sam's vast portfolio was managed for him by professional brokers in London and Sydney, who, naturally, were making plenty of money for themselves in much the same way as Sadie and the Purefoys were.

Sam had never really thought about his riches. He didn't want to think about them. He had buried himself in the horses instead. With his wealth, he could have done anything in the equestrian world, but he had chosen to do virtually nothing. It was only when Helen Garratt and her friends started talking to him that he wondered if he had done the wrong thing by burying himself in such a backwater activity as he had.

Sam was a major benefactor of several equine charities, but he had never tried to set up any venture of his own, partly through lack of advice or momentum and partly because he did not want the publicity such an activity would bring. Helen herself had been vociferous about the opportunities open to him to do something like this. Sam knew she would be pressing her case again with him should be with her on Hennessy Gold Cup day.

"Retired competition horses, Sam", she had said, "You would be just wonderful at supporting their retraining. And what about providing opportunities for young people in racing and as stable staff? There is so much you could do."

When Sam tried to protest, she had countered, "Yes, I know you give all sorts of donations. But, with your connections, you could start something new, or at least pay for someone else to extend what they are doing. You could really make a difference. John and I would be keen to help."

This conversation had taken place at the Cheltenham Festival earlier in the year. Sam knew that Helen was right, but somehow he could not find the momentum to go forward with the ideas. And meanwhile, his clever investors made his wealth grow ever greater.

The one thing that Sam would have no truck with was tax avoidance schemes. But, as his investors pointed out, founding a charity with genuine charitable objects was not a tax avoidance activity. People would benefit directly from what he had done rather than his money going into a public purse over which Sam himself had no control, except as an ordinary voting citizen.

All these thoughts jumbled themselves around in Sam's head as he sat in his study in the Grange and struggled to read through a report sent through by his stockbroking firm in London. The computer set-up in his study was simpler than that in Isabella's office and consisted mainly of an email facility and a printer. His direct instruction that all communications and reports be sent to an individual personal email address, rather than through any more sophisticated online means, had been agreed with his representative at the brokers, David Rose, and had always been followed to the letter. Sam then asked any questions and or resolved any queries on the phone with David, often asking for sections of the reports to be explained to him in great detail. The firm thought Sam obsessed with security and probably too busy to read their reports, but all he really wanted was someone who could read things to him, a process which was a lot quicker as far as he was concerned.

Sam felt unexpectedly weary. The gloomy dark day, Helen's invitation, the weird business of Frank Stanley and Isabella Hall, the complex investment reports, and the heat in Curlew's leg were all things he did not want to think about. He moved to an armchair by the fire and stared at the flames. And fell asleep.

Sadie, meanwhile, had finished preparing the feeds. Conveniently, the expected delivery arrived shortly after Kye's departure in the lorry. Finding herself with nothing immediate to do, and checking that the horses all had full water buckets, she decided to walk up to the house to spend a bit of time over a coffee with Kelly. She could see Isabella sitting in the yard office, speaking on the phone.

"If Mr Purefoy wishes to take the matter up with Mr Sampfield Peveril," Sadie heard Isabella saying, "He is welcome to do so."

"What's that cow interfering in now?" thought Sadie as she passed the office door. She decided not to tell Isabella that she had gone. Let her come and find her, if she needed her.

Isabella put down the phone, unaware that she was now alone in the yard with the horses. The work riders had long left for the day, Kye was out, Mr Sampfield Peveril was up in house, but, as far as she knew Sadie was somewhere about the yard. Time to see what Tabby Cat had to say, she thought.

Isabella clicked the computer mouse on the Racing Tips for Smart Girls icon. The cute tabby kitten popped up into its customary box in the centre of the screen.

"Hi girls," piped the kitten, "Great to see you again, isn't it, Stevie?"

Stevie's disembodied voice floated out of the speaker,

"Yay, Tabby Cat and all the smart girls! Tell you what, though, Jayce got a bit wasted last night and he's left us on our own today. Men, huh?"

"Smart girls don't need Jayce today," replied Tabby Cat, sweetly, his little mouth moving along with his fake speaking voice, "We're going to talk about pretty colours."

"Great stuff, Tabby Cat," went Stevie's voice, "Tell you what, girls, choosing your favourite colour is not a bad way to find a winning horse. And we're going to have a look at pink and blue, aren't we, Tabby Cat? Not blue for boys and pink for girls, but smart colour combos for our own smart girls."

Isabella sat back in her chair and listened to Stevie's voice, punctuated by the occasional intervention from the squeaky kitten, talking about famous racing colours and why they might be a good way to choose a race winner. Isabella did not take any notes, but listened with her eyes closed, taking deep breaths, as if trying to internalise something.

The computer dialogue and Isabella's absorption in it were interrupted by a fierce bang on the door of the office.

Isabella looked up. A tall, red headed young woman with bright blue eyes was standing in the doorway.

"Well, I'm here," she said, "And not before time. Just found this little devil wandering about the place."

The little devil turned out to be the hefty Ranger Station, who was standing next to the young woman, being held in check with a piece of baler twine looped around his neck.

"Can you put him back in his box?" asked the woman, "And preferably with a head collar on him. Where are Sadie and Kye?"

Isabella jumped up from the desk, leaving the Tabby Cat vlog babbling away to itself.

"I'm, er, I don't work with the horses," she said.

"Well, then can you go and get me a head collar at least?" replied the stranger, "I assume you know where they are. I can't just keep this monster here on a string, you know."

Isabella knew that there were head collars hanging outside each of the indoor boxes. Ranger Station should have been in one of these boxes and not wandering about the yard. She hurried over to the stable block and grabbed the collar from Ranger's hook.

The newcomer took the collar and slipped it over Ranger's head. Isabella fastened up the buckle at the side of Ranger's nose and offered the lead rope to the other woman.

"No, you take him back," said the newcomer, pulling the twine off Ranger's neck and stuffing it in her jacket pocket, "I'm here to see Curlew, so I'll come in with you. Why are Sadie and Mr Sampfield not here?"

Ranger Station was fortunately quite willing to return to his box, especially when offered a piece of carrot as an incentive, and Isabella led him in, removed the head collar and shut the door. After hooking up the head collar by the door, Isabella unclipped the lead rope and slid the clip through the bolt which held the box door shut.

"That should stop him opening it again," Isabella said.

"I thought you said you didn't work with the horses," said the other woman, "I'm Rachel Horwood, by the way."

"I don't work with the horses," said Isabella, "I'm an uh ... administrator."

Rachel raised her eyebrows, and was about to speak, when Isabella cut her short.

"I'll call Mr Sampfield Peveril from the house for you, Dr Horwood," she said, "And to answer your earlier question, Kye has taken one of the horseboxes for its MOT and I don't know where Sadie is. I'll call her mobile. Do you know where Curlew Landings' box is?"

"Yes, I'll go and have a look at Curlew," replied Rachel, "And I'm Miss, not Doctor."

Isabella did not acknowledge Rachel's last statement, but instead returned to the office. She silenced the chattering Tabby Cat, who was just reminding all the smart girls that he would be back to give them some smart ideas for Saturday's races, that is, only supposing that Jayce got out of bed in time. Stevie butted in to say she had some great ideas for what to wear, but Isabella did not wait to find out what these ideas might be.

Isabella called Sadie's mobile, the number of which she found in the office records.

Sadie answered almost at once, having recognised the yard number.

"Miss Horwood is here to see Curlew Landings," Isabella told her, "And Ranger Station's been out of his box. He's back in now, but the bolt needs attention."

Sadie leapt out of the kitchen chair where she was sitting enjoying a mug of coffee with Kelly.

"Shit," she said, "I'm on my way."

"Could someone call Mr Sampfield Peveril too, please?" requested Isabella.

"Yeah," said Sadie," Kelly will ask him to come down."

Having silenced Tabby Cat and Stevie, Isabella returned to the indoor boxes to find Rachel in Curlew Landings' box, running her hand down his off foreleg. The horse seemed pleased to see her and pushed his nose into the back of her head as she leaned over his leg. The vet was clearly used to such treatment and kept up a dialogue with the horse, warning him about his bad behaviour and harassment.

"Sadie and Mr Sampfield Peveril are on their way," Isabella told the vet, "I'll leave you to it."

And before Rachel could answer, Isabella had gone.

By then time Sam arrived in Curlew Landings' box, Sadie was walking the horse in a headcollar along the area between the boxes. The other horses looked on curiously at the sudden activity, pleased with the unexpected additional company.

"Well, he isn't lame," said Rachel, "Which is a good start. Can we take him onto the polytrack and trot him up?"

Sadie did as she was asked, and Curlew was soon trotting alongside Sadie on the small circular polytrack by the barn.

Rachel's considered view was the injury was not serious and did not arise from an underlying problem with a tendon or ligament. Sadie confirmed that the earlier treatment of hosing and wrapping the leg appeared at last to have reduced the inflammation. Sam agreed that there had been an improvement.

"I'm inclined to think," said Rachel, "That it's a knock or a bang which has bruised his leg on the outside but not broken the skin. But if you are worried, Mr Sampfield, we can get an MRI scan done very easily."

After some discussion, it was agreed that the injury would be monitored for a further twenty four hours and then a decision taken as to whether to bring the horse back into work or to have a further medical investigation. And, with that, Curlew Landings had his leg hosed down for the last time by Sadie, and Sam returned to the house to finish his interrupted work.

"So, who's the newby, then?" Rachel asked Sadie, as they returned Curlew Landings to his box.

Sadie snorted.

"Called Isabella Hall, la-di-da," she scoffed, "Some mate of a friend of Mr Sampfield's who needed a job. Bit on the side, more like."

"She's Mr Sampfield's girlfriend?" asked Rachel, astonished.

"No, not Mr Sampfield's, the friend's," Sadie clarified, "Some guy he knew at school called Mr Stanley. She meets him up at The Charlton Arms. Goes down there on a bike all the time. Always at it, they are."

"Really?" said Rachel, "She doesn't look the type. She seemed very formal and serious."

"All a big act, in my opinion," Sadie huffed, "What's she doing in a place like this, if there isn't something going on? She doesn't know the first thing about horses."

"Hmm," said Rachel, "I'm not sure you're right about that."

7

The coming ten days were due to be busy for Sam's usually relaxed and slow moving yard.

Highlander Park was entered in his first point to point on the coming Sunday, to be ridden by Sam's Peveril cousin, Gilbert. Then Sam was planning to take Caldesi Island hunting during the week, with Sadie joining him on Rooker Sunset. After that Curlew Landings, assuming he was fit, was to run in a Novice Hurdle at Newbury on Hennessy Gold Cup day. A jockey was yet to be booked to ride Curlew.

Sadie was excited by the prospect of the week's activity. Although her comfortable situation in Sam's yard suited her well, she sometimes longed for an opportunity to work in a busier yard, with horses off to the races two or three times a week and travelling far afield to interesting racecourses. Hennessy Gold Cup day was a novelty for Sadie, so she was looking forward to taking Curlew to Newbury for the day. But, first, the inexperienced Highlander Park needed to be made ready for his first competitive race.

Both Kye and Sadie loved riding the enthusiastic and extravagantly jumping Highlander. They had worked him over the jumps on the far side of the gallops and were sure he would do well so long as he did not get over-excited by the atmosphere at the race meeting. Kye had seen Isabella Hall watching him take Highlander through his paces. He was unsure why she was watching, as she never spoke to him afterwards, and his suspicions of the reason for her interest in him intensified uncomfortably.

On the Friday before Highlander's Sunday race, Gilbert Peveril arrived at the yard, ready to ride out with second lot. Gilbert was short and strong with wiry red hair and a forthright manner. He was a good horseman, successful over many years in point to point racing, his one weakness being an inclination to take risks, something which had more than once cost him an advantage in the race. On these occasions, the horses did not always understand what he wanted or became over-faced by the demands he made on them.

As the ride worked its way up the hill behind the Grange, Sam impressed on Gilbert that Highlander's inexperience and natural honesty needed to be respected, otherwise the horse might become confused and demoralised. Gilbert said that he understood.

Kye, riding Rooker Sunset, was not confident that Gilbert had actually understood Sam's instructions. He resolved to watch Gilbert carefully as he worked Highlander over the obstacles. But Gilbert cantered Highlander sedately up the hill behind Sam on Caladesi Island, with Kye and Sadie and two of the work riders following on their horses, and Kye began to feel that he had no need to be concerned.

Although the sun had been up for over two hours, the morning was gloomy and dull, with low grey cloud hanging apparently almost within touching distance above them as they reached the top of the hill. The horses were all blowing healthily as Sam led the ride forward around a track which looped behind the crest of the slope and brought them up to a row of four hurdles alongside a thick hedge.

The six horses negotiated the hurdles easily, so Sam sent them all round for a second attempt, instructing one of the new work riders to lead the ride and to push his horse more firmly into the obstacles, but otherwise seeming to Kye and Sadie to be happy with everyone's work.

The two work riders were sent back onto the flat gallop track whilst Sam, Sadie, Kye and Gilbert trotted their mounts around to a row of three steeplechase fences which lay alongside the hurdles.

"I'll take Caledsi over these first, Highlander to follow me, then Honey and Rooker to come over afterwards," instructed Sam.

The four horses took the jumps competently enough, including Highlander, who seemed to be enjoying his ride with Gilbert. The exercise was repeated twice more, at which point Sam pronounced himself satisfied and gave the string the word to return to the yard.

"Well, young Highlander seemed to go well for you there, Gil" remarked Sam, as the party was dismounting in the yard, "Come into breakfast and tell me what you think of him."

"Delighted, of course, James," responded Gilbert, and, tossing Highlander's reins to the waiting Kye, he followed Sam towards the Grange.

As Sam and Gilbert approached the boot room door, Isabella Hall opened it from the inside. She looked startled to see the two men standing in front of her.

"Oh, good morning, Mr Sampfield Peveril," she said.

"Good morning, Mrs Hall," said Sam, "Please allow me to introduce my cousin, Gilbert Peveril, who has been riding out with us this morning. Gilbert, this is my new office manager, Mrs Hall."

"Good morning, Mr Peveril," said Isabella, formal as usual.

"Pleased to meet you, Mrs Hall," Gilbert said, "But I think that we have surely met before somewhere? You seem familiar."

"No, I don't think so," was Isabella's immediate reaction

"I am sure I recognise you," persisted Gilbert, unhelpfully, "At a point to point meeting maybe, or a racecourse?"

"I think that is rather unlikely," said Isabella, obviously keen to get past the two men and to avoid further discussion, "I don't work with the horses."

"No, no," insisted Gilbert, "I thought perhaps as a guest or an owner?"

"Really not the case, I can assure you," said Isabella as she managed to manoeuvre past him and proceed on her way towards the yard office.

"Hmm, could have sworn I'd seen her before somewhere," mused Gilbert, as he and Sam proceeded through the kitchen and into the breakfast room, "Who is she, anyway? What was her name again?"

"Mrs Hall," said Sam, as Lewis followed them into the breakfast room and stood waiting to hear what they would like to eat.

The mystery of where he had previously met Mrs Hall continued to irritate Gilbert as the cousins ate breakfast together and discussed Highlander Park and other horses likely to be up against him in the forthcoming race. After about thirty minutes, Gilbert announced that he needed to be on his way and threw his napkin down onto the table.

As the two men walked into the hallway, Gilbert suddenly announced triumphantly, "I know where it was. Cheltenham."

Sam had not been following Gilbert's train of thought, and was caught by surprise by the remark.

"Cheltenham?" he queried.

"Yes, at the racecourse. The Showcase meeting in October," went on Gilbert, slowly.

Sam thought back. That meeting would have been about a week after Isabella Hall had arrived. He did not recall that she had been away from Sampfield Grange either on that weekend, or indeed at any time, for long enough to have travelled to Cheltenham for a day's racing. He said as much to Gilbert.

"Well, I'm pretty sure it was her. In fact, I know exactly where I saw her," Gilbert went on, "She was in the parade ring. I was with Roj Mortimer. He invited Pippa and me to join him to see that new horse of his run in the first. That why I thought she must be an owner or someone's guest."

"Was she with anyone?" asked Sam, curious notwithstanding his belief that Gilbert was mistaken, "I can't imagine she was standing there alone."

"No, she wasn't on her own," said Gilbert, slowly, "She was with a trainer and a chap I didn't recognise."

"A trainer?" asked Sam, now genuinely interested, "Who?"

"Irish fellow, name'll come back to me," replied Gilbert, "The other chap was tall, smart tie, cavalry type I'd say."

"How odd," remarked Sam as they proceeded towards the front door, "I'll have to ask her about it. See you on Sunday at Cuffborough, then."

The conversation between the two men had taken place in the hall just outside the kitchen door, which Lewis had left open in order to be able to hear when Gilbert Peveril left, so that he could clear the breakfast things. As a result, it had been heard in its entirety by those occupying the kitchen at the time. The exchange between the two men had meant nothing to the two work riders, who were not party to the intrigue which Sadie, Lewis, Kelly and Kye were all enjoying so much, but everyone else's ears had pricked up immediately.

"What do you make of that then?" asked Lewis, excitedly, once they had heard Sam going upstairs.

"Cheltenham racecourse and with someone who sounds like Mr Stanley too," enthused Kelly.

"Mr Peveril said they were there for the first race," said Kye thoughtfully, "We could easily find out which horses were running, the trainers and the jockeys. That might give us a clue about why she was there."

"But how did she get there?" asked Sadie, "It takes an hour and a half to drive to Cheltenham racecourse from here and she doesn't even have a car. She would have had to be out most of the day if she was going to get there and back and watch all the races. I don't remember her being out for a whole day."

Lewis had checked the racing calendar online by this time and had come up with the dates of the Cheltenham Showcase meeting. There were two, a Friday and a Saturday. Gilbert Peveril had not said on which date he had been there.

Sadie knew she and Kye had to get back to the yard, but this mystery was too interesting simply to be ignored. She sent the two work riders on their way, telling them that she would walk down to the yard later.

Lewis made some more entries onto the tablet computer which Kelly kept in the kitchen, ostensibly for ordering shopping and other housekeeping needs.

"I've got the full results of the first race on the Friday," he said, "We need to find out who owns and trains all these horses and then do the same thing for the first race on the Saturday. Maybe the jockeys too. Perhaps she knows one of them."

Realising that this research would take Lewis a bit of time to complete, the self appointed detectives agreed to confer again over lunch, always supposing that they could ensure that Isabella Hall herself was not present. Otherwise some excuse to meet later would need to be invented.

Isabella was seated, as usual, in the yard office, as Sadie and Kye passed by.

"I have an idea," hissed Kye to Sadie. He turned back to the door.

"Hi, Isabella," he said, brightly, "Do you have a list of Mr Sampfield's work appointments on yez computer?"

"Yes, I do," replied Isabella, sounding cautious.

"Sadie and me's trying to remember which point to points he went to in October," said Kye, "We think he went to the place where

Highlander is running this Sunday in October. Could yez check for us?"

Kye gave Sadie the two dates of the Cheltenham Showcase meeting, saying that he was sure it was sometime about then, but asked whether she could check the dates either side as well.

Sadie and Kye held their breath as Isabella went back through the onscreen diary. She told them that on the Friday, Mr Sampfield had not been out, as far as the diary was concerned, but that on the Saturday, he had been at a shoot in Devon. Kye named a few other dates for her to check, knowing that she would come up with nothing. Sam had been nowhere near Cuffborough point to point course during October.

"Why did you ask her that?" Sadie wanted to know, as Kye thanked Isabella, and they walked into the stable barn, the horses looking at them expectantly.

"Because she wouldn't have gone out all day if Mr Sampfield had been here," said Kye, "But he wasn't here on the Saturday, so she could have gone out and he wouldn't know."

"But we would," objected Sadie.

"Is she in that office all day?" asked Kye, "Do you know when and where she goes on her bike? She is sometimes gone for hours."

"Well, she can't have cycled all the way to Cheltenham," said Sadie, reasonably, "It's too far."

"Yes, but she could have cycled down to The Charlton Arms and gone in a car with Mr Stanley," Kye pointed out.

Sadie was still dubious.

"She would still have to be out for eight hours at least. Three hours for the travel, four hours for the races, getting to and from the Charlton Arms. That's a long time, Kye," she said.

"Well, let's see what Lewis comes up with," replied Kye, suddenly tiring of the discussion and beginning to wonder how he and Gray could get the weed and pills stowed in the secret compartment under the horsebox in time for a bit of trading at the point to point meeting on Sunday.

Unfortunately for the group, Isabella Hall joined the staff for lunch, as usual, so the conversation, such as it was, had to be restricted to neutral subjects. Even so, Lewis thought he would chance his arm with a couple of questions.

"You ever been to a point to point, Isabella?" he asked, "Like the one Highlander's in on Sunday."

Rather to Lewis's surprise, Isabella brightened up at the question.

"Yes, I have, Lewis," she said, "Although it was a long time ago."

"Anywhere round here?" asked Lewis.

"No, it was in Ireland," Isabella replied.

"Do you fancy coming along on Sunday to see Highlander run?" asked Sadie, suddenly.

"Yes, that would be lovely," Isabella replied, unexpectedly enthusiastic, "Thank you for asking me."

Kye was squirming with suppressed fury at what Sadie had just done. If Isabella Hall really had him under scrutiny, then Sadie had played right into her hands.

"What yez do that for? Asking her along on Sunday?" he asked Sadie as soon as Isabella had left the kitchen to return to the office.

"Why not?" asked Sadie, "Then we can find out if she really does know anything about horses."

Kye could not think of a suitable reply. Sadie was only continuing the detective process in which the group was already so determinedly engaged. She did not know anything about his prospective money making enterprise and he did not intend to tell her.

Meanwhile, Lewis had news for them.

"I've been through the results of the first on both days," he said, "And I've checked out all the owners and trainers. There is no-one called Hall or Stanley amongst the owners. I can't see any jockey with those names either, so that doesn't help us much. But Mr Peveril's friend, R E Mortimer, is listed as an owner of one of the horses in the Saturday race, so that must be the day that he says he saw Isabella and Mr Stanley."

"So, who were they with then?" asked Kelly, impatiently. Lewis had refused to tell her the results of his research until all four of them were together.

"Well, that's the tough bit," admitted Lewis, "There were twelve horses in the race. So that's eleven possibles, if you take out Mr Mortimer's horse."

"Mr Peveril said something about an Irish trainer," interrupted Kye.

"And Isabella just said she used to go to point to point meetings in Ireland," Kelly added.

There were two Irish trainers amongst the trainers who had entered horses in the race: Niall Carter and Brendan Meaghan. Neither of the names meant anything to Kye or Sadie.

And, no matter how hard the four of them raked over the ashes, the trail had just gone cold.

8

Although Sam was sure that Gilbert had been mistaken in his identification of Isabella Hall as the person he had seen at Cheltenham racecourse during the Showcase meeting, a niggle of doubt continued to pull at his mind. Unlike Lewis, he had not needed to look up the dates of the race meeting concerned, as he remembered them perfectly well. In particular, he knew that the Saturday had coincided with a shoot in which he had participated at a friend's estate in Devon. And he was certain that he recalled seeing Isabella on the Friday up on the gallops, apparently running along one of the hillside tracks, because he had mentioned her training activities to another participant in the shoot whom he knew to be interested in marathon running.

So, if Mrs Hall, as he continued to think of her, had been at Cheltenham races, this would have had to have been on the Saturday, he reasoned. Running in his thinking along a parallel track to that already followed by Kye and Lewis, he wondered who had been involved in the first race that day.

Sam's dyslexia had made his memory much better than that of more competent readers, but even he could not remember the complete result of every horserace in the country. He recalled Roger Mortimer's horse, because he knew the owner of the stud at which the horse had been bred, but could only make an educated guess at the likely contenders in the same race. He would have to grit his teeth and access the internet if he wished to try to find out the identity of the owner and trainer accompanying Isabella Hall that day.

Sam had to admit to himself that the shiver which had run through him on hearing Gilbert's conclusions as to where he had seen Isabella Hall related more particularly to Gilbert's description of the man he had seen with her. Sam had no idea as to the accuracy of Gilbert's knowledge of regimental ties, so the suggestion that the person concerned was a 'cavalry type' did not necessarily carry any weight. Anyone with a military bearing could have been included in

Gilbert's description. In any case, Sam decided wryly, the so-called security services no doubt had access to any amount of different ties to suit the required occasion.

Isabella Hall had been with them for only about a week at the time of the shooting event, and Sam remembered that he had mentioned to her that he would be away for most of that day. Her response had been that it would give her an opportunity to find out more about the local cycling routes. He was certain that she had been at Sampfield Grange for breakfast at least, because he had wished her luck in negotiating some of the steeper hills in the area, a comment to which she had responded with a polite smile.

As far as Irish racehorse trainers were concerned, Sam did not know any of them well. The idea of Isabella Hall, Frank Stanley and an Irish trainer standing together in the parade ring at Cheltenham racecourse began to seem increasingly ludicrous. He resolved to spend no further time on the puzzle at least until Sunday when he would be seeing Gilbert again.

Kye, who was at the same time skepping out a row of horse stalls, and therefore had plenty of time to think, was becoming increasingly worried about the implications of Isabella Hall's prospective attendance at Sunday's point to point meeting. A text message sent to Gray suggesting that they might postpone their plans for the day had met with an angry response from Gray, who needed to recover some of his financial investment as soon as possible. So Kye reassured him that he would go ahead as planned, and resolved to ensure that Isabella Hall was kept occupied elsewhere whilst his illicit trading activity was going on.

Sunday's point to point meeting at Cuffborough proved to have attracted a large and enthusiastic crowd of spectators, including numerous dogs, who were braving very windy and muddy conditions. Isabella Hall had insisted on cycling to the venue, a distance of about fifteen miles, whilst Kye and Sadie took Highlander Park in the small horsebox. Sam had driven there alone in the Range Rover. Kelly and Lewis were minding the yard in their absence.

Highlander Park could not believe his beautiful brown eyes when he arrived at the noisy and windswept event and was unloaded from the lorry by a watchful Sadie. The new horses and the gusty breeze only added to his excitement at the occasion, and he pricked his sharp black-tipped ears with anticipation and took a good look around at his highly interesting and novel surroundings.

Isabella Hall appeared on her bicycle shortly after Highlander was unloaded. She carried the machine across the muddy field towards the Sampfield Grange lorry and leaned it against the cab on the passenger side. Highlander recognised her and gave a little whicker in her direction.

"No problem finding the place, then?" said Sadie, feeling she needed to take the upper hand in some way, but not sure how to do it.

"None at all," replied Isabella, "Do you need me to do anything?"

"Want to lead him up?" asked Sadie.

"What, in the ring?" asked Isabella, "No, I can't do that. That's for you or Kye. You've done all the work with him."

"Yez saw that, then?" asked Kye, appearing from behind the vehicle.

"I did," said Isabella, "It looked good."

"You know a bit about training horses, do you?" asked Sadie, thinking she might as well try to elicit some useful information from Isabella.

"No, nothing at all," replied Isabella, rather hastily, "I just thought he looked as if he could jump over all the obstacles very well."

Kye was anxious to move Sadie, Isabella and Highlander Park away from the horsebox, so that he could get his prospective customers satisfied before Highlander's race went off.

"Mr Sampfield and Mr Peveril will be waiting for yez," he told Sadie, "Better get the horse over to them pronto."

Isabella indicated to Sadie that she would follow on behind the horse once she had changed her shoes, the cycling shoes being unsuitable for walking around on the muddy hillside.

"Come on, Landy," Sadie said to the young gelding as they set off to meet Gilbert Peveril, "You've got to do a good job for Mr Peveril. Like Isabella said, you've worked well and I think you can do this race with your eyes shut. Well, not literally," she added, just in case the horse should take her comment seriously. But Highlander was too busy having a good look at the unfamiliar surroundings.

As Sadie led Highlander Park away towards the parade ring, Kye sent out a text to those clients who had agreed to meet him at the Cuffborough point to point course that the coast was now clear for them to come to collect their orders. They were mostly stable staff from other yards, but some were locals from all walks of life who thought the Cuffborough course a less conspicuous purchase point than their local pub.

Isabella soon finished changing her cycling shoes for the pair of walking boots which she had brought in a rucksack carried on her back. She shoved the cycling shoes into the rucksack in their place.

"Kye?" she called, unable to see where he had gone.

But Kye, thinking that Isabella had gone ahead with Sadie was already under the lorry, detaching the metal container which he and Gray had so carefully installed, and in which today's supplies had been stowed on the previous evening.

Isabella saw Kye's muddy booted feet sticking out from under the horsebox and called to him again.

"Kye, is there a problem with the horsebox?" she asked, kneeling down on the ground to look under the lorry.

Kye froze with shock.

"Not sure, Isabella," he called back hurriedly, holding the box up against the chassis so that it could not be seen, "I thought I heard a rattle on the way here. Just giving it a quick check."

"I see," said Isabella, "Hope it is all right, then."

Much to Kye's relief, Isabella then stood up and walked away from the horsebox. Kye found that he was sweating. That had been too close for comfort. Had she seen anything? He wasn't sure.

Sadie meanwhile had joined Sam and Gilbert in the saddling area. As they tacked up the horse and made him ready to race, Gilbert noticed Isabella Hall picking her way towards them across the sticky ground.

"You know, James," he said, as Sam made ready to leg him up into the saddle, "I'm right about her.

"Who do you mean?" asked Sam, who was unaware that Isabella had joined them at the Cuffborough meeting.

"Your Mrs Whatsername over there," said Gilbert, pointing with his whip, "I have definitely seen her before and I know it was that day at Cheltenham."

"Well, tell me about it later," Sam told him, "In the meantime, I want you to look after Highlander Park here and bring him back in one piece, with his confidence intact too."

"Right you are," replied Gilbert, "You can rely on me, James, don't worry. We'll do well in the race, won't we young Highlander?" and he patted the horse's neck firmly. Highlander nodded his head and his ears rotated forward.

Highlander Park was still on his toes as he went out onto the course. Gilbert Peveril was well used to riding at point to point meetings and did a good job of keeping Highlander calm and focused as far as possible on the job in hand. Sadie held onto Highlander's bridle until she was sure he was as settled as Gilbert could get him, and finally let go to allow horse and rider to canter out into the face of the wind.

Sam and Sadie walked together to an earth bank alongside the finish line, which offered a good vantage point over the higher part of the sloping course. Much of the course was invisible, even from that point, but it offered the best view after that enjoyed by the commentator, who stood on a raised platform in the centre of the course. Numerous other spectators were already on the bank, dogs and children milling around their ankles, preparing to cheer the runners on. Sam noticed that Isabella Hall was standing nearby although she had not attempted to join them.

"Mrs Hall," he called out, "I wasn't aware you had planned to come along."

"I hope that is all right with you, Mr Sampfield Peveril," Isabella replied, sounding slightly put out, "Sadie did invite me."

Their conversation was cut short at this point by the announcement through the crackly tannoy system that the runners were off. The start was over to the left of the slippery earth bank on which the ragged crowd of spectators was assembled, and a huge shout went up from them as the horses thundered past from the left and disappeared around a bend and down the slope to the right.

The race commentator was rather desperately trying to keep track of the eight runners. Sadie and Sam strained to hear what he had to say about Highlander. Isabella Hall stood quietly, speaking to no-one.

"The horses are well grouped as they enter the downhill section," announced the commentator, "The blue cap of Nine Springs is showing in front and I can see Highlander Park in the red and green Sampfield Grange colours just behind. They're being chased closely by the rest of the field with little to choose between them just yet. They're coming to the first jump now."

The commentator's description was essential for the spectators on the bank to understand what was happening in the race, as the far side of the course was completely hidden from view by the slope and a line of trees.

"I didn't see them clear the obstacle," the commentator went on, thereby acknowledging that even his view of the course was partial, "But they all appear to be still standing, although Ham Hill House is beginning to lose his position behind Highlander Park."

The commentator continued in much this vein until the eight horses reappeared to the spectators' left and prepared to go around the circuit for a second time.

Frustratingly, the commentator said nothing more about Highlander Park after the horses disappeared down the slope again. He mentioned that one of the horses had refused a jump in the back straight and that another had been pulled up. Fortunately, neither was Highlander.

After what seemed to Sadie like an age, but was probably no more than twenty seconds, the amplified voice announced that the remaining horses were making the climb back to the finish line which was located immediately in front of the earth bank.

"Highlander Park and Nine Springs continue to lead the field," shouted the commentator, "This is a good battle between two experienced riders. Gilbert Peveril is getting a good tune out of the young horse and Luke Cunningham is keeping Nine Springs well up to his work."

"Come on, Landy," yelled Sadie, unable to contain herself.

Sam glanced across to Isabella Hall. She was standing perfectly still, but seemed to be muttering under her breath. Her hands were clenched into fists in front of her as if she were silently willing the horses forward.

"And that's a great jump from both horses!" shrieked the

commentator, "I think Highlander Park has landed in the lead. Yes, he has. They should be coming back into view any second."

Sam stood as tall as he could and craned his neck to see the horses appear up the slope to their left. Sure enough, Highlander Park was just ahead with an animated Gilbert urging him forward, his whip waving furiously.

Highlander Park sailed confidently over the final fence and won the race by a length. Nine Springs was second and only three other horses finished.

Sadie was ecstatic. She rushed to meet Highlander Park and Gilbert as they returned to the winner's area and stopped by the wooden post with a number one nailed to it. Gilbert dismounted, his face one huge smile. Sadie was patting the steaming Highlander madly as Gilbert removed the saddle and stood still whilst a picture was taken of the horse and his connections by the course photographer. Highlander puffed and blew and looked pleased with himself. Kye had by this time joined them too, having watched the race from the far end of the earth bank.

It took a while for Sam to realise that Isabella Hall was not with them.

"Oh, she's around somewhere," said Sadie, vaguely, too preoccupied with Highlander Park's victory to be concerned about anything else, "Kye, did you see how well he did? Isn't he clever?"

Kye nodded. He had seen even less of the race than most of the other spectators, having been preoccupied with other matters, but he had at least seen the exciting finish.

"He's a good jumper, I'll give him that," enthused Gilbert, "You two have done a first class job getting him ready."

Gilbert did not have any other rides that day and Sam had no more runners, so, once the post-race formalities had been completed and Highlander Park returned to the horsebox, Sam and Gilbert were able to resume their interrupted conversation. The wind had grown stronger and the dark clouds massed and scudded across the sky. The two men were almost shouting in an effort to hear each other.

"Your office woman," said Gilbert, "The reason I remember her was that there was an incident in the parade ring."

"What sort of incident?" Sam wanted to know, at the same time looking round to see whether Isabella Hall was anywhere in sight. He would have felt embarrassed if he thought that she suspected that he was discussing her private affairs with Gilbert.

But he could not see her anywhere.

"It was Roj's horse that caused it," Gilbert told him, "Girl brought it into the parade ring and something spooked it. A few people had to get out of the firing line pretty damn quick so as not to get kicked or knocked over. She was one of them. That's why I saw her."

"So when Mrs Hall said she didn't know you, she wasn't making it up, then?" asked Sam.

"Oh God, no," said Gilbert, "I wasn't introduced to her or anything. In fact I didn't see her again after that. I doubt she would have clapped eyes on me at all. There were a lot of people in the parade ring."

"If it even was her…" added Sam, slowly.

"Does it matter?" asked Gilbert, suddenly curious as to why Sam had shown such an interest in finding out more from him.

"Well, not really," said Sam, feeling a bit foolish, "It's just that she didn't say anything about it to me. But I'm not her keeper, just her temporary employer, so there is absolutely no reason why she should."

He was about to bring the conversation to a close, when Gilbert suddenly brightened up and raised a forefinger in the air.

"Tell you what, James, old man," he said, "Just remembered. We've got it all on camera!"

"What?" asked Sam.

"Roj's horse, acting up in the parade ring," went on Gilbert, a note of triumph in his voice, "Pips was recording it, you know, on her phone! We didn't know the bugger was going to act like that, of course. Pips was just wanting a few shots of him walking round. I'll get her to send the pics to you. I think she can attach it all to an email or something," he added vaguely.

"Oh don't go to any trouble," protested Sam hastily, "It's not important."

But it was. Sam was desperate to know the identity of the military man who had apparently been accompanying Isabella Hall at Cheltenham races.

9

Sadie had never enjoyed a week in her life as much as she enjoyed the week following Highlander Park's win at the Cuffborough point to point meeting. The members of the local hunt with whom she rode on the Wednesday were effusive in their congratulations to Sam. Sam, for his part, openly and generously acknowledged Sadie's and Kye's part in preparing Highlander for his exciting victory.

Isabella Hall had congratulated Sadie and Kye at breakfast the morning after the race. She had explained her swift departure from the point to point course as being because of her concern about the worsening weather. She had not wished to risk cycling fifteen miles in the wind and rain, especially with the evening closing in.

"You could have come with us in the horsebox," Sadie had told her, magnanimously.

"I didn't think of that," Isabella said, simply.

"You could have been in the winner's photo too," Sadie added, "It gets published, you know!"

"Maybe next time," said Isabella.

But the main focus of the week was to ensure that Curlew Landings was ready for his Saturday race at Newbury.

Curlew, like Highlander before him, responded well to being the centre of attention. He was running in a Novice Hurdle race, the fifth race on Saturday's card, which meant that he was given plenty of practice by Sadie and Kye over the hurdle run at the top of the Sampfield Grange gallops. There was no sign of the worrying leg problem of the previous week, so everyone felt hopeful that the horse would acquit himself well in the race.

Relations amongst the employees at the Grange were more harmonious than they had been at any time since Isabella Hall's arrival. Sadie had almost forgotten the intrigue surrounding Isabella and Mr Stanley, whilst Kye was beginning to breathe more easily in respect of his new business venture. Isabella had appeared to have noticed nothing unusual during their conversation whilst he was under the horsebox and did not ask him whether he had found anything amiss with the vehicle.

"The horse box was OK after all," he said to her, experimentally, on the Monday.

Isabella looked blank, and then said vaguely, as if she did not understand the reason for the comment, "Oh, um, that's good, Kye."

Sam too had found little time to spend trying to solve the conundrum of Gilbert's apparent sighting of Isabella Hall with a man who he had become convinced was Frank Stanley. His main concern was to book a suitable jockey for Curlew.

Sam was particular about the professional jockeys he employed. Gilbert was an amateur, and a relative, so Sam was familiar with his riding style and confident that they could discuss the horses honestly and sympathetically. Professional jockeys were a different matter. Their focus was on earning a living and enhancing their reputation so their attitude to the horses they rode was rather different. Sam wanted someone who would follow his instructions, particularly in relation to the positioning of Curlew amongst the runners during the race, at the same time as not over-facing the horse. Curlew was an able creature, but inclined to back off if he did not see clear daylight ahead of him when out with other horses. As a corollary of this, the horse also needed to get a good look at the hurdles as he approached them.

In the event, the decision was partly made for Sam, as two jockeys' agents, having seen Curlew's entry in the fifth race, contacted him directly. Sam did not have many runners in Listed or Graded races, but his horses were known to be well prepared and of good quality, so were an attractive proposition for jockeys already booked to ride other horses at the same meeting.

After some thought, Sam selected one of the two jockeys, a tough Welshman called Merlin ap Rhys, popularly known as the Welsh Wizard, mainly because of his ability get the best performance out of almost every horse he rode. Even if they did not win, Merlin's rides usually improved from the race in which he rode them. Merlin had a ride in the Hennessy Gold Cup, but was free for the race in which Curlew was entered. Having accepted the booking through his agent, Merlin offered to come to Sampfield Grange to ride Curlew out on the Friday morning.

Sam had handled the jockey booking himself. Isabella had taken the calls from the two jockeys' agents, but had simply passed them through to Sam when they had requested to speak to him. Consequently, Isabella was unaware of the arrangement for Merlin ap Rhys to come to Sampfield Grange until Sadie breezed into breakfast on Friday morning and told them all about it.

"Curlew's jockey's coming later," she enthused, "He's brilliant. I can't wait to meet him."

"Who's that, then?" asked Lewis.

"It's Merlin ap Rhys, the Welsh Wizard," announced Sadie, "I can't believe Mr Sampfield managed to get him for Curlew."

There was a thump from the sideboard, as Isabella Hall put down a jug of milk. Some of the contents slopped over the side onto the checked cloth.

"Watch out, there," said Kelly, crossly, looking at the mess on the cloth.

"I'm sorry," said Isabella, "I lost my grip on the handle."

"Oh, never mind that, it's just some milk, Kelly," said Sadie, wanting to remain the centre of attention, "Merlin's an amazing rider. Did he ever ride for your old yard, Kye?"

"Not in my time," said Kye, wondering why Isabella Hall was

remaining standing at the sideboard, her face looking fixedly at the blank wall.

"And we get to ride out with him!" sang Sadie, ignoring everyone.

Isabella Hall seemed to pull herself together and returned to the table with a bowl of muesli, which she ate in silence, as Sadie continued to tell everyone about various races which Merlin ap Rhys had won.

"What do you think about that then, Isabella?" Sadie eventually said to her, as the only person around the table who had not shared her enthusiasm by offering any comment.

"He sounds wonderful," Isabella said, carefully, "Curlew Landings is a lucky horse."

"I'll let you all know when Merlin gets here," announced Sadie, dancing out of the kitchen and through the boot room with a piece of toast in her hand.

The Welsh Wizard, after such an introduction, might well have been expected to arrive by dragon or on a broomstick, but instead entered the premises in a black BMW sports car which he brought to a halt in the same place as had been occupied by Frank Stanley's vehicle several weeks earlier.

Sam was already down in the yard, whilst Kye and Sadie were in the process of tacking up Caladesi Island, Curlew Landings, Rooker Sunset, and Honeymoon Causeway.

"Pleased to meet you, Mr Sampfield Peveril," said the jockey, as he stepped forward, sharp and confident, to shake hands with Sam.

"My pleasure, Mr ap Rhys," replied Sam.

"It's no Mr anythin'," said the jockey, "My name's Merlin. And you can't shorten it to anythin' else."

"Well, you'd better shorten my name," suggested Sam, slightly amused, "Sadie and Kye just call me Mr Sampfield."

Sam called Sadie and Kye forward and introduced them to Merlin. Sadie was introduced as the yard manager, and was so overawed that she could hardly speak. Kye was simply introduced by his name, Kye McMahon.

"You a conditional, then?" Merlin asked Kye, "Ride for Mr Sampfield, do you?"

Kye had to admit that he did not, and just worked as a work rider and assistant to Sadie as yard manager. He suddenly felt a bit sad as he said it, thinking of his former ambitions.

Sam explained to Merlin that they were all going to ride out together. Merlin looked at the four horses lined up in the yard.

"Which one is my ride?" he asked, "They're all nice looking 'orses, I'll say. Look fit, too."

Sadie beamed with pleasure at the compliment as though it had been made about her personally.

"Could you kindly let Mrs Hall know that we will be out for an hour, Kye?" said Sam as he prepared to mount Caldesi, having pointed Merlin towards a suspicious Curlew, who was not sure he liked the look of the stranger who was apparently intending to ride him and was shifting crossly sideways.

Kye went over to the yard office and stuck his head around the yard door.

"Isabella!" he called, "Yez'll be here on your own. We're all going out."

There was no reply. The office was empty.

"Isabella!" he called again.

The other three riders were already mounted and eager to get on their way.

"I'll follow on," shouted Kye, from the office door, "Just need to find her."

Kye's mount, Rooker Sunset, remained tied up to the ring by the mounting block, as Kye pulled out his mobile phone and called Kelly in the house.

"Can yez come down to the yard?" he said, "Isabella's not in the office and there's no-one here."

Kelly said she would come down to the yard, so Kye got himself quickly onto Rooker's back and sent him off into a smart trot to catch up with the others. He could see the three horses silhouetted against an unexpectedly blue sky, working their way along the slope above him.

"Come on, Rookie," he said to the horse as he pressed his heels into the hunter's sides, "Let's see whether Mr Magician is all he's cracked up to be."

By the time Kye had caught up with the rest of the string, they were at the top of the hill and ready to turn into the row of hurdles along the hedgerow. Sam had been explaining to Merlin Curlew's preference to have a clear sight of his hurdles and suggested that he go out first. The other three horses would follow.

Merlin accepted the suggestion without comment and took Curlew out over the four hurdles. Curlew took them all neatly and fast.

When the group had reassembled at the end of the run, Merlin asked Sam, "This 'orse is a real smart jumper. What 'appens if 'e's not at the front?"

"He seems to get discouraged," replied Sam, "It's as if he doesn't want anything in front of him. Maybe he thinks he's not winning, is my guess, and then says he can't be bothered."

"Well, we can't 'ave that, can we?" said Merlin, leaning down over Curlew's ears, "You need to get a grip, boyo, and show them what you're made of. It's not going to be all plain sailing in this race you're in tomorrow."

Sam and Merlin agreed that they would go again over the hurdle line, but that this time another of the horses would jump alongside him.

"Kye," instructed Sam, "You take Rooker over the hurdles upsides Curlew. Don't try to pass him, just stay level."

In the course of the next twenty minutes, the four riders experimented with various combinations involving the four Sampfield Grange horses: Curlew at the front on his own, Curlew at the front with another horse, Curlew at the back, Curlew being passed between the hurdles, Curlew pushed on, Curlew held back.

Sam was amazed at the amount of effort Merlin had put into getting to know Curlew. In his experience, jockeys would ask a few questions, listen to the instructions of the trainer, and then go out and do what they wanted in the race. Only very special horses aimed at big races received the sort of attention Curlew was getting.

When he commented on this to Merlin, the younger man laughed.

"That's the best bit, see," he said, "Findin' out what they can do. Don't get me wrong, I like the racing. But it's getting the 'orses to do their best, making them even better, and you 'ave to get to know 'em to do that. You got a nice set up 'ere, you 'ave. I'd like something like this one day."

The two men were riding their horses at a walk down the track back to the yard. Merlin seemed to be enjoying himself in the hazy sunshine and was happy to talk.

"That lad of yours," had said, jerking his head back towards Kye and Sadie, who were following behind, "I'm impressed with 'im. Should have thought 'e would have been on his way to being a jockey by now. Girl's good as well, strong rider, 'orses'll jump for 'er. You're lucky to 'ave those two, Mr Sampfield."

Sam was pleased to hear Merlin's assessment of his two staff. He agreed with Merlin's view of Kye and had often wondered why Kye had not approached him about becoming a conditional jockey and starting to work his way along the career path to becoming a professional rider. The reference provided by his previous yard six months earlier had mentioned Kye's potential and the owner had clearly made the assumption that entering training was the reason for Kye's move. But Kye had never raised the subject with his new employer and nor had Sadie on his behalf.

Merlin ap Rhys took off in his sports car as soon as they arrived back at the yard, saying that he needed to get to Newbury for the rides for which he was booked that day.

"See you tomorrow, Curlew," he said to the horse as he dismounted. Curlew was still not sure what to make of this new and demanding rider and snorted derisively as the smart black vehicle sped off down the track leading to the road below.

Sam stood for a while in the yard, waiting for Sadie and Kye to untack the four horses and return them to their stalls. He was thinking about Curlew Landings.

Curlew was an unusual horse for Sam's yard. Sam mostly invested in youngsters and brought them on himself. Curlew, though, had been at Sampfield Grange not much longer than Isabella Hall. Gilbert had persuaded Sam to buy the horse that summer from a friend who had run into financial problems and had decided that keeping a racehorse in training was something he could not longer afford.

Curlew Landings was five years old and had yet to gain a handicap mark. Gilbert had ridden him in three point to points the previous season and had a high opinion of his ability. He had put in impressive performances in all the races in which he had run, coming third, second and first consecutively, and seemed ready now to take his chance in a Graded race. The next day's race was a Class 3 Novices Hurdle and would be the first opportunity Sam had had to see for himself how the horse performed in a more challenging competition.

Curlew's reluctance to fight back once he had been headed was something which worried Sam. If they could not change Curlew's attitude, they would always have to run him prominently, which was a tough way to have to win any race and meant that the horse could not afford to run out of steam in the process of staying at the front. The Newbury ground was likely to be soft so it was going to be hard work for Curlew and his rider.

Sadie and Kye came towards him, surprised to see Sam waiting for them.

"Do you need us, Mr Sampfield?" asked Sadie.

"I just would be interested in your opinion. Both of your opinions," replied Sam, as they began to walk together up to the house, "Curlew is a bit of a puzzle to me, I have to say. Is he just sulky when he thinks he isn't going to win?"

"I am not sure that's the reason," Kye spoke up. He had been thinking about this ever since they had been up on the practice hurdle course on the hillside.

"My thinking, Mr Sampfield," he went on cautiously, "Is that he likes having horses behind him to give him the oomph to run away from them and make them catch him. Once they're gone past, it's no fun for him any more."

Sam regarded Kye with interest.

"That's a novel theory," he said, "But it still means we're going to have to run him at the front. Do think he can handle two and half miles in soft ground making all the running?"

Kye and Sadie had no idea.

"Well, I imagine we will find out tomorrow," said Sam, as they reached the boot room door.

Sadie and Kye remained in the kitchen whilst Sam went to his study, having asked Kelly, who was preparing lunch, to bring him a sandwich.

"I don't know why you asked me to walk down to the yard earlier," said Kelly in an irritated tone to Kye, once Sam had left the room, "Isabella was there in the office and I wasn't needed as well."

"She wasn't there when I looked," protested Kye, surprised.

"Well, she was there when I got down there," Kelly told him, "Fiddling about on that computer as usual."

"Sorry," said Kye, "She must have been somewhere else in the yard when I was trying to find her."

But he knew that she had not been anywhere else in the yard. His earlier fears resurfaced. Was she checking out the horse box whilst he and Sadie were occupied with Mr Sampfield and Merlin ap Rhys and all the work riders gone for the day?

Sam, meanwhile, was confronting some problems of his own. Having opened his email Inbox, he discovered a message from P.Peveril with the title Pippa's Pics of Roger's Horse. Having opened the message, Sam found no text apart from the title. His relatives knew that he did not attempt to read any message longer than a few words. All that he could see was an attachment.

Sam opened the file attached to the email with trepidation. A short video recording flashed across the screen. It showed the entrance to the parade ring at Cheltenham racecourse, the weighing room to the left, the horses entering and turning to their left to walk along the parade ring pathway. The second horse to enter the ring was clearly Roger Mortimer's horse, as it suddenly spooked at something before the groom who was leading it had managed to establish it on the path. Three people standing nearby were forced, as Gilbert had said, to move quickly aside to avoid being knocked over or kicked by the excited animal.

Sam replayed the recording a few times and managed eventually to stop it at the point at which the three bystanders were most clearly visible. The quality of the pictures was poor but Sam could see that the group consisted of a woman and two men. The woman could very well have been Isabella Hall, although it was difficult to be sure, as she was wearing a large hat and sunglasses, above a smart coat and leather boots. The smaller of the two men was clearly the Irish trainer whom Gilbert had mentioned. He had his back towards the phone camera, so Sam could not see his face. But it was the other man who attracted Sam's attention.

Sam could see why Gilbert had suggested that he was a military type. The man was tall and grey haired with square shoulders. He was clad in a dark grey coat, white shirt and a green tie with some kind of badge on it. A fedora hat was held in one of his hands. The other hand held a stick on which he leaned heavily.

Whoever he was, he was definitely not Frank Stanley.

10

"Eh bien, nous sommes tous prets, Georges."

The assembled group were looking at George, expectantly. In response, George shifted slightly on the hard upright chair and leaned forward, his hands clasped together between his knees. The laptop computer, which he had propped up in front of him, wobbled dangerously.

Behind George, the wine bottles lay darkly in their wooden racks along the cellar walls. The wine museum in which they were sitting was closed for the winter, but the many hundreds of bottles remained on display. There was just no-one to see them, still less to taste, admire, and maybe even buy, them from the sales desk which stood in the middle of the museum.

No-one, that is, except George Harvey and his attentive companions. But they were not interested in the wine. They knew it was there. They saw it every day. They were interested in what George was about to read to them.

George had arrived in their little community a month earlier and had initially escaped notice. This was unusual, as *les anglais* inevitably made their presence felt with braying voices and inability to speak anything other than the most rudimentary French. But George had arrived in the winter, not a popular time of year for elderly retirees, and he had come alone in a car with a Carcassonne number plate.

It had taken a week before anyone had realised that the tall, gaunt man in the most distant of the lakeside apartments was not a local, and that was because it was a week before he emerged into the damp winter air.

Guy had spotted him first, walking slowly towards along the quayside towards the canal. The mighty Canal du Midi lay dull and impenetrable between Guy and the newcomer, a laboriously engineered and now uncompromising barrier between Minervois and Corbieres. Or at least that was how Guy thought of it. Guy was on the Corbieres side and the stranger was in Minervois territory.

"Maurice!" Guy called over his shoulder, whilst keeping his gaze fixed on the other bank of the canal.

Maurice, darker and stockier than his younger brother, emerged from the door of the little wine museum, and stood beside him on the quay. The sky was grey and the wind penetrating and chill. It swept unhindered along the open quayside, rocking the boats moored in the small harbour. The boats were closed and shuttered, bumping irritably against each other, rubbing shoulders in their crowded prison.

Together Guy and Maurice watched the man approach the footbridge which crossed the canal, providing one of two points of transit through the village between the two wine regions.

The stranger walked slowly, head down. He was clad in a grey fleece jacket over dark trousers, and wore walking boots. He carried a stick, on which he leaned heavily, his left leg stiff and unbending swinging outwards from his body at every step. Despite this impediment, and the attentions of the wind, he moved steadily and purposefully, soon reaching the steps at the bottom of the footbridge.

The footbridge, unlike its older counterpart at the other end of the village, and which carried a small road, was of modern construction. It ran at an angle to the banks of the canal, the Corbieres side disgorging pedestrians just outside the museum. In the summer, the heavy wooden doors which filled the stone arch of the museum entrance were wide open, inviting passers-by to enter its dim recesses and learn about the liquid treasures it contained, helped of course by Maurice and Guy, who managed it on behalf of a co-operative of local wine producers.

As the newcomer hesitated at the bottom of the bridge, Guy noticed that the he was carrying a black bag slung by a strap over his right shoulder. His awkward gait had caused it to slip down over his upper arm. The man shrugged it up again onto his shoulder in an impatient gesture, then started to ascend the steps on the opposite side of the footbridge.

The steps were wooden with steel edges, painted blue like the handrails which rose alongside. It curved into a clean, shallow arc over the sluggish water beneath. The wood underfoot was worn and shiny. The stranger ascended the steps awkwardly but without hesitation and was soon in the centre of the bridge, where he stopped, looking first one way and then the other along the canal.

Guy knew the view from the bridge as well as he knew himself. Born, raised, and now working in the little village of Frossiac, he had spent most of the waking hours of his young life in sight of the canal. His teenage years had seen him cycling and running along the towpath, no longer used by the long gone heavy horses which used to draw their laden barges of cargo between the Mediterranean and the River Garonne.

One day Guy had run all the way to Beziers, passing the lock staircase at Frontenac and had decided he needed to keep going. The years spent working in the bars of Beziers and later in Toulouse had enabled him to acquire a wife and to recognise the potential advantages of near to his family once he and Monique had children of their own. And his brother was keen to see him back, as he had a business proposition for him, one which would keep them both occupied. And so the wine museum had come into being.

Guy could see, now that the man was closer, that he was not young. His hair was mostly grey and receding from both temples, his forehead high and large, set above heavy lidded eyes. His nose was short, straight, high-bridged. His face narrowed to a jutting chin, his mouth serious and turned down at the corners, lips pressed together in a firm line.

Guy had become practised at assessing potential customers, and judged this man to be serious, not one of the time wasters and casual lookers who often came into the museum.

Not that the museum was open today. The dark wooden doors were shut and barred. Guy and Maurice were stocktaking and planning for the new season, as they always did at this time of the year. In the evening, they would lock the wooden doors and return to Maurice's restaurant by the old bridge, where a few locals would populate the bar and watch the football on satellite TV.

It was a time of year when little happened in Frossiac and when the people, like the boats, were moored alongside the canal, waiting for the wind to change direction and the strengthening sun to awaken the canal for the summer. Those not content simply to wait sought work elsewhere, in Beziers, Carcassonne, or even Toulouse. Some, deciding it was time for a holiday of their own, joined the ski season in the distant Pyreneen resorts of Andorra and Catalunya.

The stranger's unexpected appearance had provided a temporary distraction from the brothers' time-filling activities.

The man had evidently seen Guy and Maurice standing outside their premises, as he raised a hand in their direction, and continued his negotiation of the bridge, moving competently with his stick down the seven steps which led to the stone paved area where the brothers were standing.

"*Bonjour*," he said, stopping before them, and letting his black case slide to the ground. Guy could see now that it was a computer case containing, he assumed, a laptop.

As Guy and Maurice returned the man's greeting, he took a deep breath as though about to deliver some rehearsed line.

"*Bonjour*," he said again, then, "*Je m'appelle George Harvey. Est-ce que vous pouvez m'aider, s'il vous plait?*"

"*Mais oui, bien sur*," responded Guy and Maurice, almost in chorus, whilst Guy continued, "But perhaps you would prefer to speak in English?"

The man let out a short laugh.

"Well, I would prefer it," he said, "But my wife says that I must try to speak French."

"But, your wife, Monsieur Georges 'Arvai," observed Guy, helpfully, "Is not 'ere."

George Harvey pursed his lips, a cleft appearing in his narrow chin.

"That's true, I mean *c'est vrai*," he replied, and fell silent, evidently attempting to decide what to say next.

Maurice sensed that this line of conversation might not be the best means of assisting the man with whatever problem required their help.

"Perhaps we can speak English in any event, Monsieur," he cut in, "We need to practise for the tourist season. In the winter, we sometimes forget."

"I think you are just indulging me," said George Harvey, wryly, "But I shall have to let you have your way, as I really don't think I can explain the problem in French, and we might be here all day trying to communicate with each other."

And so it was that the two brothers ushered George Harvey into the wine museum, and understood that the network connection in his apartment over by the lake had gone down and that he was trying to find a way to do some work using his laptop computer. The PC installed in the little holiday retreat was unable to function until an engineer could be sent from Carcassonne to restore the service.

George was soon installed at the reception desk, his laptop computer open before him. Maurice and Guy nudged each other, as the state of the art piece of equipment was taken from its case and plugged into the electrical socket under the desk. George saw them eyeing it and offered the explanation that he was a software developer, who wrote applications for clients back in the UK and also in Ireland.

The brothers returned to their stocktaking and the mysterious

Monsieur 'Arvai fell silent, tapping away lightly on the keyboard, pausing for thought at intervals, and occasionally consulting a textbook which he had taken from the case and which lay on the desk beside him. A mobile phone was placed beside it, but remained silent. Guy was not entirely certain that it was even switched on.

The one thing Guy was soon sure of, however, was that Monsieur 'Arvai had a handgun stowed in a pocket in the inside of his jacket. He could see the stubby shape of the bevelled grip, black and hard against the lining of the garment, which hung loosely from the man's shoulders, falling open and away from his body as he leaned forward over the keys of the computer.

Guy quietly mentioned his observation to Maurice, who had a ledger propped on a shelf at the back of the cavelike structure which constituted the museum, checking entries in the stock list. Maurice started upright against the bar stool on which he was half-seated. He would have stood up, had Guy not stopped him with a heavy hand on his left shoulder.

"*Mais, c'est dangereux,*" hissed Maurice, under his breath, "*Il est soldat, peut-etre? Ou terroriste?*"

Guy took the view that Monsieur 'Arvai was unlikely to be either a soldier or a terrorist, as he would not be sitting working quietly in a rural museum in an obscure village where there was no-one available to be fought or terrorised.

Nonetheless, they were both relieved when their visitor stood up, closed his computer, and asked, in passable French, for directions to *l'epicerie*.

The restoration of George Harvey's home internet service appeared to be a slow process, the result of which was that George appeared once again in the wine museum the following day. Once again, he sat quietly at the laptop computer, tapping away thoughtfully at the keyboard, apparently absorbed in his work. The handgun appeared to be still in place in his coat pocket.

Maurice and Guy were fascinated by this new arrival, who had provided a welcome distraction during the dull and damp December weather. When he stood up to leave, saying it was time for him to return home to get something to eat, he was invited by Guy to join the brothers at Maurice's restaurant.

Maurice was not at all keen to invite a man with a gun into his restaurant and had insisted first on consulting a neighbour who was also the local police officer. To Maurice's surprise, it appeared that Marcel Lambert knew all about Monsieur Harvey's gun, as he had produced his permit at the police station on his arrival in the area.

"It is not a problem, Maurice," Marcel assured him.

"But to have a permit for a gun is one thing," persisted Maurice, "To carry it about in a public place in something different."

"I regret that I cannot discuss this matter with you, Maurice," replied Marcel, firmly.

"So why does he have it?" Maurice wanted to know.

"Please, Maurice," the officer told him, "I cannot answer these questions. This is a matter for the police and I am not permitted to speak about it to you."

So Maurice had to be content with this unsatisfactory explanation.

George Harvey proved to be something of a success with Maurice's and Guy's wives, who were in collective charge of the restaurant and associated bar. Both of the women were consumed with curiosity as to why an Englishman should have come to stay in their remote village at an inhospitable and miserable time of year. George, who had by now abandoned any attempt to speak French, had provided the explanation that he had needed to find somewhere quiet where he could concentrate on his work.

Guy's wife, Monique, in a different environment, would probably have been a journalist, a gossip columnist, or the editor of magazines such as Hello! and OK of which she was an enthusiastic reader. As it was, she had to be content with the limited but occasionally interesting affairs of the village. The newcomer was therefore a source of new material for her, and she persisted with her enquiries.

The polite questions from Monique about Madame 'Arvai, the wife who had been mentioned the previous day, were met with a sigh and a vague reference to her possibly joining George in the Spring. This evasive answer left Monique and Claudine convinced that Mrs Harvey had left him and that he had come to Frossiac to recover from a broken heart.

But it was Claudine who obtained from George the even more interesting information that, in between pursuing his business of technical software development, he was writing a book.

"What is the book about? Is it a romance, a thriller? Or is it a boring book about computer things?" Claudine wanted to know, as she poured a second glass of deep red Corbieres for their guest.

George informed the two women that the book was a work of fiction, although, he confessed sadly, he had little experience of writing, and was struggling to make progress with the plot.

"Can we assist?" asked Monique excitedly, "I read a lot of books – detective stories and love stories are the best."

"Well, my book has a bit of both of those things included in it," said George, slowly, sipping his wine, "But I have got a case of writer's block at the moment."

"Writer's block?" queried Claudine, "What is that?"

"It means," George explained, "That I have written a few chapters of the book, and now I cannot write any more. I cannot imagine where the action of the book will lead next. I don't know what to write."

"We will be most pleased to help," Monique assured him, imagining herself taking on the role of author and inventing all kinds of exciting events to continue and improve George's book.

"Very well," said George, getting awkwardly to his feet, "I would be very happy to read to you what I have already written. Perhaps your husbands would also be interested? I would find it useful to have a man's thoughts as well as those of two such knowledgeable women."

As a result of this conversation, and somewhat against the wishes of Maurice, it was agreed that Monique and Claudine would join their husbands and George at the wine museum later that afternoon, whilst the restaurant and bar were closed, and that George would give the four of them a reading of the chapters of the novel which he had written so far.

George's gaze was fixed on the wine bottles, silent in their racks on the opposite wall. The four faces looked at him expectantly. But at that moment, George didn't see them, nor did he see the shelves, the bottles, the posters and flyers stacked on the desk, nor even the walls behind.

Instead he saw a darkened room, the bulk of a body lying on the floor, the shocked and whitened faces of men turning suddenly towards him, the smell of blood, urine, faeces, vomit, rotting wood. He was suffocating, and in the blackness he heard the twittering and whistling of unseen birds, the rush of a breeze through thick leaves. And he could feel the acid of nausea rising from his stomach into his throat.

His stick, which had been leaning against the chair, clattered to the floor and he jolted forward. Perspiration stood out on his forehead and along his upper lip.

"Georges! Are you ill?" exclaimed Guy, starting forward from his seat, whilst the facial expressions around him changed from attention to surprise and concern.

George swallowed hard and forced himself to sit upright. He raised his arm to motion Guy back to his seat.

"Sorry, it is a getting bit hot in here," he said, untruthfully, "Or perhaps it is the stress of being expected to reveal my unpublished work to my very demanding critics."

The little group laughed uncertainly, but sat back down in their chairs, expectantly.

"All right," said George, his voice becoming stronger, "I'll read you what I have written. It is a story which takes place in England, and I hope you find it exciting. It involves ambition, crime, lies and deception."

He paused, looking at his audience. He had their attention now.

11

Susan Stonehouse put her hand on the battered black Bible and read from the laminated card.

"I swear by Almighty God to tell the truth, the whole truth, and nothing but the truth."

It sounded ridiculous, like something out of a play.

The black-robed usher took the Bible from her, and she remained standing in isolation in the polished wooden witness box. To her left, the members of the jury, men and women of varied ages and ethnic backgrounds, seated in two rows in their own wooden enclosure, shuffled a little, regarding her expectantly. Some of them cast a glance at the man in the dock of the court, but most were keen to avoid his gaze.

Susan kept her head lowered. She stared at the wooden edge of the witness box in front of her. Her legs were shaking, an insistent trembling, brought on by fear, by hunger, by stress, by her thick hangover, she knew not which. Or perhaps it was by all of them.

There was a glass of water nearby, but she did not reach for it. She thought she might be sick. She knew that her daughter was watching her anxiously from the public gallery but there was nothing her daughter could do to help her. She did not dare raise her head anyway.

The old man in the dock looked at her with a hatred so powerful that it was almost tangible. Clairvoyant people might have described a thick and foul smelling shadow filling the short distance between him and the object of his venom. He was a small, bent individual with eyes so dark they were almost black. A deep vertical furrow ran between his eyebrows, two thick slashes drawn across his narrow forehead. Iron grey hair which had once been thick and soot coloured, stuck upward like a thick bush from his scalp. His nose was long and pointed, his lips narrow and turned down at the ends.

He had a prominent chin which he jutted forward contemptuously toward the miserable figure in the witness box. He was trying to stare her down, but she did not look at him.

The two officers standing either side of the prisoner could feel the bile and fury being generated from every inch of their charge's skinny body. They regarded the witness with pity. This man was as evil as anyone they had ever come across and it was self-evidently no trivial matter to be the target of his fury.

The old man had vehemently denied both the murder charge, spitting his contempt for the person who lay dead, and had dismissed with a sneer the reference to the second person who still lay comatose in hospital. He had laughed on hearing of the accident which had befallen the teenager and her pony.

Apart from these people, none of whom were in a position to give evidence, there was only one witness who could give a partial account of the events of that day. And she looked as if she might collapse.

The police officers who had investigated the ugly crimes with which the old man was charged looked on nervously and helplessly. They had given their evidence earlier that morning. A video recording had also been shown to the court, admitted as evidence despite the defence team's attempts to have the amateur recording dismissed as being unreliable and possibly faked. The ambulance crews, both terrestrial and air, and their despatcher had also testified.

But if Susan Stonehouse could not speak up, the trial would collapse and this vile individual would walk free yet again. They and other colleagues had tried hard to bring him to justice before. His crimes were unspeakable – drugs, people, he cared not what he trafficked and whom he exploited to make his greedy fortune. His surrounding gang were violent to the extent that other gangs feared them. Witnesses melted away, or were done away with, and the pathetic prostitutes, drug addicts, pickpockets, illegal immigrants, and other damaged elements of humanity made unconvincing witnesses, even if they could have been persuaded to testify. So Konstantin Paloka continued to walk free and to destroy the lives and wellbeing of others.

Until now.

Orlando Frogmore QC stood up. The numerous press in attendance in the court had enjoyed his opening speech, given earlier that day. It suited them well to have the story of Paloka's alleged repulsive deeds described so succinctly and with such economy of expression.

"Mrs Stonehouse," he began, "I am going to ask you about the events of 6 July last year."

Susan Stonehouse nodded weakly. She seemed to sway in the witness box and her hands tightened on the wooden rail in front of her. The jury, the assembled press, the court officials and those who had managed to secure a place in the public gallery all seemed collectively to hold their breath.

Her Honour Mrs Justice Grantley leaned forward from the bench above the witness box.

"You may be seated, if you wish," she informed Susan, her tone and expression neutral.

Susan shook her head.

"I'm fine standing," she stated, unconvincingly.

The man in the dock let out a sudden roar of laughter, making everyone in the courtroom jump.

"Bitch!" he shouted.

Her Honour Mrs Justice Grantley looked at him coldly, her eyes narrow beneath her wig.

"One more outburst like that and you will be removed from the courtroom," she stated baldly.

Konstantin Paloka regarded her silently, daring her to carry out her threat. The judge ignored him and turned back to look at the witness.

The incident, though, had an unexpected result. Susan Stonehouse stood up straight, turned to face the man in the dock, and said, in a loud and clear voice,

"Yes, I am ready to tell you about the events of that date."

As she spoke, she stared the prisoner full in the face. Her expression was unflinching. It was if she was looking right through him. And, suddenly, he knew she meant what she said, and for the first time in his life, a small piece of doubt in his own invincibility entered his heart.

In the public gallery, a man sitting alone took a deep breath and willed the witness to stand firm. Another man, also sitting alone, felt a cold stab of fear go through his stomach.

The mood in the courtroom now centred onto the witness box, as Susan Stonehouse began to speak.

12

The little blue and white aircraft had been a mere speck in the distance when Tammy Soper spotted it. Sitting on the back of her pony Magpie, she decided it was time to get out of the way. Magpie hated aeroplanes and Tammy was not keen to risk being carted across an airfield and into a ditch somewhere. Tammy could not understand why anyone would want to fly around in noisy little aeroplanes when horses were so much more fun.

Pony and rider moved away from the deserted airfield and entered the narrow lane which ran along its perimeter. The hedgerows were thick and overgrown, but the pilot of the aircraft could see the two of them as she brought the aircraft down towards the runway. She was glad that they were out of the way. She did not want to frighten any horses either.

Susan Stonehouse, the pilot, was fifty four years old, and, at that moment, fit and well and happy. She was looking forward to enjoying a relaxing lunch with her husband, Peter, who sat beside her in the co-pilot's seat. Not that Peter was a co-pilot, but he did enjoy being a useful passenger and getting his own enjoyment out of the time he spent in the aircraft.

Peter Stonehouse was a technologist who had made his living in the IT world. Never entirely able to distance himself from his day job, he liked to experiment with recording what he thought were the more interesting aspects of their flights on a small video camera which was set up above the instrument panel. Many of these recordings had been posted online, edited and embellished with accompanying music and commentary, some of which had seemed to Susan to be unnecessarily dramatic. But Peter enjoyed exploiting the tools and facilities available on the internet, some of which he had designed himself. Indeed it was his ability to do such things which had made their business a success, and which was now being put to good use in the new venture which he and their daughter were building together.

Susan, as an accountant, found technology to be a useful business tool, but her interest stopped there. Flying suited her well, with its systematic approach and predictable outcomes. She especially liked the process of managing the descent and landing, controlling the speed and the angle of the aircraft's nose, deploying the flaps to increase the drag on the airframe, and gradually bringing the aircraft in an orderly fashion down onto the runway. Runways at airports and larger airfields had approach systems to help pilots make the necessary judgements, but at small and deserted fields such as Little Uppingham, there was nothing except the application of the pilot's skill to ensure that the aircraft landed safely.

Little Uppingham was typical of many airfields in the South and East of England. Used intensively during World War Two, to store and fit out aircraft shipped out from Northern and Midlands factories, it had not been needed once the war was over and the intensive production and movement of aircraft within the country had ceased. Lancaster bombers had landed there once, but now it was only small aircraft such as Susan's which made use of the over-large runway. Little Uppingham was one of the more fortunate airfields, kept in use by local flying groups and interested landowners. Many similar airfields were either lying disused or had had housing estates built on them.

Susan made a neat and uneventful landing on the deserted and silent airfield. The little aircraft continued to roll forward towards the end of the runway, the sun reflecting off the surface of its wings. The wind was almost non-existent, as indicated by the faded orange windsock hanging emptily from its pole ahead of her.

"Where now then?" asked Peter, cheerfully, as the aircraft slowed to walking pace.

"The Old Grey Goose and a great lunch," replied Susan, "All we have to do is park the aircraft and we can walk into the village."

The village of Little Uppingham was less than a mile away. They had flown over the spire of its attractive stone church as they had approached the airfield.

Susan steered the aircraft through a gap in the untidy hedge and turned towards an open area of hard standing flanked by a green warehouse bearing a rectangular sign displaying the words Warner's Seeds Ltd in yellow letters. The warehouse had a large sliding door through which tractors and delivery vehicle could access the premises, and a smaller door to the side through which those on foot could enter. A white notice on the door showed the single word Office. To the left, and at right angles to the warehouse, was a small and dilapidated trailer, which could once have been a chicken shed. It too had a door, but was unlabelled.

The warehouse and the trailer alike both appeared deserted, their respective doors closed.

Two light aircraft were already parked on the hard standing to the right of the trailer, and facing the warehouse. A dirty blue Range Rover stood near the warehouse. No pilots or driver could be seen.

"Looks like we have the place to ourselves here," remarked Peter, peering around.

"It certainly does," responded Susan, turning the aircraft to the left to bring it into line with the other two, facing the warehouse office door, "But the airfield operator said that there was an honesty box for us to pay the landing fee."

This payment arrangement was not unusual at small and out of the way airfields whose owners could not afford to staff them either with a radio operator or anyone who could collect payments for the use of the field. Susan had used the Unicom safety frequency when approaching the airfield, just to let any other approaching traffic know she was there and in the hope that other users would take the same precautions. But there had been silence from the airfield and no indication that any other aircraft was operating nearby.

"I'll shut down the aircraft and you hop out and pay the landing fee," suggested Susan, "I think it's the trailer where you leave the money."

"Righto," said Peter, and, as soon as the engine was switched off and the propeller had come to a halt, he was out of the aircraft and striding purposefully towards the warehouse.

"Peter!" called Susan, "It's the trailer you need."

But Peter didn't hear her and continued on his way towards the door marked Office.

Susan did not try to call out to him again. She assumed the door would either be locked and that Peter would turn around so that she could signal to him to go instead to the trailer, or else that there would be people inside the office who could re-direct him.

In the event neither of those things happened. Instead, in the next few moments, Susan Stonehouse's comfortable and orderly world disintegrated forever.

Peter turned the handle on the office door and it opened inwards. He went inside and the door closed behind him. A few seconds later it opened again and Peter staggered out backwards with his hands in the air. There was a loud bang and Peter immediately fell over, striking his head on the concrete surround of a drain to the side of the office door. As he fell, he let out an agonised scream of pain, as his left leg buckled beneath him.

Susan heard the bang and the scream, but not the sharp crack as Peter's skull was fractured. She did see the blood spreading from beneath Peter's head and pooling around him on the ground. It looked as if someone had turned over a dark red paint pot.

Susan tried to understand what was happening in front of her. The bang had sounded like a shot or an explosion. A bomb? A gun? Here? Why? She took a step forward towards the warehouse.

At precisely the same time as she began to move, two men burst out from the office door. They were large and heavy, like weightlifters, and looked sweaty and dishevelled. One of them had some kind of bent metal bar, or maybe a car jack, in his hand. Both of them had their attention on the fallen Peter and did not see Susan, who quickly stepped backwards behind the aircraft. One of the men crouched over Peter and then said something over his shoulder to the other. Standing up, he aimed a kick at Peter's unresisting body, and called out to someone Susan could not see inside the building.

An old man came out of the door. Susan saw that in that brief moment that he was small and dark and bent. She noted his greying black hair, sharp nose and jutting chin. He looked angry, she thought, and nasty too. He shouted something at his two companions, waving them away from the man on the ground and pointing towards the Range Rover.

Susan followed their movements, instinctively concerned to keep out of their sight. She prayed that Peter would have the sense to stay still so that they would leave him alone and go. Then she could call an ambulance. She did not yet realise that Peter would not be moving anywhere.

Susan watched as the three men climbed hurriedly into the Range Rover, the two heavy types in the front, the old man in the back. The engine roared into life and the vehicle shot off in a flurry of dust towards the road on Susan's right. She could see the old man's ugly face peering out of the back window, so she remained crouched below the aircraft's wing until the car had gone behind the hedge and was out of sight.

Grabbing her mobile phone, she pressed the keys 999. As the call was connecting, she scrambled to her feet and ran towards the warehouse, where Peter continued to lie unmoving on the ground, the blood spreading wider around his head like a lopsided halo.

Up until then, things had happened quickly, unfolding in front of her with no opportunity for Susan to take any action. With hindsight, she knew later that this had saved her life. The three men who had driven off in the battered Range Rover had been too intent on what they were doing to notice her cowering behind the aircraft. If they had even thought about the fact that an additional aircraft was now parked opposite the warehouse, they would have assumed that Peter was the pilot. After all, he was the one who had got out of the aircraft and come in to interrupt what they were doing.

Susan had then, of course, no idea what they had been doing. As she ran over towards her injured husband and the full significance of his stillness and the blood seeping around his head began to dawn on her, her mind started to swim. She could see now that it was not just Peter's head which was bleeding. Blood was soaking through his jeans below one of his knees.

She dropped to her knees beside Peter's body just as the emergency operator answered her call.

"Ambulance, please," stuttered Susan, "Little Uppingham airfield. Yes, one casualty. He's fallen over and hit his head. He's on the ground. There's blood. A lot of blood."

She got the words out between gasps and sobs, but the operator understood her and confirmed that an ambulance was on its way, although from where it was coming Susan had no idea. Then he started asking more questions.

"Is the casualty conscious? Is he able to speak?"

Susan was not listening. A black mask was gathering across her vision as her brain tried to understand what had just happened. She could see Peter's head in front of her, the liquid red halo enlarging inexorably around it, but the image began to narrow to a pinpoint, as she doubled herself over her stomach and retched. Everything began to seem very far away.

The insistent voice of the operator brought her back to her surroundings. He was asking her repeatedly if she too was injured and whether or not she could help the casualty.

"I'm ok," Susan managed to gasp, "I am not hurt. My husband is the one who is hurt."

"Do you have any first aid training?" asked the operator.

"Yes. No. No." replied Susan, whose medical knowledge consisted of a CPR course done many years ago at a children's swimming club.

"Do you know how to check for a pulse and a heartbeat?" the operator asked her.

But before Susan could reply, she heard a high-pitched whinnying scream behind her.

"Oh, Christ!" she said, turning her head around to face the source of the noise.

A piebald pony was clattering towards her from the direction of the lane. The sun was behind it, so to Susan it looked like an apparition bursting out of a lighted lamp. Its reins were flying around its ears, which were folded forward over its head, the heavy saddle was swivelled round to one side, and there was a stream of blood coming from an ugly gash in one of its haunches. The pony was clearly terrified and, as far as it was concerned, running for its life. The vision registered itself in Susan's terrified vision like a snapshot.

"Caller, are you there?" the operator's voice came down the line into Susan's ear.

Susan pitched herself forward across Peter's prone body as the pony swerved crazily away from her and found itself cornered in the space between the green warehouse and the chicken shed trailer. The creature stopped, trembling, and looking around wildly for an avenue of escape. Then, suddenly, it collapsed on the ground, the one eye which Susan could see wide open and staring, a white rim around the brown centre. It gave strange gasp, an exhalation of breath, and then the eyelid came down and closed off the horrific stare. The pony's body lurched twice and then lay still.

"Caller! Caller!" the operator was saying, as Susan remained transfixed by the shocking sight of the dying pony.

"It's dead," she said stupidly into the mobile phone.

"Please, caller," said the operator, "Tell me what has happened. The ambulance is coming but you need to help the casualty. Are you saying he is dead?"

"No, the horse is dead," Susan murmured into the handset.

"The horse? Did you say horse?" asked the operator, "Did the casualty fall from a horse?"

"Not this one," said Susan, "But another person must have fallen off the horse."

"So there is more than one casualty?" the operator persisted.

"Yes, I think so," Susan felt like a machine, trying to keep itself operating in the face of conflicting inputs and demands.

"Where is the other casualty?" asked the operator.

"I don't know," stated Susan, flatly, beginning to feel overwhelmed and gradually becoming hysterical, "All I know is that my husband is bleeding to death here and there is a dead horse in front of me. I can't see the rider."

The operator knew that his priority was to try to keep her calm until help arrived but he sensed that he was fighting a losing battle. The caller was clearly highly distressed and in a situation in which she was unable to provide the information he needed. He had to concentrate on her to prevent her becoming yet another casualty.

"I have just asked for a second ambulance to come to the scene," he said, "Now I want you to listen to me. Is there anyone else around who can provide assistance?"

"No. I don't know," whispered Susan, still clutching Peter's deathly still arm, which lay limply on the concrete. He did not seem to be breathing. She wanted to tell the operator that.

But, as she tried to speak, there was a movement by the office door, which had remained open since the occupants had hurtled out. A figure crawled, slithered and dragged itself out onto the step. It was barely recognisable as a human being. Susan saw hair matted with blood, a face battered beyond recognition, the glaze of broken eyes, useless arms, legs dragged along and twisted at unnatural angles. It opened its mouth as if to speak, but no sound came out. The apparition was like something out of one of the zombie movies which Susan's daughter had once liked to watch.

If Susan could have screamed, she would have done, but she had no strength left.

"Caller? Caller?" the operator was becoming ever more worried.

"There's another one," gasped Susan, before she fainted.

"Another casualty?" asked the operator, but he was speaking to himself.

13

That was the end of Susan's own story, as related in the witness box of the silent courtroom. Orlando Frogmore QC had asked her very few questions, other than to prompt her with an occasional reminder or a request to clarify a particular recollection.

The court had already heard earlier in the day from the paramedics and the police officers who had arrived at the airfield prepared for two casualties, one of them a man who had fallen and struck his head and the other a rider who had parted company with her horse. Nothing in their briefing had prepared them for the horrific and chaotic scene which had presented itself on their arrival.

The first ambulance crew arrived at the airfield ten minutes after Susan lost consciousness and found a teenage girl impaled through one thigh on a metal fencepost in a ditch by an overgrown lane. The girl was conscious, terrified and in pain, and frantic about the wellbeing of her pony. The paramedics could see no sign of the pony but assured her that he could not have gone far and that they would look out for him. In response to their questions, the girl told them her name was Tammy and that a big blue car had come along the lane towards them at enormous speed. Magpie, the pony, had taken fright at the sudden appearance of the revving vehicle and had leapt sideways into the hedge, unfortunately just where a rusty fence post was concealed beneath the undergrowth. Pitched out of the saddle, Tammy had bounced straight onto the pointed end of the post. Magpie had sustained a serious gash to his hindquarters, and had run off towards the airfield. A trail of blood along the surface of the lane amply verified Tammy's sobbing account.

The second ambulance crew, immediately behind, passed their colleagues in the lane and entered the open area in front of the warehouse. They found one middle aged man, unconscious, lying on his back with his head against a concrete step enclosing a drain, and bleeding from head and leg wounds; a second man with multiple injuries lying on what was left of his face in a doorway nearby; an unconscious middle aged woman covered in fresh blood; and, not far away, a motionless piebald pony lying on its side with blood congealing on its flank. There was no one able to tell them what had happened, but the pony and the man in the doorway were soon assessed to be dead, whilst the man with the head injury had a weak pulse, and the woman, notwithstanding the covering of blood, appeared to be uninjured.

The police, following within minutes, found themselves pressed into helping with the casualties. Any idea that this was all the consequence of some terrible accident was soon dispelled when the ambulance crew informed them that the man with the head injury had what looked like a bullet wound to his left leg. It was obvious that some kind of deliberate violence had been involved, although both the nature of the actions and by whom they had been carried out were unclear. No-one could see a gun, or indeed any other weapon, anywhere near either of the two male casualties. The connection, if any, with the accident to the teenager and her pony in the nearby lane was also unclear.

The first response officer told the ambulance crew to touch nothing which was not strictly required for treating the casualties, and designated the area around the warehouse as a crime scene. She secured it as best she could with the limited information and resources she had available, and called for more colleagues and a scene of crime team to attend.

But before any investigation could commence, both the teenage girl and the man with the head injury and bullet wound needed urgent medical help, so the air ambulance was called and Little Uppingham airfield experienced its second landing of the day. The doctor attending with the helicopter decided that the two injured casualties, once stabilised, should be airlifted to a local major trauma hospital.

The same doctor pronounced the man with multiple injuries to be dead at the scene. The woman was unscathed, but, once brought round, incoherent and suffering from shock. The blood in which she was covered appeared to be that of the man with the head injury. The doctor managed to understand that the man with the head injury was her husband and that it was she who had called the emergency services. When asked for more information, she simply shook her head and whispered that she did not know what was happening. The doctor instructed that she should accompany the casualties in the air ambulance and told the attendant police that they would have to wait a while before asking her any questions.

The forensic pathologist subsequently called to examine the dead man did not take long to conclude that his death was very recent. It appeared to have followed a severe beating with, amongst other things, a heavy object, the details of which would be deduced once the body could be removed from the doorway and taken to a controlled environment for a full post mortem examination. Photographs were taken and the body removed.

A local veterinary surgeon called to look at the dead pony confirmed that it had died not of its nasty wound, but more probably of heart failure brought on by shock. Photographs of Magpie were taken before he too was removed, at the request of the police, by a van called from the nearest knacker's yard.

All the casualties, both living and dead, having been dealt with and the medical staff having left the scene, the police were now able to focus on the information to be gleaned from the crime scene itself. One concern was to establish whether there was a connection between the two apparently discrete events.

The incident in the perimeter lane was later graphically described in Tammy Soper's short statement and the evidence gathered by the scene of crime officers confirmed her brief story. Tammy herself had not been required to give evidence in court, as causing serious injury by dangerous driving was not the charge being faced by the man in the dock. Her statement had however, been made available to the court.

To the investigating officers, whilst the incident leading to the injury to the girl in the lane appeared to be a case of dangerous driving, whether this event was linked in any way to the three people found in the warehouse forecourt remained in question. The pony, it was quickly concluded from the trail of blood on the ground, had run, riderless, from the lane to the warehouse after it had been injured.

There were multiple tyre tracks in the area around the warehouse, some of which were from aircraft, and most of which were muddled and indistinct on the dry ground. Given that the vehicle appeared to have come either from the warehouse or from the airfield, these were carefully investigated and compared with such tyre marks as could be found in the lane.

The vehicle which had caused the serious injury to Tammy and the death of Magpie was subsequently found abandoned in a nearby town. It had been neatly parked in a residential street and reported several days later, when its presence had begun to irritate a local homeowner annoyed by the fact that it was occupying a parking space outside his home which he considered to be for his sole use. The vehicle registration matched that of an unrelated vehicle which had been stolen months earlier in a different part of the country. Unsurprisingly, the chassis number of the car itself and the registration number plate it displayed did not correlate to DVLA records.

The location in which the dead man had received his multiple injuries was readily identified when the investigating officers accessed the warehouse office. It was a small room containing a small wooden desk, two old chairs and a couple of grey metal filing cabinets. The chairs were shoved back against the wall and covered in bloody finger marks. The desk was damaged, as if by a heavy object being smashed against it, and also covered in blood and other body fluids. There were three broken teeth on the floor, two fingernails and part of a human ear, all subsequently identified as belonging to the dead man. Establishing whether any of the human detritus could point to any other individuals, particularly the injured man and his wife, was a longer and more difficult task.

Photographs of this mess had been shown to the jury during the morning together with pictures of the dead man, whose name was given as Jerzy Gorecki, and the stricken pony, which was identified as the property of a Mrs Jacqueline Soper. All the jurors had tried to assume stoical expressions, but most looked visibly sick.

Nothing found in the desk or the filing cabinets suggested anything other than the normal operation of a seed warehousing business, and the shocked owner, when contacted at a nearby farm and brought to the building, was unable to explain how his office had come to be in the state. He did not believe anyone else had a key to the office. Such security as there was had been reserved for the entrance to warehouse itself, where the stock and other supplies and equipment were stored, and to the connecting internal door between the office and the warehouse floor. The outside door did not appear to have been forced, but the lock was a common one, and he agreed that it was not inconceivable that other keys which would fit such a lock could easily have been obtained.

Soon, not only the office, but Little Uppingham airfield itself, the warehouse, and the perimeter lane became included in the area designated as the crime scene. The airfield itself revealed nothing of relevance. No information on aircraft movements at the airfield that day had been recorded. A check with the Civil Aviation Authority on the registrations of the three parked aircraft quickly revealed their respective ownership. In addition, National Air Traffic Services records showed that one of three aircraft had taken off from an airfield close to London on the morning of the day of the incident. It had proceeded through the hands of two civil air traffic control zones and thence to a nearby military air traffic zone before the pilot had announced an intention to switch to the Unicom safety frequency. This aircraft was owned by a Mrs Susan Elizabeth Stonehouse, who was also recorded at the airfield of departure as the captain of the aircraft. This confirmed what the police had by now established, that Susan Stonehouse was the female casualty at the scene.

The owners of the two, rather old, aircraft standing alongside Susan's were contacted. Neither of them had been near the airfield that day, nor had their aircraft been recently flown. The two elderly men knew nothing of the business of the warehouse and had not recently seen anyone go in or out of the premises. The airfield was simply a convenient and cheap local facility from which they could enjoy their hobby of flying their aircraft.

The operator of the airfield, a local landowner and farmer, was able to add little to the investigation, or, at least, so it initially appeared. He knew both of the elderly local pilots, although he did not know Susan Stonehouse. He confirmed, though, that Susan had spoken to him by telephone to ask permission to use the field that morning and that he had explained to her the landing fee payment arrangements. The investigating officers had not until then realised the significance of the chicken shed trailer, so that was searched too, and a ring binder recording aircraft movements was found, photographed and removed. It contained lists of the registrations of numerous aircraft which had apparently landed at the field and whose payments had been duly posted in the honesty box.

The airfield operator, when asked to look at the ring binder, confirmed that the pilots of the aircraft concerned appeared to have been conscientious in paying their landing fees, as the money in the honesty box had usually tallied with the number of aircraft listed in the records. When asked, he said he had not met any of the pilots personally but simply attended the trailer every so often to collect the money, remove the completed sheets, and replenish the paper in the ring binder. He kept at his home all the previous records of the reported landings at the field, which he also handed over to the police.

The operator was asked to report any requests received from non-local pilots to land at the field and any instances of aircraft seen landing there without prior notification. The operator seemed doubtful of his ability to do this consistently without setting a permanent watch on the field, but said he would do his best.

A significant step forward in the initial investigation was made when the search of Susan's aircraft revealed a small camera above the coaming. This camera had been working away undisturbed since Peter had switched it on during their aircraft's final approach to the airfield. It had therefore recorded everything before it, from the moment of arrival of the aircraft in front of the warehouse through to the point at which the aircraft was searched by the police. When the soundless video recording was later played back, the investigating officers were not only able to obtain the registration number of the Range Rover but they could also see the faces of those who had climbed into it.

Apart from revealing that this was likely to be car which had been involved in the accident to Tammy and Magpie, scrutiny of the faces of the vehicle's occupants made the investigating team realise with shock that this was not simply a local matter. It was at this point that the National Crime Agency became involved.

The remaining question was that of the connection between the men in the car and Susan and Peter Stonehouse. Peter appeared to have entered the warehouse office of his own accord rather than go to the chicken shed trailer to pay the landing fee. Nothing could be seen of what happened in the warehouse office after he entered, although his buckling knee and backward fall against the concrete edge of the drain were clearly recorded, as was the hurried departure of the men in the Range Rover. Susan appeared on the recording only after the Range Rover had left the scene and then she could be seen running towards the prone Peter on the ground. Magpie's final gallop to his death was shown, as was the emergence of the badly beaten man onto the office doorstep. Thereafter the video showed a static picture of three unmoving bodies, the final location of the dead pony being outside the edge of the camera shot. The next movement shown on the recording was the arrival of the ambulance crew.

Susan was not interviewed until some time after her admission to the hospital to which the air ambulance had taken her, along with Peter and Tammy. The delay arose from a combination of the need for her to provide information to the medical team caring for Peter and to allow her recover sufficiently from the sedative to be able to give a coherent account.

Susan's recollection of events was good. She was able to explain that Peter had gone to the wrong door in his attempt to pay the landing fee and that she had called out re-direct him, but without success. She was also able to confirm that she had seen no-one other than Peter until the emergence of the three men from the office doorway. She had never seen them before and did not know who they were, but she would certainly recognise them if she saw them again.

Peter, though, was not able to help the police. The bullet lodged in his left knee had been removed and the damage it had caused repaired as far as was feasible. The surgeon who performed the procedure would have liked to explain to Peter that he would be able to walk again but would probably not be running anywhere. Instead, she was obliged to give this not entirely good news to Susan, because Peter continued to remain unconscious and unresponsive.

Peter was diagnosed as having a very severe level of head injury. A CT scan revealed a depressed fracture of the skull and a subdural haematoma, requiring immediate surgery and transfer to an intensive care unit. The removal of the bullet from Peter's knee had been a minor procedure in comparison. Peter was breathing without assistance but required constant monitoring and no-one was able to say how long it would be before he woke up. Or whether he would remember anything when he did.

The National Crime Agency detectives stood ready to interview Peter should be recover consciousness, but, as the days passed, both they and Susan came to realise that Peter was not likely to be able to help their investigation nor contribute anything to their anticipated arrest and prosecution of the offenders.

In the meantime, the original investigating team police had set about identifying the owners of the aircraft listed in the airfield records and contacting them. What they discovered was unexpected. Most of the aircraft registrations listed in the book simply did not exist. Those that did exist were established as belonging to people who were able to provide witness evidence, usually in the form of their passengers, that they had indeed landed at the airfield that day. The investigating officers worked painstakingly to establish alibis for each and every one of the identified owners on the day of the incident. Eventually, all alibis had been checked, so that these known individuals and their aircraft could all be eliminated from the investigation.

All that remained unaccounted for now were the fictitious aircraft registrations. As far as the investigating team could understand, someone had gone into the trailer, entered a non-existent aircraft registration in the book, and paid the landing fee. Whether any aircraft had actually landed at the field, though, was unknown.

The operator of the airfield, when asked, was unable to shed any light on the conundrum. He did not keep any separate records of the registrations of the aircraft which landed at the field. He said, though, that he had a good idea of the numbers of aircraft which came and went from the airfield and was of the opinion that the volume of traffic indicated by the records in the ringbinder was consistent with the general usage patterns which he had observed from his farm.

The only conclusion which could be drawn from this was that some of the pilots bringing aircraft into the field had dutifully paid their landing fees but had deliberately concealed the true details of the aircraft they were flying. The entries in the book were in this way consistent with the operator's expectations and he had had no reason to query their accuracy. This information, too, was passed to the National Crime Agency.

The National Crime Agency officers knew all about the old man on the video recording. So they were able to make a good guess at the reason for the fictitious entries in the Little Uppingham airfield ring binder. Drug trafficking was amongst the many unsavoury activities in which Konstantin Paloka was involved and light aircraft arriving at an unmanned airfield in a remote location were perfect vehicles for the transportation of illegal substances into the United Kingdom. Although the filing of flight plans was compulsory for aircraft entering UK airspace from abroad, this requirement could, with a bit of care and planning, be circumvented by inconspicuous aircraft operating from small private airfields. Maintaining radio silence and flying at low altitudes also reduced the risk of detection by radar, even if anyone was maintaining a look out.

The eventual identification of the dead man lying on the office doorstep confirmed these suspicions. Jerzy Gorecki was known to the local police as a drug dealer, although they were unaware of any specific connection to the kind of organised crime overseen by Konstantin Paloka.

The combination of all this information meant that the NCA officers had adequate grounds on which to which make an arrest. Whilst the drug trafficking arrangements could not be conclusively proven, it was quite clear from the video evidence that Konstantin Paloka had been present at a scene at which a young man had suffered a violent attack leading to his death. Whether Paloka had physically participated in committing the murder it was not possible to say, but he was, at the very least, an accessory to it.

Paloka's two accomplices were also familiar to the NCA investigators, but, again, no specific offence for which they could be arrested had yet been attributable to them. Their appearance on the doorstep of the office, as shown in the images recorded by the webcam, in which one of them could be seen holding what the forensic evidence suggested to be the murder weapon, gave ample reason to suspect one or both of them of the assault which had resulted in the death of Jerzy Gorecki. The fact that one of the two men was clearly driving the vehicle which had caused the serious injury to Tammy Soper, and the death of her pony, further suggested that another serious charge could be brought against him.

So, warrants were obtained for the arrest of Konstantin Paloka, Jack Dilley and Guy Griffin, on suspicion of murder and causing serious injury by dangerous driving. Charges relating to Peter Stonehouse could not yet be formulated, as further investigation, with which it was hoped that Peter could assist when he regained consciousness, was still required. No-one other than Peter, Paloka and his associates knew what had happened in the few seconds during which Peter was in the warehouse office. That he had been shot in the leg with a small calibre handgun was not in doubt, but whether this was deliberate or accidental, and who had been holding the weapon when it was fired was not known. The gun itself had not been found at the scene, nor was it in the Range Rover when it was recovered from the residential street where it had been abandoned.

When tracked down and brought in for questioning, Dilley and

Griffin readily admitted all the charges. They agreed that they had killed Jerzy Gorecki, because he was, in their words, a fucking little shit who had tried to make money on the side for himself instead of following instructions. They agreed that they had been instructed by Paloka himself to 'teach that toe-rag cretin a lesson', but insisted that they had not been told to kill him. That had been an accident, when things had got a bit out of control. Mr Paloka had tried to stop them, they both said, but they were so angry that they had not taken any notice of him. They were both willing to plead guilty to assault and manslaughter.

As to the injury to the girl in the lane, they were sorry she had been hurt, but she had been riding her pony very carelessly in the middle of the road, possibly even speaking on a mobile phone as she did so, and Griffin, the driver, could not avoid her. They did not realise she had been injured or they would have stopped to help her. They were sure they had seen her standing uninjured by the side of the lane shouting insults after them. So, Griffin was not willing to plead guilty to causing serious injury by dangerous driving, or to the destruction of property in the form of Magpie, but he did agree to plead guilty to failing to stop after a road accident.

Konstantin Paloka himself told exactly the same story. Yes, he had wanted the young man to realise the error of his ways but his employees had gone too far. He had implored them to stop, but they were very angry at the insult to their boss's authority and had been carried away by their own emotions on his behalf. He had not seen the girl and the pony in the lane, as he had been sitting in the back of the Range Rover. So, he was not prepared to plead guilty to anything.

Although all three individuals were questioned separately over an extended period of time, the story and the attempted bargaining over the charges, was clearly well-tutored and well-rehearsed. They all stuck unwaveringly to it, the proceedings overseen in each case by a solicitor appointed by a senior member of Konstantin Paloka's apparently numerous employees.

The NCA officers needed to make a decision. The fact that the two associates were ready to plead guilty to the assault and manslaughter, if not to the murder, of Jerzy Gorecki meant that they could be disposed of quite quickly. The charges were serious enough to keep them out of circulation for a long time.

But Konstantin Paloka himself was evidently intending to continue to protest his innocence. He did not deny that he had been present at the killing of Gorecki, but his defence was that he had played no role in the fatal act and indeed that he had tried to prevent it. Similarly, he had played no role in the serious injury to Tammy Soper, and further claimed he had been unaware of the incident. It was a thin defence, but it meant any charges against him would have to proceed to a trial, at which witnesses would be required. And the officers concerned knew what happened to witnesses who tried to give evidence against Konstantin Paloka.

The questioning of the arrested men did not shed any very clear light on what had happened to Peter Stonehouse. All three men agreed that he had come into the office without warning. They all said they did not know who he was and why he was there. None of them admitted to carrying any firearm, even suggesting that Peter Stonehouse must have brought it in with him. They all agreed that Peter had fallen backwards out of the door and then down the steps of his own accord, and all three denied that they had pushed or threatened him in any way. They had certainly not shot him.

The account given by Paloka, Dilley and Griffin in relation to Peter Stonehouse did not accord with any of the known facts. Peter was clearly not in possession of a gun when he was found lying on the ground and, as his body had been in clear view of the camera from the moment he fell, no gun could have been taken from him by anyone else. In the unlikely event that he had been carrying a gun in the first place, it would have to have been taken from him, and then used against him, in the few seconds between his entering the office and falling backwards down the steps. This was difficult to credit, but remotely possible. But, so long as Peter remained unconscious, no-one could ask him for his version of events.

A conference between the NCA and the Crown Prosecution Service was called to review all this information. The NCA objectives in relation to Konstantin Paloka and his activities were also considered. Pressure was being exerted by the legal team working on Paloka's behalf to have him released without charge. The two associates, on the other hand, were clearly disposable, and could be sacrificed by Paloka if necessary.

Although the conviction of Dilley and Griffin was important, it was of little strategic use to the NCA. The hired help could easily be replaced by Paloka from within his empire. It was Paloka himself who needed to be removed from circulation. And if could be removed for a significant period of time, even if only whilst on remand for a serious crime for which no bail would be granted, this would serve their purposes. The ultimate objective would be to have him convicted and locked away for many years.

The NCA knew that they would never get a better opportunity that this one. A stroke of fate had delivered Paloka into their hands and finally given them the ammunition they had been seeking to get him off the streets and to start the dispersal of the evil empire he controlled.

So, Konstantin Paloka, Jack Dilley and Guy Griffin were all charged with the murder of Jerzy Gorecki. In addition, Griffin was charged with causing serious injury by dangerous driving, the destruction of property, and failing to stop after an accident. When they appeared in court to face the charges, Dilley and Griffin pleaded not guilty to murder, and an alternative plea of guilty to manslaughter was entered by both of them. Griffin appeared to have been advised to change his position concerning the additional charges which were put to him, and he entered a plea of guilty to all three.

The upshot was that Dilley and Griffin's pleas were accepted and they were given lengthy custodial sentences. In return for their loyalty, their families would no doubt be well looked after by the Paloka empire through the many years to come. It seemed equally likely that the stay inside the prison walls would be made less uncomfortable than it might have otherwise been, thanks also to Paloka's connections and influence there.

Paloka simply pleaded not guilty to the charge of murder. He did not offer an alternative plea of guilty to manslaughter. His case was therefore listed for trial by jury. Bail was refused, despite representations by Paloka's lawyer, citing his client's, hitherto unheard of, poor health.

The NCA and the CPS now had Paloka where they wanted. The next step was to get him convicted of Gorecki's murder. But, with Peter still unconscious, Susan alone would have to help them.

14

Susan's evidence was followed by a silence which lasted for some seconds after she had finished speaking. Even the twisted old man in the dock seemed cowed by it.

The outline of the story had been heard before, summarised by Orlando Frogmore QC in his opening address, illuminated by the evidence of the police, the forensic pathologist, and the paramedics, and supplemented by the written statements of the doctors, the vet, and Tammy Soper. The recording made by the camera in the aircraft had confirmed the sequence of events and had clearly shown the faces of the old man and his associates as they left the warehouse.

Peter Stonehouse would not be called to give evidence nor had he given a written statement, the court was told, because he remained still in a coma.

"I should like to sit down now," said Susan, breaking the silence. She did so suddenly, as though the energy had gone out of her.

Her Honour Mrs Justice Grantley spoke.

"Have you any questions for this witness?" she asked the counsel for the defence.

"I have, m'Lady," he said, as he got to his feet.

"You may put them to her in the morning," said the judge, "Proceedings are concluded for today."

And with that, she rose, and the Clerk called for the court to rise with her. The members of the jury were ushered from the courtroom, having already been told to enter into no discussion with each other or anyone else about the case. A few of them cast sympathetic glances towards Susan, but most of them kept their eyes on the floor, at least until the man in the dock had been escorted away to spend a further night in custody.

Outside the door of the courtroom, Susan had a short discussion with Orlando Frogmore, who told her she was doing a good job, and not to worry about the cross examination in the morning.

"Just stick to the facts," he reminded her. "Don't get drawn into any speculation or arguments. Don't be upset or angry if he challenges your evidence. It's not personal. That's his job."

Susan nodded, suddenly weary again. Orlando had already told her this earlier in the day, in case the cross examination had happened that same afternoon.

Once the lawyer had gone, Susan sat on one of the leather covered seats in the gallery outside the courtroom for a few minutes, watching people from the numerous courts in the enormous old building walk past her. She wondered what would happen to her next.

Susan's life was in tatters. She felt like a ghost, a nebulous and transparent replica of her former self. She had been fit, strong and successful. Now she felt ill, weak and exhausted. Her reflection in the mirror that morning had been of a defeated, grey haired old woman whom she did not recognise.

Peter was far away in the same hospital to which he had been taken seven months ago by air ambulance. Susan knew that any news she sought about him would be just the same – no change. The hotel in which she was staying during the trial was a short walk away but she did not feel like making the walk just then. She would wait until her daughter called her.

As she sat absorbed in her gloomy thoughts, she felt, rather than saw, that someone had come to stand by her side. She looked up and found that a tall man was waiting motionless beside her. She did not recognise him, but he clearly knew who she was.

"Mrs Stonehouse, I believe we can help each other," he said quietly.

Before Susan could respond, he handed her a plain white business card.

"Call me when this is over," he added, then turned and walked away.

The episode passed so suddenly that Susan was not sure that it had really happened. She looked at the card in her hand. It had one word printed on it in capital letters. ICE. Underneath was a mobile telephone number.

"What does he want?" she thought, "Is this some kind of sick joke?"

She wanted to throw the card into the nearest bin, but could not see one anywhere nearby. So she stuffed it into her handbag and stood up. The man who had given it to her was nowhere to be seen.

As she walked down the wide stairs leading to the entrance of the court building, her phone trilled in her bag. Hastily, she pulled it out and looked the little screen to see who was calling. It was her daughter.

"Hi, Stevie Stone!" she answered, using the name which had appeared on the screen.

"Hi, mum," said the disembodied voice, "You did well today. I heard it all from the public gallery. It will be all over tomorrow and we can get back to our lives again. Now, how about I take you out for the evening?"

Listening to her daughter's determined attempts to cheer her up, Susan decided to respond in kind.

"Good idea," she said, trying to inject some enthusiasm into her voice, "I'll meet you in the usual place. And make sure you find somewhere with decent wine!"

"Excuse me, madam," a voice said from behind her, "You dropped this."

A uniformed security guard was handing her the little white card which the stranger had given her a few minutes earlier. It had fallen out of her bag when she pulled out the phone.

"Oh, yes, thank you," said Susan, vaguely, as she took it.

She looked at the card again. ICE. Why would anyone give her a card with that written on it? Maybe it was intended as a piece of advice, telling her to stay calm. She put the card into her purse where it would be safer. The tall stranger watched her from the top of the stairs and breathed more easily. He did not fancy having to repeat this charade another time.

Susan knew she had to face a cross examination in the morning. She also knew that this was just a staging post in her journey towards an uncertain future. In one way, the court case had been useful, representing a target which she had to meet. It had given her a focus, something to achieve.

Once she had learned more about the man who had been arrested and charged with the crimes for which he was on trial today, she was determined that she would do her level best to get him convicted. The many other crimes for which he was responsible could not be proven in the court, but being an accessory to the murder of the young man in the warehouse office would be enough to put him in prison for a long time. His incarceration would enable the police, she had been told, to work on gaining evidence to charge him with more crimes, enough to keep him in prison for the rest of his life. And, at the same time, to start to dismantle the evil empire which he controlled.

The fact that this gangster was responsible for Peter's terrible injuries and for the death of a young girl's beloved pony was only part of her incentive. People like him ruined the lives of others, and if she could play a part in stopping that from happening, then at least some good would have come from the unexpected destruction of her own life and Peter's.

As she walked out of the imposing front entrance of the historic court building, a small group of waiting paparazzi spied her and snapped numerous photographs. The January late afternoon gloom made the flashing bulbs appear even brighter and more intrusive than they usually were.

Susan kept her face grim and expressionless as she walked past them to the place where her daughter would be waiting for her. They had agreed that it was important that no pictures of them together should appear in the news and gossip media. Susan knew that she was a target, not just for the press, but for Paloka and those he controlled, and the less her family was included in that target, the better. Peter was at least safe in the Intensive Care Unit of a distant hospital, and their other daughter was somewhere where even Konstantin Paloka could not touch her.

"So what's going to happen tomorrow?" asked Stevie Stonehouse, known to the social media world as Stevie Stone, when they sat down together at an unobtrusive table in a relatively quiet wine bar, two large glasses of chilled Chablis in front of them.

"Well, I get cross examined," said Susan, taking a large gulp of the wine, "And that is the end of the case for the Crown. After that, the defence will call its witnesses. But there aren't any. That depraved old bastard has said he won't testify, which won't matter, as he would have only told them a pack of lies anyway. Then the lawyers make their speeches and the judge gives directions to the jury. After that, the jury members go out to discuss things and reach a verdict. Job done."

Stevie Stone looked at her mother, hunched on the chair with the glass of wine clutched in her hand. She didn't like seeing her like this. Stevie had been used to her mother being a strong and capable individual, one on whom Stevie could lean when she needed help, as she often had. But now things had gone into reverse, and she was the one providing the support.

"That's good," she stated, firmly, "Then we can focus on Dad."

"For all the good it will do," replied Susan, flatly.

"You can't think like that, Mum," Stevie told her, not for the first time, "You have got to believe he will come round. Then we can ..."

"Get back to normal?" asked Susan, "I don't think so."

"Well, we will have to make a new normal then," said Stevie, "I've got my new business now and we can work together on that."

Susan took another mouthful of wine and pulled herself back together with a determined sigh.

"Yes, you're right," she said, rather unconvincingly, but at least, she thought, I've said it. "And, tell me then, how is it all going?"

The answer was that Stevie Stone's little business was progressing slowly but surely. It involved a crazy combination of horse racing, apps and social media.

The concept was simple. Horseracing, whether flat or jump, was an ancient and established sport, which over the centuries had meant many things to many people: for some it offered the opportunity and ambition to breed or own the best and fastest horses, for others it was a way of earning a living, whether by riding, training, or as stable staff, and for yet others it provided an fascinating and addictive source of entertainment and something on which to make a wager. Whatever had been good or bad about it, it had always been inclusive, and never boring.

More recently, though, thanks to its portrayal in the traditional media, horse racing had become increasingly associated in the public mind with billionaire sheikhs, exclusive and expensive events such as Royal Ascot, involving well-heeled upper class people and fat cat business owners, arcane terminology, and the need for specialist knowledge and wealthy connections. At the opposite end of the spectrum of impressions, it was associated with more accessible but atypical events such as the Grand National, with High Street betting shops and their customers, internet gambling, and heavy drinking by men in cheap suits. Above all, it – and whether 'it' was the horse racing itself or the gambling on it - was seen as a sport enjoyed by old, or at least older, people and those people were usually men.

To Stevie's mind, this was the worst of all worlds. Families with children were put off by the aggressively presented advertisements of the bookmakers which showed carefully imaged male pub-goers, girl-oglers and wife avoiders strutting through the streets in blokey groups. Young people and teenagers were further deterred by the perceived age demographic, the old-fashioned communication styles, and the mumbo jumbo and volumes of statistics produced by TV racing commentators. Ordinary families shied away from the perception of upper class expense and privilege set alongside pushy nouveau rich businessmen whose low end businesses they recognised and to whose wealth they knew they had contributed. Taken together with the braying accents of many trainers and owners, and the increasingly evident truth that one had to be a member of a royal household, either British or Middle Eastern, or the owner of a rip-off business, to participate effectively in this sport, many people came to the conclusion that horse racing had little chance in the competition with more widely appealing sports, such as football, and even rugby, tennis or athletics.

Stevie had looked at the sports coverage in both traditional and online media and decided that for a sport to be popular, people needed to be able to identify with it, perhaps even to the extent of participating in it themselves at some level. Footballers and football club managers were household names, both in the sporting press and the gossip outlets of social media. Athletes, and players of rugby, tennis and cricket had ordinary, but interesting sounding, personal lives, which were talked about and subject to speculation. Things went right and wrong in their lives in ways which everyone understood – marriage, a new baby on the way, putting on weight, feeling stressed, a divorce, the death of a close family member. Racing coverage was mainly restricted to discussions about big races, aimed at knowledgeable punters, and associated interviews with trainers of whom most people had never even heard.

But on Grand National Day, everything changed. Suddenly, the horses became household names. The same horses had of course been racing regularly throughout the preceding winter, but this had never brought them to the attention of the general public. But now, there were news and online features on where they lived, who trained them, how and by whom they had been acquired, and interesting little snippets of stories about them were sought out and publicised. Who knew until then that one of the favourites had been foaled on an allotment owned by an ordinary group of enthusiastic villagers? Or that a jockey had recently come back to racing after beating apparently terminal cancer? Or that another fancied horse had not long ago been left for dead after a serious training injury? Or that one of the jockeys' wives was expecting their first baby on the day of the race? Suddenly, everyone was interested in everything about the event and its participants and everyone had an opinion as to who would be the winner. Significant numbers of people who never went anywhere near the sport could even name a Grand National winner from the past, not to mention at least one of the famous fences.

The Grand National, a race which had been discredited and nearly discontinued at a time within living memory, was now, and likely to remain, the most popular and well known and supported horse race in the country. People who would never normally go near a High Street betting shop ventured inside and asked the counter staff for help in placing their bets. The counter staff for their part enjoyed meeting some new and different customers, customers who actually needed and wanted their help, instead of the regular gamblers who sat on the stools in the shops every day staring at the screens and placing bets on everything including virtual horse and greyhound racing. Sweepstakes were organised in workplaces, drawing in further interest from even more potential viewers, all keen to see whether the horse they had drawn fell at the first fence or was still in eventual contention at the Elbow.

Less happily, the race had attracted opposition from those concerned about animal welfare, leading to heated debates about whether or not the race should be banned. Well publicised reviews of safety whenever horses died in the race only added to the general public knowledge of the event. The regular, though relatively infrequent, deaths of horses at other jumps races and point to point meetings throughout the National Hunt season reached a much smaller audience.

Above all, Stevie had concluded, the grip of the race on the general public was not just to do with its unusual length, terrifying fences and carnival atmosphere, but also to the fact that people got to know something about the personalities involved, whether horses, the jockeys or trainers, and became interested in them. The only races that could touch it in the popular imagination were the Derby, possibly the St Leger, and perhaps the Cheltenham Gold Cup.

Clearly, it would not be possible to sustain that level of popular interest in races, whether jumps or flat, throughout the year but there were keys which could be turned in order to get more people involved.

Stevie had noticed, for instance, bored girlfriends trailing around after their menfolk at race meetings, apparently seeing attendance at the race meeting solely as an occasion on which to get drunk. The younger men, she thought, fell into two categories: those who came to drink and gamble and those who had some connection with the horses, owners or trainers. Stevie could see that many of the stable staff were in the same age range as these bored female attendees, but there was no communication or connection between the lives of the two groups.

Children too were almost entirely absent from racecourses. Some racecourses made efforts to attract families, offering fairground attractions, animal displays, falconry, and sideshows. This certainly gave the adults the idea that a racecourse could be somewhere to bring their children to be entertained, but the drawback was that it did not involve the children in the horse racing itself. Stevie had been at a racecourse one day at which a group of primary schoolchildren and their teachers were being introduced to the racecourse operation by a guide. She had noted how interested most of the youngsters were in learning the horses' names, matching the colours printed in the racecard to the jockey's silks, finding out who the people were who were standing in the middle of the parade ring, and wanting to know who was leading the horses along the path and why they were doing it. There was nothing mentioned about gambling or anything which suggested that the race meeting was about more than finding out who was the fastest runner, just like any human athletics event.

Stevie was a relative newcomer to horse racing. Perhaps that is what had made her look so carefully at what was going on around her. Two things had happened to bring the sport forcibly to her attention. One was taking a job in a High Street betting shop when she needed extra money as a student. The other was the unexpected gift to their family of a racehorse.

The in-house staff training offered by the bookmaker had been well organised and of excellent quality. Stevie had quickly qualified as a shop manager. As a student, she was not available to work for the company full-time, so she acted as a relief manager, working in various betting shops and outlets at unpopular times or when other managers were off sick. She worked in every type of location, from top end addresses, looking after customers who had money to burn, at premier league football stadiums to which corporate box holders brought rucksacks full of cash to launder, railway stations where punters were passing away the waiting time for their trains, right through to impoverished areas where homeless people spent the cash they had just begged for in the street on hopeless bets which had no chance of coming in. The bookmaker, for its part, taught her how a betting book was constructed, and used its computer systems to make sure that anyone successful enough to make regular money from the book was soon discouraged from placing any more bets.

The experience, in short, had revealed the unappealing workings of every spectrum of the betting community. But it had also told her why people were so fascinated by it.

There was a new target market there, one which the bookmakers had ignored on the basis that it had no knowledge, no money and no interest. Stevie thought that the bookmakers were wrong. Young women had money and interest. And knowledge could be acquired. Someone just needed to talk to them.

So that was just what Stevie Stone was doing now. Peter had helped her set up all the technology and her former employer had been interested enough in the potential of the venture to agree to sponsor it for a year.

"You'd better not drink too much, Mum," said Stevie, warningly, as she heard her mother order another two glasses of wine.

"I don't think it will make much difference," replied Susan, glumly, "I couldn't feel more confused and tired than I already do. But you're right. We'll go and eat something now and then I'll try to get some sleep."

15

The next day in court was every bit as unpleasant as Susan had anticipated.

Jeremy North-Taylor, QC was representing the defendant. It was not a role he was enjoying, but that was irrelevant. He would still carry it out to the best of his ability and in accordance with his client's instructions. Not that he much cared for the client, who seemed to him both sinister and lacking in any human empathy.

Her Honour Mrs Justice Grantley having reminded Susan that she was still under oath, Jeremy North-Taylor stood up to start his cross examination.

"Mrs Stonehouse," he began, "Are you someone with a good imagination? Are you good at inventing stories?"

"Not really," said Susan, blankly, "I'm an accountant."

There was a ripple of laughter from the public gallery and the press area. Mrs Justice Grantley looked up and glanced sternly around the courtroom, which caused the laughter to subside suddenly.

"Well, maybe a comedienne, then?" said Jeremy North-Taylor, seizing the chance she had created for him with her comment.

"What is your question, Mr North-Taylor?" said Mrs Justice Grantley, pointedly.

"When you arrived at Little Uppingham airfield, Mrs Stonehouse," the defence barrister continued, "What or whom did you expect to find there?"

Susan was nonplussed.

"I don't know what you mean," she said hesitantly, "It was just an airfield with nobody there. I didn't expect to find anyone or anything."

"So, you had no knowledge that my client and his employees would be at the airfield?" Jeremy North-Taylor went on.

"No, I did not," said Susan.

"But your husband had arranged to meet Mr Paloka there, had he not?" Jeremy North-Taylor stated.

Susan stared at him.

"Meet him?" she stammered, "No."

"You know that for a fact, do you, Mrs Stonehouse?" asked the barrister.

"Well, yes, of course. Why on earth would my husband want to meet someone like that?" Susan said.

"I am asking the questions, Mrs Stonehouse," said Jeremy North-Taylor.

There was a short silence, in which Susan stared helplessly at Jeremy North-Taylor and then at the old man in the dock, who smirked back at her with a contemptuous grin on his face. Orlando Frogmore was speaking with one of his juniors, his brow furrowed in surprise. The police officers who had investigated the case and were following the case from the body of the court looked at each other with concern.

"Mr Paloka maintains that your husband arranged to meet him at Little Uppingham airfield, and furthermore that your husband told Mr Paloka that you would be flying him to the meeting," said the QC.

Susan was aghast.

"Then Mr Paloka is a liar!" she said heatedly, "How dare he make a statement like that. That my husband, who is still unconscious in hospital, would want to have anything to do with him? Why would he?"

A stir of noise and movement was now rippling through the courtroom. Jeremy North-Taylor pressed on.

"My client says that your husband came to kill him," he stated.

This statement had the effect that Jeremy had intended, as a gasp of shock echoed round the walls. Susan was sure she heard her daughter shout "No way" from the public gallery.

"My client had always maintained that your husband was carrying a gun when he entered the warehouse office," Jeremy North-Taylor went on, "Do you know anything about that, Mrs Stonehouse?"

"No, nothing at all," Susan replied, bewildered and flummoxed by this unexpected allegation, "My husband doesn't own a gun."

"Where is this line of questioning leading, Mr North-Taylor?" Mrs Justice Grantley intervened, "Mr Stonehouse is not on trial here and neither is Mrs Stonehouse. It is your client who is on trial for the murder of Mr Gorecki."

"M'lady," replied Jeremy North-Taylor, "My client's position is that his employees killed Mr Gorecki, a crime to which they have already pleaded guilty and been sentenced."

"I understand that perfectly well, Mr North-Taylor," replied Mrs Justice Grantly, frostily, "But what does this have to do with your line of questioning to Mrs Stonehouse?"

"I am seeking to show, m'Lady, that Mrs Stonehouse was fully aware of, and even involved in, the attempted murder of my client," said Jeremy North-Taylor, "And that her evidence is unreliable and should be treated as such."

"Well, please get to that point promptly," the judge told him.

"Certainly, m'Lady," said Jeremy North-Taylor, and turned back to face Susan.

"Mrs Stonehouse," he said, "Did you or did you not fly your husband to Little Uppingham airfield on 6 July last year."

"Yes, I did," said Susan, "But not…"

"Allow me to continue," interrupted Jeremy, "And did he or did he not go into the warehouse office as soon as you arrived rather than to the trailer where the landing fee was to be paid?"

"He did," said Susan, "It's on the camera recording. But it was just a mistake."

"There is nothing on the recording to suggest any hesitation on his part," Jeremy North-Taylor stated, sounding as if he was speaking to someone of limited mental capacity, "So why do you say it was a mistake? He looks like someone who knows exactly what he was doing."

"He did know what he was doing," snapped Susan, "He just went to the wrong door, that's all. He was going to pay the landing fee."

"I suggest to you Mrs Stonehouse," went on the barrister, "That Mr Stonehouse went to a pre-arranged meeting in the warehouse office with Mr Paloka. I suggest that he threatened Mr Paloka using a gun which he had brought with him in the aircraft and that Mr Paloka and his employees were acting in self defence when they tried to protect Mr Paloka and unintentionally caused Mr Stonehouse to fall down the steps. I further suggest that the gun which Mr Stonehouse had brought and was aiming towards Mr Paloka was fired by him by accident as he fell. The bullet hit him in the leg, after which you removed the gun from Mr Stonehouse's possession when you were apparently attending to him on the ground and put it in your pocket. You then disposed of it at some point later and in some place far away from the airfield. No-one searched you for a concealed weapon at the scene, did they?"

"Well where is the gun now, then?" Susan said, angrily.

"You tell me, Mrs Stonehouse," replied Jeremy North-Taylor.

Orlando Frogmore, rather belatedly, the fascinated onlookers thought, got to his feet.

"M'lady," he said, "These accusations against my client are without any basis in fact. In particular, the defence has advanced no argument whatever to indicate why Mr Stonehouse would want to kill Mr Paloka nor why Mrs Stonehouse would become an accessory to such an act."

"Mr North-Taylor?" queried Mrs Justice Grantley.

The defence barrister turned to face Susan.

"Mrs Stonehouse," he said, "Who is Marion Stonehouse?"

"She is.. was.. my husband's sister," replied Susan, slowly.

"How did she die?" asked Jeremy North-Taylor.

"She died as a result of taking cocaine which was cut with garden fertiliser," Susan stated baldly.

"And how did she obtain that cocaine?" her interrogator went on.

"I don't know," said Susan, "But I guess you are intending to tell me, aren't you? I can see that this is some trap that you are setting for me."

"No trap, Mrs Stonehouse," replied Jeremy North-Taylor, "You know that your husband was determined to find out where his sister had obtained the contaminated cocaine. Using his considerable IT skills, he spent much time and effort tracking down the various sources from which it might have been obtained. And he decided that one of those sources was Mr Paloka. So he contacted Mr Paloka, with a concocted business proposal and arranged to meet him. His intention was to kill him at that meeting and you were to assist him in doing so by covering his tracks. But it all went wrong, didn't it?"

"Is this your client's defence?" shouted Susan, before Orlando Frogmore could intervene again, "I have never heard anything so pathetic in my life. If he's going to make up a pack of lies and rely on the fact that my husband is not here to defend himself against them, then at least he could make up a tale that anyone over ten years old would find credible. Look at him ... how could anyone believe anything that depraved old monster had to say!"

Susan was shrieking now, beside herself with fury. Mrs Justice Grantley was attempting to intervene, Orlando Frogmore was asking for an adjournment so that his client could be given some time to compose herself, and a whole roomful of round eyed onlookers was buzzing with shock at this new twist in an already dramatic story.

In the midst of the hubbub, the old man in the dock rose to his feet.

"Filthy bitch!" he screamed at Susan, "I don't need to waste my time on people like you. As if your husband, whatever his name is, could have killed me! He was nothing and nobody. I would not waste my time talking to some scum like him!"

This abusive and hate-laden intervention had the effect of silencing the courtroom.

Mrs Justice Grantley took advantage of the pause. She ignored the defendant, who had sat back in his seat with a satisfied smirk on his ugly face.

"Mr North-Taylor," she said, "Is your client intending to take the stand to substantiate this story?"

"No, m'Lady," replied the barrister," My client considers that the facts speak for themselves."

"And do we have any evidence to support the claim that Mr Stonehouse arranged a meeting with your client?" the judge continued.

"No, m"Lady," was the response.

"And do you have any more questions for Mrs Stonehouse?" asked Mrs Justice Grantley, finally.

Jeremy North-Taylor indicated that he did not. He knew the defence was ridiculously weak but it was the one upon which his client had insisted. His client's infuriated tirade from the dock had not helped him either.

Orlando Frogmore was asked if he wished to ask any further questions of Susan, and, beyond asking her to confirm again that she knew nothing of any meeting with Mr Paloka and had certainly not seen or disposed of a gun, he had nothing further to ask. By this time, Susan was shaking with rage and shock, and he could see that there was little more to be gained by keeping her in the witness box.

The judge indicated that the court would rise for lunch and that she would give her summary and directions to the jury when she returned.

As the news media subsequently reported, Konstantin Paloka was found guilty of the murder of Jerzy Gorecki by unanimous jury verdict. The weak defence had clearly had no impact on the jury who had preferred to believe Susan Stonehouse's version of events. The police and the CPS heaved a collective sigh of relief.

Paloka was sentenced to life imprisonment.

The defence advanced by Paloka through his barrister did, though, have another effect. The accusations made against Peter and Susan Stonehouse were reported by the media as was the tragic tale of the death of Marion Stonehouse, a stunning beauty and professional musician who had allowed a recreational drug habit to get the better of her. Many readers sympathised with the notion that her brother would want to kill someone who had been responsible for ruining her promising life.

Susan knew that the story about the gun was entirely fabricated, a last vicious attempt by an evil old man who knew he was cornered and wanted to do the maximum damage whilst he still had the chance. There was no doubt that, had Peter not unexpectedly entered the warehouse office that day, Paloka would never have been convicted of the murder of Jerzy Gorecki. But Paloka's nasty act of vengeful spite had inserted a small shard of doubt in her mind which she needed to extract and discard. But, whilst Peter remained unconscious, she could not speak to him about it.

The news quickly became old news, and Susan returned to her former ruined existence, trying to run her company by day, drinking too much and insomniac by night, and waiting hopelessly for her injured husband to wake up. The white card given to her by the stranger in the courtroom remained untouched in her purse, forgotten.

But the outcome of the trial was not old news to everyone. Someone was still determined that the single shard inserted into Susan's mind was not enough. They wanted to make her suffer yet more.

YOU SHOULD JUST DIE, YOU BITCH was the first anonymous message to appear in her email box. WE WILL MAKE SURE YOU DIE – SLOWLY AND IN PAIN was the second. WE WILL RAPE YOU FIRST LOTS OF TIMES. YOU WILL BE BEGGING TO DIE was the third.

The same messages were posted to her Facebook page, together with photographs of dead animals entangled with barbed wire. Links to perverted pornographic sites were added to her online messaging accounts. WE ARE ALWAYS WATCHING YOU read yet another message.

Susan reported the messages to the police officers who had brought the charges against Paloka. They had no doubt that Paloka was the source of them, not personally from his prison cell, but through an intermediary. His vast empire would contain many IT specialists and hackers who could carry out his dirty work.

"Paloka has two sons," one of the officers told Susan, "They will be continuing his activities until we can cut the links with them too."

Susan struggled to understand.

"Does this mean I have been through all this for nothing?" she asked, wearily.

"Not at all," said the officer, hurriedly, "But this is a massive and well established web of corruption and it will take a while for us to cut through it. Getting Paloka into prison is a serious blow to what he has built up, but it is not going to finish things on its own."

"So, why are they sending this stuff to me?" asked Susan, "I can't do anything more to harm them."

"It is to stop anyone else who is thinking of acting against them," was the answer, "They want to show what they do to people who harm them."

"And who are 'they'?" asked Susan.

"Paloka's two sons, Aleksander and Egzon," the police officer told her, "He has been boasting in prison that his sons will come and kill you. That's why we are still keeping you under constant police protection."

"How the hell am I meant to live like this?" Susan asked herself, when the officers had left the once happy family home which had now become a guarded prison in which she lived in permanent solitary confinement.

Worn down by the burden which her life had become, and unable to see what there was for her to look forward to, Susan one morning emptied out her handbag looking for painkillers to quell her habitual hangover. She rummaged angrily through the contents until a sudden burst of rage caused her to throw it on the floor. Coins spilled and rolled out over the bedroom carpet, as her purse flew open, and out of it also fell a small white card. ICE, it said, followed by a mobile phone number.

"ICE," thought Susan, her foggy brain for the first time recognising the significance of the word, "In Case of Emergency. That's what it means."

She pondered, staring at the black print.

"Well it's a real bloody emergency now," she thought, and, grabbing her mobile phone, she called the number on the card.

Her call was answered straightaway. And, once the person who answered it had explained who he was, Susan was glad that she had called.

During the next fortnight, three things happened.

The first was that Konstantin Paloka was murdered in prison, his throat expertly cut by an unknown assailant with a serrated knife apparently taken from the prison kitchen. An urgent security review was called for and promised. The death threats to Susan escalated as a result of Paloka's death.

The second was that Peter Stonehouse's condition deteriorated suddenly. Having remained unconscious for over six months, he finally suffered a cardiac arrest and could not be revived. With his wife on the verge of a nervous breakdown, no funeral was arranged, and his ashes were scattered privately at the crematorium to which he had been taken from the hospital. By the time the media heard about it, it was all over.

The third was that Susan Stonehouse held up the entire Edgware branch of the Northern Line one busy, dark and freezing February morning by throwing herself on the rails at Golders Green Underground station. Although she received prompt medical attention at the scene and in an ambulance, she subsequently died and her ashes joined those of her husband in the grounds of the crematorium.

16

"And that's what I have written so far," said George, closing the lid of the laptop and looking his rather shocked audience in the face, "And now I don't know what happens next, so I can't write any more."

The afternoon reading of the unfinished novel had been quite a laborious process, as George had frequently had to stop to explain words and concepts with which his French listeners were unfamiliar. The sky outside had gradually darkened into a crepuscular gloom, whilst the wind had subsided enough to produce a dank silence which slowly settled onto the quayside outside the museum's heavy door. It was as if the breath had been pressed out of the atmosphere and left the little village struggling for air.

"This is a very .. let us say, very tragic story, Georges," said Monique eventually, "Everyone is dead."

"Well, not quite everyone," George corrected her.

"But all important characters are dead," Monique went on, "Suzanne and Peter are both dead and so is the terrible criminal. It is good that the criminal is dead, of course. But who is left to carry on the story?"

"Yes, Georges," said Guy, "Surely this is the problem? Perhaps the man, Peter, should not die. Perhaps he could recover? And then his wife will not want to kill herself."

"But, if Peter recovers, then what would happen?" asked George.

"Well, we will find out the truth about the gun," said Monique, "Suzanne will be able to ask him about it. And she will also ask him whether he has truly gone to meet the evil criminal in the office at the airport."

"But what if she too is involved in this, as the lawyer says?" asked Claudine, "If her husband went to kill the criminal, the criminal is now dead, so their mission is accomplished. That means that there would be no more story to tell."

"So, they must be dead then, so someone can avenge them?" asked Guy, "But who is left to do that?"

"They have two daughters," said Maurice, unexpectedly. He had contributed nothing to the discussion so far, and had seemed unconvinced by the whole exercise, staring at the ceiling whilst George was reading the story and appearing not to pay attention.

"Yes, that is true," exclaimed Monique, "One is the daughter who supported her mother and bought her wine - Chablis, bah - and told her about the new occupation she has with the horse racing. And the other daughter is ... who is the other daughter, Georges?"

"I haven't written a part for her yet," George replied, "All I have said is that she is somewhere where Paloka and his people cannot touch her."

"Where can that be?" asked Guy.

George shrugged.

"This is something which can be decided in the course of the story," he said.

The debate continued for a while, until Maurice reminded his wife that the bar needed to be opened and that she and Monique could continue their discussion at home if they wished. The two women departed, promising George that they would think hard about how the story he had written might be continued, and preferably in a more cheerful vein, perhaps with handsome boyfriends or husbands being invented for the two daughters.

George was left alone in the wine museum with Maurice and Guy.

"Well, I will return home now," said George, sliding his computer back into its carrying case and then levering himself out of his chair using his stick, "Thank you all for listening to the story and any ideas that you have will be gratefully received."

"Monsieur," said Maurice, "Why do you carry a gun? There can be no reason for you to have a weapon in such a place as Frossiac."

Guy was horrified by his brother's sudden and direct question.

"Maurice…." he began, and then subsided as his brother held up his hand in a silencing gesture.

George Harvey was by this time on his feet, the computer case in one hand the walking stick in the other. He put the black case down onto the chair, and leaned with both hands on the stick.

"Ah, you saw that, did you?" he said to Maurice, looking the other man full in the face, "I am not very good at hiding it, am I?"

"But what is it for?" asked Maurice again, "It does not make me happy that strangers bring weapons into my business premises. You must understand that, Monsieur."

"I certainly do understand it," said George, "And I am sorry if I have caused you distress. I will not bring the pistol with me again. Indeed, I think there will be no need for me to come here again, as I am assured that the broadband service will be restored at my home this evening."

"But you have not answered my question," persisted Maurice, "I am happy, of course, that you will not be bringing it here but you have not said why you have it."

A sudden frown caused George's wide forehead to crease and his eyes to narrow.

"With respect, Monsieur," he said, formally, "That is not your affair. Please accept my thanks for your help and hospitality and also thank your family on my behalf. As I said, I shall return home now."

Before Maurice or Guy could say anything else, George Harvey picked up his computer case, swung round on his stick and walked slowly and purposefully out of the door and towards the steps of the footbridge.

"Why did you do that?" asked Guy, angrily, "You have offended him with your questions."

"Because it is not right that someone should come here to our village with a gun," replied Maurice, who had in fact been rather unnerved by George Harvey's abrupt response.

"But you said yourself that Marcel had assured you that he had a permit for it," protested Guy, "And Georges is right. It is not your business."

"Why should anyone carry a gun?" Maurice went on, as though Guy had not spoken, "To kill someone, to threaten someone … or … what?"

"Well," said Guy, "It could be to defend himself. Perhaps he is afraid someone will come to his house to steal something. He cannot walk well, as you can see, so perhaps he has the gun to help his confidence that he can frighten away any burglars."

"Or perhaps," Maurice continued, "To carry a gun is part of his job."

"What, you think he is from the police?" asked Guy, "But he is an Englishman. Why would English police be here in Frossiac? Or maybe he is someone working with the French police? Maybe it is something to do with English tourists? Or maybe there is some English criminal who lives in this district and he is here to watch that person?"

The brothers wrestled with the problem for a while, but no suitable explanation was agreed upon. Eventually, they locked the door of the wine museum and walked in the near darkness along the Corbieres bank of the canal towards the old bridge. George Harvey had long disappeared over the footbridge to the Minervois bank and had been swallowed up by the oncoming night.

"One thing I do know," said Guy, as they approached the lights of Maurice's bar and were able to glimpse the screen of the television on which a football match was being shown, "Monique is going to be very upset if we do not see Monsieur 'Arvai again."

Maurice, for his part, was quite sure that he himself would not be at all upset at if he never saw George Harvey again. The last thing he wanted was foreign police officers nosing into his affairs. He needed to make a few calls that evening, he thought to himself.

Monique and Claudine were indeed most upset to find that George Harvey would not be joining them in the bar that evening.

"But we have many ideas for him!" exclaimed Monique.

The bar was quiet that evening, the only two paying customers being absorbed in watching the televised football match. Maurice excused himself, saying he had work to do, and went upstairs to the large apartment which comprised the upper floor of the ancient building. Monique, Claudine and Guy remained together in the bar. Unusually, the four adults were free of family commitments. Maurice and Claudine's two teenage sons were on an educational trip to Paris whilst Guy and Monique's young daughter was staying with Monique's parents in Carcassonne.

"I am sure we will see him again tomorrow," said Guy, not entirely convinced that he was correct. He did not understand why Maurice should have treated their new and unexpectedly interesting friend with such hostility.

"Well, we have been considering how we should approach this problem," Monique carried on, fortunately not noting the hesitation in Guy's tone.

"Yes," chipped in Claudine, "We must return to the basics."

"And what are the basics?" asked Guy, accepting the glass of beer which Claudine set before him on the dark wood of the bar. Twinkling lights looked up at him from the polished surface.

"These Stone'ouses," stated Monique, "Why are they at the little deserted airport in the first place?"

"You are asking me?" replied Guy, "I think the story said that they went there to eat lunch at an English pub."

"But is that really true?" asked Monique, "The whole episode could have been set as a trap for the criminal, to entice him there and kill him, as the lawyer said? As we heard, the sister of Monsieur Stone'ouse has been killed by contaminated drugs. The police did not do anything do prevent this because the criminal was too powerful. So, the family members have taken the law to themselves to avenge her."

"And now, because of the decision at the trial, they have been successful," went on Claudine.

"Well, not really," objected Guy, "They are both dead, as we have already said."

"But this is a story, Guy," said Monique, "Perhaps they do not have to be dead. George could change the story."

"We have said this, again, already, Monique," replied Guy, suddenly becoming tired of the unfinished novel of Monsieur 'Arvai, "If they are not dead, then there is no story. The criminal is dead, the Stone'ouse family has received no blame in the court of law. So what then is there left to happen?"

"This is the whole point," said Claudine, excitedly, "If the Stone'ouse father and mother are not dead, then the sons of the criminal will come for them and …"

"And what, Claudine?" asked Guy, "Kill them? And so we are back to the same problem."

Whilst his family was wrestling with the gradually less absorbing problem of the ending to Monsieur 'Arvai's novel, Maurice had made a call to his main business contact within the wine co-operative.

"Good evening, Jean-Philippe," he began, "Or perhaps not such a good evening. I believe we have a difficulty."

Maurice swiftly related the story of the unexpected appearance of George Harvey at the wine museum and the discovery that the visitor was carrying an apparently permitted gun of which the local police were fully informed. He did not mention the reading of the unfinished novel but simply referred to George Harvey's use of the wine museum broadband service.

"You permitted him to connect his computer to the internet through your broadband?" the man he had called almost shrieked.

"Why not?" asked Maurice, "I was attempting to be helpful. I did not know he had a gun at that time."

"Have you never heard of spyware?" asked Jean-Philippe.

Maurice had not, but was soon given to understand by an increasingly frantic Jean-Philippe that spyware was something which could be installed remotely onto a computer system to provide information about the contents and activity of the computer.

"You think this is what he had done?" asked Maurice in a horrified whisper.

"You have said yourself that you believe that he is a police officer," shouted Jean-Philippe, "What do you think?"

"My God," said Maurice, "What do I do now?"

"Do not use the computer at all until I tell you it is safe," instructed Jean-Philippe, "In the meantime, tell me, where does this Georges 'Arvai live?"

Maurice quickly gave directions to the holiday home where he believed George Harvey to be living and Jean-Philippe cut the connection with a curt instruction to him to do nothing to arouse any suspicion on anyone's part that the unwelcome Englishman might be a police officer.

So Maurice went downstairs to the bar to find, much to his relief, his brother begging him to change the topic of conversation to anything other than the solution to George Harvey's case of writer's block.

The following morning, Maurice decided to get up early and take a walk over towards the small lakes by the holiday homes where George Harvey was living. It was still and sunny day, for a change, and light gleamed sharply from the unruffled surface of the water. Maurice was able to see very clearly the little group of houses in one of which George Harvey was living.

But as he came closer, he could see that there was no-one at home. The car with the Carcassonne number plate was gone and the front door was standing wide open to the elements.

17

At about the same time as Maurice was staring in horror at the open door of George Harvey's apparently abandoned holiday home in Frossiac, Sam was arriving back in the Sampfield Grange yard from riding out with first lot. The weather had relented somewhat from its recent predilection to damp grey gloom, and weak winter sunshine was warming the green folds of the hills above the estate.

Sam was in an optimistic mood. It was now almost two weeks since Hennessy Gold Cup day and the success which Curlew Landings had enjoyed on his debut appearance at the Newbury races that day still brightened the mood of Sam's unambitious and comfortable yard. He could see Curlew in the barn, being untacked by Sadie, who was still speaking to the horse as though he was a minor superstar.

The plan to run Curlew Landings prominently had worked well. Merlin had started Curlew at the front and had aimed to make all the running. Curlew had loved every minute of it and his stamina had shown no sign of giving out, even in the soft going on the course that day. On the run in, there were three horses, including Curlew, fighting it out for first place. Merlin and Curlew made a good fist of the battle, eventually ending up winning by a short head. Best of all, Curlew had shown no signs of backing off during this tough challenge. Sam's most difficult problem now was where to take the horse next, in particular whether he should aim for another novice event or step up against more experienced horses. But this was a problem he was happy to have.

Merlin too had been highly pleased with the horse, particularly since he had had a disappointing experience in the Hennessy Gold Cup. Sam had left the Garratt box to go down to stand in the centre of the parade ring with Helen and John prior to the Gold Cup race. It had been a relief to be away from the rather overpowering atmosphere created by Helen's and John's talkative friends, who had pumped Sam for information about horse breeding and racing and then had become more interested in their lunch and accompanying alcoholic drinks than in watching the racing. A couple of the party had joined

John in the wet and cold of the parade ring, but most had preferred to remain in the box.

"Sam, darling," said Helen, when he had mentioned this on their way down the stairs from the box, the others having elected to take the lift, "You have to remember that these are John's professional associates. He's a musician, remember? Not everyone lives and breathes horses like you. They've come here for a day out. And, by the way, you still haven't given me an answer about that charity project I told you about last month."

Alto Clef was a large and distinguished grey creature with a long stride and a big scopy jump. This had sometimes worked to his disadvantage in the past, as he tended to give his fences too much air and thus to waste valuable time as he crossed above them. But his size and galloping speed made up for these drawbacks, as well as his capacity to run without difficulty in soft or heavy ground. Alto Clef appeared from the information on the big screen to be going off third favourite.

The field as a whole had consisted of fifteen horses, many of them well known and popular with the punters. It had also included a number of Irish trained horses, one of which was Merlin's mount for the race. Sam had been curious to find out the details of the horse to be ridden by Curlew's jockey and had consulted the race card as he stood in the ring watching the horses being led round in a mostly calm and stately procession by their grooms.

Sam's dyslexia did not prevent him reading racecards, which tended to follow an established format and to contain predictable information. Even so, he had had to concentrate. When he had eventually found Merlin's name in the race listing, he had noted that the horse he was riding was called Tabikat and that it was trained in County Meath by Brendan Meaghan. Sam had been surprised to see Merlin booked to ride for an Irish trainer. The owner of the horse was given as Levy Brothers International, which sounded more like a Jewish-owned business of some kind rather than an Irish racing syndicate. The breeder's name had been given simply as E Foley.

Although Sam had heard of the trainer, who was quite prominent in Ireland, the breeder's name had been unknown to him. The name Tabikat did, however, sound familiar, although Sam was certain that he had never come across the horse before. The racecard had said that the dark brown gelding, which Sam could now see at the far end of the ring, was by Tabloid News out of a mare called Little Kitty Cat. No information was given about the dam's sire.

Tabikat himself had soon came past the position where Sam had been standing and Sam had stepped forward to get a better look at him. Helen and John and their friends had been busy discussing the magnificent Alto Clef with their trainer, and had not noticed Sam's preoccupation with the other horse.

Tabikat had been without exaggeration one of the most arresting horses Sam had seen in a while. His dark coat had shone as if it had been cleaned with boot polish and he had held his head high as he had stalked around the parade ring looking neither left nor right. He was not a big horse but had looked athletic and bright, full of energy and power, muscles rippling under neatly executed and rather unusual quartermarks. The young groom who led him had walked quietly and briskly along, like a humble servant completely overshadowed by her beautiful charge.

So absorbed was Sam in looking at the gorgeous Tabikat, moving alongside the horse as he walked, that he had not seen a young woman standing nearby until after he had bumped into her.

"I do apologise," he had exclaimed, hurriedly, "That was entirely my fault. Are you all right?"

"I'm fine," had replied the young woman, sounding amused, "It takes more than that to knock me down."

"I was just looking at this horse," Sam had explained, "I've not seen him before."

The woman had regarded Sam with interest. She had large brown eyes, Sam had noticed, and her hair was tucked up into burgundy coloured felt hat with a wide brim.

"That's Tabikat," she had said, "But I expect you know that much already."

"I do," had admitted Sam, "But my jockey booking for the next race is riding him in this race, so I was curious."

"Your jockey booking," the woman had repeated, "Are you a trainer or an owner?"

"Well, both, actually," Sam had told her, "The horse is Curlew Landings."

"James Sampfield Peveril, Sampfield Grange," the young woman had declared, as if reading from a list.

"Oh, you know of me?" Sam had asked, surprised at the ease with which she had identified Curlew Landings.

"Well, it's my job to know," the woman had replied, "I am a racing tipster."

"Ah," Sam had said, "And what do you make of Tabikat's chances in this one?"

"He's in with a shout," his informant had replied, "He's relatively exposed but most of them are in this field. The ground suits him and he's got a good jockey on his back. Distance not a problem. Trainer in form. Good temperament, holds his own in races."

"And Alto Clef?" Sam had asked, "What do you make of him?"

"In with a chance of a win, certainly a place," the woman had stated, "But, hey, what's all this with the questions? I charge for my tips, you know."

Sam had seen she was only half-joking with him, but had not been able to resist one last question.

"And Curlew Landings in the race after this?" he had asked.

"You know better than I do," the woman had answered, laughing.

At that moment, the bell had rung for the jockeys to mount, and Sam had realised that he really should be with the Alto Clef group who were now about twenty yards away. He had turned to say goodbye to his new acquaintance, but she had walked off already.

In the event, Alto Clef had come third in the Hennessy whilst Tabikat came in fifth. It was a disappointing race for both horses, as a multiple fall at the cross fence the second time round had seen both horses hampered, with Tabikat and Merlin in particular needing some fancy footwork to avoid being brought down. By the time they had recovered, some of those more fortunate in running had streaked ahead and could not be caught before the finish line.

Merlin had still been annoyed when Sam had caught up with him before Curlew's novice hurdle race.

"Bloody shame, that was," Merlin had said, crossly, "That 'orse has got some engine and it jumped like a stag. Safe, too, good brain. Tell you what about that Paddy trainer, 'e knows what 'e's about. The 'orse was a fit as a fiddle."

"How come you were riding him, Merlin?" Sam had asked, as they watched Curlew Landings walk around the parade ring with Sadie, the horse's eyes out on stalks.

"Oh, reg'lar jockey's out injured," Merlin had told him, "Someone called up Jacko from some backwater place in the peatbog and asked me to take the ride."

Jacko, less usually known as Jackson Argyrides, was Merlin's agent.

"Any'ow," Merlin had gone on, "I am now looking at your young boyo 'ere to give me a win."

And Curlew Landings' subsequent excellent performance had put out of Sam's mind any further thoughts about Tabikat and Brendan Meaghan.

Sam had arrived back at Sampfield Grange first, half an hour ahead of the horse lorry. He had previously asked Lewis to record the television coverage from Newbury that afternoon so that he could watch Curlew's race once he arrived home. But he also wanted to review the Hennessy Gold Cup race itself. The bad luck in running experienced by Alto Clef had left the horse's connections, at least those who cared about such things, very upset. Their main concern had been to find another race in which the horse could run before the end of the year.

Sam, when Helen had asked his opinion, had said that this was a matter for their trainer. But Helen had insisted on having his views too, so he had reluctantly agreed to give a comment, whilst reminding her at the same time that his thoughts should only be considered a last resort if they were undecided.

The choices, as far as Sam could, see, having mulled it over on the way home, lay between a couple of Grade 3 chases at Ascot and Cheltenham in December or the King George VI Chase at Kempton on Boxing Day. There had also been some options at Northern courses, but he knew that Helen's husband preferred not to travel too far from London. The Welsh National, also scheduled for Boxing Day, had been another Grade 3 option, but possibly too far away for Sir John. The King George was a double step up from the Hennessy and, as one of the major races in the calendar, likely to put Alto Clef up against the top staying chasers presently in training. There was also the variation between the Classes and their handicapping arrangements to take into account.

Sam was not used to making such decisions but he had taken Helen's request seriously and had sat down in front of the TV with a glass of whisky and determined to do his best.

After a bit of fiddling about, Sam had managed to get the recording to the point at which the horses for the race were being led around the Newbury parade ring. He had been able to see himself standing with Helen and John and their friends, their Lambourn-based trainer talking to them earnestly as they had watched Alto Clef. He had seen himself moving away from them to follow Tabikat's progress, but then the camera had moved away to another part of the parade ring.

One of the TV presenters had been roaming the parade ring, interviewing the trainers and owners of the two or three leading fancies. Sam and the Alto Clef party had not been included in this, but Sam had been able to see them standing further away behind the people to whom the reporter was speaking.

After some time spent looking at the main contenders in turn, the camera had started to follow Tabikat, whilst the offscreen commentators had talked briefly about his chances in the race. The shot had happened to include the point at which Merlin had been legged up into the saddle by the trainer, Brendan Meaghan.

But Sam had not been looking at Merlin. He had been looking at the trainer. Although, once again, he had had only a back view, he had been pretty certain he had seen this back view before. It had been the back view of someone getting out of the way of Roger Mortimer's horse at Cheltenham racecourse less than a month before.

And, just as he had recognised the trainer as Brendan Meaghan, another piece of the jigsaw had suddenly slotted into place inside his head. Sam had now remembered where he had heard the name Tabikat before or something which sounded like it. It had been the name of the ridiculous talking kitten which gave racing tips on Bethany's computer. And who else had said they were a racing tipster that day at Newbury? The young woman with whom he had collided in the parade ring.

The recording had progressed to the coverage of the race itself. The first part of the race was, as he well remembered from watching it from Helen's box, routine, nothing much happening, all the horses except those off their game or stymied by the ground, still in contention. It had been coming into the back straight for the second time that it had begun to hot up.

As the horses had approached the cross fence, there had been nothing to suggest a problem, but someone had got it wrong and a mid air collision had resulted in two horses going down, with yet another unseating its rider. As Sam had seen already, Alto Clef and Tabikat had been both shunted sideways and both of them had had a hard job to stay on their feet. It was impossible to say where they would have finished had that incident not taken place.

Whilst Sam had been reviewing the Hennessy Gold Cup race in preparation for calling Helen with his thoughts, Kye had driven the horse lorry containing the much praised Curlew into the yard. Kye had been surprised to see Isabella Hall emerging from the darkness of the office to greet them. Her face in the headlights had looked pale and set, but she had seemed animated enough.

"Well done, really great stuff, Sadie and Kye," she had called out as the two stable staff descended from the horsebox cab, "Mr Sampfield is here already. He went up to the house. Lewis has recorded everything from the TV this afternoon, so you can all watch Curlew's race again."

Kye and Sadie had had the horse unloaded and into his stall quicker than ever before. Curlew, for his part, had seemed indifferent to all the praise and attention and had stalked like an over-affected actor into his stall, concerned only about being fed. The exertions of the race had seemed not to have bothered him one bit.

Isabella Hall had been more engaged and animated that evening than the Sampfield Grange staff had ever seen her. Kelly had arranged food for everyone when they returned, so the grand showing of Curlew's race had taken place in the kitchen.

Lewis had set up the TV recording to start at the preliminaries to Curlew's race, inasmuch as these were shown between the commercial breaks and coverage of the races at other courses.

"You look good there, Sadie," had declared Kelly, as the televised Sadie had walked around with Curlew Landings, adding, rather unnecessarily, "And there's Mr Sampfield," as Sam had walked across the TV shot to leg Merlin up into the saddle.

"Oooh, look, that's Merlin," had exclaimed Sadie, happily.

Kye had sat moodily in the corner as the race had been run and re-run on the television screen. His dealing of weed and pills from the horse box in the Newbury car park had gone well, and he had resolved to slip off to see Gray the next day to share the proceeds and order more supplies. Out of the corner of his eye he had watched Isabella Hall, who had been sitting next to Sadie, listening to her frequent exclamations alternately about the skill of the jockey and the brilliance of the horse. He was irritated about Sadie's obvious infatuation with Merlin ap Rhys, but he had been genuinely worried about Isabella Hall.

Kye didn't trust Isabella Hall at all, he had decided, and he had found her association with the mysterious Mr Stanley difficult to fathom. To him, it seemed fake. If they were having an affair, there must surely have been more convenient circumstances in which to conduct it instead of taking work in a backwater racing yard and cycling off for assignations at a local pub all the time, and the sort of pub where people were likely to gossip about unusual strangers. And if she had been with Mr Stanley at Cheltenham racecourse, surely that too was a pretty public sort of place to be seen with a lover whose existence you had apparently gone to such lengths to hide? It didn't make sense.

Whatever Isabella Hall was, she had no place in a country racing yard. She was definitely up to something, he had decided, and he needed to make sure it did not involve him. He had resolved to speak to Gray about having her followed.

18

Since Hennessy Gold Cup day, Sadie had been harbouring a guilty secret. Well, not that guilty, she reasoned to herself. She was a single woman who could do as she pleased.

In the aftermath of Curlew's win, Merlin ap Rhys had sought her out. Kye had come over to collect the recovering Curlew from the unsaddling area to take him back to the horse box. Sadie had stayed behind with Mr Sampfield for a few minutes to receive her employer's compliments on her preparation of the horse, and then had waited outside the weighing room for Merlin to come out. He had no further rides that day, she knew, and would be preparing to go home.

Merlin had been talking to some fellow jockeys as he had appeared in the doorway, but, spotting the eager Sadie, had immediately parted company with them and come over to speak to her.

"You done a real good job there, girl," Merlin had said to her, "That 'orse is going places now, for sure."

As Sadie had smiled and thanked him for riding Curlew so well, Merlin had taken her by the elbow and led her towards the side of the grandstand. The crowds had thinned out by now as only one race remained to be run, and no-one had taken much notice of two young people talking by the wall. Merlin had been wearing dark glasses and a black leather jacket with the collar turned up and was unlikely to be recognised by anyone other than the most observant punter.

"That Kye your boyfriend, then?" Merlin had asked her.

"No, not really," Sadie had told him, "Just works with me. We get on OK."

"That's good," Merlin had said, "Great girl like you would be wasted on 'im."

Merlin had had his arm around Sadie's waist now, and the bone and muscle of his body had pressed against her side. Sadie had felt as if she was being leaned against by a bulldozer. She had stepped back and found the wall of the grandstand behind her.

"Looks like you're between a brick wall and a hard on," Merlin had said, unashamedly mixing metaphors, and before Sadie could answer, he had leaned in to her and covered her mouth with his. Sadie felt his tongue forcing itself into the back of her throat. And he had not been joking about the hard on either. She could feel that too.

Stepping back, Merlin had laughed at Sadie's confused expression.

"This is no place for it," he had said, "We'll be seeing each other again, you and me, and then we can get a room, as they say."

"OK," had gasped Sadie, not sure whether she was flattered or not by his inelegant approach.

Merlin had planted a kiss on her forehead and walked off. Sadie had wandered slowly back to the lorry to find Kye impatiently waiting for her.

"Where have you been?" he had asked.

"Just saying goodbye to Merlin," had replied Sadie, not entirely untruthfully.

"Can't take anything away from him as a jockey," had said Kye, "But he's a smooth sod with that daft Welsh accent."

"I think it's nice," had replied Sadie, climbing up into the cab of the horsebox.

As Sadie and Kye had driven through the late afternoon darkness towards Sampfield Grange, Sadie had stolen a sideways glance at Kye's set face. She had wondered whether he was really interested in becoming a jockey at all. He seemed more concerned about spending time tinkering with the horsebox than getting involved with the horses once they were at an event. Perhaps he really was destined to be a motor mechanic after all.

Almost two weeks later, Sadie was still waiting to find out where Mr Sampfield would finally decide to declare Curlew Landings. There were a couple of point to point meetings to keep the other horses occupied, so there was work and travelling for them to do, but Merlin ap Rhys was obviously not going to be found at points. Isabella Hall had, on Mr Sampfield's instruction, entered Curlew Landings in two Novice Hurdle events at Cheltenham and Ascot in December. Mr Sampfield would have to make up his mind soon, she knew, as the declarations for the Cheltenham race would have to be made the following day.

Sam himself, watching Curlew being led back into his stall by Sadie, was well aware of this impending deadline. Curlew had worked well that morning, and, Rachel, the equine vet, had declared him fit and well after his Newbury race. There was no sign of a recurrence of the worrying heat in his leg from a few weeks ago.

As Sam walked into the yard office, he decided to ask Mrs Hall to declare Curlew for the Cheltenham race.

"Good morning, Mr Sampfield Peveril," Isabella Hall greeted him, "I have a message for you to call a Mr Brendan Meaghan sometime this morning. His secretary said he would be available until about 2.00pm."

"Brendan Meaghan?" queried Sam, in surprise, "Did they say what it was about?"

"I am afraid not," replied Isabella Hall, "His secretary said he wanted to speak to you personally."

"Very well, I will call him from the house," said Sam, taking the piece of paper which Isabella Hall was holding out to him, "And could you be ready declare Curlew for that race at Cheltenham too, please?"

"Of course, Mr Sampfield Peveril," replied Isabella Hall.

"Mrs Hall, I do wish you would call me Mr Sampfield, as the other staff do," said Sam, suddenly, "Using both family names really is such a mouthful."

"Yes, whatever you prefer," replied Isabella Hall, "But I must also ask that you stop calling me Mrs Hall. It sounds so …. odd to me."

"What would you like me to call you?" asked Sam, "What do Sadie and the others call you. Isabella? Or something shorter?"

"No, Isabella will do," replied Isabella, "Only my husband has called me by any other name."

This was the first occasion on which Isabella had mentioned her husband. Sam realised that he had been assuming that she was divorced. The picture of Isabella Hall, the military man with the walking stick, and Brendan Meaghan at Cheltenham racecourse flashed into his mind. An idea suddenly occurred to him.

"Is Mr Hall involved in horse racing?" he asked, suddenly.

Isabella looked as surprised as her immobile face would allow.

"No," she replied, carefully, "Why?"

"I wondered if you knew Brendan Meaghan," replied Sam, feeling that he might be about to paint himself into a corner.

"Why should I?" asked Isabella, staring at him.

Because I saw you standing with him at Cheltenham racecourse, Sam wanted to tell her. But, of course, he was not absolutely certain the woman had been Isabella Hall, and, even if it had been, the unknown man could have been anyone and not necessarily her husband.

"Oh, I just wondered if you could shed any light on why he might have called," Sam responded, hurriedly.

"I am afraid not, Mr Sampfield," Isabella replied firmly, "And, by the way, there is no Mr Hall. He's dead."

Sam walked up to the house with a strong feeling that he had been unintentionally discourteous, even hurtful, to Isabella Hall. If her husband was recently dead, that might well explain her reserved and distant manner. At the same time, though, her statement that she did not know Brendan Meaghan was patently false, if indeed it was she who had been standing with the Irish trainer on that day at Cheltenham races. He shook his head in exasperation, and, not for the first time, thought he should call Frank Stanley on the number he had provided in the event of a problem to demand an explanation. But, was this really a problem? He didn't know.

Settling into a chair in his study, he dialled the number on Isabella's piece of paper. A female voice with a strong Irish accent answered the call and, after he had told her who he was, appeared to hand the phone directly to Brendan Meaghan himself. Sam had the impression that the two of them had been waiting in their office, or wherever they were, for him to call.

"Mr Meaghan," Sam started, "You asked me to call you."

"That I did," Brendan Meaghan answered, "I am wanting to know why you are taking one of my best horses?"

"One of your best horses?" Sam reacted with shock to this unexpected question, "What do you mean?"

"You mean to say you don't know?" the other man exclaimed disbelievingly, "The owners informed me this morning. They're sending Tabikat to you."

"Tabikat? To me?" Sam knew he sounded like a parrot, but could not think of anything else to say.

"Well, I would not be calling you otherwise," the trainer went on.

"But a horse of that calibre…." Sam's voice tailed off, "When?"

"Look, he's entered in the feature chase at Leopardstown after Christmas," stated Brendan, "And then he's to come to you."

"I see," said Sam, bewildered by the information.

"Look, we need to talk, and not on the phone," went on Brendan Meaghan, "If you're to take the horse on there are some things you need to know. Are you to be at Cheltenham this weekend?"

"Well, yes, I have a novice running on Saturday," replied Sam.

"Good, then I will meet you on Friday evening 7.00pm in the restaurant at the Queen's Hotel. The table's booked in your name," said Brendan shortly, and the line went dead.

Sam stared at the telephone handset for a full half minute before returning it to its cradle. He found that his hand was shaking. He could not grasp what had just happened. An established Irish chaser was about to be transferred from a top Irish training yard to Sampfield Grange. It didn't make any sense. Brendan Meaghan had said that the owners had requested it. But he did not know the owners. Who were they? Some Jewish-sounding business was all he could recall from the racecard at Newbury.

At that moment, the telephone on his desk rang. Sam snatched it up, thinking that Brendan Meaghan might be calling back with more information. But it was not Brendan Meaghan. It was Sam's investment broker, David Rose. Sam had forgotten that he was due to call that morning.

"David," Sam said, before David could tell him anything else, "Do you know anything about Levy Brothers International?"

"You're not thinking of investing in them, are you?" said David surprised, "As far as I know, it's a family owned business. A bank. No shares available."

"No, that's not the reason I asked," Sam replied, "I've just been told they are sending a racehorse to me for training."

"A racehorse?" was David's response, "I didn't know they were into that sort of thing. They're in property development and international commodities trading as far as I know."

"Could you find out something more about them for me?" Sam asked him, "It's very odd to have a horse owned by a bank. I suppose if it's a family firm that may explain it. Some tax thing, maybe?"

"Wouldn't know," replied David, "But I'll make some enquiries."

Sam's subsequent regular discussion with David about his financial portfolio served to calm Sam's nerves a bit. As the conversation came to an end, Lewis knocked on the study door.

"Would you like a bite of lunch now, Mr Sampfield?" he asked, "Oh, and Isabella gave me this letter for you. It was in the office but you came up to the house without taking it."

Sam held out his hand to take the smart white envelope. He could already guess what was inside. As expected, the single sheet of notepaper contained the blue and gold letterhead of Levy Brothers International, the name printed in both English and Arabic. Sam was certain it was Arabic, although the name of the bank appeared to be Jewish, which struck Sam as odd. The message it contained was short and to the point. It asked if Mr Sampfield Peveril would kindly accept Tabikat, a seven year old bay gelding, into training at Sampfield Grange from the first day of the following month. On the assumption that this was acceptable, the bank would contact his secretary to make the necessary arrangements. The present trainer, Mr B Meaghan of County Meath Republic of Ireland, had been informed of the proposed change.

Sam had a distinct feeling that he did not have any choice in the matter. Someone, somewhere, had decided that the change of trainers was going to happen, and his, and probably Brendan Meaghan's, opinions were not relevant. Whoever it was had judged their target well. No trainer in his or her right mind would turn down the offer of a horse like this one. Sam could not shake off the thought that Isabella Hall had something to do with this, but he could not for the moment see what that could be. Granted she had watched his horses being exercised out on the gallops, but she was hardly in a position to be advising remotely located racehorse owners on a change of trainer on that basis.

"I'll come into the kitchen for lunch," he told Lewis, "I have some news for the staff."

And, as Sam was imparting the news of Tabikat's impending arrival to an incredulous Sadie, Brendan Meaghan was speaking to a tall man who was sitting in his office, a stick propped by his side.

"Did that sound convincing enough for you?" Brendan was asking.

"Absolutely perfect," replied the other man, "You should be on the stage."

Brendan Meaghan grunted.

"I want that horse back in one piece after this is all over," he said, firmly, "That Sampfield Peveril fella had better know what he's about. You don't mess with a Cheltenham Gold Cup contender at this stage in the season."

19

Brendan Meaghan's gruff instruction – Sam really could not consider it an invitation - to meet the following evening meant that Sam was obliged to travel to Cheltenham on Friday afternoon. Curlew Landings was declared for the fifth race on the Saturday card, so Kye and Sadie would bring him to Prestbury Park, as originally planned, on Saturday morning. Merlin had already confirmed through his agent his availability to ride the horse again at that meeting.

Isabella had seemed to have no difficulty in securing a room for Sam at the Queens Hotel, which made Sam wonder, cynical as he was now becoming, if it had already been booked in advance. On reflection, Sam thought it inadvisable to challenge her about this, so instead took the opportunity to ask whether Levy Brothers had been in touch concerning the final details of the arrangements to take on Tabikat in the New Year. When Isabella had answered in the negative, he made it clear to her that he wished to speak personally to whoever called from the bank.

"Yes, of course, Mr Sampfield," had replied Isabella, her face expressionless.

Sam had had an unsettled journey to Cheltenham. His feeling that he was being manipulated had become stronger, but he was unable to understand why. Sam was convinced that Frank Stanley and Isabella Hall were somehow involved in whatever was going on, but to what end was completely unclear. As he worried and nagged at the problem in his mind, his smart Audi sports car responded without hesitation to its driver's requests for more speed on the M5, as though arriving earlier at his meeting with the Irish trainer would get Sam a quicker answer to his questions.

As Sam left the M5 and joined the A40 towards Cheltenham, a red traffic light caused him to come to a halt outside the site of GCHQ. The circular building occupied a prominent position to his left and was surrounded by rows of parked cars. For a supposedly secret facility, it was very visible and prominent, thought Sam, wondering if Frank Stanley was one of the many people who appeared to work there.

Unexpectedly, his phone rang. As he moved off from the lights outside GCHQ, Sam heard on the in-car speaker the welcome voice of Helen Garratt, who had called to tell him that John and the trainer had decided to enter Alto Clef in the Welsh National. John had family in Cardiff, so a day out at Chepstow during the festive season would be a great opportunity for a reunion. Sam congratulated them on the decision and said that he would try to ensure that he watched the race on the television.

"Oh, no, Sam, darling," Helen contradicted him, "You're coming to join us. We can't do it without you to support us."

Sam gave a non-committal answer and said he was just arriving in Cheltenham, so would call her later. Wishing him good luck, Helen rang off. Sam had been half-tempted to confide in her his concerns about what was happening to him, but decided to wait to see what Brendan Meaghan might have to tell him before taking any action. Helen was a good friend, and one of the few people whom he could trust to give him impartial advice. Most people always had one eye on his wealth and the other on his horseracing connections. Perhaps he should have married her after all, he thought, half-seriously.

Sam was now waiting in the restaurant of the imposing Queens Hotel, which overlooked the attractively planted and grandly named Imperial Gardens in the centre of Cheltenham, at the table booked in his name. Sam had already checked the card for the races at Prestbury Park that afternoon and noted that Brendan Meaghan had two runners. At this time of the year, though, all the races were over by four o'clock in the afternoon, so there was no reason for the trainer to be late for the enforced appointment.

An attentive waiter asked if Sam would care to order a drink but Sam told him that he would wait for his fellow diner before ordering anything. The dining room was quiet at that time of the evening, strategically lit and warmly relaxing. But Sam felt anything but relaxed. In his jacket pocket was the report which David Rose had sent through by email to him that morning, the report about Levy Brothers International.

As was his custom, Sam had not felt equal to trawling through a financial report on a company, however succinctly prepared, and had called David on the phone as soon as he had received it that morning.

"Just give me a summary, David," he had said, and David had done just that.

The bank called Levy Brothers International, it appeared, was based in Bahrain and London, thereby explaining why the letterhead appeared in both Arabic and English. It was entirely owned by an Ephraim Levy and his two sons, Daniel Levy and Isaac Levy. The Levys appeared to be resident in Bahrain, despite being Jewish, being prominent members of the small Jewish community based there over many centuries.

Levy Brothers' main business appeared to be in financing the construction of top end properties in London and the Middle East. It also had a successful commodities trading floor, mainly dealing in precious metals and ores and oil futures.

The fact that Sam had never heard of the organisation suggested that involvement the racing industry, either as a sponsor or an owner of such facilities as a stud or a major training yard, was not part of the bank's enterprises. He had not heard of any of the Levy family as individual owners either, including in flat racing, which was the more likely of the two racing codes to attract serious money of the sort that this enterprise clearly had at its disposal.

"What I don't understand, David," had said Sam, when his broker had summarised the financial information which described a very successful and longstanding family enterprise, "Is why they have a single racehorse in training in Ireland."

"Beats me," had replied David, as Sam envisaged the broker

shrugging his shoulders and spreading his hands as he sat at his expansive desk in the City, "Hobby horse for one of the boys, maybe?"

"Boys?" had queried Sam.

"Looks like Daniel's twenty five and Isaac's eighteen," had replied David straightaway.

"Doesn't seem like the sort of hobby for a baby banker," Sam had said.

"Well, they don't seem to be bankers, not yet anyway," David had told him, "Daniel is an automotive engineer and works for Harlow Motosport F1 and Isaac's still a student."

None of it had made any sense to Sam. Maybe Brendan Meaghan could tell him more.

As if summoned by Sam's thoughts, a short stocky man in a grey tweed jacket suddenly occupied the chair opposite Sam's.

"Sampfield Peveril?" enquired the newcomer.

"Mr Meaghan?" asked Sam in return.

"That's good, I'm at the right table," said the other, and, sitting back, waved a fierce hand towards the hovering waiter.

"What'll you have?" he asked, as the waiter approached.

Sam opted for a gin and tonic whilst the other man asked for a glass of water.

"I don't drink," he stated, apparently to forestall any questions from Sam, then, to the waiter, "Bring the menu, would you, now?"

As Sam opened his mouth to speak, Brendan held up a warning finger.

"No business talk until I've eaten," he said.

Sam took the hint but could not think of any other topic he had in common with Brendan Meaghan but horses and the weather.

"Good day's racing today?" he asked, carefully, "How was the going on the course?"

Brendan Meaghan looked directly at Sam. His eyes were a faded blue and sunk into a sea of wavelike wrinkles which sat above reddened cheekbones which spoke of a life spent in an inhospitable outdoors. His nose was sharp and pointed and his mouth sunk down into his prominent jaw. He looked older than Sam had expected.

"Tomorrow's likely to come out better," was all Brendan said, after which enigmatic comment he remained almost completely silent until he had consumed two courses consisting respectively of vegetable soup and rare steak, waving away the offer of dessert with disdain.

Sam was fascinated by his new acquaintance and ate his own, rather more interesting meal, accompanied by a glass of claret, in silence, wondering what would happen next. Perversely, he suddenly found he was beginning to enjoy the mystery in which he had become enveloped.

Brendan, having satisfied his hunger, became more friendly.

"I prefer to do one thing at a time," he told Sam after consuming his plate of steak at record speed, "Now we can talk. If you are finished, that is?"

"Yes, of course," said Sam, "I am fascinated to hear what you have to say."

The other man looked at him suspiciously, as if suspecting some sarcasm in the comment.

"See now, Mr Sampfield Peveril…" he began.

"Please," said Sam, "Give me at least the opportunity to tell you that I am usually known as Sam."

"Sam, then," continued Brendan Meaghan, "Listen, we need to talk."

"I agree completely," Sam told him, looking around at the nearby restaurant tables, which were beginning to fill up with chattering diners, "Shall we see if we can go somewhere quieter?"

"That's already arranged," Brendan told him, and stood up abruptly.

The attentive waiter appeared immediately.

"My guest and I are going to the meeting room now," Brendan told him. As he spoke, he signalled to a couple sitting at a table on the other side of the dining area, "If we need anything, my secretary over there will tell you."

Sam felt as if he had been thrown suddenly onto the back foot. He had not been aware that Brendan Meaghan's staff had been observing them from within the restaurant.

"Look here, Mr Meaghan..." he began.

"Brendan," said his companion.

"Brendan, then," said Sam, "I have been very patient, but I am getting rather irritated by this charade. I should like to know what on earth is going on here. I have not asked to take on this horse, you know, and I am relying on you to tell me."

"To be sure, you are," replied Brendan, after a short pause, "If you'll go to the room with me, I will tell you everything you need to know."

"Need to know, or want to know?" asked Sam.

"Well now, everyone wants to know more than is necessary,"

replied the Irishman, enigmatically, and walked off towards the exit to the restaurant. Sam was left with no choice but to follow him.

As Sam sat back in the comfortable chair provided by the Queens Hotel, ready to listen to whatever Brendan Meaghan had at last decided to say to him, Kye was sitting on a stool made from an empty oil drum in the rather less salubrious surroundings of Graham Colvin's workshop.

"You'll get some good business for us at Cheltenham tomorrow," Gray was almost physically rubbing his hands together in anticipation.

"Yeah, I've called around and there's plenty of trade waiting," Kye told him, adding, "But I'm still bothered about that cow up at the boss's office."

"The posh sort on the phone?" asked Gray, whose only contact with Isabella Hall had been when she had booked the horse box in for its, albeit unknown to her, specially enhanced MOT.

"Something's not right about her," went on Kye, his paranoia, learned from the days with the HGV servicing outfit, beginning to get the better of him, "I think she's watching me. And she's weird. Goes out cycling all over the place. Lewis and the others think she's meeting a bloke, but I don't think so. I reckon she's a bizzy."

"You sure?" asked Gray, anxiously, not expecting this conclusion.

"Course I'm not fucking sure," replied Kye angrily, "If I was sure we'd know to stop this game for a while. But it's good money. I don't want to stop if we don't have to."

"Tell you what," said Gray, "We could follow her and see where she goes."

"For fuck's sake, Gray, she's a serious bike rider," said Kye fiercely, "Even if I had a bike, I couldn't keep up with her."

"I wasn't thinking of a bike," replied Gray.

"What then?" asked Kye.

"I've got a drone," said Gray, smugly.

Whilst Kye and Gray were discussing the problem of Isabella Hall, Sadie was lying on the bed in the Sampfield Grange cottage enjoying a satisfying fantasy about the naked body of Merlin ap Rhys. After two weeks of remembering, and possibly exaggerating, that delicious hard on of his, she was at last going to see him again tomorrow. With any luck she'd see the hard on again too. This time she was going to make sure it was put to good use.

But whilst Sadie was weaving a lascivious story about herself, Sam was listening to an entirely different and unexpected story being told to him by Brendan Meaghan.

20

The evening sky was bright with a late setting sun when Eoghan stood by the five barred gate of the most southerly field of his small farm. A breeze lapped lazily across the tips of the deep grass. It shimmered quietly, rippling over the land which fell away gently in the direction of the sea. The sea was not visible from here, but, on windier days, its sharp edge could be felt in the air which rushed across the slopes of the farm and buried itself amongst the mountains behind.

Eoghan had been born in the farmhouse, as had his four older brothers. Growing up amongst the daily drudgery of the isolated farm, he had learned to work hard, and to take his opportunity to learn when he got the chance.

No-one had sought his contribution. It had just been taken for granted. The farmhouse in those days was long, dark, and smoky, full of the deliberate slow movement of men accustomed to the outdoors, too big and clumsy to fit comfortably amongst the assorted chairs and tables, pots and pans, stoves and fire irons around which the family revolved. Eoghan, the last, and the most talented, of the Foley progeny grew quietly into his place, his presence scarcely disturbing the routine established over many generations of Foleys, O'Sullivans, and Scannells.

Eoghan's mother had fed, clothed, and then left, him to himself. She had loved him, as she had loved all her sons, but she had been busy. And, as Eoghan came to learn later, she had been grieving. A household of men and farmhands to be fed, she had spent her life tending hens, collecting their eggs, wringing their unresisting necks, set on the unrelenting treadmill of plucking, boiling, roasting, washing, scrubbing, frying, folding, carrying, collecting, sweeping, a pivot for the tedious activity which pushed the household around its existence of everlasting drudgery.

Eoghan had watched her from the hearthrug until he had been old enough to take his place in the structure of the Foley family world.

And he had grown up, not sullenly submitting to the yoke of drudgery, like his brothers, but resentful, scratchy, and prone to outbursts of rebellion which had brought blows down on his back and head, and threats, not just idle ones, of thrashings and beatings for failure to take his share of the family burden. His father had been a taciturn and resentful man, carrying a burden of rage and disappointment against some unseen enemy.

In Eoghan's youth, the work had been done with the assistance of the horses kept in the ramshackle barn beyond the farmhouse kitchen. There had been three of them. Like the rest of the household, they were mostly taciturn, sinewy and inured to the tough conditions in which they lived and worked. But they were also warm, friendly, and happy to accept Eoghan as a stablemate during the long and rainswept nights when he huddled against their matted coats and stared at the sharp points of the stars as they appeared between the scudding clouds. Their soft breath and sudden harrumphs soothed the churning turmoil in Eoghan's head and provided the one place in his restricted world where he could sleep. If his family missed him from the house, they did not say. And he did not care. Eoghan was a true creature of the farm and the stables.

At twelve years old, Eoghan had grown into a small, tough and wiry boy, with a scruffy thatch of black hair and sharp blue eyes. By now, school was behind him. His teacher had recognised the latent intelligence in the boy, his unexpected facility with arithmetic, his unlearned affinity with animals, his resentment of authority. But the teacher too was disaffected by the environment in which he had been forced to work, and, after some half-hearted attempts to penetrate the hard shell which the boy had built around himself, he had relapsed back into the indolence bred by lack of challenge and an inability to motivate himself to do more. The teacher had a degree from the University College in Galway, but had made the mistake of inheriting a lazy disposition and then compounding it by failing to find a wife who might have arrested his inevitable decline into drink, gambling, and loneliness.

Lack of energy and dehydration from a night spent emptying a bottle of whiskey had shortened the teacher's temper. Attempts to challenge his authority were met with brutal reprisals and most pupils shrank from contact with him. The school was small, and the dull pupils were intermittent attendees, as most families saw no use for anything more than the educational basics for their children. They were children of farmers and farm workers. They would never need anything beyond what the farm needed. There was value in being able to read and write and count. There was no value in learning about other lands, other times, other languages, or savouring the verse and music written by foreigners with unpronounceable names. Music and dance they understood, but that was not learned at school. And history was inbred in them all as being about wickedness of the British and all the evil that had stemmed from that.

Any teacher worthy of the profession would have challenged this view. But this teacher was not ambitious for his pupils and had inevitably come to see things from the parents' viewpoint.

Only once had Eoghan and the teacher breached the barrier which lay between them. Eoghan, re-entering the classroom after the end of the school day to retrieve a bird's egg left behind in his rickety desk, had been surprised to find the teacher poring over a newspaper spread across his desk. A cane lay across the newspaper, the teacher using in as a ruler to mark lines on the black typed surface.

So engrossed was the teacher in his task that he did not at first notice Eoghan entering the half lit room. The windows faced west. It was winter, and the sun was low on the dusky hills which obscured the sea from view. Lumps of deep grey cloud lay plastered across a coral sky, the sunlight spilling erratically around their glowing edges.

As Eoghan hesitated in the doorway, the teacher looked up. The light was behind him, and to Eoghan he appeared in outline, a smoky apparition, features invisible. As Eoghan froze, the teacher spoke.

"Come here, boy," he said.

Eoghan knew better than to disobey an adult. And so he approached.

The newspaper on the desk had been covered in lists of closely typed names and figures. Eoghan had seen the name of the local town, Gleannglas, at the top of the first column, but the other names were unknown to him.

A rumble of thunder had sounded from beyond the hills. The gloom of the deserted classroom had thickened. Eoghan and the teacher were silent, locked together in the fading pool of light, staring at the newspaper.

The teacher had pointed at one of the names in the list. Kerry Rebel, it said.

"Is that you, Eoghan?" the teacher had asked, "Are you a rebel or a winner?"

Eoghan had not understood but had nodded obediently, wondering what he meant.

The teacher had laughed, a short bark, cut off suddenly, as a flash of lightning had illuminated the little building.

"Well, you still have your chance," he had said, standing up.

He had started to fold up the newspaper, but had stopped.

"You have it, farm boy," he had said, "Let me know if you can make something of it – and of yourself."

Eoghan had been left in the classroom with the newspaper. He had folded it carefully and tucked it into his dirty jacket. He had walked home through the whipping rain, with the sound of thunder in his ears, the name Kerry Rebel running through his head like the recital of a charm against the evil magic of the darkening evening.

After the long climb up to the farm, voices were shouting, muddy water running through the yard, and there were cattle to be got in from the churned up fields. The horses and the men were shouldering their burdens and hauling their heavy loads, and Eoghan slipped in amongst them all, and became part of them once again.

Later that night, he hid the bedraggled newspaper amongst the hay bales in the barn, and slept amongst the horses. Kerry Rebel, Kerry Rebel, went the wind across the roof. And Eoghan slept.

Two of the three horses on Eoghan's farm were solid, heavy draught types, dull coated, resigned and locked into the work of the changing seasons. Ploughing, harrowing, sowing, muck spreading, harvesting, drawing loads of hay, logs, carts filled with pigs, sheep and poultry, they were involved in it all.

Eoghan, from the time he could lift the tack, became their stable boy, taking over the role from his next oldest brother, Gearoid, who disappeared to join the work of the fields and cattle. As Eoghan was the youngest, the stable lad role never passed on again, and, once he had left his unambitious school for good, Eoghan became the farm's horseman.

The third animal was a Connemara pony mare, once bright eyed and still even tempered. Her job was to pull the cart which took members of the family up and down the rutted track between the farm and the town of Gleannglas, a journey of some five miles. As soon as Eoghan could be trusted to drive her and the cart alone, the driver's job was his.

Eoghan had never been shown how to ride a horse. Horses were for working, so he had been taught how to ready them for work, how to feed them to ensure they had enough energy to work but not enough to rebel against their masters, how to clean their tack every night so that it lasted as long as possible before needing to be mended or replaced, and how to check for injuries which might turn bad and stop the horses from working. The horses all went shoeless, so no farrier attended the farm to check their feet, and that too became Eoghan's job. He was told, and embraced like a religion, the one rule about horses' feet. There was nothing more important than keeping them in good order.

If the draught horses ever loved any human being, which seemed unlikely amongst the unending drudgery of their lifestyle, they may have loved Eoghan. But the Connemara pony became his true friend. And it was she who taught him how to ride.

Eoghan's mother, emerging for once from her post in the kitchen, had watched her youngest son, now thirteen years old, hitching up the complicit pony to the cart one morning. A load of small logs, chopped by Eoghan's brother Gearoid the previous night, lay neatly stacked in the cart, several trays of eggs on top of them. It was a dull day, a soft stream of air drifting beneath pale grey clouds, which seemed stuck above the hills beyond the farmyard.

"Eoghan!" called his mother, "Eoghan! Will you hold the mare here and pay me heed for a while?"

Eoghan had been surprised. His mother, small, sturdy, wrapped up like a package in a brown shawl over a shapeless skirt, came forward and put her hand on the pony's shaggy rump.

"This Tarragon," she said, "is here to teach you if you want to learn."

Eoghan stayed silent, puzzled, wondering what his mother meant. He had never heard any of the horses called by a real name before.

"Your uncle says she is a safe one to ride," she went on, "She was brought here for your sister."

Eoghan knew about his sister. She had died before he was born. No-one was allowed to speak of her, but he knew her name, Branna, because it was on her gravestone. His mother went to see her on her infrequent but regular trips into the town, his father driving her in the cart, the pair of them hunched together over their hands, his father's holding the reins which lay across the bay pony's back, his mother's holding something, he knew not what, clutched in her fingers.

Mention of his dead sister was unusual, frightening even. But his mother seemed strangely determined to continue, so he waited to see what would happen next.

"My family", his mother went on, "are horsemen. They said we got it from the tinkers, but we were never part of that life. My father was a master blacksmith. He made everything from the fire. He made shoes for the grand horses of the rich. My brothers all went for smiths or drove the jaunting carts. There were others, but they're gone now."

She tailed off for a while, as if out of breath. Eoghan stood still, petrified. The sky and the dull clouds bore down on his head. His mother had never spoken of her family before. He knew his only uncle, Callan, the driver, and his jaunting cart in the town, but there had never been any others.

"You're the same as them," resumed his mother, "I know how you take up with the horses. But there's no use in it if you are not able to ride them. Take Tarragon out of her shackles and she will show you how."

With that, Eoghan's mother had seemed exhausted, and had shrunk back into the farmhouse, leaving him staring after her, the pony and cart, with their eggs and logs, suddenly seeming far away.

On the slow journey into the town, Eoghan's mind ran over and round the forbidden memory of his dead sister, rubbing and nudging at the meagre information, trying to eke out of it some explanation of why she was no longer there. He knew she would have been ten years older than him, had she not been gone by the time he was born, and was now just a name in the list of his siblings, slotted in between Colm and Diarmuid, the second and third of the Foley brothers.

As the cart creaked and rattled its way along the wet track under the motionless grey sky, he wondered what his sister would have been like. She wouldn't have been asked to work in the fields. Would she have helped his mother in the farmhouse? Would she have ridden the patient Tarragon across the high fields, both of them breathing in the soft air from the sea, or, perhaps it would have been in the stormy weather, soaked through to the skin, and laughing at the elements. Would Tarragon have been her special friend, a riding pony, instead of a drudge pulling a cart?

And what did his mother mean about Tarragon teaching him how to ride her? He had never seen Tarragon with anyone on her back. It had never really occurred to him that she was there to be ridden, like the smart horses he saw rich people riding around the paths and tracks in the hills.

Eoghan and Tarragon had trodden the familiar track into Gleannglas twice a week for over a year now, since he had turned twelve years old and was free of the need to attend school. The journey was reassuringly predictable. A quiet start up on the top of the hills, no other living being to be seen, the shadows of clouds decorating the fields, the calls of his brothers as they worked fading into the silence where the sky met the land. Eoghan and his pony and cart were a silhouette against the line of the hill as they moved gently and inevitably down into the valley where the town lay.

As they neared the town, the route became busier. The farm track came to an end and joined a narrow lane with a firm surface. The pony's pace would quicken at this point, and sometimes Eoghan imagined himself driving a jaunting cart, a paying passenger lounging in the back instead of logs and eggs.

The cart passed the little school which the dispirited teacher had finally abandoned shortly after Eoghan's departure. But Eoghan had eventually understood what was in the paper which the schoolteacher had given him. It was a racing paper and the list which the teacher had been studying so carefully had been a list of horses entered for a race in Leopardstown.

The paper had been interpreted for him in the barn by Eoghan's oldest brother Enda. Enda was thirteen years older than Eoghan, a powerfully built young man whose dark soul seemed to meld seamlessly into the land. Eoghan would see him out on the hills, sometimes at night, when Enda seemed to disappear into the darkness and return many hours later with not a word said about where he had been. Eoghan could see Enda's comings and goings from his sleeping place in the barn, but he kept silent. He knew Enda knew he could see him and he knew that Enda didn't care.

One evening, after Eoghan had stabled the draught horses, and given them their feed, he had moved some hay bales in readiness to fill the manger, and found the forgotten paper. Kerry Rebel and the drumming rain on the farm roof had returned at once into his thoughts. His mother had not yet called the men in for their evening meal, so he sat down upon the hay bale and opened the paper. The light was fading fast from the early spring sky, but Eoghan's blue eyes were strong and he could read the words and numbers and pick out the colours with ease.

"Leopardstown 3.05", he first read carefully, the unfamiliar name meaning nothing to him. This line was followed by information he did not understand about what seemed very large amounts of money. Beneath that was a list of strange names with a picture of a coloured shirt and hat next to each of them, along with more numbers and unfamiliar names, this time names of people, he thought. At the top of the list of strange names, Eoghan saw the words Kerry Rebel, with the teacher's dark pencilled marking scored underneath. The other names in the list had not been mentioned by the teacher, and seemed to have escaped the attention of his pencil. These words included such oddities as Bright Jack, Castlemaine Lad, The Lively Spark, Padraig's Fancy, and Mammy's Boy.

Eoghan had not been able to make any sense of it. Such was his concentration that he had not heard his brother Enda enter the barn until he heard Enda's breath puffed out in a long whistle.

"And so my little horseboy brother fancies his chances at the Leopardstown races, is that it?" Enda had said, apparently amused.

Eoghan had frozen at the realisation that Enda had seen him with the teacher's paper, expecting some kind of retribution for his lack of attention to the horses. Instead, to his surprise, Enda had sat down beside him on the hay bale.

"That Kerry Rebel", he said, pointing to the teacher's marked selection, "He's something special, now. He comes from Mallows, you know, home bred and all. Is that why you picked him out?"

Eoghan shook his head dumbly. He had never heard of Mallows. He didn't know what Enda was talking about.

Enda, for all his roughness and secretive nature, had a soft spot for his baby brother. His private name for him was The Colt, although he had never spoken this aloud. He knew his mother would never allow the use of anything other than her children's given names. She considered it bad luck. All except his dead sister of course, whose name was never to be mentioned at all. Branna, the lost one.

Enda had been a child of about Eoghan's present age when his sister had died at the age of nine. Named after a bird, she had flown away and left them. The Colt looked a bit like her, he thought.

"It is a racing paper, Eoghan" he offered, "Do you not know that?"

Eoghan shook his head again, looking down at the barn floor.

Enda took the paper from Eoghan.

"Look," he said, "Leopardstown is the name of a famous horse racing place a long way from here on the other side of the country. And this is a racing paper showing what races are to be run there. This is an old paper now, so the races are over."

"Races for horses?" said Eoghan, hardly daring to speak.

"That's it, horse races," went on Enda, "These are the names of the horses that will run in the race and here are the names of those who will ride the horses. Your Kerry Rebel is to be ridden by Cormac Meaghan and he's the favourite to win."

Eoghan had not heard Enda speak for so long about anything but the work of the farm, which usually caused him to lapse into moody silence after a few sentences. Enda seemed to be about to say more, but the call of their mother could be heard across the farmyard, a tin tray banged with a spoon to reinforce her voice, and the unexpected conversation had come to an end.

Tarragon broke unbidden into a light trot as the cart approached the town, causing Eoghan to shake the conversation with Enda out of his mind and to concentrate on the tasks awaiting him. The logs and eggs were to be dropped at Aunt Brigid's house, ready for the market, and replaced with those things which his mother wanted Aunt Brigid to send up to the farm. Eoghan never knew how his mother sent the messages to her brother Callan's wife, as his mother could neither read nor write. It was only years later that he realised that Enda was the messenger, calling in with the orders on his evening visits into the town. But, at the time, it seemed mysterious and strange to the isolated Eoghan.

Aunt Brigid had little to say to Eoghan that day, seeming preoccupied with problems of her own devising. Uncle Callan was nowhere to be seen. At this time of year, business for the jaunting carts was scarce and Callan often joined up with his brothers in the farriery trade. In answer to Eoghan's question, Aunt Brigid grunted something about himself being at the racecourse and out of her way for the present, and thank God for that.

Tarragon had turned from the lane by the school, its windows reflecting the afternoon sun, which had slowly groped its way through the blanket of dull cloud, and into the farm track. Eoghan was dreaming over the reins. The racecourse. He would like to see the races, he thought. His lost sister Branna returned to his thoughts and he pictured her riding Tarragon on the racecourse. But perhaps racehorses were not like Tarragon, though, or the draught horses, or even like Uncle Callan's smart black cob in the traces of the jaunting cart.

Tarragon suddenly stopped dead in the centre of the track. Eoghan was jolted unpleasantly back into the present, gathering the reins automatically and shaking them smartly.

"Get on then," he ordered the horse.

Tarragon stood her ground and Eoghan could now see why. A girl was crouched in the long grass at the side of the track. A girl about his own age with long dark hair curled against one side of her face, the hair on the other side behind her ear, from which dangled the gold hoop of an earring.

Branna. That was Eoghan's first thought. This is what he had imagined Branna to be like and now here she was. He stared, unable, like Tarragon, to move.

The girl jumped up from the grass and stood before him on the track. She wore a faded red dress and a little rabbitskin jacket. There were sturdy black boots on her feet, like boy's boots, but with a couple of red ribbons where the laces should be.

"I have been watching you," she stated.

Eoghan was unnerved. His dead sister, watching him.

"I see you every time you come with the pony along this way," the girl went on, "She sees me, but you see nothing."

"Branna?" came out of him as a hoarse croak.

"What's this with Branna?" the girl answered, surprised, "I am Caitlin."

"Caitlin, then," repeated Eoghan, his panic beginning to subside, adding, more normally. "What do you want then? A ride in the cart?"

The girl looked offended.

"Not at all," she retorted, "I have come here to teach you to ride the pony."

Eoghan was speechless.

"That one, she's a riding pony," went on Caitlin, authoritatively, pointing at the stationary Tarragon, "The likes of her should not be pulling that old thing". She gestured contemptuously towards the cart.

"And how would you know what she should be doing?" retorted Eohgen, nettled by the girl's confident statements.

"Because I do," replied Caitlin unhelpfully, adding, "You can call me Cait if you like."

"Why, and what sort of a cat are you that makes out she knows about other people's horses?" said Eoghen, determined to hold his ground against this unexpected adversary, "You look like a kitty cat to me, a little kitty cat."

The girl tossed her head, the gold hoop of the earring swinging against her neck.

"Well, do you want to ride her or not?" she said defiantly.

Eoghan knew she had him there. He did want to ride Tarragon, now that Caitlin had put the idea into his head.

"Very well, then, Kitty Cat," he said, trying to retain the upper hand by repeating the childish name. He jumped down from the cart and started to remove Tarragon's tack.

Caitlin watched him speculatively.

"You have no riding tack for her then?" she asked. It was a rhetorical question. Both of them knew that the cart harness was the only tack Tarragon possessed and the only tack Eoghan had ever put on her.

Tarragon was soon free and standing untacked, still in the centre of the track. The sun glowed dully behind a thin film of cloud. There was no wind and the air was thick with the dampness of the earth and grasses. It felt like a spell about to be broken.

The two young people pushed the cart to the side of the track. Tarragon stood like a statue as Eoghan put his arms around her neck and pulled himself awkwardly on her back, wondering what the pony would do. But Eoghan was small and light and Tarragon hardly seemed to notice him. He got his legs on either side of her body and

202

put his hands in her mane.

Caitlin produced a piece of ribbon from somewhere inside her jacket and looped it round the pony's neck. It looked like the same ribbon that she used for lacing her boots, Eoghan thought, watching the girl's dirty hands with their stubby fingernails deftly fashioning a loop at the end of the thin strip of fabric and threading the other end through it.

"Sit up on her, now," instructed Caitlin, holding the end of the ribbon, "Sit straight up on your backside, so she knows you're there."

Eoghan did as he was told. Tarragon shifted slightly beneath him.

"Now," went on Caitlin, "Squeeze your legs against her sides and she will walk forward for you."

Eoghan pressed the sides of his skinny calves against Tarragon's dark brown flanks. The pony obliged him by moving forward a few steps whilst Eoghan rocked back on top of her.

"Keep your balance," ordered Caitlin, "You have to move with her. Feel her as she walks and be part of the walking. You are part of her, not a sack of old seeds."

Eoghan's first riding lesson went on for half an hour. Even Caitlin had to admit that he was a quick learner. The years with the horses had paid him well, and his slight, wiry frame quickly adapted to Tarragon's movements. The pony moved freely beneath him as they walked and trotted up and down the cart track. Caitlin had long let go of the end of the ribbon and Eoghan was steering Tarragon easily using his weight and his legs. Tarragon responded readily to his familiar voice and seemed pleased to be rid of the bit in her mouth, shaking her black mane and snorting softly.

After about an hour, Caitlin announced that the lesson was finished for the day. Eoghan reluctantly slipped down from the pony's back. Together, they pulled the cart back onto the track and restored

Tarragon to her customary role.

Eoghan, released from the dream in which he had existed during the unexpected riding lesson, became suddenly aware of how far the sun had moved since he had first set out on his homeward journey.

"I have to be on my way now," he announced, awkwardly, whilst everything in his being urged him to remain in the dull sunlight on the track with the strange girl. Tarragon shifted restlessly, resenting the loss of freedom, and keen to be home.

"I know you do, horseboy," Caitlin replied, "But you'll be along here again soon enough. I'll watch out for you."

Before Eoghan could speak again, she turned abruptly away, and pushed her way through the ragged hedgerow at the side of track. He watched her running down the slope of the rough field on the other side, a tiny figure flitting between the grazing cattle. He saw her hop over a stile and then she was gone.

Eoghan expected his mother to be annoyed at his late return, but, to his relief, she said nothing, as he unloaded the baskets sent up to the farm by Aunt Brigid and put them on the kitchen floor. By the time he had stabled and fed Tarragon, his father and brothers and the draught horses were coming in from the fields, and Eoghan became busy. The tack was dirty and the horses tired. His family had little to say.

Eoghan retreated to his usual private world with the horses. Going mechanically about his tasks, he was able to think about the day's unexpected events. They made no sense. Who was the girl and why did she think he should be riding Tarragon? There was no use in riding her, although he had to admit to himself that he had liked it better than driving the cart.

Above all, though, he knew without any doubt in his mind that he wanted to do it again. As to seeing the odd girl, he was not so sure. He felt that she had been making fun of him in some way he could not quite understand. But, he thought, maybe she was a bit daft and didn't mean any harm. Jumping out on people about their business on the farm tracks was an odd thing to do, surely?

But, she was going to help him ride Tarragon, so he supposed he would have to put up with her. He wanted that more than anything now.

"A daft kitty cat, she is, that's all," he grunted contemptuously to the oblivious horses, until his mother banged the tin tray which called the family indoors to eat.

The next time that Eoghan was loading the cart for the town, his mother simply handed him Tarragon's riding tack. It was done in silence and Eoghan accepted the unfamiliar items without speaking. There was a neat brown leather bridle with a shiny bright jointed snaffle bit. And there was an apparently unused leather saddle, cut – although Eoghan know nothing of it at the time - for jumping. Clean metal stirrups with straps threaded through their top edges were attached on either side.

Eoghan put the tack in the cart along with the eggs and the logs and went on his way. His mother turned away before he left but he knew she still stood there for minutes after he had guided Tarragon from the yard. Eoghan could see her, as if he had eyes in the back of his head, like the horses did. She was still, quiet, dark, and unmoving. She seemed to be looking at the far horizon, beyond the overgrown lane along which Eoghan was about to travel.

"I will be back with the news from Aunt Brigid," Eoghan called, as he clicked Tarragon forward on their way.

He had never said that before, but the silent gift of the riding tack had unnerved him.

"And I shall be glad to hear it from you, Eoghan," replied his mother.

At the time, the comment meant nothing, but it was to haunt Eoghan for years to come. He never saw his mother stand or speak again after that day.

The weather on that fate-marked day was warm and bright, a small breeze ruffling Eoghan's black hair, as he sent Tarragon on with the cart down the rutted track. Tarragon seemed interested in everything around her and tossed her head from side to side as the cart rocked along, bumping from one dried-out muddy tussock to another. Eoghan needed to pay close attention to keep her straight along the best part of the going.

Eoghan and the cart soon passed the point where Caitlin had surprised him on the track a few days before. There was no sign of her. He looked carefully in the bushes and hedgerows, just in case she was waiting to jump out on him, but he saw nothing. Tarragon appeared not to see anything either, so they continued on their way to Aunt Brigid's house, a small knot of disappointment forming in Eoghan's stomach.

Aunt Brigid seemed distracted and also appeared to have company in the house. As Eoghan unloaded the logs and stacked them in a neat pile by the back door, he caught a glimpse of Uncle Callan in the parlour of the little stone house which he shared with Aunt Brigid and their three daughters. Uncle Callan was not alone. He was standing looking towards someone who Eoghan could not see. The unseen person was addressing Uncle Callan, who was nodding vigorously in response.

For some reason, Eoghan thought of the unhappy schoolmaster who had given him the racing paper. The voice sounded a bit like his, a different way of speaking, quicker and more forceful than the duller, mellowed tones of his father and brothers. But then, Uncle Callan glanced up and caught sight of Eoghan standing silhouetted by the light shining from behind him into the front door. He held up a hand and the invisible speaker became immediately silent.

Uncle Callan came along the dim stone passageway towards Eoghan.

"What's your business here, child?" he asked, his manner hostile.

Eoghan was confused. Uncle Callan knew him well enough, and certainly too well to address him that way.

Eoghan was about to speak when Aunt Brigid appeared from the yard, where she had been allowing Tarragon to drink from a bucket, and stood behind him.

"And now, Eoghan," she said, "I will give you your load for your mother."

Uncle Callan appeared to relax.

"I see now it is you, Eoghan," he said, "I was blinded by the light, sure enough. Look, you send your mother my love."

Uncle Callan turned away and went back into the parlour, closing the door on himself and the unknown visitor.

Aunt Brigid seemed keen for Eoghan to be gone. The cart relieved of its load, she handed Eoghan a large bag full of paper-wrapped items for his mother. If she noticed the saddle and bridle beneath the sacking in which Eoghan had placed them, she made no comment.

The hasty departure suited Eoghan. He had no wish to wait around in the town and was keen to get back on his way in case Caitlin might decide to put in a belated appearance.

And so she did, at exactly the same spot where she had surprised him the last time. Her appearance was much the same, except that the washed out red dress had been exchanged for a green one, which looked equally old and wretched.

"You brought her tack then?" the girl demanded, before Eoghan could open his mouth.

Eoghan nodded towards the cart.

"In there," he said, excitement welling up in his throat.

The sun emerged from behind a small cloud and its light flashed from the bit as Caitlin picked up the bridle. Eoghan soon had the cart harness off Tarragon and Caitlin proceeded to put the unfamiliar bridle onto the pony. Tarragon rattled crossly at the new bit, and flung her head around, but Caitlin's gentle persistence paid off, and the bridle was soon in place.

"Hold these, while I put on the saddle," ordered Caitlin, pushing the reins into Eoghan's hand.

Putting the saddle onto Tarragon proved more of a problem, as she skirted irritably sideways. Eoghan stroked and patted her neck and eventually the job was done.

Caitlin tightened the girth.

"This is her own saddle?" she asked Eoghan.

Eoghan shrugged.

"This is the only one I have seen," he offered.

"Well the fit is not so good," stated his companion, firmly, "If it is hers, she was younger and in better condition when it was made for her. Next time we will have a blanket to go beneath it."

"I can ride her without the saddle," said Eoghan, aware that time was moving on, and anxious to get on the pony.

"That you will not," said Caitlin, running the metal stirrups down the leathers and fastening the buckles. Everything was new and shiny, the leather itself stiff and clean looking.

"You'll be no jockey that way," she added.

"Jockey?" asked Eoghan, taken aback, as usual, by her forthright statements.

"Well, that is what we are doing here, is it not?" the girl responded, turning her green-eyed gaze on him.

"I don't know what we are doing at all," said Eoghan, feeling rather desperate, "I want to ride the pony, nothing more."

The girl eyed him speculatively.

"For sure, you don't know much, horseboy," she said, "You are here to be made into a jockey."

Eoghan at this time in his life knew very little about jockeys or indeed about horse racing at all. He knew that some of the boys from his school had taken part in pony races across the hills above the town. But he had never had a pony to race, so had not been part of this exciting sounding activity.

"The pony racing?" he asked, "I can take Tarragon for that?"

Caitlin's eyes opened wide, and rounded like a cat's. She almost spat.

"Pony racing, pffh!" she scoffed, "Not at all. It is real racing you are going to be doing."

Eoghan remembered the racing paper which the teacher had given him. He tried to regain some control of the conversation, which was beginning to frighten him, the girl talking so authoritatively about things of which he knew nothing.

"At Leopardstown then?" he asked.

Caitlin laughed.

"Yes, if you like," she said, "But we need to start here at home. At the racecourse in the town."

Eoghan knew there was a racecourse in the town. His Uncle Callan and brother Enda went there. But he had not thought it the same type of place as the exotic sounding location in the racing paper. And, yet, he recalled, the name Gleannglas had been printed in the racing paper. So perhaps it was the same kind of place.

Whilst he was pondering this, Caitlin motioned to him impatiently to get onto the back of the increasingly restless Tarragon, and his second riding lesson, this time with a saddle, began.

Eoghan never saw how far the sun moved during the next two hours, nor how it gradually became obscured by thickening cloud. The bright day began to fade into a dull gloom and a small and insistent wind picked up from the remote ocean and moved through the grasses and trees which surrounded the two diminutive figures and a bay pony on the hillside.

As Eoghan reluctantly got down from Tarragon's back, Caitlin having signalled that the lesson was at an end, the pony suddenly flicked her head around, her eyes widening with fear.

"What is it, now, Tarragon?" asked Eoghan, rubbing her neck, whilst Caitlin ran the stirrups up the leathers and began to remove the saddle.

Then he heard it too – an insistent buzzing sound from further up the track which gradually developed into a full throated roar.

Caitlin had the saddle in the cart and Eoghan was grappling with Tarragon as she heaved and pulled against his grip on the reins, when Enda appeared over the brow of the track above them riding on a motorcycle.

Tarragon was beside herself with fright at the appearance of the strange and noisy machine. She twisted and reared backwards and it was all Eoghan could do to hold onto her.

The two youngsters stared in surprise as the noisy motorcycle approached. Eoghan had not even known that Enda owned a motorcycle, but his first thought was that Enda had come to stop him riding Tarragon.

Enda came to a halt beside them, and the sound of the motorcycle lessened as Enda throttled back the engine. Tarragon recognised Enda and became a little calmer, standing stiller, but tensed and ready to run if the strange contraption came any nearer.

"Eoghan!" yelled Enda, "Get that pony and cart out of the track, for the love of God!"

Eoghan hastened to obey his brother's instruction, saying nothing, his heart beating erratically in his skinny chest. Caitlin grabbed Tarragon as Eoghan moved the cart so that Enda could squeeze the motorcycle alongside, his muddy boots propelling it along, as the engine idled.

"Get back up to the farm, now, Eoghan," ordered Enda, as he shoved the bike along the rutted track, "Ma is taken bad. I am going for the doctor."

Eoghan had no idea what he meant, but the instruction was clear enough. As Enda roared off down the track, sending Tarragon into another frenzy of plunging and tugging, he became aware of Caitlin standing alongside him.

"Come on," she urged, softly, her usual sharp tone gone from her voice, "I will help you."

Between the two of them, they pushed the now calmer Tarragon between the cart shafts and changed over the tack. Eoghan's fingers were shaking as he fastened the buckles. Caitlin put the riding tack into the cart and hopped up onto the seat beside him.

Eoghen set Tarragon off up the hill and the two of them rode together in silence until they reached the farmyard. The sun had gone from sight behind the thickening film of cloud, giving a dead glow to the stone buildings around them.

"I will see to the pony," said Caitlin, "Go in to your mother."

Eoghan stumbled into the farm kitchen. The fire had gone out and his mother was nowhere to be seen. He pushed past the long eating table into the small room beyond where he knew his parents sat in the evening.

His mother was half seated, half slumped down in a floral patterned armchair near the small window which overlooked the hill over which Eoghan and Caitlin had just travelled. His father was kneeling on the floor beside the chair.

"Aoife, Aoife," he repeated softly.

As Eoghan came nearer, he realised that his mother looked different. Her face seemed to have collapsed on one side, her mouth looked slack and crooked, and her eyes seemed darkened and watery. She was trying to reply to his father, but seemed to have difficulty speaking.

"Enda has gone for the doctor," his father was saying, "He will come to you soon."

Eoghan's arrival had gone unnoticed by his father, and Eoghan was not sure whether or not he should say anything. But something in his mother's unfocused gaze seemed to alert the older man to Eoghan's presence. He turned.

"Come sit by your mother, Eoghan," said his father, moving back from the chair.

Eoghan walked forward and crouched by the chair.

"Ma, I rode the pony," he blurted out. He thought she would want to hear that, he knew not why.

Behind him, he heard his father's boots clumping across the stone floor and out of the room. His mother said nothing, so Eoghan put both his hands onto her arm and sat silently with her, as the evening sky darkened outside. At some time, Caitlin came into the room, and sat on the floor alongside him, leaning her head against his back. She too said nothing.

Eoghan and Caitlin, through the many years later, could never recall how long the three of them had remained in that room until the doctor arrived. Sometimes it seemed an age and sometimes they remembered it as minutes. They seemed to exist within an unreal world bounded only by the walls of the room. Eoghan could feel his mother's pulse throbbing weakly under his fingers as he held her arm. He could hear Caitlin's even breathing and the weight of her head against his spine. His father did not return, but Eoghan somehow knew he was outside the door in the kitchen and that Colm, Diarmuid and Gearoid were there too, all sitting in silence.

It was dark when the doctor arrived. He came on the back of Enda's motorcycle. No four wheeled motor vehicle could get up the track to the farm in those days.

Eoghan registered the doctor's arrival but his next conscious memory was of waking up in his usual bed in the stable. The horses were all there, snuffling in their mangers. There was no sign of Caitlin. The sun shone weakly between the planks of the wooden doors.

Shaking the sleep from his head, Eoghan wondered if he had dreamed the events of the previous evening. But, once outside, he knew he had not. With the sun as high as it was, everyone should have been out in the fields, including the horses. But the horses were still indoors and, in the farmhouse, so was everyone else – everyone except his mother.

The men were seated around the table. They had empty plates before them, and seemed to have finished eating some time ago. Enda saw Eoghan hesitating in the doorway.

"Come and be seated, Eoghan," he said. So Eoghan took his place at the table, and was given a piece of bread and a mug of milk. Someone at least had milked the cows that day, even if nothing else had happened.

"There is nothing more to be done," Enda said then, addressing their father, as if resuming a discussion which had been interrupted by

Eoghan's entrance.

"That being so, we must return to work," the older man responded, and, motioning to his sons, began to rise from his seat.

As they went out, Eoghan, gulping down the milk and stuffing the bread into his pocket, made to follow them.

"Not you Eoghan," said Enda, stopping him, "Not now."

Eoghan sat down, confused. The horses might be needed.

"Gearoid will see to the horses," Enda told him, as if reading his mind.

"Enda, where is Ma?" Eoghan blurted out.

"In the hospital in the town," said Enda, "She has had a stroke."

Then, seeing from Eoghan's confused expression that he did not understand, Enda added, "It is an illness in the brain. It means she cannot walk or talk. Some of her body does not work any more."

"Will she come home?" asked Eoghan. But he already knew from Enda's expression that their mother would not come home.

On that day, Eoghan's charmed existence came to an abrupt end.

When his mother left the hospital, some days later, she went to live at Uncle Callan's house. His father took Tarragon and the cart down to the town now, so that he could visit her. And so, Eoghan's riding lessons were over already.

Confined to the farm now, Eoghan took over many of his mother's duties, tending to the hens, milking the cows with the help of whichever one of his brothers was available that day. And he prepared the food. His efforts were limited to putting out milk, bread, eggs and ham on the table, but no-one seemed to mind the limited diet.

Enda seemed now to be running the farm and organised the work for everyone.

A new drudgery engulfed them all, overshadowed by their mother's absence and their father's unspoken grief.

Then one day, Tarragon and the cart came home alone. Eoghan, collecting eggs from the little flock of hens behind the farmhouse, heard the clattering of the cart entering the yard and knew that it sounded different. Tarragon would usually come to a neat and quiet halt by the gate, waiting to be untacked. But today the cart wheels continued to shift about on the stones as Tarragon whinnied for attention.

Only one of Eoghan's brothers was within hailing distance. Colm was in the cow byre, washing down the walls and floor. Eoghan ran into the little stone building, calling for him.

Stopping only to release Tarragon from her traces and push her into her stall, the brothers ran down the track towards the town. Less than halfway there they found their father. He was lying on the ground, flat on his back, as if felled by a knock out boxing blow to the jaw.

Colm was the tallest and strongest of the Foley brothers. With an exclamation which could either have been a sob or a cry of rage, he lifted his father up in his arms and started walking back up to the farmhouse.

"Go for the doctor, Eoghan," he said.

Eoghan ran the rest of the way into the town. He had no idea where the doctor lived, so he went, breathless and frightened, to Aunt Brigid's house. Aunt Brigid sent him into the kitchen where his mother was sitting propped up by cushions in a wooden chair.

"Sit with her Eoghan," she said, "I will go for the doctor. Do not leave the house."

Eoghan did as he was told and crouched by his mother's chair, just as he had on the evening when she had experienced her devastating stroke. He tried to get his breath under control, but his heart continued to pound as though about to break out of his heaving chest. His mother's silence and immobility finally calmed him down, and he placed both hands on her arm and touched his forehead against her arm.

"It's Dad, Ma," he whispered, "Colm found him on the track. Tarragon came home and told us."

To Eoghan's surprise, his mother moved her other hand and placed it over the top of his. And then, laboriously, she spoke, her words slurred but recognisable.

"Eoghan, all will be well. You will do as Enda says."

She relapsed into silence and became still again. Eoghan felt drained of all energy, and remained still alongside her. He longed for the feel of Caitlin leaning against his back, but she was not there, and worse still, he had no idea where to find her.

Then within a week, both of Eoghan's parents were dead, and the farm passed into Enda's control.

21

Under Enda's stewardship, the farm changed out of all recognition. Cocooned in his own limited world with the horses, Eoghan was unaware of the extent to which he had been living the lifestyle of a previous era. Most farms in western Ireland had been mechanised long ago and horses were no longer the engines of their daily work.

A tractor replaced the draught horses and a small truck replaced Tarragon and the cart. Enda's motorcycle was used for journeys which did not involve loads. The rutted track along which Eoghan had guided Tarragon was rolled by a heavy machine which belched and ground its way up the track, whilst all remaining ruts were filled with the crushed stones which were then laid on the top. A surface of dark and smelly material, which Eoghan realised was the same as that used to cover the streets of the town, was laid down.

Enda bought two bicycles on one of which Eoghan soon learned to freewheel down from the farm into the town, although the return journey was harder work. He looked out for Caitlin along the way, thinking that she too might enjoy riding on one of these new, to him at least, machines. But there was no sign of her.

At the funeral of his parents, who had departed their remote little world within a day of each other and were buried together in the local churchyard, Eoghan thought he had seen Caitlin. A small figure was occasionally visible in the gloomy trees overhanging the dilapidated stone wall which bounded the graveyard. But he could not be sure it was her, and, when he looked again, the fleeting shape was no longer there. The thought then struck him that the figure might be Branna's ghost, so he stopped looking and thought about his parents. They would be pleased to be with Branna, he thought to himself, and that made him feel better.

The arrival of the road and the machinery signalled the departure of Eoghan's other three brothers. Colm, Diarmuid and Gearoid were still young enough to seek a living elsewhere, and had no wish to remain on a remote and backward farm. They departed together one day, once Enda had secured from the town the services of the farm workers he still needed.

In spite of the death of his parents, this was a good, though short-lived, time in Eoghan's life. The horses, although no longer working on the farm, still remained there. Enda could have sold them for meat, but, unsentimental though the work-hardened brothers were, the longsuffering horses had been part of their daily drudge, and deserved to benefit from the new world which the farm was now entering.

So the two draught horses were put out into one of the top pastures where they could see the sea and breathe the soft air, and no more strain was put upon their backs and shoulders. It was summer now and they could stay there all day and night. Eoghan would go up each morning and evening to ensure that they were safe, and they rewarded him with a dazzling display of seemingly youthful acrobatics and high kicks around their new territory. It made him laugh to see their huge bodies launching themselves into the air like ponies. Then they would come to the gate to talk to him and he talked back to them, missing their warm companionship during the night. He was no longer allowed to sleep in the stable barn, and lived in the house with Enda and, until they left for their new lives, his other three brothers.

Tarragon, now that the cart was no longer in use, had no role to play in the work of the farm. Eoghan, fearful that she might be sold, summoned up the courage to ask Enda if he could continue to ride her. To his surprise, Enda agreed, stipulating only that Eoghan was to look after her and the draught horses and that these activities should not interfere with his duties on the farm.

Eoghan's duties were, though, becoming increasingly limited, as Enda hired new workers to take over the work formerly done by his father and brothers. A young woman was brought in to prepare meals, see to the poultry and clean the farmhouse, soon occupied only by Enda and Eoghan. Work was started to construct living quarters out of an old feed store. Construction materials and unfamiliar interior fittings were regularly brought up the track from the town.

The farmhouse itself was not spared the modernisation process, with the installation of a cooking range to replace the open fire and chimney ovens used by Eoghan's mother, together with the purchase of new utensils and associated cooking paraphernalia. The gloomy living room where Eoghan had sat with his mother and Caitlin had been painted with a whitewash and the dingy furniture replaced with new. Electricity was run through overhead wires up to the farm and light fittings installed in every room. A bathroom with a flushing toilet was put in. Eoghan had thought such things existed only in the town, but it was now clear that they could be had at home too.

As Eoghan's only regular work was with the now redundant horses, he soon became a kind of odd job boy, assisting the three building workers who came up from the town each day, and listening in fascination to their unfamiliar conversations about their lives and families.

Had Eoghan been older or more versed in the ways of the world, he might have wondered where Enda was finding the money to pay for all these improvements and changes to the way the farm was run. But Eoghan was ignorant of such things and his trust in Enda was as complete and unconditional as that which he had given to his parents.

Tarragon too was thriving in her new environment. Eoghan rode her with increasing confidence around the fields and little tracks close to where the draught horses cropped the grass. He remembered Caitlin's comments about the fit of the saddle and took a folded blanket to protect Tarragon's back and withers from any rubbing. Once, he let Tarragon jump over some logs which had been left at the edge of a copse ever since the day his father had died. Such was their success with this new manoeuvre that they amused themselves trying to jump a variety of different obstacles which Eoghan created by restacking and rearranging the logs into ingenious shapes of ever increasing height.

All this Eoghan and Tarragon did alone, learning together through a process of trial and error. There was no sign of the ghost of Branna, which Eoghan firmly believed was because his parents were now able to look after her. Nor was there any sign of the more tangible figure of Caitlin, and Eoghan gradually stopped looking for her. He fell from Tarragon's back on numerous occasions whilst they were learning to jump together, and on those occasions was glad that Caitlin was not there to laugh at his feeble efforts.

Eoghan's solitude was broken only once, when he saw the shape of a tinker's van making its way along the ridge of the hill beyond the pasture where the draught horses lived. He knew the tinkers had horses with them because they called to the draught horses, which whinnied back a greeting. Even Tarragon raised her head to listen to the conversation, but, deciding that the jumping was more interesting, ignored the invitation to get involved.

After a few weeks of this new and benign lifestyle, Enda and Eoghan found themselves alone in the farmhouse one early Autumn evening. The nights were coming in earlier now and the farm was ending one season and beginning to plan for the Winter and for next year's Spring. Enda was often out during the evenings, roaring off down the new road on the noisy motorcycle. Tarragon, stabled by the gate, had ceased to fear this machine and now turned her head away with casual indifference as it passed by.

On this evening, though, Enda had remained at home, sitting at the kitchen table, working his way through mysterious looking papers with the assistance of the newly installed electric light. Eoghan was well used to being alone with his own thoughts, and simply sat nearby, thinking alternately about what he and Tarragon could do together tomorrow, puzzling over unfamiliar topics of conversation he had overheard between the builders, and, it had to be said, wondering whether he would ever see Caitlin again. He was keen to show the little Kitty Cat what he and Tarragon were now able to do. It would be hard for her to be so scornful of him now, he thought triumphantly.

Without really meaning to, he suddenly said to Enda, "Tell me Enda, what is a bookie?"

Enda jumped.

"And why would you want to know that, now?" he asked, rather sharply.

Eoghan was too taken up with his question to notice Enda's tone.

"The men who are building the rooms in the feed store," he said, "They talk about things all day and one of them said that the bookies had sucked him dry and his family would not eat until you paid him again."

Enda seemed to relax a little on hearing this explanation by Eoghan.

"Well, that is his own fault entirely," he said, "He should be thinking about his family before going to the bookies."

Enda then began a patient explanation about horse racing, betting, and the roles in this of various participants, including the mysterious bookies. He talked about breeding and bloodlines, about famous and not so famous horses and jockeys, and how such a man as the builder came to be involved in all this, even though he had probably never sat on a horse in his life.

"It can be the ruin of you, little brother," said Enda, finally, "Or it can make you for life. Or more usually a bit of both."

Eoghan listened in open-mouthed fascination to this narrative.

"Can anyone be a jockey?" he asked, "Is any horse allowed to enter a race? What about Tarragon and me?"

"Look, Tarragon is not really a racehorse," said Enda, kindly enough, "Racehorses are special horses, owned only by rich men and women. But there is no reason why you cannot be a jockey. Indeed, it is what we all have in mind for you, so it is."

Eoghan was not sure who Enda meant by "we all" but a more urgent problem presented itself.

"But how will I get a racehorse?" he asked, simply, "You said only rich men and women can have them. We are not rich."

"If you are a good enough jockey, these men and women will bring their horses to you to ride," Enda told him, "And they will pay you well too."

Before Eoghan could ask any more questions, Enda seemed to make his mind up about something, and held up a silencing hand.

"No more questions now, horseboy," he said, "Because tomorrow you can go and learn about it for yourself."

Having said that, he returned to his paperwork and Eoghan resumed his silent thoughts.

At Gleannglas racecourse the next day, Eoghan had never seen so many people in one place. Enda paid for tickets at an entrance protected by metal turnstiles, which fascinated Eoghan, who had not come across such contraptions before. The man behind the counter by the turnstiles seemed to know Enda well and greeted him by name, adding,

"And your Uncle Callan is here before you."

Enda grunted in response and the two brothers passed through the creaking turnstiles into the racecourse grounds.

People of all ages were strolling, standing, or hurrying around a large open area beyond which Eoghan could see wooden railings and various white painted buildings. One of them, higher than the others, had steps at the side, on which a few people were filing up and down.

Large noticeboards with information about the races that afternoon were attached to the sides of some of the buildings. Behind them, the familiar green hills of Gleannglas rose up against a dull, grey sky. A watery sun was struggling to penetrate the static clouds. Between the buildings and the hills lay the racecourse itself. The course was roughly an oval shape with flattened sides and ends. Eoghan and the other racegoers were situated towards the end of one of the long sides. Painted wooden fences separated the spectators from the course itself, but the further side had no fences, and the limits of the course were delineated by thick woodland, which had been cut back to create a running line. The clustered trees provided a smooth curve back around toward the buildings, where they were replaced by fencing once again. The woodland side of the course was higher than the point at which Eoghan was standing, whilst the fenced side of the course was completely flat and straight. Most people were standing in the area where the buildings were located but a few had walked across the course into the centre.

Eoghan could see that obstacles had been erected at various points around the course. Unlike the logs over which he and Tarragon had practised, these obstacles seemed to be made of hedgerow and brush, piled up and lashed together. Some were a lot bigger than others.

After an initial explanation of the function and location of the parade ring and an instruction to Eoghan to watch all the races carefully and learn as much as he could, Enda seemed keen to be free of Eoghan's company. Eoghan saw him join a group of men standing near a row of bookies' stumps, as Enda had told him they were called. The bookies had blackboards, which looked like smaller versions of those used at the school, on which they chalked up lists of names and numbers, whilst shouting out loudly and persistently to passers-by. Eoghan realised that this must be the betting Enda had told him about. He wondered if the workman who had lost all his money would be here today instead of working up at the farm.

A sudden booming and crackling sound made Eoghan jump. A disembodied voice floated across the heads of the crowd, which was rapidly growing in size. The voice welcomed everyone to the racecourse and informed them that the first race would take place at 1.30. Eoghan had no watch, but a large clock above the entrance showed that the time was ten past one.

The aimless milling of the crowd seemed to be replaced by a general movement in the same direction, and Eoghan, for want of any other purpose, followed behind. He found himself moving towards the parade ring which Enda had previously pointed out. His small size enabled him quickly to wriggle through the people in front of him until he was standing by the wooden rail surrounding the ring. Opposite him, horses were being led onto the track which lay around the inside of the railing.

Eoghan had never seen such beautiful horses. There were ten altogether, and each of them had its own groom to lead it around by the bridle, and some even had two grooms. Most of the horses were bay, like Tarragon, although two were chestnuts. All of them were tall and long legged with strong, confident strides and clear wide eyes. Their ears twitched inquisitively, as they took in, and then ignored, the various admiring and critical scrutiny of the spectators. They all wore coloured rugs over what Eoghan could see was a saddle beneath.

As each horse passed Eoghan, he breathed in their scent and longed to reach out and touch them. Behind the horses, the centre of the parade ring was filling up with people. He wondered who they were and whether anyone was able to go into the ring with the horses. But he could not see how to get into the ring from where he stood.

The identity of the people in the ring was soon made clear to Eoghan as a result of his hearing a conversation which took place above and behind his head.

"I see Mr O'Dowd is come to watch today," said one voice.

"They say he paid five thousand English guineas for that horse," responded the other.

"That is a serious sum of money," commented the first voice, sounding impressed, "He must think a lot of the horse, he surely must."

Eoghan, listening intently to their continuing discussion, soon deduced that Mr O'Dowd was the elderly man who had just entered the parade ring accompanied by several other smartly dressed people who stood around in a little group in the central area. Other similar groups were collected together in various places around the grassy area. So these were the owners who paid other people to ride their horses, thought Eoghan. He could see now that Mr O'Dowd, who was leaning on a stick as he conversed with the other members of his party, was far too old to ride the horse himself, although some of those around him seemed younger.

After some minutes, during which the ten horses continued to walk around the parade ring and more groups of people assembled in the ring, the crowds behind Eoghan gradually thickened. Then the jockeys entered the parade ring. Each of them was dressed in a patterned shirt of different colours, all of them very bright, rather like the coloured pictures in the children's story books which Eoghan had been given to read at school. The jockeys were walking and talking together as they arrived, but soon dispersed, each of them joining their own expectant group in the parade ring.

Enda had told Eoghan to learn what he could, so Eoghan concentrated on Mr O'Dowd's group. Mr O'Dowd's jockey was dressed in green and yellow colours and wore a green covered hat with the strap undone and hanging by his chin. Eoghan noted that the jockey, who looked very young, shook hands with Mr O'Dowd. Another man in the group, who was wearing a brown hat with a brim, then spoke to the jockey, nodding his head vigorously, whilst the jockey nodded back. Eoghan wondered what they were talking about.

The voices behind him struck up again.

"And he's left the horse with Scannell, even so," one of them said.

"Who's the jockey, then?" asked the other, "I don't recollect him."

"Meaghan's the name," said the first voice.

"Not Cormac, surely," exclaimed the second.
"No, no, to be sure," replied the other speaker, "This is a conditional,

his cousin I believe. Brendan Meaghan. Fifteen years of age."

Eoghan stared at Brendan Meaghan. This jockey was not much older than he was himself. And he was riding what the voices seemed to think was a very expensive horse.

"Well, I suppose Mr O'Dowd and Mr Scannell know their business," said the first speaker, sounding doubtful.

As they spoke, the jockeys began to break away from their groups and each approached one of the horses. The grooms, recognising them, slowed their charges down and removed the rugs, and the jockeys were soon mounted on the horses, legged up into the saddle by helpers. The grooms walked with the horses until they left the ring and then let them canter away as they reached the racecourse. Rugs were left scattered in the parade ring, to be picked up once the horses had been sent on their way.

The departure of the horses brought about a general move towards the buildings by the racecourse, which Eoghan realised were where the spectators would stand whilst watching the races. An open area in front of the buildings was also available and Eoghan found himself carried towards this by the renewed movement of the crowd. He wriggled his way once again to the front and stood with his chest pressed against the wooden rail.

The horses meanwhile had made their way towards the far side of the course. Eoghan could see the bright colours of the jockeys' shirts against the duller background of the trees. The echoing voice from the loudspeaker continued to give information about the horses and Eoghan was able to work out that the horse belonging to Mr O'Dowd, and ridden by the teenage jockey, was called Bristol Gold.

After a few moments, during which the horses circled slowly around and various adjustments were made to the tack of some of them, the race began. The ten horses formed a ragged line as a man with a yellow flag waved them forward. Then, at some signal invisible to Eoghan, they suddenly surged forward and broke into a gallop.

As the horses moved in a tightly packed group away to the left, Eoghan saw that they were approaching one of the lower obstacles. The combined shape of the collected horses and jockeys rose and then fell as they negotiated the hurdle. Their speed and stride continued unbroken as they forged onwards towards the end of the far side of the track.

The loudspeaker voice was excitedly telling the spectators about the progress of the race. People around Eoghan were calling out and cheering, repeating the names of the horses they were following. Another hurdle was cleared by the still tightly grouped horses, after which they all turned along the shorter end of the track, where another hurdle awaited them.

There was a shriek from the loudspeaker and a collective groan from the crowd, as one of the horses dipped to the ground over the third hurdle. The remainder of the field ignored the event and continued onwards, whilst the fallen horse scrambled to its feet and rushed after the other runners. The unseated jockey, dressed in red and white, sat up on the grass, appearing dazed.

Eoghan was glad that it was not Bristol Gold which had fallen. He could see the bay horse, identifiable by the jockey's green and yellow shirt, in the middle of the group of straining horses, now rounding the bend to his left and approaching the tightly packed spectators.

The noise around Eoghan increased to a roar as the horses approached. Eoghan could hear their hooves thudding through the ground, the rattling crash as they slammed through the top of the next hurdle, the jockey's voices as they shouted and yelled at their mounts and at each other.

The horses shot past Eoghan's position by the rail and were off towards his right to jump the next hurdle, the riderless horse still streaking determinedly after them.

No more horses fell in the remainder of the race, but the runners slowly began to spread apart as they worked their way along the far side of the course, or the back straight as the gabbling voice on the loudspeaker called it. Soon the horses were once again approaching the spectators, in front of whom, Eoghan now understood, the race would finish. The muttering and cheering around him once again swelled up to a frenzied roar, some people even screaming and jumping about in their excitement. Eoghan was not used to being in such crowds, but, far from being frightened, the emotion of the people around him caught him up, and he began to shout and cheer too.

Eoghan cheered for the only horse whose name he knew, and that was Bristol Gold. He could see the horse, still amongst the leaders, with his young jockey balanced in the irons, doubled over the horse's neck, whip flailing in his hand.

The drumming of the hooves came nearer and the chaos and noise in the spectating stands increased to an unbearable level. Eoghan yelled his encouragement to Bristol Gold as loudly as he could, even shouting the jockey's name as well. He knew the jockey could not hear him, but Eoghan also knew that what he was watching was a team effort, and that the horse and his jockey were a single entity at that moment, striving together to reach the finishing line in front of the other horses.

Suddenly the race was over. Bristol Gold came third. The loose horse had by now caught up with the remainder of the field and flashed across the winning line alongside the leaders. A few more horses galloped past the winning post whilst others trailed slowly behind them, having given up their efforts to catch the leaders.

At that moment, Eoghan felt a sense of elation and anti-climax tumultuously mixed together, something he was to feel many times in his coming career. Strangely, too, though, he felt a flicker of dread. He did not recognise, or try to understand at the time, this feeling which would be repeated again many times in the future. But it would wake him in the night, even in old age, with its confused images of Enda, Mr O'Dowd, the colours worn by Brendan Meaghan, the crowd pressing at his back, the loose horse running pointlessly towards the winning line, and, most of all, the five thousand English guineas paid for Bristol Gold.

The crowds were dispersing around him now, intent on finding the next piece of excitement in their afternoon. Eoghan was left leaning against the white wooden rail, feeling as if he had been punched. Turning round, he saw that the horses were leaving the racecourse and proceeding in a slow procession towards the previously deserted parade ring. The grooms had reappeared alongside each of them, and had taken hold of their bridles, leaving the jockeys to sit quietly on top. Some jockeys spoke animatedly to the grooms and to the other people who appeared alongside the moving horses. Others sat silently, looking dispirited. Some of the horses seemed bemused, plodding along obediently in a manner Eoghan recognised from his years with the draught horses. They had done their work, and were now waiting to be told they could rest. But here they were surrounded by noise and excitement rather than by the tedium and drudgery of the farm. Fine, beautiful, and cared for with the same dedication which Eoghan had shown his own equine charges, they were working horses nevertheless.

As the horses and their retinues reached the parade ring, three horses separated themselves from the group, Bristol Gold amongst them. Eoghan joined that section of the crowd which was moving towards the part of the parade ring reserved for the winning horses. There the three horses and their accompanying parties were cheered by all those who had supported them during the race.

The winning horse was called Charcoal Burner. The people surrounding the victor, whose groom pushed a bucket of water under his nose, hugged each other and patted the steaming animal with enthusiasm. The jockey's hand was shaken by various men and women as he removed the saddle from the horse's back.

The winner's position was a joyous and triumphant scene, to which most of the nearby spectators were attracted. They whooped, applauded and stamped their feet as a prize was presented to the owner of Charcoal Burner, a woman wearing a smart red coat and matching hat.

Eoghan's gaze was, though, fixed on Bristol Gold, who was standing near a post with a small sign with a figure three nailed to the top of it. Brendan Meaghan had by now dismounted and was engaged in animated conversation with Mr O'Dowd and the man in the brimmed hat. They seemed happy and pleased, all of them clapping the others on the back. Eoghan tried to get nearer to hear their conversation, but caught only the phrase "a sure prospect for the future" or something similar.

Attention had by now turned to the next race. Already more horses were entering the parade ring, and Charcoal Burner's victory had become a thing of the past.

Eoghan watched seven races that afternoon, but, to him, none was as exciting as the first one. He looked for Mr O'Dowd and Brendan Meaghan again in the parade ring before each race, but they did not reappear, and new horses, jockeys, owners, supporters and winners took their places.

As the horses returned to the parade ring after the last race, Eoghan felt a hand come to rest on his shoulder. It was Enda.

"And how is my little horseboy brother enjoying the day's racing?" asked Enda, unexpectedly good humoured.

"I am enjoying it very well," replied Eoghan, "and indeed I should like to come here again," he added hurriedly in the hope of taking advantage of Enda's good mood.

"And so you shall," stated Enda, rather grandly.

Eoghan thought Enda's manner strange. He did not recognise then that Enda had been drinking.

"But now," Enda went on, "I have business to attend to here in the town, so you shall need to return home without me this evening."

Eoghan remembered that Enda had put one of the bicycles in the back of the truck which they had used to travel to the racecourse. He nodded obediently to Enda and made his way to where the truck was standing outside the interesting green turnstiles.

And by the truck he found Caitlin. She was wearing the same red dress she had worn on the day he met her, the same boots on her feet, laced with the same ribbon. It was as though his mind had conjured her up again from his first sight of her on the farm track.

Caitlin grinned at him, her gold earrings catching the dull light from the low sun which was pushing a few feeble rays from beneath spreading grey clouds.

"So you have been to the races today, horseboy?" she said, "And did you win any money from the bookies?"

Eoghan was immediately thrown into his usual state of confusion by her confrontational manner.

"And what is this, then?" Caitlin added, pointing at the bicycle which was lying in the back of Enda's truck, "Has Tarragon thrown you to the ground one too many times?"

Eoghan did not know how to answer so many questions all at once, so he simply said, "Why are you here?"

"I am here to see you, of course," retorted Caitlin, seemingly nettled by his question.

"Well now you have seen me," said Eoghan, "And I will be needing that bicycle to go home."

"Suit yourself," replied the girl, and she turned on her heel to walk away.

"No, look, come back," called Eoghan, frightened by the effect his words had had. The last thing he wanted at that moment was for her to leave.

"You can ride the bicycle, if you want," he added.

It worked. She turned back to face him. And for the next hour, the two of them behaved like the children they still were, riding the bicycle in circles around the truck, screeching to a halt and almost pitching over the handlebars, sitting backwards on the saddle, perching on the crossbar, until they were both exhausted. The light was fading from the sky in a watery glow above the horizon.

"I have to go home," Caitlin announced.

"And where is that?" Eoghan asked, suddenly aware that he knew little or nothing about her.

"With my Dad and sister," offered Caitlin, unhelpfully.

"And where might they be?" persisted Eoghan.

"Right here at the racecourse," Caitlin said, laughing.

"You live here at the racecourse?" asked Eoghan, incredulously.

"Indeed we do," Caitlin told him, "Our Dad is one of the workers here."

"And what does he do?" Eoghan wanted to know.

"He is a farrier," Caitlin replied, "But he does other things too, mending things and the suchlike," she added, vaguely.

As Eoghan opened his mouth to ask more questions, intrigued that it was possible for anyone to live in such an exciting place, Caitlin turned on her heel and ran off, not in the direction of the turnstiles, but to an iron gate set further along in the wall. She opened it quickly, slipped through and was gone.

Eoghan stared after her for a while, wondering whether he should follow, but, in the end, he decided that perhaps the horses would be needing him at home. He picked up the bicycle from the ground and began the slow uphill journey back to the farm.

The farmhouse was in darkness when he reached it. For once, Eoghan suddenly missed his mother. Not that she had had much time to spare for him, but at least she had been there. Even when he was there, Enda was not the same.

So Eoghan did what he had always done. He went out to Tarragon's stall in the barn and let himself in. Soon he was asleep in the straw, whilst Tarragon snuffled and shifted nearby and blew her warm breath above his head.

Enda, when he returned much later, was not pleased to discover that Eoghan was asleep in the barn. But he was tired, and problems were preying on his mind, so he left Eoghan where he lay and went into the farmhouse alone. Lying in the dark, Enda decided that changes needed to be made. He had many commitments to fulfil, and the time was coming when he would be called upon by those to whom he had made promises. And the first of these was his wife.

Eoghan was woken in the morning by the sounds of the farm and wondered whether Enda would be angry with him for sleeping in the barn. He talked to Tarragon for a while and told her they would go out together to visit the draught horses in the field. Then he went into the farmhouse to find Enda.

But Enda was gone already. The daily woman said that he had set out into the town in the truck soon after she arrived. She gave Eoghan a bowl of porridge and a mug of milk, then left him alone in the kitchen as she went off about her work.

His breakfast quickly eaten, Eoghan helped himself to some bread and cheese, which he stuffed into his jacket pocket, and went to tack up Tarragon. After visiting the draught horses, who, as usual, were happy to see them, Eoghan and Tarragon made their customary way up to the high tracks and fields, jumping over everything they found in their path. When they tired of that, horse and boy drank together from a cold little stream which gurgled and tumbled through a small rocky ravine well out of sight of the farm.

This was their own special stream, and Eoghan had thought that no-one else knew of it, until one day he had seen the tinkers' horses drinking there with two boys standing alongside them. Eoghan had been too shy to go and speak to them, although Tarragon had called out to the strange horses and they had called back. But the tinkers were nowhere to be seen today, and Eoghan and Tarragon had their stream to themselves once again.

As Eoghan and Tarragon descended the hill above the farm, Eoghan could see that Enda's truck had returned. People were standing in the yard, and, as he approached, he could see that one of them was Enda. With Enda stood a man Eoghan had never seen before, together with a woman with red hair wearing a brightly patterned dress, and – his stomach lurched with the shock – Caitlin.

The waiting people were talking together, but all looked up as Tarragon clattered into the yard, letting out a little whinny as she recognised Caitlin. Eoghan slid down from Tarragon's warm back, and stood holding her bridle, unsure what to do or say.

Enda took the red haired woman by the elbow and stepped towards him.

"Eoghan," he said, firmly, "This is Niamh. She is my wife."

Eoghan said nothing. He had not known Enda had a wife. He could not understand how Enda could have a wife who did not live at the farm. Married people usually lived in one house and had children with them there. And why was Caitlin here? And who was the strange man?

Niamh came toward Eoghan and put her hands on his shoulders. Eoghan flinched at the unfamiliar contact and looked down fixedly at the ground. Niamh stepped back.

"Hello, Eoghan," she said, quietly, "I believe you are already acquainted with my little sister, Caitlin."

Eoghan nodded dumbly, not daring to look at the silent Caitlin.

"And here is my father, Diarmuid," Niamh continued, looking towards the man, who Eoghan could now see was grey haired and had a deeply lined and sun worn face.

"It is good to meet you at last, Eoghan," Diarmuid said slowly, and Eoghan raised his head slightly to meet his gaze.

It was from that moment on that day that Niamh and Caitlin came to live at the farm.

Once Eoghan had overcome his shyness, he learned that Enda had married Niamh some time before the death of their parents, but that she had not been welcome at the farm. His parents did not approve of her father's employment at the racecourse. They had wanted Enda to marry a farmer's daughter who could have joined his mother in running the farmhouse. But Niamh was an educated girl, who had studied at the college in the next town, and they could see no use for her. Her training as a bookkeeper, a job she did at the racecourse, was of no use they could see to the running of the farm.

So Niamh stayed with her father and sister in their little house by the racecourse and Enda came there to see her when he could. Enda's intention had been to leave the backward farm and to make a new life with Niamh, pursuing some other more rewarding occupation. But a number of events, not to mention promises extracted from him by Uncle Callan, had caused his plans to change. Now, in the fading light of the late Autumn afternoon, it was still not clear to Enda that he had made the right decision. But he was committed now to his chosen course, and had no option but to make the best of it.

Niamh became to Eoghan both the mother and older sister that he had lost. Niamh not only made sure that he was clean, clothed, and fed, but she gave him books to read and encouraged him to talk to her. From the ignorant and silent horseboy, Niamh did what the disenchanted teacher had failed to do. She drew out a bright and lively personality, a quick mind, and a voracious appetite to learn. Niamh nourished Eoghan's natural ability with horses through books containing information about their care and their training.

Some of the books were veterinary textbooks, others were history books, and some were made up stories. Eoghan's reading skills were rusty, but soon improved with Niamh's help. Caitlin too was encouraged by Niamh to read and so the house gradually acquired enough books that shelves were required to hold them, and improved lighting was installed that winter by which to read them.

Niamh's father Diarmuid remained in his accommodation at the racecourse. A widower of ten years, he was glad to have his two daughters settled at the farm, especially Caitlin, whose wildness often troubled him. Niamh was a sensible girl, he thought, apart from her strange decision to marry a man whose house she could not enter until his parents were dead, but Caitlin was not the type to go to college to learn. Perhaps the life of the farm would suit her better, he hoped. And she had a boy of her own age for company.

Diarmuid knew that Caitlin had been teaching Eoghan to ride Tarragon. Enda had discussed it with him, not because Enda thought Caitlin would be a suitable teacher, but because Diarmuid had once been a jockey and that was the trade which Enda had in mind for Eoghan. Diarmuid had declined to take on the project himself and suggested that Caitlin might be of service.

"She is a good young horsewoman herself," he had told the doubtful Enda, "Her old pony is gone now, and we will find a new one for her when we can, but in the meantime she can occupy herself with giving your brother some skills."

And so, Caitlin had been sent to introduce herself to Eoghan, which she had done in her own way on that warm day a few months earlier on the farm track. Eoghan's mother had known that Enda had found another youngster to help Eoghan learn to ride Tarragon, but she had not known of the connection with Enda's wife. Enda was not sure whether she would have objected, but he thought it better to remain silent about this detail. His mother, belatedly, had realised that Eoghan needed to learn to ride if he was to be of any help to the family, and that the ghost of Branna must no longer be allowed to stand in the way.

Eoghan's riding abilities had improved beyond measure since his last meeting with Caitlin, but he was self-taught. If Enda's plans were to bear fruit, he would need more expert help. So Enda risked another roll of the dice, and found a new pony for Caitlin.

The pony was another Connemara mare, a younger version of Tarragon. A boy from the town rode her up to the farm one misty Autumn morning, just as it was getting light, and left her tied to the gate. Uncle Callan had bought her in a livestock sale. She was skinny and undernourished, but sound and tough. She stood by the gate and shrieked for attention, until Eoghan, ever alert to the cries of horses, ran from the farmhouse, thinking that Tarragon was calling him. Instead, Tarragon was looking out of the barn, snorting crossly, her face reflecting her disgust at the noisy youngster who had disturbed her comfortable existence.

Caitlin, clad in a shapeless nightgown, followed Eoghan across the farmyard. Together, they untied the pony and led her into a stall next to that occupied by the irritated Tarragon.

Caitlin rubbed the pony down with a handful of straw, patting and soothing her. Eoghan brought hay and a bucket of water, filled from the farmyard trough. The pony settled down soon enough, and she and Tarragon were almost friends by the time their two youthful carers had left the barn.

"We are a good pair of horse grooms, you and I, Miss Kitty Cat," said Eoghan, on whom Caitlin no longer had her former silencing effect.

"So we are, indeed, horse boy," agreed Caitlin.

They agreed to call the new pony Branna, and both laughed aloud to think that the horses loved them and that there would be nothing else in the world for them to care about once they were all together in the hills above the farm and the rest of the world did not exist.

But Enda, watching them from the window, knew that the rest of the world did exist and also that it could be very bad.

"We need to move these children away soon," he said to Niamh, who was lying still and quiet in the bed behind him.

"I know that," she responded, quietly, "But you have made your pact with the devil and it may already be too late."

"Eoghan will go to Mallows," replied Enda, "And Caitlin back to your father. Uncle Callan cannot force all this upon them too."

Niamh could say nothing. But she watched Eoghan and Caitlin from the window, and her heart sank in her chest.

22

That summer, Eoghan went to Mallows and remained there for five years. Arriving there as a skinny lad with a passion for horses and a magical glimpse of the world of racing stored in his as yet untouched soul, he left the place which became his second home as a strong and knowledgeable young stud groom and a jockey with two wins to his name.

Mallows in those days was a mixed stud and racing yard. Set in the hills to the south of Gleannglas, its peaceful estate extended over sloping green meadows and rutted, meandering tracks. The sea was visible from the tops of the higher slopes and the salt in the air could be tasted by those who cared to venture upward over the undulating grassland. In the lee of the slopes were the paddocks and buildings of the stud and stableyards, enclosed by neat wooden fencing and populated by many horses and a smaller number of people.

Eoghan was brought to Mallows in the open back of Enda's truck, his few possessions stuffed into a new rucksack which Niamh had given him. Caitlin rode with him whilst Niamh sat in the front with Enda. Niamh was pregnant and sat upright by Enda's side, one hand lying over her swollen abdomen and the other holding the frame of the truck's open side window.

Caitlin and Eoghan were busily making plans for the ponies. Although Niamh had, for reasons of her own, misgivings about Caitlin remaining on the farm, Enda had pointed out that Niamh would need help when the baby arrived and that Caitlin was required to look after the ponies. Eoghan's concern was that Caitlin could not take the ponies out together, whilst Caitlin assured him that she could ride one and lead the other. It was not the same, but at least meant that neither Tarragon nor Branna would be left behind at home.

"And a ride over to Mallows is not so far," said Caitlin. But they both knew that in reality it was a long way.

Although the life at Mallows might have seemed harsh, with early morning starts, the need for round the clock care of the pregnant and foaling mares, and continuous physical work during the day, by comparison with Eoghan's hard childhood, his working circumstances seemed normal to him. He would have been happy to sleep with the horses, which were some of the most beautiful creatures he had ever seen, the sleek and glossy stallions to whom breeders brought their mares, the mostly sweet natured brood mares who wandered happily in the lush paddocks with their inquisitive foals, and the gelded horses, kept and trained for racing. But that was not allowed.

So Eoghan moved into a world which revolved entirely around horses and it suited him very well. Although he missed Tarragon, Branna and Caitlin, his new environment, and what he could learn from it, filled his every waking thought and the ponies and his young sister-in-law were pushed into the back of his thoughts. Although they were no more than ten miles distant, they could have been in another universe.

Mallows was owned by Tadhg Brody and had a regular staff of around twenty people. Four of those people were apprentices, of which Eoghan was one. The other three were teenage boys a little older than himself. One of these, Eoghan was fascinated to discover, was Brendan Meaghan, the young jockey who had ridden Bristol Gold into third place at the Gleannglas races. Another was Oisin Cassidy, a red headed and gap toothed boy, whom Eoghan remembered from his now almost forgotten days at the town school. The third apprentice, Ronan Brody, was the son of the owner himself. He was a sharply spoken and aggressive lad, who did not hesitate to remind the other apprentices of his special status amongst them.

Eoghan's strange upbringing had turned him into an easy going individual who accepted other people for what they were. It had never occurred to Eoghan to judge or offer comment on anyone else. As a result, he got along well with the other three lads, just as he did with the horses. Despite having brothers close to him in age, Brendan, Oisin and Ronan were the first three male friends and companions Eoghan had ever had.

The four apprentices lived in a small extension to the main farmhouse, for a farm is what Mallows originally had been, and their welfare was overseen by Ronan's mother, Caoilinn. Cai, as she was known, was horrified to discover from Enda, whose details she had recorded as being Eoghan's guardian and next of kin, that Eoghan's parents were both dead and that his youthful sister-in-law Niamh was the nearest thing he had to a mother. Cai also noted the presence of a bright looking young girl who stood with Eoghan, bravely holding back tears, as Enda signed the papers which would bind Eoghan to his apprenticeship at Mallows.

"This is my sister," Niamh explained, when Cai asked about the youngster.

"I think she will miss her stepbrother," said Cai.

"Indeed she will," said Niamh, as the two youngsters went to fetch Eoghan's bag and bicycle from the truck, "But Eoghan needs to learn his trade. And he will be home once a month."

As things turned out, Eoghan became the least of Caoilinn Brody's concerns. The hidden resentment felt by her own son at being treated as if he were just one of the other apprentices, together with the increasingly rebellious moodiness of the young Brendan Meaghan, were to prove more of a trial to her than any difficulties Eoghan could have presented.

Ronan and Brendan liked to slip away whenever they could to make their way into Gleannglas. As Eoghan's bicycle had been brought from the farm in Enda's truck, and as Eoghan had no concept of ownership of anything other than the horses at Enda's farm, the bicycle was soon appropriated almost exclusively by Brendan as a means of transport to get him into the town. Ronan had a bicycle of his own, so the two boys were soon able to make plans together to get themselves away from the tedium of the stud farm and into the more exciting environment of the Gleannglas pubs. Not that the boys were allowed to drink in pubs. But there had been nothing to stop their friends and their friends' older brothers from smuggling bottles full of beer and whiskey to them out of the pubs' back doors, particularly since Ronan seemed to have the money to pay for it. And there were plenty of Gleannglas girls who were willing to spend time with boys who had money to spend.

Had Cai known what the two boys were up to, she would have certainly prevented it. But Ronan and Brendan always had excellent alibis, which came in the form of Eoghan and Oisin. Eoghan was not interested in hanging about the back doors of the pubs of Gleannglas and had as yet no curiosity about girls. Oisin had had too much experience of an alcoholic father, who had regularly returned home in a drunken rage ready to beat up Oisin's longsuffering mother, to want to go anywhere near a pub.

But it was Eoghan's path in life which was most changed by an incident which arose from these secret excursions by Ronan and Brendan. It happened on one night during the second of Eoghan's five years at Mallows. A spring storm was blowing in from a fierce and heaving Atlantic Ocean when Cai announced in the farmhouse kitchen at breakfast time that she and Tadhg would be away from home that night giving comfort to the family of a relative whose child had died. The establishment was to be left under the charge of the chief stud groom, an elderly and deaf individual who lived with his wife in one of the farm cottages. The other employees either lived out in the nearby area or else were resident in the farmhouse itself. The four teenage boys in the little whitewashed extension were housed on their own and largely unobserved.

As Cai and Tadgh drove away along the flat rutted track in Tadgh's truck, Ronan and Brendan exchanged glances. No-one would notice at all if they slipped out of the establishment for most of the evening. But, by the time the evening came, it was pouring down with wild rain, huge drops of freezing water driven by angry winds over the hills behind the farm. The horses were safe in their boxes and Eoghan and Oisin, along with the other staff, had retreated, soaking wet, indoors.

Ronan and Brendan were not to be deterred by the appalling

weather.

"You can surely not be cycling anywhere in this?" Oisin asked them, when they announced their intention to go into the town.

"Not at all," replied Ronan, "We will drive in by using the horsebox."

"You are able to drive the horsebox, are you?" asked Eoghan, surprised by Ronan's statement.

"Of course I am able to drive it," said Ronan, "And there'll be no horses in it, so it will be easier."

Following this brief discussion, Ronan and Brendan set out into the dark and wet of the evening, leaving Oisin and Eoghan behind in the fuggy damp of their farmyard apartment.

Many hours later, when Eoghan had long been asleep and the gale outside the walls was still blowing itself into a frenzy, a hand shook him roughly by the shoulder. It was pitch dark in the room and Eoghan could not see who had roused him.

"Oisin?" he said, uncertainly.

The sudden flare of a struck match lit up the room and Eoghan found himself looking into the terrified face of Brendan Meaghan.

"For the love of God," hissed Brendan, "You have to help us, Genie. Ronan has run the horsebox into the ditch on the main road. He's blind drunk and he's hit his head. I can't move him."

Eoghan could hear Oisin snoring away in his bed on the opposite side of the room. Pulling on his shirt and work trousers, he grabbed a waterproof coat from the passageway and followed Brendan into the rainswept farmyard. A dull nightlamp illuminated the yard and the entrance from the road. One of the three Mallows dogs was waiting outside, having heard Brendan's return, but, seeing that the humans were members of the family, it made no sound. Eoghan patted the dog's wet back and whispered to him to go back and lie down. The dogs were used to stud staff getting themselves up unexpectedly in the night to tend to foaling mares, so quickly settled down again together in their stable corner at Eoghan's command.

Eoghan and Brendan found and lit two of the hurricane lamps which served the stud staff at night, and set off together along the stormsoaked road. Water streamed underfoot in all directions, and the force of the wind almost pushed them over as they leaned into it, each with one hand covering their faces, the other holding the lamps. Water, as if thrown in buckets, hurled itself onto their heads. Neither boy spoke. It was impossible to be heard.

The stricken horsebox was about a mile along the road. It was almost invisible in the wild darkness, tilted at a crazy angle into the ditch, one of the wheels twisted sideways on the road surface, the other three sunk into the mud of the water-filled ditch. Ronan was in the driver's seat, slumped forward, his head resting on the grubby steering wheel.

The two boys had been made fit and strong by their daily work, but getting Ronan out of the damaged vehicle was an almost superhuman task. Drunk and unconscious, Ronan was a dead weight. In vain did Brendan slap him in the face and urge him to waken. Brendan was still half drunk himself, but he soon began to realise that it was more than the drink which was preventing his silent friend from waking up.

"We need to get him home," Eoghan panted, trying to make himself heard about the screaming gale, "Then we can send someone for a doctor."

"No doctors," yelled Brendan in Eoghan's ear, "No-one must know about this."

"But he is hurt, Brendan," Eoghan shouted back.

"We take him home and we look after him," Brendan screamed angrily, "If anyone knows about this, then my time here is finished.

It is all very well for Ronan himself. He will own Mallows one day. They cannot send him away. They can send me away. And you."

Eoghan stared at the soaked and streaming face of Brendan. Brendan's wide brown eyes were like those of a terrified horse. In his mind, Eoghan saw Enda and Niamh at home, expecting the best of him. And there was Caitlin, Tarragon and Branna, who all needed him to ride with them. The wind whirled around his head like a banshee.

Wordlessly, he shrugged Ronan from his slumped position on the road, and got one shoulder under his arm. Brendan did the same on Ronan's other side. Together they staggered and hauled Ronan along the waterlogged road, the wind shoving them forwards, until they reached the yard. The dogs came out once more to greet them, and watched soundlessly as Ronan was dragged into the building, where Oisin awoke, blinking with shock, asking what was going on.

Eoghan and Brendan on that night made and carried out a plan which was to bind them together in a lifelong conspiracy. Oisin was threatened on pain of death to say nothing, a request to which he readily agreed, knowing that his future too was at the mercy of Ronan Brody's family.

Ronan was undressed and shoved into bed by the joint efforts of the three boys. His outer clothes were hung in the entranceway to dry inasmuch as this was possible in the grim conditions. And the sound of the wind outside drowned out any of the noises which might have alerted the other staff to the fact that people were up and about at that time of night.

"All four of us have been here this evening and all through the night," Brendan pantingly told the other two, as he and Eoghan stripped off their wet clothes and hung them up in turn, "We have not stirred anywhere other than into the yard when we were checking on the dogs. We know nothing of the horsebox. Tomorrow morning we get up as usual and do our work just as if everything is the same."

Eoghan's mind was still on Ronan's comatose condition.

"What about Ronan?" he asked, "What if he does not wake up in time to work?"

"We do his work for him," Brendan told him, "Bryan over there won't know which of us has done the boxes, so long as they are all done by the usual time. If he does notice, we can tell him Ronan has been ill during the night and we are helping him out with his work."

But Bryan, the geriatric chief stud groom, noticed nothing. The lads all looked the same to him and he had his own work to attend to. None of the other staff remarked on Ronan's absence, even when Brendan took food back to the room in case Ronan should wake. But Ronan slumbered on, as the storm blew itself out, and calm returned to the Mallows yard.

The absence of the horse box was not noticed for some time. No use was made of it during the following day and it was only when Tadgh and Cai returned in the afternoon that anyone realised that it had gone from its customary position behind one of the barns. Tadgh and Cai had passed it on the road and recognised it as their own.

It was only the terrible weather of the night before which saved Brendan and Ronan from being discovered. No-one had heard the horsebox leave the yard, indeed no-one had seen anything. It was concluded that the vehicle must have been stolen and abandoned after it ran into the ditch. The fact that it was facing towards Mallows along the road did somewhat undermine the logic of this explanation, but no-one could come up with a better one.

Ronan, fortunately for all involved, opened his eyes by midday and seemed none the worse for his experience, of which he recalled very little. His head hurt badly, an inconvenience which he went to some heroic lengths to disguise, once the truth of what had happened was related to him.

The incident had a profound and lasting effect on Brendan Meaghan. Both boys understood and acknowledged their debt to Eoghan. But it was Brendan who vowed never to drink alcohol again.

The following summer, Tarragon died.

Throughout the first three years of his tied apprenticeship at Mallows, Eoghan returned home regularly once every month. During those years, Enda and Niamh had produced a young family, two lively little girls named Aiofe and Daimhin. For the first time in his life, Eoghan felt the warmth of returning to a family home, a place where people cared about and welcomed him. The only time he felt uncomfortable was when Uncle Callan took the trouble to call in on the family. Uncle Callan would look appraisingly at Eoghan and ask him pointedly about his progress as a jockey. For some reason, it made Eoghan feel as if he was being watched, even though nowadays he hardly ever saw Uncle Callan.

But Uncle Callan was a minor ripple in the enveloping pool of an otherwise happy time in Eoghan's life. Eoghan and Caitlin would take the ponies out into the hills, just as they had when Eoghan lived at home. Their routine was unvaried, as they visited their special haunts, and waved to the travelling tinkers who traversed the eternal ridges of the undulating countryside around the farm. Tarragon and Branna called out loudly to the travellers' black and white ponies, and the travellers' ponies called jauntily back to them. Come with us, they seemed to be saying, we have more freedom than you.

Eoghan had learned of Tarragon's death through a message left with Cai by Niamh. Cai had enough compassion to realise the impact that the death of the elderly pony, which had taught her young stud groom and aspiring jockey to ride, would have on a kind young man such as Eoghan. She told him that he could go home for a couple of days if he wished.

Eoghan found the visit more traumatic than comforting. His childhood companions, the draught horses, had both been put down the year before, having become increasingly arthritic and unable to cope with the outdoor conditions. But Eoghan had not had the deep connection with them which he had had with the loyal Tarragon.

Kindly, Enda had not sold her carcass for meat, so Eoghan and Caitlin were able to see Tarragon buried on the hill behind the farm.

The two teenagers stood rigid, side by side on an unfairly blue and sunny day whilst the black earth was shovelled over Tarragon by two of the farm workers. Eoghan felt as if his soul had been wrenched out of his throat, which hurt unbearably, and there was nothing which Caitlin could do to penetrate the silence in which he enclosed himself. Branna too, stood restlessly with them, not understanding where her equine companion had gone.

Tarragon's worn tack remained hanging on its usual nail in the barn. No-one had dared to touch it whilst Eoghan was there. Unseen by anyone, Eoghan took from the bridle a small green and red plaited ribbon which Caitlin had once attached to the headpiece and put it in his pocket. Every time he thought of Tarragon, he closed his hand hard over the tatty and precious trophy, and hoped that Tarragon was now being looked after by his long dead sister, after whom they had named Caitlin's pony.

Eoghan returned to Mallows determined to immerse himself in his progressing career as a jockey. Caitlin watched him walk down the farm track with scarcely a backward glance and was shocked to feel a dull ache of loneliness begin to creep into her heart. Tarragon had been the connection between the two youngsters, and now Tarragon was gone. Eoghan had his new life at Mallows. Niamh had her husband and children. Diarmuid, her father, still had his life and friends at the Gleannglas racecourse.

Early the next day, in softly emerging sunshine, Caitlin tacked up Branna and they set out together into the warm emerald hills above the farm. Stopping only briefly to let Branna drink, Caitlin left the special stream behind, and followed the ridge from which the tinkers' ponies had called out to them. Caitlin and Branna did not once look behind them and were soon gone from sight of the awakening farm. The only trace of Caitlin was a small neat note on the kitchen table in the farmhouse which told her sister not to worry about her.

In vain did Niamh and Enda search the locality for Caitlin. Enda even drove the farm truck to Mallows in the hope that Caitlin might have shared her plans with Eoghan. But Eoghan knew nothing.

"Who's this Caitlin then?" asked Brendan, once Enda had left, having extracted from Eoghan a promise to let him know if he should hear anything from Caitlin, "Your girlfriend, is she?"

But Eoghan gave Brendan a look from brimming blue eyes which contained such pain that Brendan regretted his flippant words.

"She taught me to ride," was all that Eoghan said.

In the final year of Eoghan's time at Mallows, Tadgh's focus was on making best use of him for his racing owners. Brendan had by now left Mallows to join the racing yard of his older cousin, Cormac Meaghan, now a newly established trainer. A successful jockey, he had ridden out his claim and could no longer take useful weight off the backs of the Mallows horses in the handicap races in which Tadgh liked to run them at Gleannglas and other not too far distant Irish racecourses.

Ronan's talents did not lie in race riding, although his skills as a bloodstock manager and breeder, and heir apparent to Tadgh as the owner and operator of Mallows, had developed more promisingly. Tadgh and Cai were relieved by this outcome, knowing more than Ronan imagined about his wild behaviour of the last few years. At the age of twenty, Ronan became the assistant manager at Mallows. Oisin too had now left Mallows and had returned to Gleannglas to assist his increasingly decrepit father in the running of his shambolic horse dealing business.

Eoghan, now eighteen years old, was already recognised as a talented young jockey and a number of Tadgh's owners were keen to have him ride their horses. One cold October afternoon, Eoghan was entered at the Gleannglas races to ride a smart gelding called Spice Lodge. Eoghan knew Spice Lodge well as one of the livelier horses in the Mallows yard, and felt sure that they could do well together in the hurdle race which Tadgh had selected for them.

Eoghan had visited Gleannglas racecourse on a number of occasions since the first exciting day on which he had seen Bristol Gold run into third place with Brendan Meaghan on his back. But his duties so far had been limited to those of a groom and to leading horses up in the parade ring for others to ride. He had competed in a couple of amateur races at point to point courses, but this was the first occasion on which he had been booked to ride in a race under official rules.

Eoghan did not feel nervous at the prospect of riding Spice Lodge in the race. Instead, he felt confident and energised by the task ahead of him. Tarragon's special ribbons were tucked into an inner pocket of his riding breeches, where he always kept them, like a precious charm. As he entered the racecourse in the front seat of the Mallows horsebox, he briefly caught sight of the spot at which he and Caitlin had ridden on their bicycles on a day which now seemed like a lifetime ago. Suddenly, he could see Caitlin in her worn red dress and beribboned boots, wobbling precariously on the handlebars of the old bike, now rusted and unused in Mallows yard, shrieking with laughter as he tried hopelessly to catch her. It was the first time he had thought of Caitlin in months, and the thought made him catch his breath suddenly. Where had she gone, he wondered.

Spice Lodge's race was the second on the card. The spectators' area of racecourse was filling up quickly as the first race was completed and the victorious horses returned, sweating and steaming, to the winners' enclosure. From the window of the little white wooden building which served as the weighing room, Eoghan caught sight of Enda and Uncle Callan walking together towards the parade ring, ready to look at the horses which would shortly be coming out for the second race. Uncle Callan was speaking urgently to Enda as if telling him something important, and Enda was nodding and gesticulating impatiently as if to say that he understood and did not need to be told again. Eoghan saw Niamh and the two little girls following behind them, dressed in warm coats and knitted hats against the chilly Autumn air. He could see that Niamh was pregnant again, her coat unbuttoned at the front to make space for the swollen bump that was the baby.

As Eoghan came out into the parade ring, he caught Niamh's eye and waved to her and to his young nieces, the older of whom waved enthusiastically back. Enda's attention was caught by the movement, and he too lifted his hand in Eoghan's direction. Uncle

Callan said something to Enda, and laughed, although Enda did not seem to be amused by the comment.

Mounted on the increasingly agitated Spice Lodge, Eoghan had to concentrate all his attention on the bay gelding, which had decided that it did not like being stared at by so many people and would rather be anywhere but the parade ring at Gleannglas racecourse. It took all Eoghan's skills and patience to keep the horse calm as Tadgh repeated the instructions which he had already drummed into Eoghan the evening before. Don't let him get to the front. Keep him covered up. Try to keep him calm. Spice Lodge's owner, a local farmer in a pea jacket and thick cord trousers, stared glumly at Eoghan and the horse and said nothing.

Once beyond the white wooden railings, and out of earshot of the worst of the noise being made by the spectators, Spice Lodge seemed a bit calmer. The dull tones of the racecourse loudspeaker did not seem to bother him, Eoghan realised, but the chaotic chattering sound of the milling racecourse attendees was unfamiliar and frightening. Spice Lodge had been to the races before, but to smaller meetings than this one, so this experience was a new one for them both.

Eoghan stroked the bay gelding's neck as they cantered down to the start, which was at the further end of the course, well away from the grandstand area. There were six other horses in the race, all ridden by jockeys more experienced than Eoghan. He was the only claimer in the race. In the weighing room, the other jockeys had talked amongst themselves and Eoghan had been left largely to his own thoughts. This had suited him, as he had no idea how to approach his fellow riders, or even whether he should attempt to engage with them.

Eoghan kept Spice Lodge separate from the rest of the field as the runners milled around near the starting line. He heard the other jockeys calling out to one another, but did not realise that one of them was speaking to him, until a big chestnut horse came up alongside him and its rider spoke to him in an impatient voice.

"Hey kiddo, you deaf or somethin'?" said the other jockey.

Eoghan's throat went dry and he found that he could not speak. He just shook his head dumbly. The other man laughed, not unkindly, and moved away.

Eoghan's subsequent recollection of the race was that it was finished before it started. Knowing that Tadgh was far more experienced than he, Eoghan followed his riding instructions to the letter. But Spice Lodge did not like being held up behind the other horses and dragged savagely at the bit as the field passed the grandstand for the first time. Eoghan tried to speak to him soothingly, but the horse was not listening. The other jockeys were shouting and yelling around him, and he began to think that he would prefer to be deaf. The shouting seemed to consist mostly of obscenities and curses.

Luckily for Eoghan, Spice Lodge was a good hurdler, and, notwithstanding his tugging and pulling, managed to get himself over the hurdles cleanly and without tripping. As they rounded the bend into the back straight, Spice Lodge's vicious hold seemed to slacken a bit, and he dropped his head slightly. Eoghan began to feel as if he had some control at last, but the change in the horse's behaviour also spelt disaster as far as the rest of the race was concerned. Try as Eoghan might to keep the tiring Spice Lodge going forward, the horse had burned so much energy fighting the contact that his reserves for finishing the race were quickly depleting. It took all Eoghan's emerging skill to bring the horse home in fourth place, an achievement which was assisted by another horse falling at the last.

Eoghan was disappointed, as he pulled the panting Spice Lodge to a halt. All the fizz seemed to have gone out of the horse, and it walked back to the parade ring quietly enough. Eoghan jumped down and unfastened the girth. The glum farmer looked ever glummer as Tadgh commiserated with Eoghan over the defeat. Eoghan did not dare to say anything to Tadgh in front of the farmer who had placed his faith in both of them, but he resolved to speak to Tadgh about the running tactics once they were back at Mallows. He was sure that the horse could have done better.

As Eoghan walked towards the weighing room, Niamh, who was standing by the white rails, called out to him.

"You did well, Eoghan. You'll win the next time."

"That I certainly will," thought Eoghan, as he smiled wanly at her, "This will not happen to me again."

He was glad that the mocking Caitlin was not there to see his defeat.

Eoghan's career as a jockey lasted eight years. Known universally as Genie Foley, he rode out his claim with Mallows and then moved across the country to join Cormac Meaghan's yard as second jockey to Brendan. When Cormac had no rides for him, he rode for other trainers until he was eventually able to venture out on his own, and be tied to nobody.

Eoghan never again allowed a trainer to dictate to him the running instructions unless he agreed with them. Some trainers objected to this and refused to book him for their horses. Eoghan was not always right. But he stuck to his opinions, and his instinctive experience with horses, together with an obsessive determination to watch and research the past performance of the horses he rode, made him successful and respected. The agent he employed to work on his behalf did to have to try too hard to ensure that he was rarely short of rides.

The time at Cormac Meaghan's successful training yard opened Eoghan's eyes to the existence of the rest of the world. The yard was a busy and active place, unlike the peaceful rural quiet of Mallows, full of young people who laughed and shouted to each other as they worked. Horses came and went through the yard, bought and sold by ambitious owners who were keen to see their investments run successfully at the top racecourses in Ireland and even beyond.

Eoghan, with his unfamiliar Kerry accent, shy manner, and untidy black hair shading his bright blue eyes, was like a magnet to the female stable staff. Although they were impressed by his riding skills and by his unconcealed determination to win every race he entered, it was Eoghan himself that they wanted. Eoghan was elusive and different and fascinating. So, Eoghan's life in his time as a jockey was characterised by a series of short term romantic relationships, none of which satisfied him, nor, ultimately, the young women involved.

"It was like he was always thinking of someone else when we were in bed together," complained one of his disappointed partners to her sympathetic, and slightly jealous, friend, "But when I asked him, he said there was nobody."

"That's just his way, then," said the other girl, "Horses and nothing else, I suppose it is. Still sexy, though ....." she added wistfully.

Genie Foley was first approached to stop a horse in the early years of his career and angrily made it clear that no sum of money would induce him to do so. The compulsion for him and the horses to win races on their combined merits was too important. His refusal was so adamant that he was never approached again and continued his successful career unhindered by scandal or corruption.

Then, one day, in what was to become his final year of racing, Enda contacted him. Eoghan was by then living in a smart modern flat overlooking the sea on South side of Dublin. It was a late winter Sunday and he had no rides that day. The early morning sun was shining brightly through the expansive bedroom window and the clear air was punctuated by the occasional sound of hectoring gulls. It was as yet early in the day, and Eoghan's latest squeeze was sleeping soundly in the bed beside him. Eoghan looked at her motionless back and traced his finger gently along her spine wondering what they would do today to fill the empty time. It always felt empty when there was no racing.

The telephone rang in the next room. Eoghan slid from the bed and was surprised to hear Enda speaking to him through the telephone receiver. His brother contacted him only rarely and his first thought was that something was wrong, perhaps with Niamh or one of the children. Or else, just possibly, that Caitlin had returned.

But it was none of those things. Enda came almost straight to the point.

"You are riding Singing Bamboo at Leopardstown this week, are you not, Eoghan?" Enda asked him.

"I am, Enda," replied Eoghan, surprised. He knew that Enda had followed his career but only to the extent that it was reported in the racing newspapers. Enda was a farmer and had four children and a wife to support. His excursions to the races were limited to Gleannglas racecourse and did not extend to the bigger courses on the other side of the country.

"We would like it if he did not win," stated Enda, his voice sounding odd.

Eoghan was unable to speak for a few seconds.

"What do you mean, Enda?" he asked, "Who can you mean by 'we'? Surely, Niamh and the children cannot want me to lose a race?"

"No, not Niamh, for sure she is very proud of you, little brother," mumbled Enda.

"What is this about then, Enda?" asked Eoghan, "Is it money you need? I can send you money. God knows, I have plenty now."

Enda seemed unable to speak and Eoghan thought he could hear a hastily caught sob from the other end of the line.

"Enda? Speak to me, please," Eoghan called into the phone, the feeling that something terrible was about to happen welling up inside him.

"Look, Eoghan," Enda said eventually, "I was wrong to make this request of you. Good luck in the race."

There was a click as Enda cut the connection. As Eoghan replaced the receiver thoughtfully, two slim arms encircled his waist from behind and a warm body pressed itself against his naked back and buttocks.

"Everything all right, Genie?" asked the girl.

Eoghan remained thoughtful.

"Let's go back to bed," he said eventually, which was just what his companion had hoped to hear.

In the event, Singing Bamboo did not win his race, having been brought down at the last by a loose horse which ran across the field and cannoned into him. Eoghan had been left sprawled on the ground as the remainder of the field thundered past. Even Singing Bamboo scrambled quickly to his feet and ran off after them.

Two days later, Eoghan opened a letter, which was written in capital letters on lined paper torn from a notebook. It said WELL DONE GENIE. LEE HO IS NEXT.

Eoghan contacted Enda straightaway. Niamh answered the telephone.

"He is outside in the barn," she told Eoghan, hesitantly, in response to his unusually curt demand to speak to his brother.

"Get him indoors," Eoghan ordered her.

Neither Niamh nor Enda had ever heard Eoghan speak angrily.

"Whoever is wanting me to stop the horses," Eoghan raged at Enda down the telephone, "Tell them that it will not happen. Ever."

Eoghan slammed down the telephone receiver, leaving Enda and Niamh staring at each other in shock in the farm kitchen.

"What will become of us, Enda?" asked Niamh, her voice shaking.

But Enda did not know.

Lee Ho duly ran to victory in his next race. Another note to Eoghan was delivered, expressed in less complimentary terms POOR CHOICE GENIE. PUT IT RIGHT ON LANGHAM LIGHT.

Eoghan had no idea what to do. There was no way of telling who was sending the notes. He was sure it was not Enda but it was clear that Enda was somehow involved in what was happening. If it were not for his concern about Enda and his family, Eoghan would have had no hesitation in going to the police or to the racing authorities. There was no question that his loss on Singing Bamboo had arisen from an unavoidable accident and it was a matter of record that Lee Ho had won his most recent race. No wrongdoing could be attributed to Eoghan.

So Eoghan consulted Brendan Meaghan. Brendan's view was that Eoghan should turn the notes over to the police.

"There might be fingerprints or something such," he said, doubtfully.

"And there might not either," replied Eoghan, "And what if they are Enda's fingerprints, if so?"

Brendan had no more idea of what to do than Eoghan did, so they resolved to do nothing, and see what happened. This decision was to prove disastrous.

Langham Light was a big, long striding bay chaser, which Eoghan was due to ride at Navan in early April. The Cheltenham Festival in England, where Eoghan had had three rides, was over, and the Punchestown Festival, where Eoghan was expecting to add to his winning record, was looming later in the month. The ride at Navan was a routine piece of work for Eoghan, the horse having been trained by Cormac Meaghan. Brendan himself was riding at the same meeting and they travelled to the racecourse together. Eoghan told Brendan that he intended to do his best to ensure that Langham Light won his race.

What happened in Langham Light's race made headlines in the

racing press, although not for the right reasons. Rounding the first bend in the lead on second circuit and approaching an open ditch, Eoghan found himself blinded by a flashing light, as if from sun reflecting off a mirror. Worse, Langham Light was temporarily blinded or at least distracted by the sudden glare, and failed to take off at the fence. The horse crashed through the top of the birch and landed awkwardly on its side. Eoghan was catapulted from the saddle and landed with his full weight on his left knee. As he tried to roll away, another horse came over the fence and in its efforts to avoid the stricken Langham Light, stepped with full force on Eoghan's already injured knee and shattered the bones to pieces.

Eoghan was left screaming in agony on the ground. He had effectively been kneecapped and would never ride in a race again. Langham Light fared even worse, and was put down on the course.

Eoghan was pumped full of painkillers and taken to hospital, where doctors operated on the shattered knee. Eoghan would walk again, but would need a metal brace to support his knee. His stay in hospital was as brief as he could make it and whilst he was there, his bed was attended by an array of shocked ex-girlfriends, fellow jockeys and, when Eoghan told the story of the flashing mirror, by the police.

But worse was to come. When Eoghan returned to his flat with its grand sea view and the attentions of his latest loving girlfriend, the telephone rang once again. It was Niamh. Eoghan could hardly understand what she said, so hysterical was she, but he eventually learned that Enda was dead, shot in the chest with his own shotgun by Uncle Callan, who was now under arrest.

"This is my fault," Eoghan said, tears running down his face whilst his uncomprehending girlfriend started at him in shocked silence.

"You must not say that," Niamh told him fiercely, "This is not your doing. Enda and Uncle Callan have made their own trouble."

"I will come home," Eoghan told her, "You are my responsibility now."

And once Eoghan could walk again, he did return home. The smart flat in Dublin was sold, the pretty girlfriend looked around for another jockey to keep her happy, and Eoghan's agent regretfully crossed him off his books. The Punchestown Festival went ahead without him.

Eoghan never really discovered the full extent of what Enda and Uncle Callan had been doing. Uncle Callan's trial could not be conducted in public for reasons of national security and it was equally unclear what information Uncle Callan was apparently able to offer at the trial in order to obtain a reduced sentence for his nephew's murder. All that Eoghan knew was that his brother had tried to protect Eoghan for as long as he could before the pressure to recoup the investment made in the farm and in Eoghan's training had become too great.

The operator of the fatal mirror at Navan racecourse was never found.

Eoghan now found himself responsible for a remote hillside farm and a shocked and grieving widow with four young and confused children who had lost their father. It was a far cry from his comparatively easy life in County Meath and Dublin, but the burden he had inherited gave him a feeling of calm purpose which he had not experienced for some years. The burning desire to win horseraces had left him on that terrible day at Navan racecourse and now he turned his mind to what he might do with the farm.

One warm May evening, Eoghan walked slowly down the familiar track which led from the farm down into the town. His leg was beginning to strengthen but the knee brace, he now knew, would be with him in some form for the rest of his life. He had refused to use a stick or crutch and had made his way out of the farmyard gate, past Tarragon's old stall, now a storeroom. The green and red ribbon was in his pocket, as it had always been, now even more tatty and frayed.

The sun was sliding slowly down behind the greying hills to his right when he saw a small and distant figure ascending the track on foot and approaching him slowly and inexorably from below. The person stopped at the side of the track by a clump of long grass, turned towards the sun, and raised a hand to shade its eyes. Eoghan stopped and watched, holding his breath.

As the figure turned again to ascend the track, he saw it was a young woman with long dark hair, tied back from her face. The woman was small and slim, not unlike the girlfriends who had kept him so enthusiastically entertained in Dublin, and was dressed in neat blue jeans and a white shirt. And she had gold hoops dangling from each of her ears.

As Eoghan started to move carefully again down the track on his damaged leg, the young woman came forward to meet him.

"Hello, horseboy," she said.

Eoghan stood perfectly still and looked unwaveringly at her, afraid that this vision was produced from his imagination.

Caitlin stood in front of him.

"I've been watching out for you," she said.

Eoghan said nothing, but reached forward and put his hands on her slender waist. Caitlin laid her head on his chest.

They stood there in silence, not daring to move, as the sun descended into the distant ocean. A blanket of warm darkness began to fall around them. And the ghost of Tarragon slipped quietly away for ever.

23

For many years to come, Eoghan would have nightmares about the fall at Navan racecourse which had ended his successful career as a jockey.

In the early days following his return to the farm, the pain from his damaged knee kept him awake, and when he did fall into an uneasy doze, he saw the flashing light in his eyes and felt again the movement of the hard galloping Langham Light beneath him. He saw the grey sky as it whirled above his head, heard the scream of the horse as it landed with a sickening thud on the ground, and experienced again the searing pain in his shattered knee as the next horse ground it into the turf. He saw Langham Light trying and failing to get up, the medical staff running towards him, while the light flashed and flashed again. In his dream he saw that it was Uncle Callan who was holding the light and Enda was beside him, a bloody hole in his chest, and Uncle Callan was raising the gun towards Eoghan.

Eoghan would wake in a sudden shock, with an anguished shout of pain and fear, which could be heard by everyone in the house. Caitlin, beside him in the bed, would stroke his head, murmuring soothing words, and kissing his sweating forehead, until his heart rate slowed again and his breathing returned to normal. But he did not easily go to sleep again.

Over the years, Eoghan slowly began to have better dreams. The exhilaration of watching Charcoal Burner winning the race in which Brendan Meaghan had ridden Bristol Gold at Gleannglas many years ago was one of these. Eoghan sometimes even woke believing he was a naïve thirteen year old boy once again, and all his life as a jockey was still before him.

The difficulties facing Eoghan's young household were considerable. Niamh was not yet thirty years old and had four small children. Eoghan and Caitlin were two years younger, but Eoghan was still fighting nightmares and trying to come to terms with his damaged body. They had youth on their side, but little else.

The local community in Gleannglas were well aware of what had happened to Enda, and there were some who sympathised with Uncle Callan, and regarded Enda as a traitor who had got what he deserved. Aunt Brigid had already left the town accompanied by the youngest of her daughters, the others having married and moved on. But most people were shocked by the undeserved misery which had been visited on Enda's widow and young children. And many of them admired the bravery with which Eoghan had left his career in racing and shouldered the burden of caring for them. For sure, Eoghan could no longer be the jockey Genie Foley so well known from the racing papers, but he could, they thought, have more easily stayed with his friends in County Meath and earned a living as a trainer. The arrival home of the missing Caitlin had also not gone unremarked, and some wondered whether she had been in the County Meath with him too.

Eoghan became something of a minor celebrity in the town, welcomed at the racecourse by trainers and jockeys who wanted his advice. Tadgh Brody proposed to him a role as assistant trainer at Mallows, knowing that Ronan had no interest in that side of the business. Oisin Cassidy, now in charge of the horse dealing enterprise left to him by his long deceased father, even offered Eoghan a share in his business.

The practical support the Foley family received from their neighbours was helpful to Eoghan and the two sisters. It supplemented the money obtained from the sale of Eoghan's Dublin apartment, but they needed something sustainable. And so, after much planning and thought, they decided to scale down their farming activity and to go into the hotel trade. Grants and subsidies were becoming available to help Irish businesses, particularly those in rural areas, and Niamh's quick brain and business knowledge enabled them to take advantage of some of these.

Over the ensuing years, the three young entrepreneurs built a business based on holiday cottages, offering associated activities for those wishing to immerse themselves in a quiet rural environment where they could relax and unwind from their busy lives in the cities. Eoghan used every contact he could remember from within the racing world, with the result that guests began to come from far and wide, from America, Europe and the Middle East. Those skills which Eoghan and the two sisters did not possess themselves, they found from within the Gleannglas town. The emergent establishment, which they agreed to call Enda's Farm, offered guests everything from pony trekking and hiking to arts and crafts, yoga, and the opportunity to eat fresh and traditional country food.

Eoghan never asked Caitlin where she had been in the ten years since she had taken Branna up into the hills. Caitlin had little to say about it, although it soon became clear to Eoghan that she had travelled abroad during that time. Caitlin now spoke French and Spanish and had learned to play the guitar, all skills which came in useful in their new business as country hoteliers. She had extensive knowledge of the canals and waterways of England and Europe, something which Eoghan learned only when he heard her in discussion with a guest. She also had a small tattoo of a horse and jockey on her right buttock, which Eoghan discovered on the unforgettable first night after her return.

Eoghan was well aware that he had no right to ask Caitlin anything. He could only feel privileged that she had chosen to return to him and dearly hoped she would not leave again.

Only once did Eoghan gain any insight into Caitlin's recent past. Eoghan was a young and fit man, so his knee, with the assistance of more surgery and the insertion of new pins, soon grew strong enough for him to be able to ride again, although the days of riding with short leathers and balancing over the neck of a racehorse were behind him. But he and Caitlin could now go out with the pony trekkers together, and sometimes, when no guests were needing them, they would go out alone, pretending that they were children once again, exploring the hills and streams just as they had done at that idyllic time all those years ago with Tarragon and Branna. Then they remembered that they were not children any more, and could make love on the grassy slopes in the warm sun. All their own children were conceived there.

The travellers still appeared at intervals on the hills above Enda's Farm. Eoghan and Caitlin's new horses were Connemara ponies too, and they called to the travellers' ponies just as Tarragon and Branna had done. But once, the travellers stopped, and some turned their heads towards where Eoghan and Caitlin sat on their horses on the windy slope below, and one of them pointed. A male figure detached himself from the group and came down the hill towards them, sitting aside a piebald cob.

As he approached, Eoghan could see that the man had dark skin and curly black hair flecked with grey. He wore an open necked black shirt and well worn jeans. The black and white pony stopped obediently before them. The man ignored Eoghan and spoke directly to Caitlin.

"*Catalina,*" he said, and waited.

Caitlin sat immobile on her pony and gave a small nod. The man jerked his thumb at Eoghan and said,

"*El caballerito?*"

Caitlin nodded again, and the man laughed.

"*Bueno,*" he said, and turned his pony away without a further word.

"*Adios, Arnaldo,*" said Caitlin, as if to herself.

Although Eoghan and Caitlin never married, they had three children together. Niamh did not marry again, and remained at Enda's Farm even when her children were all grown. Over the years, Niamh's children had made many friends amongst the guests who stayed on the farm and they received invitations to travel and stay in places all over the world. It was a far cry from the narrow, secluded and unworldly upbringing which their parents had experienced.

Shortly after Eoghan's fortieth birthday, something entirely unforeseen happened, an event which was to change the course of his life once again. It occurred on a gloomy Autumn evening when there were few guests at Enda's Farm. The ponies were turned out in the paddocks and Eoghan was standing by the farm gate wondering whether to replace the rain-worn sign which announced the name of Enda's Farm to the arriving guests.

Eoghan could see a brown horsebox making its way up the track towards the farm.

"That looks like Oisin's horsebox," he said to Caitlin, who had come out to stand beside him. Everyone else was indoors.

The distant vehicle grew gradually bigger as it approached the farm, arriving in the yard with a triumphant rattle and squeal of brakes. Eoghan could see Oisin sitting in the driver's seat.

Oisin jumped down immediately from the cab. He looked agitated.

"Genie, I need your help," he said, without preamble.

Whatever Eoghan had been expecting from Oisin, it was not a request for help. Although Eoghan and his family had earned a living from their holiday business, they were not wealthy, and life was still an uphill struggle to remain solvent.

"If it is money you need, Oisin," said Eoghan, "You know I am not able to help."

Oisin became aware that Caitlin was standing silently beside Eoghan. Oisin had always been rather unnerved by Caitlin. People said she was a bit crazy, like her old father who had worked at the racecourse, and that she had been away with the gypsies for years. There was talk of her and Genie making love in the open air on the hills, like rabbits, where anyone could see them. But, for all that, Oisin thought that Caitlin was beautiful and that he would have been happy to have her in his bed, or even stretched out alongside him on the chilly hillsides, come to that.

"Good evening, missus," Oisin said hurriedly to Caitlin, hoping she could not read his mind, and, then, turning his attention again to

Eoghan, he went on, "It's not money I need, Genie. I want you to take a mare from me. She's in the box here."

"Of course I can take her," said Eoghan, not understanding why Oisin was so upset, "Are you short of somewhere to keep her at home?"

"No, I need you to take her for good," Oisin told him, "She's a gift, if you like. She's yours, or your, your... wife's, if you want."

Before Eoghan or Caitlin could say anything else, Oisin darted round to the back of the vehicle and unfastened the ramp. He carefully led out a beautiful throughbred chestnut mare with a white blaze, who looked around curiously at her new surroundings.

Whatever Eoghan had been expecting to come out of Oisin's lorry, it was not a horse of this calibre. He was assuming that the animal would be one of Oisin's usual riding or harness horses or maybe a pony.

"What's this, Oisin?" he said in surprise, "This is surely not one of your horses."

"To be sure, she is," replied Oisin, sounding nettled, "I bought her fair and square from someone who could not afford to keep her. She's top quality, too."

"I can see that," replied Eoghan, as Caitlin stepped forward to take hold of the mare's headcollar from Oisin, "And why would you want to make a gift of her to us, then?"

Oisin's face crumpled.

"I'm finished, Genie," he said, "The bailiffs are coming tomorrow to take everything I have. But this mare, I cannot let her go to pay the debts. So if she comes to you, they will not find her. I've written in the books that you have bought her from me."

Caitlin was stroking the mare's neck and speaking softly to her.

"And she's in foal," Oisin added, as if that would clinch the deal, "To Alakazam."

"Alakazam? From Mallows?" Eoghan asked, not believing he had heard correctly.

"Yes, and it's not paid for, either," Oisin went on.

"What isn't? The covering?" asked Eoghan, slowly beginning to understand.

"I told Ronan that the mare was not in foal, so he has not asked me for payment," Oisin told him, in a rush of words, "But, she is and I cannot tell him that or he will want the money or else the mare instead."

In this strange way, Eoghan came to acquire the first of the brood mares which would establish him a breeder in the local area. When he discussed it with them, Caitlin and Niamh had both said they were willing to continue to run the ongoing holiday business whilst Eoghan set out on his new venture. They all thought that the visitors would love seeing the new foals when they came. But most of all, as Caitlin said, it would enable the horseboy, as she still called Eoghan when they were alone together, to return to his true vocation, not to mention making use of the learning he had gained all those years ago at Mallows. And he had three growing sons, the oldest now about the age which Eoghan had been when he had first encountered Caitlin on the old farm track, who could help him.

They called the thoroughbred mare Cait's Gift, as Oisin had insisted that the animal had no other name than Maire, which Caitlin did not consider nearly grand enough for such a lovely creature. It was of course unlucky to change a horse's given name, but they reasoned that Cait's Gift was really just a factual description of what the mare was to them, rather than being a new name.

Cait's Gift, or Kat's Gift, as she later came to be officially called when the need for her name to be recorded was eventually required, was not typical of the mares from which Eoghan started to breed.

Mostly, the horses he produced were riding horses, bred from commoner stock than Maire. Some of the mares and their progeny were kept for the use of the visiting riders at Enda's Farm, whilst others were sold at sales and to dealers such as Oisin had once been. The confused state of the records at Oisin's business had been such that no-one missed Maire amongst the horses which were confiscated by the bailiffs and she remained at Enda's Farm for the rest of her life.

Eoghan was intrigued about the bloodline of Cait's Gift, who looked as classy as anything that he ridden in his racing days. But Oisin could not, or would not, tell him anything more about her, and Eoghan soon decided that it was probably better to remain in ignorance.

Cait's Gift's filly foal arrived on bright windy day in April. Eoghan had not been present at a foaling since the days at Mallows, but Caitlin helped him, showing a calm confidence in what she was doing which made Eoghan realise, not for the first time, how little he still really knew about his enigmatic and beautiful life partner. Their oldest boy, Enda, was also there to see the miraculous newborn creature finally slither wetly onto the straw. After a few nudges, she was soon up on wobbly legs and suckling from her rather surprised dam, who seemed not quite to understand what had happened to her.

Young Enda, breathless with amazement at this new experience, said that it reminded him of the farm cats with their kittens, and then wondered why his mother laughed when his father said that they should called the new foal Little Kitty Cat.

"I once called your mother Little Kitty Cat," Eoghan explained to his son, "When she was about your age."

"When you spoke to me at all…." added Caitlin, and Eoghan shook his head ruefully at the memory of himself as a tongue-tied lad driving a pony cart.

Little Kitty Cat grew up amongst the other horses on Enda's Farm, but only Eoghan and Caitlin knew that she was special and different. Although her lineage on her dam's side was unknown, it was clear from the start that she was something unusual. Oisin had said that the foal was a daughter of the stallion Alakazam at Mallows and Eoghan could well believe this. Ali in his day had been a strong staying flat horse, dark brown with a white star on his forehead. He had run well for two years for his owner before his chances of moving onto hurdling had been set back by injury, and he had been sold to Mallows as a stud horse. Ali's progeny had generally done well for their owners, as Eoghan discovered when he checked the records. A project was beginning to take shape in his mind.

Oisin came up to see the foal once she was old enough to be out in the summer fields with her mother. He was working now for Ronan as a stud groom at Mallows.

"You should have a share in her," Eoghan told him, as they leaned on the barred gate, watching the foal, whose coat was already darkening, following her mother around the field.

"No, Genie, I'm bankrupt," said Oisin, "Someone who wants money from me would only try to take her from us. She's yours now."

"Tell me about the stallions standing at Mallows now," Eoghan said, "Are any of them related in bloodline to Alakazam? Or," he added pointedly, "to Maire?"

Oisin understand Eoghan's point immediately and assured him that neither of the parents of Maire was related by blood to any of the other Mallows stallions, at least not in the last three generations.

Little Kitty Cat grew up in the midst of the family and guests at Enda's Farm. All the horses kept there had to be accustomed to people and not be easily upset by the antics of boisterous children. Little Kitty Cat's secret parentage did not mean she was treated any differently, and none of the visitors who exclaimed with pleasure over the foals and young horses who came to greet them when they arrived at the farm noticed that she was at all unlike the other horses. But, as she grew older, Eoghan knew that he would have to send her away for training. Although Alakazam's form as a racehorse was a matter of record, Cait's Gift was a mare of no account at all, and he needed to know more about what her first progeny could do. So he decided to bring Brendan Meaghan into his plans, in part, at least.

Brendan and Eoghan had remained friends ever since the terrible day of the devastating accident at Navan, and Brendan had watched with fear, and later relief, Eoghan's road to recovery and eventual financial and personal stability. Brendan had visited Enda's Farm on numerous occasions, first bringing his new wife, and later their children too, to stay during the little time he could spare from his work at the Meath training yard. Brendan had now joined his cousin as assistant trainer and expected to take over the yard when Cormac had had enough of it.

Brendan's wife had been one of Eoghan's many female admirers in his racing days, and had been curious to see what had happened to the quiet and attractive country boy whose racing career had been ended so tragically.

"My God," she said to Brendan, as they lay in their bed in one of the neat new cottages during their first visit, "Would you look at that wife of his? She is something else. And they have known each other since they were children together. No wonder he didn't want any of us, with her waiting for him at home."

"Now I don't think she was exactly waiting for him," objected Brendan, who well remembered the terrible day when a frantic Enda had come to Mallows searching for the missing Caitlin, "And she isn't his wife even now."

"Oh, it is all sooo romantic," had sighed the new Mrs Meaghan, much to Brendan's annoyance.

Eoghan called Brendan over to see Little Kitty Cat when she became officially two years old. It was a cold and windy day and several of the Foley horses were running energetically around one of the paddocks by the now widened track up to the farm. Eoghan explained carefully, without wishing to tell any direct untruths, that, although he had no official record of the filly's bloodline, and that she was therefore registered as a non-thoroughbred animal, he had been told that she came from good racing stock through her sire's line. He pointed out her dam, Cait's Gift, to Brendan, saying that the mare had come to him already in foal and that he knew nothing of her background. Eoghan did not mention that it was Oisin who had brought her.

"Will you take Kitty for training for a while, Brendan?" asked Eoghan, "Just to see whether she is any good? If not, then I'll have her back here with the others."

Given that both Cait's Gift and Little Kitty Cat were registered as non-thoroughbred horses, Brendan thought the whole enterprise to be rather hopeless, based as it was on an unsubstantiated comment about the apparently unknown sire, but his desire to help his friend led him to agree.

When Eoghan spoke to him about training fees, Brendan would hear none of it.

"I owe you a big debt, as you know, Genie," he said, "This is one way I can start to repay it."

So Little Kitty Cat was registered to race and stayed at the Meaghan yard for three years, during which she confounded Brendan's misgivings as to her potential by winning three races and being placed in several more.

"She's a very good mare. It's a shame she's no pedigree," Brendan told Eoghan over the phone after Little Kitty Cat's second win, "Are you sure you can find no record of her bloodline?"

Eoghan was able to say truthfully that he could not. After all, he only had Oisin's word for it that Cait's Gift had been covered by Alakazam and indeed whether this was even Alakazam's foal. It occurred to him, somewhat belatedly, to ask himself why Ronan had agreed to have one of his top stallions cover one of Oisin's mares, especially when he might have guessed that Oisin might not have been able to pay the necessary fees. The racing performance of Little Kitty Cat suggested that the information given to him by Oisin could well be true, but there was genuinely no available proof one way or the other. A DNA test could reveal the truth, but that was out of the question in the circumstances.

So Little Kitty Cat continued to race as a non-throughbred horse and came back to Enda's Farm as a successful six year old with recorded form in Irish racing. Eoghan's plan was to breed from her, but he needed to find the right stallion. And this breeding needed to be above board and recorded and to be with a registered thoroughbred stallion from the Irish Studbook.

Eoghan knew what characteristics he was looking for in the horse he intended to produce. He wanted a strong staying chaser, reminiscent of the promising Langham Light, whose life had ended along with Eoghan's career in the mud of Navan racecourse. His researches led him to consider stallions at studs all over Ireland and beyond, but he eventually decided that his best chance lay with a local stallion called Tabloid News, currently standing at Mallows. After all, Ronan had long owed him a favour.

Oisin had left Mallows stud suddenly two years before and Eoghan had no idea where he had gone. Ronan had grumpily assumed that one of his creditors had caught up with him and that Oisin had decided to make himself scarce. For all his chaotic approach to business, Oisin was a competent stud man and could easily make his skills available to employers in more distant locations where his creditors might not be bothered to search for him.

Ronan was surprised to be contacted by Eoghan about bringing a mare to Tabloid News.

"This is a bit out of your league, surely, Genie," Ronan said, rather pompously.

"Is my money not good enough for you then, Ronan?" asked Eoghan, even though he expected that Ronan would not be getting as much as he expected out of the arrangement.

"To be sure, it is, of course," blustered Ronan, "And you are an old and valued friend into the bargain."

"That's good," replied Eoghan, "Because a bargain is what I am looking to you for."

In the end, in consideration of the events of the stormy night now many years in their shared past, Ronan agreed to the covering of the mare Little Kitty Cat by the great stallion Tabloid News for less than half the normal fee. As a result, just under a year later, a dark and healthy colt was foaled.

Eoghan and Caitlin called him Tabikat.

24

Sam had agreed with Brendan Meaghan that Tabikat's transfer to Sampfield Grange would take place on New Year's day. Brendan had two runners in the New Year card at Cheltenham, and, even though Tabikat was not one of them, the horse was to travel to the course alongside his stablemates. Sam himself had no entries at the festive Cheltenham meeting, but was happy to take the Sampfield Grange horsebox to the course to collect his new charge. Accompanying Tabikat on his journey was his regular work rider, Claire O'Dowd, who was to be seconded to Sam's team until the end of the month to assist with Tabikat's training programme.

Tabikat had run creditably in the Leopardstown steeplechase a few days before, finishing in fourth place in a competitive field. He had come out of the race fit and well, and Brendan was confident that he had a realistic chance of running into a place in the Gold Cup at the Cheltenham Festival in March, so long as he was kept up to his regular work programme and stayed healthy.

"He's the easiest horse in the world to train," was one of the many statements which Brendan had made to Sam by telephone over the three weeks since they had sat in the Queens Hotel together whilst Brendan had recounted the unexpected story of Tabikat and his breeder, "Look, he's home bred, as you know, and his behaviour around people is second to none. He's a good attitude, intelligent, and works well, whatever you ask of him. An example to some people, he is indeed."

Sadie was doubly excited by the plan to go to Cheltenham races on New Year's Day. The prospect of having a true star in the Sampfield Grange yard was thrilling enough, but the opportunity it offered to meet up with Merlin ap Rhys whilst collecting the new horse was the icing on Sadie's much anticipated cake.

Sadie's meeting with Merlin at Cheltenham when he had ridden Curlew Landings in the Novice Hurdle three weeks earlier had been disappointingly brief. Merlin had been too busy that day with his riding commitments to spend time with Sadie. Their paths had crossed only whilst Sadie was leading up Curlew before the race and again when she was looking after the horse once the race was over. Curlew had run determinedly at the head of affairs in a much more competitive field than that which he had encountered at Newbury, but had faded whilst tackling the hill at the end of the course and had been passed by two other horses. Worse than that, he had been found to have sustained a cut to his near foreleg, from which blood had been trickling as he crossed the finish line. Whether he had cut into himself or whether the cut had been caused by contact with one of the hurdles had not been clear. The racecourse vet, having inspected the wound after Sadie had hosed it down and Merlin had gone to weigh in, thought that the injury was superficial, but had advised a scan to be sure than no tendons were damaged. Curlew himself had seemed reassuringly untroubled by the injury but had enjoyed the fuss made of him by Sadie as she had bandaged his leg.

Merlin had come briefly over to the stabling area to obtain news of the verdict on Curlew's injury and to put a consoling arm around Sadie's shoulders, in which he had somehow managed to include squeezing one of her breasts as well. He had had to return to the weighing room to prepare for his next ride, but had ensured before he left her that Sadie had recorded his number in her mobile phone.

"Get Mr Sampfield to give you a day off and come see me," he had told her, as he had run back towards the weighing room.

Kye had been busy getting the horsebox ready for the return journey, hastily repacking the goods he had not had time to sell, and, fortunately for Sadie, had noticed nothing of her exchange with Merlin.

Sadie would have liked to have stayed after the race meeting was over, but Sam had been insistent that Curlew should be taken home promptly, so Sadie had boarded the lorry alongside Kye, feeling irritable about her thwarted plans but highly delighted that Merlin had wanted to see her again, and for a whole day too.

Sadie had kept Merlin's number handy in her list of contacts and had discovered from him that he expected to have three rides at Cheltenham on New Year's day. She had negotiated the following day as a holiday, telling Sam that she had been invited to stay by a friend in Cheltenham after the races finished.

Merlin had been encouraging about the prospect of spending some time together after the races were over. Sadie had explained that the purpose of her attendance was solely to pick up the horse which Merlin had ridden in the Hennessy Gold Cup, so her time, once the horse was loaded into the horsebox, would be her own.

"Tabikat going to Mr Sampfield, 'is 'e?" Merlin had said, sounding surprised, "Didn' see that one coming. Mr Sampfield using the reg'lar jockey still, would you know? He's a good ride, that one. If Mr Sampfield wants me to ride 'im in the Gold Cup, I'd jump at the chance, you tell 'im I would."

Sadie had had to admit that she knew nothing of Mr Sampfield's plans for the horse other than that he was being aimed at the Gold Cup.

"But I'll make sure he knows what you said, Merlin," she had assured the jockey.

"You're a great girl, you are," Merlin had replied, "Can't wait to get my 'ands on you again at Cheltenham."

Accordingly, on New Year's morning, Sadie was sitting in a frenzy of anticipation in the lorry alongside Kye on the way to Cheltenham. They were travelling faster than would have been usual on their way to the races, as today the horsebox was empty, and Kye, as the driver, did not have to worry about the comfort and security of any equine passengers.

Both Kye and Sadie had been preoccupied with their own concerns over the Christmas period, otherwise each might have noticed a change in the other's behaviour. Kye had tuned out Sadie's constant gushing references to Merlin ap Rhys, feeling more irritated than jealous, simply thinking that Sadie still had a schoolgirl crush on the apparently charismatic jockey. Kye had no notion of what had happened between Sadie and Merlin at Newbury racecourse nor how much Sadie had been attracted by Merlin's unconcealed sexual interest in her.

Kye, for his part, was still wondering what to do with the unexpected information about Isabella Hall which had been captured by Gray's drone.

The drone had been a smart red device sporting four small propellers, situated as if at the four corners of a square, with a spider like body in the centre housing the camera. It was controlled from a hand held console, which had a cradle into which a mobile phone could be inserted. From the forecourt of the workshop, Gray had demonstrated to Kye how the drone's height and direction could be controlled using two small levers, operated simultaneously with each of his hands. The images collected by the camera during its remotely controlled travels were streamed back to the screen of the mobile phone. It had all seemed very straightforward. But there had been one major snag. The video streaming range of the drone was limited to about two kilometres, so, if Isabella Hall's journeys took her beyond this range, as Kye was sure that they would, it would still be necessary to follow Isabella in a car, although at least this could now be done from a safe distance.

This requirement had meant that both Kye and Gray needed to be involved in the tracking, Gray operating the drone whilst Kye drove the car. Co-ordinating their own work arrangements with Isabella's outings on her bike was always going to be difficult. Nevertheless, they had eventually managed to track Isabella's cycle rides on two separate occasions. And what they had discovered was quite different to anything which Kye had anticipated.

On the first occasion, Isabella had set off from Sampfield Grange on a cold and windy afternoon during which broken white clouds with grey edges skittered across a pale blue sky. An anxious sun hovered just above the skeletal trees, casting an ineffective light over the rain soaked countryside. The wind had presented some challenges to Gray in controlling the drone, but he had managed to track the apparently unsuspecting cyclist successfully throughout her uneventful ride of about fifteen miles around the tracks and narrow lanes near Sampfield Grange. Isabella had followed a roughly circular route and Kye had been sure that on her arrival back at Sampfield Grange she had had no idea that she had been followed.

"Well, that di'n tell us much," Gray had grunted as the mobile phone screen in the drone console showed a picture of Isabella Hall getting off her bicycle in the Sampfield Grange yard, "She's just riding around the place, going nowhere, doing nothing. She training for something, is she?"

Kye had had to admit that this had looked very much like an exercise ride by someone preparing for an event of some kind.

"Lewis and I think it's just a cover," he had explained hastily to Gray, "She doesn't always just go riding round for exercise. She goes somewhere, I'm sure of it. Lewis, Sadie and Kelly think she's off meeting a bloke, but I reckon there's more to it than that."

"Well, we'll give it another try," had said Gray, who had quite enjoyed the process of secretly tracking and filming Isabella Hall. The drone had been an expensive purchase and he had already become bored with flying it around aimlessly without any objective in mind. The outing with Kye had made him feel as if he was doing something exciting, as if he were a secret agent or something equally glamorous.

On the second occasion, Isabella had initially taken the main road which led towards the local town and The Charlton Arms. Kye was beginning to think that the suspicions of the Sampfield Grange staff about meetings with Mr Stanley were about to be confirmed, when Isabella had suddenly turned off the main road and cycled along a hedge-lined lane with which Kye was unfamiliar.

"Where's this go, then?" he had asked Gray, as they had approached the turning, which, rather ominously, appeared to be called Dagger Lane, several minutes after Isabella had started to cycle along it ahead of them, the little drone recording her progress between the hedgerows.

"Nowhere, really," Gray had replied, "There's some farms along there and an old airfield, but that's about it. It comes out somewhere over Warnock way after that."

The picture on the mobile phone screen had shown Isabella pressing on doggedly along an increasingly narrow track spattered with mud and grass laid down by the thick wheels of tractors and farm vehicles. It had looked treacherously slippery.

As Kye had nosed Gray's car over the mud, he had had a sudden fear that Isabella would think better of pursuing her ride along the unsuitable lane and would stop and turn back. This would put them in a difficult position, as there was no place where they could easily turn the car around, and they would then run the risk of coming face to face with their quarry. She might even spot the drone, which had so far remained behind her and therefore in effect out of sight. Kye had begun to run through possible explanations of their presence which he could trot out to her in the event that his forebodings were realised.

Isabella, however, had showed no sign of turning back. So Kye had continued nosing the car carefully along the muddy thoroughfare, until the drone's camera had sent back an image showing that Isabella had stopped in the centre of the lane and dismounted from her bike. As Gray had shifted the position of the drone to ensure it remained out of her line of sight, Kye had brought the car to a halt in a convenient gateway into a ploughed field.

As the car engine had idled, Kye and Gray had heard the sound of an engine. Looking around at the lane behind them and even into the field, they had not been able to see any sign of a vehicle. The sound increased in volume and then ahead of them above a line of trees on a slope beyond a bend in the lane, Kye had spotted a small aircraft approaching them, silhouetted against a dull grey sky. Its downward trajectory had suggested that it was coming in to land.

"Look at that, Gray," Kye had exclaimed, tapping Gray's arm and pointing at the oncoming aircraft.

Gray had swung the camera of the drone around to pick up the aircraft. It had appeared to be a single engine aircraft coloured blue and white, its tricycle landing gear ready for touchdown.

"Must be going into Old Warnock airfield," had commented Gray, "Don't usually see much except microlights goin' in there. Usually it's just model aircraft geeks that use it."

"Isabella must have seen the plane too," Kye had told him, "She's stopped her bike. Is she by where the airfield is, Gray?"

"Yeah, I'd say so," Gray had said, turning the drone round to pick up Isabella and her bike.

But Isabella had been no longer in the lane and it took Gray a minute or two to work out that she had gone along a footpath which led into the back of airfield, the main entrance to which was on the further side of the field near to the village of Warnock and accessed by a rather better means of approach than the narrow and muddy Dagger Lane.

Kye had cautiously re-entered the lane and edged the car along it towards the point at which Isabella had entered the overgrown footpath. Gray and the drone had continued to follow her as she had proceeded on foot across the grass, half-pushing and half-carrying the racing bike.

The aircraft had touched down now on the paved surface of the runway, which seemed in better condition than might have been expected at such a rarely used facility. It had come to a halt at the end of the hard standing and the unseen pilot had shut down the engine. The single propeller had whirled to a stop and there had been a sudden silence.

"I'm going to get out and have a look," had said Kye, "You keep the camera on her, but don't let her see it."

"That's gunna be tricky," Gray had warned him, nervously, "I dunno which way she might turn. And that pilot, he might see us too."

"Well, keep your distance," Kye had instructed him, as he had left the car and proceeded on foot along the little path to the airfield. Reaching the end after less than fifty metres, he had crouched behind the hedge and watched Isabella Hall and the pilot.

The pilot had emerged from the aircraft and walked forward to embrace Isabella. Isabella had left her bicycle at the edge of the runway and had sprinted forward into the pilot's wide armed embrace.

But, clandestine though this meeting clearly had been, it was not the meeting of lovers which Kye had expected to see, albeit it at The Charlton Arms rather than a chilly airfield. For a start, the pilot had been a woman, and their embrace had not been that of lovers. It had looked more like that of a couple of friends who had not seen each other for some time greeting each other with enthusiastic smiles and excited gestures. The two women had immediately started an animated conversation, but Kye had been too far away to hear anything they said, even if their words had not been carried away from him on the stiff wind into which the small aircraft had just landed.

Kye knew nothing about aircraft, but he had tried to imprint a picture of the machine into his mind and also to memorise the registration number painted on its side – G STON. He had been conscious of Gray's drone hovering somewhere nearby and had hoped that it too would be recording a clear picture of the aircraft.

Meanwhile, the two women had climbed into the aircraft together, and Kye wondered if they were intending to take off again. But, it seemed that they had climbed into the front seats solely to get out of the persistent wind and appeared to be sitting in the aircraft talking together.

Kye had remained where he was for about ten minutes, during which Isabella had showed no sign of emerging back onto the runway to collect her bike. He had been progressively getting increasingly cold and stiff and just considering returning to the warmth of the car when the aircraft door had been pushed open and Isabella Hall had emerged. She had appeared to be taking leave of the pilot, and had waved towards the aircraft as she had jogged back towards her bike.

Kye had jumped to his feet and sprinted back along the lane. Leaping into the car, he had started the engine, saying to Gray,

"She's coming back. We need to get out of here, quick."

Not knowing which way Isabella Hall was likely to turn once she was back in Dagger Lane, Kye had elected to continue along the lane, guessing that Isabella would return the way she had come now that her mysterious meeting was over. He had been right. The drone's video stream had showed Isabella turning right out of the footpath and, once on her bike again, retracing her route towards Sampfield Grange.

As the blue and white aircraft had taken to the sky again above the lane, Kye had eventually found a farm entrance in which to turn the car around, and had followed about a mile behind the cyclist, until he reached the main road and had been able to make his way to Colvin's Motors.

Gray had agreed to download the video recording of the afternoon's work and had said he would email it to Kye so that Kye could look at it more carefully on his own phone. But although Kye had secretly reviewed the recording dozens of times when there had been no-one else around to ask him what he was doing, he was no nearer to understanding what was going on.

Driving the Sampfield Grange horsebox North on the M5, he considered again the implications of what he had seen. First, the meeting between Isabella and the aircraft's pilot was clearly pre-arranged. Second, Mr Stanley did not appear to be involved in the meeting, at least not in person. Third, Isabella had evidently been to the airfield before, as she had cycled to the half hidden footpath without any hesitation. On the face of it, it could just have been a meeting between two friends, although a cold and deserted airfield seemed an odd place to meet. If the meeting was just a social event, surely it could have taken place in rather more conventional and comfortable surroundings. But maybe the two women did not wish to be seen for some reason.

Gray had offered to try to find out more about the aircraft itself from a friend who was a plane spotter. The helpful friend had confirmed from his photographic records that he had seen that particular aircraft, a Piper Archer, twice before, once at Old Warnock airfield and once at Gloucestershire Airport, located between Gloucester and Cheltenham. The friend was not a frequent visitor to either airfield, so could not say if these were the only occasions on which the aircraft had visited them.

But the piece of information which was of most interest to Kye was the date on which the aircraft had been spotted at Gloucestershire Airport. It was the same date on which Isabella and the man who Sadie and the others were sure was Mr Stanley had been seen by Gilbert Peveril at Cheltenham races.

"So that's how she got there," Kye had breathed, when he was given this information by Gray over the phone.

"Got where?" had said Gray, who knew nothing of the apparent sighting of Isabella that day.

"It's a long story. Tell you another time. Thanks Gray."

Kye had rung off hurriedly, before Gray had been able to give him the other piece of information which he had extracted from his friend, namely the details of the owner and home location of the small aircraft. So Gray had texted these details instead to Kye. The owner, it appeared, was a Ms Elizabeth Baker and the aircraft was based at Elstree Aerodrome just North of London.

"Must be a mate of hers," Kye had texted back not knowing what to make of this additional intelligence.

Kye was less concerned with learning about the aircraft and its owner than in deciding whether it indicated any threat to himself and his illegal money making activities. He had already decided not to share what he had learned with Sadie, Lewis and Kelly for fear he might be asked about his relationship with Gray.

After agonised discussion, greed had got the better of Kye and Gray, with the result that they had decided to go ahead as normal at Cheltenham races on New Year's Day. Kye had checked the previous day that Isabella Hall was not planning to accompany him and Sadie to the racecourse. Isabella had indicated that she would be remaining at Sampfield Grange all day.

The coast therefore appeared to be clear, so why did he feel so uneasy?

Kye would have felt even more uneasy if he could have heard the conversation in the aircraft that day between Isabella and the pilot.

"There's a drone following you," the pilot had said, "I saw it as I was on final."

"Yes, I know," Isabella had replied, "It's that lad from Sampfield Grange. Kye McMahon. And his mate from the garage. Kye sells weed and God knows what else out of the back of the horsebox at the race meetings. The other chap supplies him. Kye thinks I'm some sort of investigator who's on his case. He's like a cat on hot bricks every time he sees me. It would be funny if it weren't so irritating."

"Are you going to do anything about it?" the other woman had asked, "I can see him now, in the hedge over there, you know."

"Oh God, what a pain," Isabella had sighed, "We may have to warn him off. I'll speak to Frank. He might be able to make use of him. We have a pretty good hold over him with this drug dealing going on. Our stuffed shirt of a Lord and Master at the Grange would have him off the premises in two seconds if he finds out."

"That bad, your boss, is he?" had laughed her companion.

"No, he's not so bad," Isabella had replied, also laughing, "He's just rather old-fashioned and narrow minded. He's quite sweet and polite really, like someone out of a costume drama. His staff and their hangers-on really take advantage of him. He needs an introduction to the real world, I think. Perhaps Frank can sort him out after Cheltenham in March."

At this, the other woman's face had become serious.

"This is all a hell of a risk, you know," she had said.

"I know," Isabella had replied, "But we can't go back now. It's too late. Frank says they've already taken the bait."

25

Whilst Sadie and Kye were making their way to Cheltenham, separately preoccupied with their respective personal concerns, Sam was some way ahead of them, speeding in the black Audi up the M5. He reached the racecourse well ahead of the crowds of mainly local people who would soon be streaming towards the roundabout near the main entrance, eagerly looking forward to a great day out at the races. A drab and dismal sky with hints of rain in the air did not appear to have put off the earlier arrivals and Sam could see the warm clad pedestrians chatting cheerfully amongst themselves as they neared their destination. It all looked like a lot of fun, Sam thought, rather enviously, conveniently forgetting that a good number of the people he was observing would gladly have exchanged places with him, if only for the chance of driving his expensive car.

Sam had arranged to spend the day with Brendan Meaghan, whose three horses had arrived at Prestbury Park the previous evening. Brendan's staff had taken the horses, Tabikat included, out onto the course for some exercise earlier in the morning. When Sam joined him, Brendan was in the redbrick stable area and in an unexpectedly good mood. He introduced Claire O'Dowd, a pale and bespectacled girl with an untidy mass of black hair, who would be returning to Sampfield Grange with Kye later in the day.

"I'll be wanting Claire until my two are back and ready to travel," Brendan warned Sam, "Tabikat will have to wait here for them."

The last time Sam had been at the racecourse had been on the day of the race in which Curlew Landings had picked up his injury. An examination by Rachel of the injured horse once he was home at Sampfield Grange had confirmed the racecourse vet's diagnosis that, although the injury was nasty looking, it was superficial.

"It doesn't even need stitches," Rachel had said, "And he can go on with his usual exercise programme, so long as we protect the wound and allow it to heal."

Since that day, Sam had been gradually digesting the background information which the Irish trainer had given him about Tabikat on the evening before Curlew's race. He had come to the conclusion that, although the lengthy and eloquent account had answered a number of his questions, it had only served to raise new ones. In particular, Brendan's story had not explained how the horse came to be owned by the Bahrain based Levy Brothers, nor why they had wanted their top Irish chaser to be transferred from Brendan Meaghan's large and successful yard to a small operation such as Sampfield Grange.

Isabella Hall had done as Sam had asked her to do when a representative of Levy Brothers International had called Sampfield Grange to make the arrangements for the payment of Tabikat's various fees, and had asked the individual concerned to speak directly to Mr Sampfield. The conversation had, though, been uninformative. The caller had merely said that he was an accounts assistant acting on instructions from his head of department, and was unable to provide any insight into the reasons for the decision to send the horse to Sampfield Grange, nor, indeed, who had made it.

"Look, the answer to that question is easy," Brendan said when Sam asked him about the horse's owner as the two men walked behind one of Brendan's horses as it was led along the rubber surfaced horse walk towards the saddling and pre-parade area, "Niamh Foley's eldest daughter Aoife is the wife of Ephraim Levy and the mother of his two sons."

Sam had not expected such a simple answer and struggled with the very notion of this information. It seemed an unlikely marriage between a rich Jewish banker and a country girl from County Kerry.

"How did they meet?" he asked, eventually.

"Now, I told you that Eoghan's family went into the business of holiday cottages," Brendan reminded him, "I'm told that Ephraim used to go on holiday there with his family as a young man."

"So Ephraim bought the horse from Eoghan?" asked Sam.

"Well, now, that I cannot say," Brendan responded, "It seems to me that there was more to it than that. For a start, the Levy Brothers bank was not the sole owner of the horse when he first came to me. Although, to be sure, they were the ones who paid the bills."

"So who else was involved?" asked Sam, intrigued.

"As I recall," the other man replied, thoughtfully, "There were two other owners. I don't recollect the names. It will all be in the papers which Claire will give you."

"So who comes to see Tabikat when he races?" asked Sam.

"Most usually some employees from the bank," Brendan replied, "It's a grand day out for them, I should say."

More puzzled than ever, Sam left Brendan and Claire to their tasks with Brendan's now rather fired up runner in the first race. It seemed bizarre to Sam that someone, even a banking family, should own such a successful racehorse and never come to watch it race. He had spent the day after Boxing Day with Helen Garratt and her husband's large and enthusiastic family, watching Alto Clef run into second place in a hard slog of a Welsh National, and could see the pleasure and excitement they all had in their horse's success. The memory reminded him that Helen had asked to come to Sampfield Grange to see him in two days' time. She wanted to talk about her idea for a charity again.

Once Brendan's horse was walking the parade ring, being led around by the evidently unflappable Claire, Sam found himself standing with the runner's connections in the centre. He had another question to ask Brendan. It was a question which he had hesitated to ask, but one to which he was desperate to know the answer. He took his opportunity once the horse had been mounted and the little group was on its way down to the course, the connections walking ahead and talking amongst themselves.

"Do you know, by any chance, a woman called Isabella Hall?" he asked Brendan.

"That's not a name I know," replied the trainer, after a pause during which he appeared to be turning the name over in his mind, "Who is she and for what reason do you think I might know her?"

"My cousin Gilbert thinks he saw her with you here at the Showcase meeting," replied Sam, deliberately ignoring the first part of Brendan's question.

"The Showcase meeting, did he indeed?" Brendan mused aloud.

"Yes, she was with a man, an older man, very tall, smart tie, using a walking stick," said Sam, describing the figure he had seen on Philippa Peveril's photographs.

Brendan seemed to be trying to decide what to say. Eventually, he spoke, choosing his words carefully.

"I was here at the race meeting, to be sure," he said, "But I have no notion of the person you are describing."

At that point, the owners of Brendan's runner turned to speak to them and Sam was unable to pursue the matter any further. But he was puzzled. He could not believe that Brendan did not remember anything at all about the people he had been with in the parade ring at the Showcase meeting, particularly since the three of them had so nearly been knocked over by Roger Mortimer's spooked horse. So why was he lying about it?

Once all the horses had gone out onto the course, Sam excused himself, and returned to the trainers' car park where Kye was in the process of parking the horsebox in the furthest end of the available area. Sadie jumped down from the box, eyes glowing.

"Hello, Mr Sampfield. Is Tabikat here?" she asked.

Sam walked with Sadie to the stable where Tabikat was looking interestedly over the half door at the race day activity going on around him and perhaps wondering why he was not part of it. One of Brendan's stable staff had remained with Tabikat whilst Claire was down on the course, and proudly showed his warmly rugged and magnificent charge to Sadie and Kye.

"He's beautiful," breathed Sadie, as Tabikat inclined his mahogany coloured head towards her. Tabikat nodded in agreement and allowed her to fondle his velvety nose.

"I can't wait to ride him, Mr Sampfield," Sadie enthused. She seemed a bit put out when Sam explained about Claire's month long stay at Sampfield Grange.

"It's as if they don't trust us, Mr Sampfield," she exclaimed, ignoring the presence of the waiting Irish groom.

"That's not the case, I assure you, Sadie," Sam tried to convince her, although he was inclined to agree with her assertion, "Tabikat is a valuable horse and we are preparing him for one of the top races in the calendar. It's not our usual business. We need all the advice and help that we can get. I know that I do."

"So why are they sending him to us, then, Mr Sampfield?" asked Kye, curiously.

Sam only wished that he knew. It was the very question to which he had not received an answer either from Brendan Meaghan or from the employee of Levy Brothers International. Instead, he said,

"Mr Meaghan's groom won't be available to travel until after the last race. So why don't you two go off and enjoy the day? I asked Isabella to arrange admission for you both."

As Sam left them for the parade ring, where he was expecting to join Brendan once again, Kye told Sadie that he needed to return to the horsebox, saying that he had things to do and that he would join Sadie later. Sadie was too preoccupied with her own prospective activities to ask him any questions. And Kye was too relieved that she was not going to stick around the horsebox to question the reason for her lack of interest.

Sam, conscious that he had missed the running of the first race, made his way back along the horse walk. The runners for the second race were now in the pre-parade area but he was not able to see any sign of Brendan Meaghan or Claire O'Dowd. Noting that Brendan's other runner was not due to run until the fourth race, he guessed that Brendan might have gone up to the bar. Not fancying the crush and noise of an indoor facility, Sam decided to walk along to the parade ring to see whether he knew any of the trainers who had runners in the second race.

"Hello, it's Mr Sampfield Peveril, isn't it?" a female voice said from behind him.

Sam swung round. The speaker was the young woman he had met at Newbury on Hennessy Gold Cup Day. She was wearing the same burgundy hat and her brown eyes contained a hint of amusement at Sam's obvious surprise.

"Got any tips for the smart girls today?" she asked before Sam could say anything.

Sam laughed.

"I thought I recognised you at Newbury," he said, "Stevie Stone, isn't it?"

"Well done," said the young woman, also laughing, "But I wouldn't have thought my little corner of the great horseracing industry would be something to interest a traditionalist such as yourself."

"It doesn't," said Sam, and then, realising that he had sounded ill mannered, hastily added, "I mean it's not really aimed at me, is it? But my office manager used to follow your tips, I think. You and your talking cat were on her computer in the yard office."

"That's good news," Stevie Stone replied, "Jayce and I have got to earn a living somehow."

"I have to say," said Sam, "That you sound rather different in person than you do on the screen. That's all an act is it, the slang and so on? Could I assume that Jason might actually be a public schoolboy?"

"No, Jayce is definitely not a public schoolboy," Stevie said, laughing, "He's a retired accountant from Billericay. He's knows his stuff, though. I think he's enjoying being portrayed as a feckless young man."

"But," Stevie went on, "What are you doing here today, Mr S P? You don't have any runners."

"I've come here to collect a horse," replied Sam, not really sure why he was telling this stranger about his affairs, "In fact it's the horse we were talking about when I was with you in the parade ring at Newbury. Tabikat."

"One of Brendan Meaghan's horses coming to you?" said Stevie, raising her eyebrows, "That's a bit of a coup for you, isn't it?"

"I really am not sure," replied Sam, "I have to confess I have not the remotest idea why he has been sent to me. Brendan says that the owners made the decision out of the blue."

"Owners, that's the Levy Brothers nowadays," commented Stevie, "They're an unusual family."

"Do you know them?" asked Sam, surprised.

"I do," said the young woman, "Although it's a while since I have seen any of them."

"Can you tell me anything about their ownership of Tabikat?" asked Sam eagerly, "Brendan Meaghan was rather vague about it all."

"Sure can," said Stevie, "But I'd rather do it over a drink."

The jockeys were by now coming into the parade ring ready to mount up for the second race. As Sam was about to respond with an offer to take Stevie to the Owners and Trainers bar, a familiar Welsh voice addressed him.

"Nice to see you, Mr Sampfield," Merlin called out as he passed Sam and Stevie on the way to join the connections for whom he was about to ride, "I 'eard about Tabikat comin' to you. I'd be pleased to ride 'im again, if you want me."

Sam acknowledged Merlin's offer with a nod and a brief word of thanks. Merlin looked quickly at Stevie, but showed no sign of having recognised her.

"I'm impressed," said Stevie, "Good news clearly travels fast today."

"Hmm," said Sam, gesturing his guest politely towards the parade ring exit. As they walked towards the rail, he noticed Sadie leaning against it, eager eyes fastened on Merlin ap Rhys. Stevie followed Sam's gaze.

"That one of your staff?" she asked, "She's certainly infatuated with Merlin the wizard man, whoever she is."

"Really?" responded Sam, looking at Sadie with interest, "I've booked Merlin a couple of times for one of my novices. Sadie Shinkins there is my yard manager. The two of them have ridden work together at Sampfield Grange, that's all."

"I think it might be a bit more than that," said Stevie, amused by Sam's lack of perception.

"I think I might need that drink," replied Sam, who had suddenly realised the identity of the friend with whom Sadie planned to spend the following day.

Stevie and Sam left Sadie behind and made their way over to the Owners and Trainers bar. A few people greeted Sam as he entered the bar and steered Stevie towards a small table. Brendan Meaghan did not appear to be there. Once Stevie was sipping her glass of Chablis and Sam had a measure of single malt whisky before him, they were able to resume their conversation.

Stevie reiterated the information already given to Sam by Brendan concerning the relationship between Eoghan Foley's family and the Levys. The horse, she said, had been taken on by the Levys at Eoghan's request, mainly because Eoghan could not himself afford to keep a horse in training, especially with a top yard such as Brendan Meaghan's.

"Brendan said that there were other owners involved," said Sam.

"That's true, but not any more," replied Stevie.

"Oh? What changed? Did something happen?" asked Sam.

Stevie put her glass carefully down on the table.

"Yes, something did happen," she said. Sam noticed that her hand was shaking.

Stevie took a deep breath.

"The other owner died," she said, quietly.

"Who was the other owner?" asked Sam.

"Her name was Susan Stonehouse," Stevie stated baldly, "She was my mother."

As Sam took in this information and tried unsuccessfully to decide what to say in response, Kye was having an unsettling experience of a different kind.

Having sent out a few texts to potential customers he knew were waiting around the racecourse, he had become aware that someone was watching him. A woman wearing faded jeans and a fleece jacket, and, notwithstanding the dismal weather, dark aviator style sunglasses, was standing in the car park, hands in her pockets, pretending not to be watching the horsebox. Kye looked towards her a couple of times and caught her eye, which caused her quickly to look away.

Kye was sweating. His customers were about to arrive and he could hardly hand over their purchases with this nosy character watching on. He knew he had to do something to get rid of her.

Deciding that direction action was the only option, he turned round suddenly and walked quickly up to her. The woman didn't move.

"Yez looking for someone?" he asked, aggressively, staring her in the face.

"Yes," replied the woman, apparently unbothered by his direct challenge, "I'm looking for yez, Kye McMahon. You're muscling in on my boss's territory."

26

The day and a half which Sadie spent with Merlin ap Rhys exceeded her highest expectations.

Sadie had waved off a strangely subdued Kye, together with Claire O'Dowd, in the horsebox, the lordly Tabikat having loaded calmly and without any trouble. Sadie had told Mr Sampfield that she would be back in time to ride out on the morning of the day after next, to which he had merely nodded and told her to enjoy her day off. Looking forward to some unexpected freedom, she skipped happily off to find Merlin's black BMW.

Merlin had rides at Ffos Las racecourse the next day and then at Wincanton the day after. His plan was to return to his house near Chepstow that night. Sadie could, if she wanted, come to the races with him the following day and he would return her to Sampfield Grange in the course of his journey to Wincanton.

Merlin took the scenic A48 route to Chepstow and Sadie suddenly found herself feeling a bit out of her depth. His left hand resting on her thigh, Merlin was asking her opinion about the day's racing. Sadie managed to muster up a few thoughts on the winners but fell silent after a while. She became suddenly conscious that she had worked nowhere else other than Sampfield Grange and that her racing knowledge was very limited compared with that of Merlin.

Merlin took a glance at her from the corner of his left eye. He could feel that her thigh muscle had tensed under his hand and saw that she was looking fixedly out of the front windscreen. He thought he had assessed correctly that she was no timid and shrinking virgin, and was certain that she was attracted to him, so this was unexpected. He decided that he needed to move onto safer ground where she would feel comfortable.

"Tell me," he said, "'ow's Curlew Landings?"

Sadie visibly brightened up and gave him an animated account of

Curlew's progress and the fact that Mr Sampfield hoped to have him fit for a race at Taunton later in the month.

"He thought he'd find something a bit less scary for him this time," she said.

By the time they reached Chepstow, Merlin knew everything there was to know about the Sampfield Grange horses. Sadie was relaxed and chatty and he felt confident of a great night ahead.

He was right. They had scarcely got through the front door of the neat terraced cottage before Sadie launched herself at him, with the result that they had ended up making love on the hall floor. Merlin was so turned on by her unexpected enthusiasm that he came uncontrollably within seconds.

"I'm sorry, *cariad*," he said ruefully to Sadie, as they lay on the hall carpet, "That was no fun for you. I'll do better later. You're a bit of an 'andful, you are."

"That's all right," replied Sadie, pressing herself into his shoulder as he tried to calm down, "I liked it."

"You sure?" asked Merlin, "Not much 'appened. You mean you like it all over quick, then?"

Sadie's wide blue eyes looked back at him in surprise.

"Isn't it always like that?" she asked, simply.

Merlin didn't know what to say.

"Let's get up off this 'ard floor," he said, eventually, "And you and I can 'ave a bit of a chat."

Seated in the quarry stone floored kitchen, clothes hastily recovered, a mug of hot tea made by Sadie, in his hand, Merlin asked, choosing his words carefully.

"So what do you like doin' when you 'ave sex, then?"

Sadie looked embarrassed.

"What do you mean?" she asked, "I just like it normal, like, you know, nothing weird."

Merlin had long ago learned that the secret to making women want more sex with him was to find out what they enjoyed and give them plenty of it. But he was not sure he could work out what Sadie enjoyed.

"Is there anything you don't like doin', then?" he tried, instead.

Sadie thought for a bit.

"Well I don't like being bashed about," she said eventually, "And I don't like watching lesbian porn much."

"That it?" asked Merlin.

"Well, I'll watch the lesby stuff with you, if you like it," Sadie said hurriedly, fearing that she might have said the wrong thing, "You can choose what we do."

"OK," said Merlin, taking a deep breath, and wondering what sort of miserable types Sadie had previously had in her bed, "I think I get the picture. I've got some good ideas for things I think you might like doin'. But you 'ave to promise me something. You 'ave to promise me that you'll tell me if you don't like something. And if you do like something, then promise you'll ask me to do it again."

Sadie looked happier.

"Can we go upstairs now?" she asked.

The next few hours turned out to be very exciting. Sadie was certainly no prude, and put plenty of energy into her lovemaking. But, as Merlin had deduced, her previous partners had been unadventurous and selfish lovers, and Sadie herself had not had the imagination to expect or demand anything more from them. Merlin's more interesting tactics were met with an enthusiastic response to the extent that Sadie soon had practical experience of a whole list of inventive positions and activities.

Eventually, at about midnight, an exhausted Merlin called a halt. They had left the bedroom only once during the evening to get something to eat and drink. A day's race riding followed by four hours of highly active sex were enough even for him.

"Look, *cariad*," he said, "I 'ave to ride tomorrow, so I need some sleep. So do you."

Merlin had two rides at Ffos Las the next day. The rides were both in the middle of the card, so an early start was not required and they would have the whole evening to themselves.

Both Sadie and Merlin were used to waking early, so, even though they had been wide awake and energetic until midnight, there was plenty of time for repeating a couple of the more novel ideas before breakfast and the car journey towards Swansea. The weather had deteriorated during the night and heavy rain was sweeping across the surface of the M4, needing the windscreen wipers of the car to be working at double speed. The rainstorm abated a bit during the afternoon, but the going at the racecourse was deep and heavy and the races proved hard work for both horses and riders.

Merlin was not sure that he had managed to shower all the mud off himself at the racecourse, which he rather unwisely mentioned to Sadie, as, in the car on their way back towards Chepstow, she started to unfasten the belt and top button of his jeans.

"That's OK, if I find any I'll just lick it all off," she told him. "Like chocolate sprinkles on an ice cream cone."

For the next few minutes, it was all Merlin could do to keep the car on the road.

Sadie's educational day and half came to an abrupt end when she and Merlin set out early the following morning eastwards along a spray soaked M4. Sadie had to be back early to ride out, so it was still dark when they quietly closed the door of Merlin's terraced cottage and set out into the wet and dismal blackness. The cottage had been the scene of yet another adventurous night, as a result of which they had left behind a broken washbasin in the *en suite* bathroom, Merlin having been leaning against it whilst Sadie washed the rest of the non-existent mud off the parts of his body which she had been unable to reach in the car.

"Will you come in and see Curlew?" asked Sadie, trying to return herself to some sort of normality, but not wanting Merlin to set off on his way to Wincanton.

"Well, if Mr Sampfield is all right with it," Merlin replied, "And I can 'ave a look at Tabikat too. "oo's takin' him out then this morning?"

Sadie told him about Claire O'Dowd. Merlin quickly searched his memory and was relieved to realise that she was not amongst his previous sexual conquests. He did not want his performance in bed to be the subject of discussion between two female stable staff at Sampfield Grange.

As Merlin and Sadie were progressing on their reluctant journey, both Kye and Sam were also wide awake and grappling with their own problems.

Kye had been seriously frightened by the words of the woman in the Cheltenham racecourse car park. His retort of "Who's yez boss then? Tell him to come and say that to me face," had been met with a derisive laugh, as the woman had walked off without a backward glance.

Fortunately, he had been able to prevent his prospective clients coming to the horsebox by texting to them the single word Bizzies.

Kye had found it difficult to make himself behave as normal with

Claire O'Dowd on the journey back to Sampfield Grange. Luckily, she had seemed to be a girl of few words and sat quietly in the lorry as it had nosed through the darkening evening down the M5. Kye had been glad of the presence of the precious horse in the box, which had forced him to concentrate on keeping his driving smooth and steady. He had realised, to his surprise, that he missed Sadie's company and wondered about the friend she had gone to see in Cheltenham. She had never mentioned knowing anyone in the picturesque Regency town.

Claire O'Dowd had supervised the unloading of Tabikat from the horsebox and had led him into the stable which had been prepared for him by Kye before they had left for the races that morning. The horse had walked grandly into the box, looked carefully about him, then turned slowly round to face towards the stable door, where he had stood stock still like an aristocrat viewing his estate. The other horses had looked curiously towards the newcomer and Tabikat graciously inclined his beautiful head towards them all.

Tabikat had got to see something of the Sampfield estate when Claire rode him out with Sam, Kye and some of the work riders in torrential rain the following morning. Tabikat had appeared entirely unbothered by the unpleasant conditions, which, as Claire put it, were normal for the horse, coming from the West of Ireland, as he did. Kye had then passed a restive day, somewhat calmed by the routine nature of his usual tasks, wondering when he could get away from the yard to talk to Gray.

Claire had moved into the second bedroom in the cottage. Lewis and Kelly had been agog to know all about the gorgeous Tabikat, a subject on which Claire was willing to talk for as long as anyone would listen, so Kye's silence at mealtimes went largely unnoticed. Now Claire was sleeping soundly in the next bedroom as Kye tossed and turned in his cold bed, wondering what to do.

What did the woman mean by her boss and his territory, he wondered. Was this some local Cheltenham drug dealer or did the unknown person's influence spread to other racecourses as well? He and Gray had plans to pursue some business at the race meeting in

Taunton in two weeks' time, where Curlew Landings was due to run. And Highlander Park was entered in another point to point at Cuffborough the week after. This was good business which they could not afford to miss. On the other hand, Kye had seen what gangs in Toxteth could do to people who crossed them, and he didn't like what he had seen. Rural Taunton was not Liverpool but this did not mean that the influence of such nasty people could not be felt there.

Lying in a rather better appointed bedroom inside the Grange itself, Sam was awake early and still attempting to make sense of all he had learned at Cheltenham races and from the paperwork which Claire O'Dowd had deposited with Isabella Hall in the yard office. Sam had established that Claire herself had worked for Brendan Meaghan for only six months and had little personal knowledge of Tabikat's history.

On his return from riding out on Tabikat's first day at Sampfield Grange, Sam had quickly come to rather obvious conclusion that the horse needed to work with horses of a similar calibre if he were to continue to experience the level of challenge and fitness needed for success in his Gold Cup race. Accordingly, he had asked Isabella to put a call through to nearby trainer Ranulph Dicks, whose large and well appointed yard included a number of horses destined for the forthcoming Cheltenham Festival. Ranulph had been intrigued to hear about the transfer to Sam's yard of Tabikat, a change which had not yet attracted any interest from the racing press, and had acceded immediately to Sam's request to bring Tabikat over later in the week to work with Ranulph's horses.

As Sam had finished his conversation with Ranulph, he had noticed, lying on Isabella's desk, the folder of paperwork which had arrived with Tabikat. A package which he assumed contained the owner's racing silks had lain unopened on a nearby chair.

"Have you had time to take look through all that?" he had asked, "Is it in order?"

"I am not entirely sure I can answer that, Mr Sampfield," had replied

Isabella, "I don't really know what information to expect."

"Well, there should be the horses' initial registration papers, issued when he was foaled, his equine passport and an export certificate, for a start," Sam had told her, "And then all the medical and training records that Mr Meaghan will have kept."

Iabella had looked quickly through the paperwork.

"Those are all here, Mr Sampfield," she had said, "And there is a change of ownership record as well."

"Really? What does it say?" Sam had asked, interested to see whether the paperwork confirmed the story which Stevie Stone had told him.

"It says," Isabella had said, slowly, "That the horse was initially owned by Mr Eoghan Foley and then by Levy Brothers International. And then, about four years ago, two additional owners were added: Captain T K Stonehouse and Mrs S E Stonehouse. But these two people were only involved, it seems, until about eighteen months ago. Now Levy Brothers are the sole owners again."

Sam had listened to the information without comment and had gone on to explain to Isabella the notifications she needed to make to Weatherbys now that the horse had been moved to Sampfield Grange. But he had been intrigued by what Isabella had just read out. Who was Captain T K Stonehouse? Susan Stonehouse's husband, perhaps? If so, then why had Stevie Stone not mentioned him when she had spoken about the death of her mother? He would have to remember to ask Stevie the next time he came across her at a race meeting.

Sam's discussion with Stevie at the racecourse had come to an abrupt end when Brendan Meaghan had suddenly appeared and sat down with them at the table in the Owners and Trainers bar. Stevie had said a brief Hello to him and had risen to her feet.

"I have to get moving," she had said, "These vlogs don't make themselves and we need Tabby Cat to get Jayce's tips out there to the smart girls."

The memory of the conversation with Stevie had made Sam think of the icon on the computer in the yard office.

"Have you ever heard of Stevie Stone? I met her at Cheltenham yesterday," he had asked Isabella.

Isabella appeared to be thinking hard before replying.

"Is she the woman on the Racing Tips for Smart Girls vlog?" she had asked.

"She is indeed," Sam had said, "Have you ever followed her tips? The thing's on your computer there. Bethany seemed to use it."

"I'll have to pay attention to it in the future," had replied Isabella, politely, "Maybe she will mention Curlew Landings and Tabikat."

During Sam's restless night, the rain had continued to fall, but, as a watery dawn broke over the drenched countryside, the clouds parted to allow a feeble yellow sun to climb slowly into a pallid sky above the eastern copses of the Sampfield estate.

Arriving in the yard, Sam was pleased to see that a smiling Sadie was back and ready to ride out and that Merlin ap Rhys was standing in the yard with her.

"Good morning to you, Merlin," Sam said, suddenly feeling cheerful, "Have you come to ride out with us today?"

"If you'll 'ave me, Mr Sampfield," Merlin replied, "I'll get my gear on."

"Yes, yes," said Sam, expansively, "You take Curlew out. Get him used to you again. See how the leg's healed. Kye can ride Rooker today."

As the sun climbed slowly above the crest of the slope, the string of six horses mounted the track which led to the ridge of the rolling hill above the Grange, feeble shadows flickering along the ground behind them. Sadie led the ride on Honeymoon Causeway. Claire rode immediately behind on Tabikat with Merlin on Curlew Landings alongside. Behind them came the work riders on Highlander Park and Ranger Station, followed by Sam and Kye on Caladesi Island and Rooker Sunset respectively. Morning birds whistled from the trees as the horses passed them by whilst small creatures quickly rustled themselves out of harm's way in the thorny undergrowth alongside the track. The breath and body heat of the horses and riders condensed in the chill air until the little party was enveloped in mist and their outline faded into the background of the clouds gathering along the distant skyline.

Isabella Hall watched the string go from the window of her flat above the garage. Her mobile phone gave a sharp ping. She looked at the screen. XX it said. XX she typed back.

27

The January sun was slowly warming the sluggish surface of the Canal du Midi when George Harvey returned to Frossiac. As before, he arrived without announcing his presence, the only sign of his resumed residence being the car with a Carcassonne number plate parked outside the furthest of the secluded holiday homes by the reed studded lake.

Since the day in December when he had stood looking at the open door of George Harvey's house, Maurice had been busy protecting his back. As Jean-Philippe had instructed, Maurice had made no further use of the computer housed in the tranquil gloom of the canalside wine museum. Maurice had told Guy that there was a virus on the computer and that the nephew of Jean-Philippe would be coming to clean the computer and check for any other problems. In the meantime, Guy was instructed not to access the computer for fear of exacerbating any problems. Fortunately, Guy was not an experienced user of technology and had accepted the explanation with exasperation but without argument.

Jean-Philippe had moved quickly following his receipt of Maurice's telephone call. The first thing he had done was to send his nephew Thierry to the wine museum the following morning, thereby lending credence to Maurice's story. His second action had been to make enquiries of friends and contacts in Carcassonne and the surrounding area to see if George Harvey could be located there.

Thierry, an acne-faced youth with lank brown hair hanging in greasy curtains down to his shoulders, had spent most of the morning tapping on the computer keyboard and scrolling through lists of code which had appeared on the screen. He had brought with him a laptop computer from which he had downloaded various programs and installed them on the wine museum equipment. Eventually, Thierry had pronounced himself satisfied that the computer, and the local area network to which it was connected, were fully functional and clean of viruses. He had quietly told Maurice that he had not been able to find any spyware, or indeed malware of any kind, on the system. And so, the computer could now be used without fear.

Thierry had also left with Maurice a printed list of the transactions which had been carried out by George Harvey whilst using the museum's network and the names of the files which George had accessed. Thierry had told Maurice to let him know if any of these files contained information which might be 'of concern', as Thierry mysteriously put it.

Unfortunately, Thierry's competence as a software technician was no match for that of George Harvey. The piece of software which had been installed on the museum computer by George Harvey, by means of the connection of his laptop to the museum's network, could not have been found by any of the commercially available spyware and malware detection applications available to Thierry. George's resident bug was buried deep and thoroughly disguised, and had therefore remained safely in place, and ready to do its work, after Thierry had gone complacently on his way home.

Maurice had been keen to review the printout as soon as possible. He had told a disinterested Guy that he needed briefly to return home to fetch some documents which he had mistakenly left there. Guy had accepted the information with a shrug and had told Maurice to take his time. Very little was happening in the museum, after all. So, Maurice had hurried along the footpath towards the stone bridge, the printout folded small in his trouser pocket. He had headed for a secluded wooden bench located further along the canal towpath, set around a gracious shallow bend which had hidden him from the view of anyone crossing the bridges in the village. No-one would see him there except perhaps the occasional passing cyclist or walker. And they would not be interested in what he was reading.

The printout, when Maurice had unfolded it and laid it flat on his lap, had consisted of a list of searches apparently made by George Harvey, the addresses of websites which he had accessed, and the names of document files on which he had been working. Maurice had not entirely understood everything he was reading, as the information had been in English, but even he could not miss the one feature which the searches, websites and file designators had in common. It had been the name Susan Stonehouse.

As far as Maurice could work out, George Harvey had been writing and researching his unfinished novel whilst he was sitting in the museum. This did not at first seem to be a problem, as George had made no secret of the fact that he was writing a novel. But, the more Maurice had thought about the information at which he was looking, the more puzzled he became.

The first difficulty had been that George Harvey had definitely said initially that he was a software developer rather than an aspiring author. Maurice had not known how he would be able to tell whether George had been writing software whilst sitting in the museum, but there was certainly no evidence of it on the printout in front of him. The second issue had been that George had been apparently searching the internet for the name Susan Stonehouse. But Maurice had understood that Susan Stonehouse was a fictional character, so there would be no reason to search for her name. Even if the character were based on a real person, that person's name would surely be the subject of the search. But yet, there it had been in black and white on the printout – Susan Stonehouse. Perhaps George had been simply checking that a real Susan Stonehouse did not exist before using her name in his story. But this would surely not require such extensive searching as George had appeared to have carried out.

A third feature which had attracted Maurice's attention was the nature of the websites which had been accessed. They had all appeared to be British news websites, from television companies such as the BBC and Sky News to newspapers including The Times, The Daily Mail and The Sun. Again, the search term Susan Stonehouse had been used to penetrate further into these sites in search of information. And, the final thing of note was that the names of the files on which George Harvey had been working had all included the letters and words 'SS Book Ch' followed by a number, which Maurice had speculated could refer to the chapters of the book in which Susan Stonehouse was a principal character.

Puzzling his way through this information, Maurice had eventually come to two conclusions. The more welcome of these was that George Harvey did not appear to be interested in the wine museum's tax records. The less reassuring one was that a mystery surrounded the story which George Harvey had read to them the previous day. Perhaps it had not been a story after all.

Maurice had remained sitting in his place for some time whilst the sky had slowly drained of colour and the orange sun had slid further along its downward trajectory, flickering its way through the trees on the opposite bank. None of this information explained why George Harvey was carrying a gun, unless – and Maurice had not wanted to think about this – he was somehow connected with the true story of Susan Stonehouse and had needed either to protect himself or, worse, was perhaps hunting someone down. But why was he here, in a tiny village miles from wherever the place was in England that all this had happened? The obvious and innocent explanation was that George Harvey needed peace and quiet in which to write his book, but this was somewhat belied by the presence of the unwelcome weapon.

Maurice had sat up suddenly on the uncomfortable bench. He was not thinking clearly, he had told himself. The simplest solution would be, of course, to do the searches and check the websites for himself.

Maurice had walked briskly back along the towpath towards the museum. Guy had clearly tired of waiting for him and the heavy wooden door was locked when Maurice reached it. Maurice had let himself in and switched on the computer. Sitting on the wooden seat before the screen, he had typed Susan Stonehouse into the search engine.

A list of references had popped up on the screen. They were all in English, as Maurice had expected. He clicked the mouse onto one of them at random and was rewarded by the appearance of a news report from The Sun. The report had been headed TRAGIC SUE IN DEATH LEAP and had continued "Morning commuters at Golders Green Station in North London were left reeling in shock when a grieving widow threw herself onto the line in front of a packed Tube train. The desperate woman was Susan Stonehouse, whose sensational evidence at the Old Bailey saw evil gangster Konstantin Paloka put away for life. Police refused to confirm reports that brave Sue had received rape and death threats from online trolls."

The news item had contained more details, but this introduction had been enough for Maurice, whose command of written English was less secure than his ability to speak it. He had racked his brains to remember other details from George's story, eventually deciding to copy the name Konstantin Paloka from the news article. The articles which he had found after searching on Paloka's name, led him to the names Little Uppingham airfield, Peter Stonehouse, Jerzy Gorecki, Tammy Soper, Jack Dilley and Guy Griffin, names which he had thought he remembered from George's story.

There had been no doubt about it. George Harvey's story had been no fiction. The people and the activities were real.

As Maurice had pondered the significance of his research findings, his mobile phone had rung. Jean-Philippe had been on the other end of the line wanting to know if Thierry's printout had indicated whether George Harvey had been doing anything which might have affected their business arrangements. Maurice had been able to respond truthfully that there was nothing of any concern to Jean-Philippe on the printout.

"He appears to have been doing research for a book he is writing about events which happened in England," Maurice had told Jean-Philippe.

Jean-Philippe had not been interested in the English book and had instead told Maurice that he had consulted various people in Carcassonne and had learned two things. The first was that George Harvey's internet service had been finally reinstated that morning, which accounted for the door of the house being open, whilst the technician was at work there. The second was that George had left Carcassonne airport at about the same time, on a flight bound for Dublin.

"Yes, he said he worked for clients in Ireland," Maurice had told him.

"I think we have no problem, then," had said Jean-Philippe.

"Apart from the gun," Maurice had reminded him.

After ending his conversation with Jean-Philippe, Maurice's phone had rung again almost immediately. This time it had been Claudine, wanting to know why Maurice was not yet at home.

Maurice had wandered back home along the canal bank, wondering what he should tell Claudine about George Harvey and his writings. Claudine had been as yet unaware that George had left Frossiac and certainly had no access to the information provided by Jean-Philippe about George's departure to Dublin from Carcassonne airport. In the end Maurice had decided to say nothing, and to deal with the issue if and when George Harvey returned.

George Harvey eventually made his reappearance in Frossiac known when, several weeks after Maurice's discovery, he walked into the stone floored bar by the picturesque bridge one evening in late January and ordered a beer. Claudine was ecstatic to see him.

"Where have you been, Monsieur?" she exclaimed, "We have been missing you and also thinking about your story."

"I had to leave to attend to some urgent business," George told her, leaning his stick against a nearby table and accepting the tall glass of cold beer.

As George settled onto a wooden stool at the bar, Maurice and Guy opened the door and stepped inside. Their timely arrival was no coincidence, as George had spotted them locking up the door of the wine museum and had ensured his arrival in the bar coincided with theirs.

"Look who is returned!" exclaimed Claudine.

Maurice and Guy stepped forward to shake hands with George Harvey.

"It is good to see you again," Guy told him, "Perhaps we can help you to finish your story now."

Maurice remained silent, unsure what he should say. He was the only person who knew that the apparently fictional story was based on true events.

"I am not so sure now that that is necessary," George replied, "I think that I have managed to make some progress on my own."

"Is that so?" asked Claudine, "Then, I will call for Monique to join us and we can all hear what has now happened to the characters in the story."

"I do not think that we need to ask Monsieur 'Arvai for that information," Maurice spoke up.

"And why not?" asked Guy, "We have heard so much about this story already."

"Because Georges' book is a *roman a clef,*" Maurice stated, quietly, "Which means that the story is true. There is no need for us to invent the information. We will be able to read about it on the internet."

Everyone stared at Maurice.

"How do you know this, Maurice?" Claudine asked, stopped in the act of calling on her mobile phone to summon Monique to the bar.

"I know it," replied Maurice, "Because Thierry, when he came to fix the computer after Georges left us on that day last year in December, showed me the record of the work which Georges has done. The people in his story are real people and the events are true events. You can read about them in the English newspapers."

George Harvey spoke up.

"I can see that your computer expert has found me out," he said, slowly, "But, Claudine, do please call Monique. I need to explain to all of you what I am doing here."

George Harvey's explanation, when it came, appeared straightforward enough.

"Maurice is correct that the story I am telling is a true one," he said, "I knew Peter and Susan Stonehouse personally for many years. Now that they are gone, I am like a father to their daughter, Stevie. The truth of what happened to them needs to be told and not left buried and forgotten in old newspaper reports. Their memory needs to be kept alive."

George picked up his glass and took a swallow of beer before continuing.

"But you have heard for yourselves," he went on, "what happened to Susan when she spoke out against Konstantin Paloka in the courtroom. She received death threats and her life was made into a living hell. Paloka's son vowed to hunt her down and kill her with his own hand. In the end, she could not live in such circumstances, so she took her own life. Paloka himself had always maintained that Peter Stonehouse intended to kill him, and anyone who dares to say otherwise in public will find themselves in the same position as Susan Stonehouse."

George's audience remained silent.

"So," George continued, "I have come here to a small and quiet village a long way away from the events which I am describing in my book. There is no reason why anyone will suspect that a disabled man seeking peace and quiet in which to write a novel is doing anything which may connect him to such dangerous people."

"But, Monsieur," said Monique, who, like the others, was unsure how to react to this explanation, "If you are so concerned that you may be threatened, why should you read the book to us? Why not keep the narrative a secret?"

"That is a good question, Madame," George replied, "But the difficulty for me is that I am not an experienced writer. It was important to me that someone should hear the story for the first time and provide me with a reaction to it. Then I could see whether or not I had told the tale well enough that people would be interested in it and how it might end."

"And the gun, Monsieur?" asked Maurice, eliciting a startled reaction from the two women, who had not been aware of any gun being involved in the emerging mysteries associated with George Harvey.

"Is to protect me in the event that Aleksander Paloka may find me," George stated, baldly.

As the four French villagers struggled to absorb the information George had just given them, George quietly finished his beer and set the glass down on the polished bar top.

The trap in the wine museum computer had been set. Thanks to the interference of Maurice and Thierry a few weeks earlier, it had been primed. And George had returned to Frossiac in anticipation of it being sprung.

The ending of the story was about to write itself.

28

Egzon Paloka rarely went outside nowadays. There was really no point. Everything he needed was here in this windowless room. There was a skylight, but it was rarely opened. It was too difficult for him to reach it now and he didn't want anyone else climbing about the place and disturbing his carefully arranged empire.

Egzon liked to think of his surroundings as his own version of the flight deck of the Starship Enterprise. Not that the consoles in the foetid room travelled anywhere, let alone into outer space, but from his seat on his personalised command centre, Egzon had the whole world at his fingertips. If he had really wanted to look at the stars, there were myriad astronomy programs which he could access to give him an unrestricted view of whatever constellations he wanted to see, with no need for him to bother with cumbersome telescopes or favourable weather or optimum times of the year.

Egzon had already explored the stars through the technology available on his earthbound flight deck and had seen everything he wanted to see. His explorations thereafter remained domestic and he sought entertainment in other ways. Conventional television and movies, pornography, and gambling had all been tried, but he had tired of them. Online games against unseen opponents provided more of a challenge to the active brain which presided over an inert body now covered with ever expanding layers of fat. He often had several of these games in progress at any one time, always aiming to reach the highest levels and to defeat the most skilled of the available opponents. He always won. No-one had more time than Egzon spend on such pursuits.

The trouble with these games, Egzon soon decided, was that they were fantasy. He needed something real against which to pit his technologically sharpened wits. Joining an active community of hackers, phishers and trolls provided him with a source of interest for a while and taught him some new skills, but he was not interested in making money through confidence trickery and blackmail, or in sending nasty abuse to unknown people. Even hacking into banks and businesses and creating havoc became boring after a while.

Egzon had watched with fascination the rise of the dark web and applauded those who manipulated it to achieve their personal ends. Terrorists, child pornographers and depraved paedophile rings, the sellers of illegal drugs and other destructive evils were all able to further their ideologies and ply their trades with relative impunity. Egzon did not want to join in any of these activities. They were not to his personal taste. What fascinated him instead was the battle which he could see was developing between these vile purveyors of evil and the combined forces of world government agencies determined to defeat them. This was a true life battle and one in which Egzon fancied playing a part.

Konstantin Paloka, unlike his younger son, had been highly interested in the opportunities afforded by technology to further his criminal activities. So, like it or not, Egzon had been obliged to work with the dark web to create avenues through the ethernet to pursue his father's evil trade. Creating these avenues had been simple, but the thrill for Egzon had lain in protecting them, preventing their detection by using ever more ingenious security, moving and closing them down when the opponents came too close, and developing destructive virtual weapons with which to fight back.

Konstantin was dead now, despatched by the knife of a fellow prisoner in faraway England. Egzon knew about this, and the events which had led up it, through listening to the constant newsfeed which was streamed to one of the many screens around him. His older brother Aleksander had been with his father at the trial at which he had been convicted, watching proceedings from the public seating which the British authorities kindly provided for anyone wishing to watch their arcane justice system in action, if action was the right word for something so slow and ponderous.

Aleksander had been close to their father, having been groomed since childhood to inherit his parent's works and all that went with them. Aleksander was strong and hard, as vicious and evil as his father. Egzon, by contrast, was introverted and silent, dismissed by his father and older brother as a useless family hanger on until the possibilities offered by the internet had become evident. And then Egzon had become useful. Pale and maggotlike, the pudgy and unappetising Egzon was able to take on global forces that were beyond the reach of Konstantin and Aleksander.

The days after the death of his father had been a frightening time for Egzon. Not that he cared for his father, who had made no secret of his contempt for his weak and blubbery offspring, but Egzon feared what his brother might do now that he was in charge. Egzon was not so naïve as to think that, if the law enforcement authorities in the United Kingdom of Great Britain and Northern Ireland could put his father into prison and get his throat conveniently cut by a mysterious attacker, they would stop there. They would come after Konstantin next and it would not be long before they found Egzon too. The fact that he was in Albania would not protect him.

Aleksander had been half mad with rage when he had returned to Tirana from London following the imprisonment of their father. He had ranted with fury about the police, the lawyers, but above all about the two British people he held responsible for Konstantin's conviction.

"Peter Stonehouse and Susan Stonehouse," he had screamed at Egzon when Egzon had made one of his rare trips away from his flight deck into the living rooms of the extensive walled and guarded estate where the Paloka family resided in the South Eastern suburbs of Tirana, "They have done this to our father. Scum and cowards, like the police."

Egzon knew of these unfortunate people from the news reports. He knew that Peter Stonehouse was in a coma in hospital but that his wife had had the unexpected courage to stand up against their father and what he stood for and had as a result secured his conviction for murder. Just one murder amongst the many for which Konstantin had been responsible, but it was that one which had finally brought him to some semblance of justice.

But it was the murder of their father in the British prison which had sent the simmering Aleksander over the edge. His rage had crystallised into the white hot fury of grief. Not grief for his father, but grief for the fact that he had been thwarted. He was determined on revenge against Susan Stonehouse.

Konstantin vowed that Susan Stonehouse would die and that she would die by his hand. Egzon's practical suggestion that a professional hitman should be hired to do the job was received by his brother with spitting contempt.

"But she will surely be guarded by the British police?" Egzon said, tentatively, "And the British police will also be watching you. They will have you in their sights, Aleksi, now that our father is gone."

"The British police are fools," snapped Aleksander, "They are more interested in rules and writing reports than in doing their real job. The person who is responsible for this is that bitch, Susan Stonehouse. Without her, the police would not have done anything."

"Then how will you kill her?" asked Egzon, interested in spite of himself.

"I will make her suffer, truly suffer," Aleksander ranted, "She will want to be dead, she will beg to be dead. She will want to kill herself. But that cannot happen. That would be too easy for her. I want her to see my face when I kill her."

Egzon waited for his brother to calm down. Once he was calmer, Aleksander's vicious brain would start to work. And so it did.

Aleksander was well aware that he needed to lie low in Tirana for a while. Although he had expressed his contempt for the British police, he was well aware that the UK authorities were not so incompetent, or corrupt, as he would have liked them to be. But that did not mean that he was going to let Susan Stonehouse off the hook. So, he instructed Egzon to start a trolling campaign against her.

"Do everything you can to make her life a living hell," was his directive to Egzon.

For Egzon, this was a simple assignment. He had quickly found his way into Susan Stonehouse's email account and social media pages. Flooding these with vicious messages and pornographic and sadistic images was quickly accomplished. He even set her laptop computer to switch itself on at random times during the night and to emit harrowing shrieks like an animal being slowly murdered. Inventing more and more ingenious ways of tormenting his victim became an interesting creative challenge which kept him amused in between his usual task of ensuring the protection of his brother's online trading empire.

The only drawback, as far as Egzon was concerned, was that he could not see the effect that his activities were having on his victim. He had found many pictures and news items about Susan Stonehouse freely available on the internet and had amused himself by altering and defacing some of these, but since the trial and subsequent death of his father, no more such reports and profiles had appeared. The news media had lost interest in her.

Egzon was well aware that in the UK, there were many CCTV cameras which scanned the public streets to assist the law enforcement authorities in preventing crime and catching offenders. He hacked his way into the Metropolitan Police system with little effort and soon found the images from the area where Susan Stonehouse lived. The grainy images showed her frequently walking from her home in the morning towards an Underground station, a police bodyguard close behind her. But the bodyguard had not been able to prevent the appearance of the image which popped up on Egzon's screen one morning, showing Susan Stonehouse leaping into the path of an oncoming train and disappearing beneath it.

Egzon looked at the image in disbelief. It looked as if his fun with Susan Stonehouse was at an end. Her husband had died from his injuries two days earlier and he had enjoyed sending humorous messages about this event to Susas's iPad, showing an image of Peter's face with a large stake through one eye, and the message FUCK YOU BITCH plastered underneath. Worse, though, would be Aleksander's reaction when he found out. Now he would never get the chance to travel to England to kill Susan Stonehouse himself.

In vain did Egzon point out to his brother that he had in effect killed Susan Stonehouse by hounding her to her untimely death. Aleksander had wanted something much more up close and personal than a sad suicide on a dismal winter morning. But there was nothing more to be done, so Egzon and Aleksander turned back to their old business once again. Aleksander had his hands full ensuring the loyalty of his father's senior henchmen following Konstantin's demise, and Egzon knew that it was in his own interests to help his brother. He had no idea what would happen to him if he lost Aleksander's protection. The same thing which had happened to their long dead mother, probably.

Many months passed, during which Egzon almost forgot about Susan Stonehouse. The little flurry of news following her death had quickly died away and nothing new appeared concerning her anywhere in the internet. Egzon left a few web spies in useful places to alert him to any activity relating to his erstwhile prey, but it had seemed pointless. If she was dead, there was nothing to be gained by vandalising her online presence. She was beyond the reach of anything he could do.

So Egzon remained on his flight deck and resumed his battle with global security services. The distribution of child pornography was a major part of the Paloka web presence, not least because of the opportunities it offered for the blackmail of those who used it, or could be made to appear to have used it, and who might otherwise have stood in the way of such lucrative business activities as people smuggling and cybercrime. The security forces in the UK and elsewhere seemed to have stepped up their war against the distribution of this vile stuff and Egzon needed to work hard to maintain the existence of the channels through which it was distributed.

The rolls of fat around Egzon's neck and abdomen grew still larger and his ability to stir from his disgusting den became so limited that he now needed assistance simply to rise from his reinforced chair. Then in the December following Susan Stonehouse's death, one of his web spies sent him an unexpected message.

The message was garbled. The web spy appeared to have found something of interest somewhere in Europe, but the little piece of software had been blocked and disabled before the message could be formatted into anything which made sense. The name Susan Stonehouse was the only thing that appeared clearly. Egzon worked carefully on the message. It had not come from a conventional source such as a news website, but appeared to have been embedded in some sort of encrypted file.

As Egzon considered what to do with the information, a second web spy reported in, sending him a similar message before it too was destroyed. The second spy seemed to have been a little more successful, however, and Egzon was able to trace the source of the information it had relayed. He was interested to discover that it had come from a police file held by the British security services.

Egzon decided to say nothing to his brother until he could find out more. Calling upon all his knowledge of the systems used by the British intelligence services, he poked and hacked his way towards the sector which had been accessed by the now defunct web spy. His efforts were rewarded when he found his way into a heavily encrypted file which told him that Susan Stonehouse was not dead but alive and living with a new identity under a witness protection scheme. Unfortunately for Egzon, the secret file which he accessed was booby trapped, and vanished irrecoverably immediately he attempted to delve further into its contents.

Egzon debated what to do next. Giving his brother this news would be likely only to bring further pressure onto himself as Aleksander would insist that Egzon move heaven and earth to find out the new identity of Susan Stonehouse and where she was to be found. Egzon was well aware that the triggering of the booby trap on the file would have alerted the British authorities to the fact that someone had found out about Susan Stonehouse's continuing existence. If Aleksander were to return immediately to England to seek her out, the British authorities would take action to protect her, probably changing her location and her identity yet again. And this time, aware that someone was looking for her, they would take more care to protect their information from hackers such as Egzon.

Egzon decided to wait. For a few weeks, nothing more happened, and he began to think that the trail had gone cold. Then another of his spies started to sing and this time there was no encryption or garbling of the messages it sent back. Someone somewhere in the South of France was accessing newspaper reports not only about Susan Stonehouse but about everything connected with the episode which had led to the death of Konstantin Paloka.

Although the information was comprehensive, it was not particularly helpful. Egzon was, for some reason he could not understand, unable to get an immediate fix on the location of the computer from which the information had been accessed. Every time he got near to pinning it down, the connection to the site appeared to drop out. Egzon could not decide whether this was being done deliberately by a firewall or whether the local broadband service itself was so unreliable that it was unable to support anything other than the most minimal traffic. He experimented with trying to access the information at different times of the day, and eventually succeeded in locating the source of the information to a node in Carcassonne.

Egzon had never heard of Carcassonne, and had to take some time out from his hacking activities to research it, in the hope that a connection with Susan Stonehouse might suggest itself. He discovered, somewhat to his mystification, that it was a medieval town in the Aude department in the Region of Languedoc Roussillon in the South of France. It was located, he learned, in the Aude plain between the Atlantic Ocean and the Mediterranean sea and to the North of the Pyrénées. He viewed attractive pictures of the Cité de Carcassonne, a medieval fortress apparently included on the UNESCO list of World Heritage Sites. The town's main business appeared to be tourism and wine-making. Amongst other things, Egzon learned that it was situated on the Canal du Midi, an amazing feat of seventeenth century French engineering which enabled the transport of goods directly between the two bodies of water without the need for a lengthy journey around the Iberian peninsula. No longer used for trade, it was a major tourist destination, attracting visitors from all over the world, visitors who wanted to spend a leisurely time travelling slowly up and down the 240 kilometres of picturesque waterways, either on small boats or by cycling along the towpaths once used by the heavy horses which formerly drew the laden cargo barges. And all along the canal were hotels, restaurants, wineries and other businesses which kept the local citizens in a lucrative livelihood servicing the needs of the visitors.

Egzon thought the place sounded rather attractive. Its rural location certainly suggested why the broadband service might be so unreliable. But it was unclear why anyone in that area should be accessing old news reports about events in distant England over ten months earlier. Was Susan Stonehouse located there with her new identity? But why would she risk revealing her presence in such a clumsy and easily detectable way? Certainly someone was taking an interest in her story, or perhaps in one of the other characters associated with the events concerned. The web searching activity continued quite persistently over a period of two or three days in December and then abruptly ceased.

Having made further efforts to pinpoint the computer network which had used the services of the Carcassonne node, Egzon decided to wait a little longer before reporting back to Aleksander. For all he knew, this activity could have no connection with Susan Stonehouse's new identity and location. It could be someone simply researching the reports of the case, a journalist perhaps, although it was hard to see what could have prompted someone in such an unlikely location to do so.

As before, several weeks passed by with no further activity from the remote site. Egzon began to think that the trail had been false and that conducting another search though the British security services files might prove more rewarding. And then, one day in late January, the web spy, which he had installed to watch the Carcassonne node, woke up and told him that a computer in a little village called Frossiac was indicating that Susan Stonehouse's story was being accessed once again. This time, the local firewall did not appear to have detected the spyware, and the connection did not drop out. Egzon had no difficulty hacking into the computer concerned, which seemed to be full of records of the contents of a wine cellar and the associated sales made by the owners. The business appeared to be a wine museum and sales outlet owned by a man named Maurice Vacher.

Egzon could not fathom at all why a French wineseller should be interested in the story of Susan Stonehouse. But he knew that the time had come to tell Aleksander of his discoveries. Someone would need to visit Frossiac to find out just what was going on there.

29

Claudine Vacher was surprised to see the smartly dressed young man crossing the little stone bridge and moving purposefully towards her still half-shuttered bar. She felt a passing shiver of apprehension. The man had an official look about him, as though he were an inspector of some kind, maybe a health inspector, come to check that hygiene regulations were being followed at her establishment. No-one else would come to Frossiac wearing a sharp city suit.

"Good morning, Monsieur!" she greeted the visitor brightly, as he walked in his well polished black leather lace up shoes towards the cluttered counter on which she had been stacking newly washed glasses ready to arrange on the mirrored backed shelves behind her. It was as yet too early for lunch and the bar was deserted.

Now that she could see him more closely, Claudine revised her opinion of his possible status. Notwithstanding the expensive suit, the young man looked sleazy, black hair slicked back from a narrow forehead, dark and hooded eyes glancing carefully around the room. But he spoke politely enough.

"Good morning, Madame," he greeted her, a slight North African edge to his voice, "I wonder if you could assist me? I am looking for a wine museum operated by a Monsieur Vacher. My business colleague has recommended it to me."

Claudine was not expecting a request for directions, but could see no reason not to give them. But, as the young man turned and left the bar with a brief word of thanks, she sent a quick text message to Maurice, whom she knew to be alone at the museum that day whilst Guy was out visiting suppliers.

Un client est arrive. Un vrai chevalier d'industrie!

Meanwhile, the man unflatteringly described as a spiv, had taken the path on the Minervois side of the canal and soon approached the blue railed footbridge opposite the museum.

Youssef was somewhat bemused by the assignment he had been given. Normally resident in Toulouse, he was a small time drug dealer and pimp, propping up a remote corner of the Paloka empire. The call from his boss in Bordeaux had come to him late the previous evening. The instructions were strange. He was to go to a small wine sales outlet in a remote village in the Aude, a village so small that he had had to look up on an online map, and ask some questions of the owner. The questions were not the sort of questions Youssef usually asked. These questions were to be polite and discreet, not reinforced by any threat of violence or retribution. Maurice Vacher, the person being questioned was, on the whole, a respectable businessman, although Youssef had been informed that he was running a tax scam, knowledge of which could be used to pressurise him gently should he prove difficult to deal with. But the objective of the exercise was simply to ask the questions courteously and then report the answers back to headquarters. And, incidentally, Youssef needed to look like a respectable person, possibly the owner of a restaurant which needed good Aude wines on its *carte*.

The footbridge, once Youssef had climbed the slatted steps, gave him the best view of the approach to the target premises. Youssef never approached any premises without first checking the means of escape, preferably identifying more than one route, and ensuring that no-one else was observing what he was doing. Concealed in the small of his back, beneath the tailored grey jacket was a small handgun. His instructions had been to go unarmed to the museum. But Youssef felt exposed without his gun, so took it anyway.

Youssef could see that the stone arched wooden door to the museum was open. A soft wind ruffled the waters of the canal beneath the bridge, small gleams of sunlight glancing off the shallow ripples. As he had walked along the path alongside the canal, he had noticed houses over to his right, behind a still and empty pool. A few waterbirds had been nosing around in the reeds, chattering quietly to one another. A cluster of small boats had been tugging dispiritedly against their moorings nearby.

The quiet and emptiness of the whole scene was something unfamiliar to Youssef. He resolved to go quickly into the wine outlet and ask his questions promptly. The silence of the little place, coupled with his unfamiliar form of dress, was beginning to make him uncomfortable.

Youssef descended the wooden steps of the bridge, attempting to affect a businesslike appearance. He crossed the threshold of the wine museum and found himself plunged into an unexpected gloom. Although it was far from bright outside, the contrast between the cellar-like environment and the clear view from the bridge made him blink several times, before he spied a man standing by a counter towards the back of the museum.

"Good morning, Monsieur," the man greeted Youssef, as Youssef struggled to make out his features. He looked stocky and dark haired, but otherwise friendly and unsuspicious of his visitor.

"Monsieur Vacher?" asked Youssef, walking forward.

"Yes, I am Maurice Vacher," replied the other man, "Have we met before?"

Youssef searched through his carefully prepared lines.

"I regret, no, Monsieur," he replied, "But you and your wines have been recommended most highly to me by a business colleague."

"This is very good news," exclaimed the other man, "And may I know to whom I am speaking?"

Youssef, fortunately, had been prepared for this question. He produced one of a number of cards which he carried with him which described him as Hamza Mehdi, the proprietor of a Moroccan themed restaurant in Toulouse.

"Monsieur Mehdi," said Maurice, warmly, "How may I be of assistance?"

"Your wines have been recommended to me most highly," Youssef continued, "I should like to discuss whether we may consider doing business together."

"But of course," replied Maurice, "And who is it who has been so kind as to recommend my wines to you?"

"She is an English lady," replied Youssef, "Her name is Suzanne Ston'ouse."

He stumbled over the unfamiliar name, but, as he had been told, watched the other man narrowly to see how he reacted.

Maurice Vacher seemed surprised to hear the name.

"Suzanne Ston'ouse?" he said, copying Youssef's pronunciation, "Are you able to tell me how that is written?"

Youssef was prepared for this question too. He handed Maurice a small card on which he had written the name.

"She is also one of the best customers of my restaurant," Youssef explained, helpfully.

Maurice looked thoughtfully at the card.

"We have a number of English customers here," he said, slowly, "But I cannot remember a lady with this name. But it is possible that my brother may have taken the order. I regret that he is not here today."

Youssef was not quite sure how to respond to this comment. But, before he could say anything else, Maurice made a suggestion.

"One moment," he said, "I will look into our computer system and see whether I can find her name amongst the list of our regular customers."

Maurice moved towards a computer screen which was standing at the end of the counter.

"Please," he said, "May I see the name again so that I can be sure to spell it correctly?"

Youssef handed him the card and Maurice typed in the name. During a pause whilst Maurice scrolled through a list of names, Youssef heard someone enter the museum behind him. Turning round, he saw tall man standing in the doorway and leaning heavily on a walking stick. The light was behind the newly arrived visitor and Youssef could see nothing of his features.

Maurice looked up from the computer.

"Please be seated, Monsieur 'Arvai," he called to the newcomer, "I will be with you shortly."

The tall man acknowledged Maurice with a wave of his free hand and sat down on a low wooden chair near the museum entrance.

Maurice turned his attention once again to the computer. After a few seconds, he spoke again to Youssef.

"Monsieur Mehdi," he said, "I am sorry but I can find no record of any customer of this name. Perhaps she is known by the name of her business instead?"

Youssef had no idea whether this was an avenue which he should explore, but even if it were, he had no idea how to take matters further. The only name he had been given had been that of Suzanne Ston'ouse. An uneasy feeling was beginning to prick at the back of his neck, warning him that he risked becoming trapped between the helpful owner of the cavern-like wine premises and the big man who was now sitting close to the door.

Youssef's urgent objective now was to extricate himself from his discussion with Maurice as quickly as possible and to report back to his boss that there had been no information to be obtained from the proprietor of the Frossiac wine museum.

"That is unfortunate, Monsieur," he said, "Perhaps I may have come to the wrong premises in error."

"But nevertheless, Monsieur," responded Maurice, "Maybe it is possible for us still to do business together."

"I regret that will not be possible," replied Youssef hurriedly, "I have been instructed to deal only with the business recommended by Madame Ston'ouse."

"How unfortunate," replied Maurice, "But could I persuade you nevertheless to sample some of our stock? Perhaps Monsieur 'Arvai would care to join us?"

Marurice signalled towards George, who rose from his chair by the door at the invitation.

"I regret, but no," insisted Youssef, "I must consult with my superior about this problem before proceeding with any discussion."

"That is a pity," said Maurice, "Perhaps you could let me know if I could be of service in the future. I will keep your business card in case you should change your mind."

After that, things moved surprisingly quickly. Youssef stepped, with relief, towards the door of the museum. Walking into the relative brightness of the outdoor world, he did not see George's stick outstretched across his path until he had fallen over it. He did, however, see at close range the stone flagged floor of the wine museum, whilst at the same time feeling Marcel Lambert's knee in the middle of his back followed by Marcel Lambert's hand removing his gun from beneath his jacket. And then he heard the sounds of the three police officers who suddenly stood above his head with their semi-automatic weapons.

Maurice Vacher had never been in the museum at all. Maurice had been suddenly and immediately summoned with papers delivered by no less a person than Marcel Lambert, the local police chief, to attend the office of the local tax inspector. And, as Guy was absent,

Marcel Lambert had kindly and conveniently agreed to wait in the museum during Marurice's enforced absence.

George Harvey retrieved his stick as the four police officers hauled Youssef to his feet. George looked towards the computer on the counter. As he expected, the screen had gone dark but the flashing light on the box below showed that the processor was working furiously.

The little viral warrior which had been planted by George several weeks earlier was now launched on the second phase of its mission. Locating the path which Egzon had used to access its host, the aggressive virus started its journey back towards the Carcassonne node. The firewall of the Carcassonne node recognised the malign presence and stopped its onslaught for the two seconds which it took the worm to burrow its way through a conveniently created hole and to explode the equivalent of a small bomb in the wall's innards. The Carcassonne node went down, creating chaos in homes and businesses around the local district. But the vicious virtual attacker was now on its way to Tirana, faithfully retracing the steps taken by Egzon some forty eight hours earlier, and so made its relentless final approach to Egzon's flight deck where it destroyed everything in its way before blowing itself up in a final blaze of online glory.

Egzon's ghastly and heartstopping scream of rage was heard throughout the many floors and salons of the Paloka residence. Guards with dogs came running to his basement room, guns at the ready, but they found no-one there except Egzon. Egzon was slumped backwards in his huge chair, his jaw slack, one side of his face collapsed, saliva drooling from his blubbery lips. His blue eyes were wide open and staring.

The flight deck screens were dark, except for one. That screen was lit with a lurid red light.

FUCK YOU EGZON it said.

30

Isabella Hall lay on her back on the well-sprung double bed in the main guest room of The Charlton Arms. The room had been recently redecorated and furnished to reflect the well-touted and commercially exploited heritage of the establishment as a coaching inn. Two Georgian sash windows, draped with red and gold leaf patterned curtains, looked out on to the nearby crossroads at which cars queued from four directions to negotiate the circular traffic island topped with a medieval cross which stood in the centre.

Seated in a comfortable armchair by one of the windows was Frank Stanley. He bore little resemblance to the formally dressed figure who had appeared unannounced at Sampfield Grange almost four months earlier. Today he was reprising the unlikely role of cycling coach and suspected secret lover to Isabella Hall, and so had dressed in a grey sweatshirt, tracksuit bottoms and branded trainers. His dark hair with its grey streaks had been styled with hair gel, which Isabella privately thought was an improvement. His bright blue eyes were looking at her now.

Isabella was still wearing the green and white cycling gear in which she had arrived at the hotel half an hour earlier. Her white and silver helmet lay on a table by the bed, her black cycling shoes arranged neatly on the floor beneath the tables.

They were waiting for a message. Until it came, they had to fill the time.

"Subject to the confirmation which we are expecting, I think this is the last time we need to meet face to face," Frank was saying.

"Face to face, that's a bit of a joke," commented Isabella, rubbing her fingers behind her ears, where the scars had faded into white lines which no longer needed to be so carefully disguised by her odd hairstyle.

"Still painful, is it?" asked Frank.

"No, not any more," Isabella replied, "My face just feels a bit stiff, that's all. I can't smile like I could, even if I wanted to. But I suppose the poker face has come in handy in keeping the people at Sampfield Grange off my back. They just think I am a stuck up cow."

"You're still confident none of them suspect anything?" asked Frank, not for the first time.

"No, I'm not completely confident," replied Isabella, "But, to go through the usual list, Lewis and Kelly are solely focused on ensuring that the household is run on their terms, so their main concern has been checking that I am not a threat to their personal powerbase. I did cause them some annoyance by getting rid of that slimy accountant, but I really could not stand by and see Mr Sampfield being made a fool of like that. I realise that he is very rich, but that's not the point."

"Ripping old Sam off, are they?" Frank asked, sounding amused.

"Well, not seriously," conceded Isabella, "But he really doesn't see what is going on around him. It's not just the dyslexia which you told me about. He just seems so .. so.. well, not exactly introverted, but as though he is just living for himself, working within small horizons, sort of … solitary, really, as if the rest of the world doesn't affect him."

Frank remained silent.

"Lady Helen Garratt, his friend, she's tried to galvanise him into doing something, you know," Isabella went on, taking advantage of Frank's silence, "She came to the Grange three weeks ago, to talk to him about some charity she wanted to start and to ask for his help with it. She asked me to come in and take notes of the formal part of their discussion, because she knew Mr Sampfield wouldn't write anything down. She had some wonderful ideas about retraining retired racehorses and setting up a school for young stable staff brought in from inner city areas. He said at once that he'd finance it, but that isn't what she wanted. She wanted him to take charge of it, share his expertise, help the young people to plan careers for themselves."

"And what did Sam say about it?" asked Frank, interested, in spite of himself, in the information Isabella had recounted.

"He said he'd think about it and let her know after Cheltenham," replied Isabella, "I can see his point. He's quite worried about the responsibility of Tabikat. And he's still bothered about the reason for the owner's decision to send Tabikat to Sampfield Grange, as if it is some kind of trap or set up aimed at him. Fortunately, he hasn't seen the silks yet. I've put them away in the flat."

"And what about the other staff?" Frank asked, returning to the purpose of their discussion.

"Well, Sadie, the yard manager, is absolutely besotted with Mr Magic Merlin ap Rhys," Isabella told him, "It's put Kye's nose right out of joint, as she was keeping his bed warm until then, but that's all stopped now that Merlin is around. Which has been a bit of a problem for me, by the way, as I have had to keep myself out of Merlin's sight. I thought he might have seen me at Cheltenham when Brendan asked him to ride Tabikat in the Hennessy. If he did, he probably just thought I was one of Brendan's owners, but I couldn't risk him seeing me at Sampfield Grange. Stevie said he didn't recognise her on New Year's Day, but he did go past in a hurry. Sadie, though, she wouldn't notice anything that wasn't two inches in front of her face. After Merlin, it's the horses and her family, nothing else."

"Lizzie mentioned a problem with Kye McMahon," Frank prompted her, shifting in the armchair, as the sunlight broke through the clouds and shone into his eyes, "Have we sized him up now?"

"I don't really know how much of a problem he is," Isabella replied, "As you know, I told Lizzie that he's got a business going with the chap from the local garage, selling weed and stuff out of the back of the horsebox. That doesn't really matter to me, except that it makes him jumpy. He's pretty bright and streetwise, so he's probably seen more about me to make him suspicious than the others have. I know for sure that he was watching me texting out one day when things weren't going so well and I got a bit weepy. The others just think that I'm sending you *billets doux,* but I am not sure that Kye has fallen for the story about our relationship. Lizzie will have told you that Kye and his mate were tracking me with a drone and they did follow me to the airfield that day. I don't think Kye has the remotest idea of anything that's really going on, but he does seem to think that I'm on his case, and that could cause us a problem, I suppose?"

Isabella had finished her analysis of Kye with a question, but, before Frank could comment, she went on, animatedly.

"That's what's such a shame about that whole set up at Sampfield Grange. Your Mr Sampfield, good old Squire Sam, treats them all like family retainers. He thinks that providing them with roof over their head and paying them pittance wages is enough. He doesn't seem to see them a real people or want to invest in them as individuals with a future in the industry he claims to love so much. Sadie is a talented horsewoman and yet there she is, stuck in little backwater with no prospects. I overheard some comments from Merlin about how lucky Mr Sampfield was to have Sadie and Kye, and I thought that may have shaken him up a bit, but he's forgotten it all already. He'd chase Kye off the premises if he knew Kye was drug dealing, but Kye needs someone to look up to and give him some ambition and then he wouldn't need to do anything like that. Mr Sampfield shouldn't be waiting for Kye to ask him about being a jockey. Mr Sampfield should suggest it himself and pay for the training. And he should let Sadie have some experience at a bigger yard for a while."

"You're really taking an interest in these people, aren't you?" said Frank, surprised, "It's not necessary, you know. In fact, it would be better if you didn't. You won't ever have to see them again in a few weeks' time."

Isabella laughed, half-heartedly.

"And they won't ever have to see me again, either," she said, "Especially not if I'm dead."

"Look," said Frank, "I know this is difficult and frightening. But we've just done the equivalent of crossing the Rubicon and we can't go back now."

"Thank God for public schoolboys!" said Isabella, an edge of hysteria creeping into her voice, "Always some conquering hero you can pull out of classical history to act as an exemplar to stir the troops into action. Who am I then? Caesar's wife? Beyond reproach whilst everyone else can behave as badly as they want?"

Isabella swung her legs angrily off the bed and disappeared into the bathroom, slamming the door behind her.

Frank Stanley looked towards the door, slightly concerned. He was well aware of the stress she was under but he couldn't have her going flaky on him now. If only George would text in. But both his and Isabella's phones had remained stubbornly silent.

Frank took advantage of the pause in the conversation to pick up the bedside phone and order tea to be sent up. Whilst he waited, he pondered whether he need take any action in relation to Kye McMahon.

Following Lizzie Baker's report, he had had Kye's background investigated. The connection with the Liverpool HGV smuggling racket was tenuous and Kye seemed to have got himself out of the emerging situation before becoming personally implicated in anything. The yard where he had worked remembered him as a good worker and a potential talent as a jockey, which seemed to bear out what Isabella had told him.

Frank had requested that an officer be assigned at Cheltenham racecourse on New Year's Day to keep an eye on Kye. The officer had been one of those on regular plainclothes duty at the course, and had reported back that a woman had been openly watching Kye. Some kind of confrontation had happened between Kye and his observer, which had resulted in Kye shutting up shop for the day. The officer did not recognise the woman, whom he described as "hard faced and not a local", but, he said, she certainly seemed to have put the wind up Kye. A similar watch had been kept on Kye at Taunton races a week ago, but the woman had not reappeared at that venue although Kye's sales activities seemed to have been suspended, perhaps for fear that she might turn up.

Gray's drone had been temporarily grounded by a mysterious fault which had developed with its tracking system. Gray had been in angry dispute with the manufacturer for most of January.

A knock on the door interrupted Frank's train of thought. Hastily he rumpled up the hitherto undisturbed bedclothes and opened the door to admit a young woman carrying a tray on which a teapot and china were set out. Her eyes were as wide as saucers as she entered the room, noting everything she could about the scene, ready for reporting back to her fellow workers downstairs.

Frank was not sure whether Isabella had heard the arrival of the waitress from her position in the bathroom. He did not want her to come back into the room unprepared for someone else to be present. Remembering his intentionally unconvincing role as Isabella's pushy cycling coach, he called out to her in a firm and authoritarian tone.

"Isabella! Come out now. I've ordered a legal high you can take even for racing. It'll show all clear on any drugs tests."

The waitress quickly put the tray down on a small circular table by the window and made her escape, ears burning.

Frank wished that making Isabella feel better was as simple as giving her a cup of tea. He had considered asking for some whisky to go with the tea, but it would hardly have fitted his assumed role, and both he and Isabella needed to keep a clear head. Maybe the earlier reference to the Rubicon was over dramatic and cliché'd, but their plans had certainly reached a point of no return.

And then, just as Isabella emerged reluctantly from the bathroom, both his phone and hers emitted simultaneous pings. The text messages were identical and appeared to be from an unknown number. They both said XXX.

"George has done it," said Isabella in a scared whisper. Clutching the phone, she texted XXX in reply.

But Frank had also received a second message from another source. The tea forgotten, he stared at the little screen unable immediately to decide what this additional piece of information might mean for their plans.

"What is it Frank?" asked Isabella, "Has something gone wrong?"

"Far from it," said Frank, "Egzon is dead. Sounds like a stroke or a heart attack."

Isabella looked at him, her fear showing, inasmuch as was possible, on her immobile features.

"Oh…" she gasped, and sat down suddenly in the chair by the window.

"I think we can expect Aleksander over here soon," said Frank, businesslike once again, "It won't take him long to make the connection with Susan Stonehouse."

Isabella nodded, saying nothing.

"You need to get back to Sampfield Grange," Frank went on, "Everything is working out exactly as we wanted. Just keep it together and it will go to plan, you'll see."

Isabella drew a deep breath and reached for the cycle shoes and helmet.

"And don't worry about Kye and the others," Frank told her, "I'm keeping an eye on the situation."

"And Mr Sampfield?" asked Isabella, "Are you keeping an eye on him?"

"What do you mean?" asked Frank, sharply.

"He's a man not used to being faced with a challenge," Isabella told him, "You're just relying on him to do the right thing. I know that he's an old friend of yours and you know him better then I do, but I still think there's a risk that he could just down tools and ask the owners to move Tabikat to another trainer. You need to keep him onside."

Frank wrinkled his forehead, wondering what she might have guessed, but she was walking towards the door.

"See you at Cheltenham in March," she said, simply, and slipped out onto the landing.

Isabella ran down the stairs, right into the path of Graham Colvin.

Gray was coming into the hotel to pick up a set of keys for a van which he was due to service. He and Isabella passed so close to each other in the narrow lobby that it was impossible for Isabella to get past him unseen.

"Good afternoon, Mr Colvin," Isabella said politely, moving towards the door as quickly as she could.

Gray was too surprised to say anything, and remained standing at the reception desk staring after her departing back. Then he turned round, just in time to see Frank Stanley coming down the stairs.

So this is Mrs Hall's fancy man, he thought.

31

Sam had had a disappointing afternoon at the late January Cuffborough Point to Point meeting. Gilbert had ridden Highlander Park into second place in a slightly stiffer contest than that of some three months earlier. This time, only Sadie had been standing on the muddy bank to watch Gilbert and Highlander streak over the finishing line, beaten by less than half a length by a smart up and coming grey ridden by Ranulph Dicks' tough looking daughter Amelia. Sam himself had watched proceedings from a seat next to the overworked judge in his already cramped box.

Kye had excused himself from the spectators' earth bank, saying that there was a mechanical problem with the horsebox which required his attention before they set off home. Sam had felt mildly exasperated to hear this news, wondering aloud whether it was time to replace the vehicle, and Sadie had asked pointedly what they were paying Graham Colvin to do. Kye had assured them both that he was just being cautious. But both Sam and Sadie were separately forming the impression that Kye was really not interested in Highlander's racing career.

Gilbert Peveril had been disappointed with Highlander's second place, but, generously, could not fault the horse's performance.

"Bit of rotten luck running into that Dicks horse here today," he had told Sam, as they had made their way back towards the crowded little parade ring, Gilbert still on Highlander Park's back.

Sadie had been leading the sweating horse, who truly had, as Gilbert put it, worked his white socks off during the race. The said white socks had now been spattered with claggy mud. Sadie had been telling Highlander that she would soon wash the mud off and have him looking all bright and clean again. But Highlander had had his nose down towards the ground and looked as if he didn't care.

"That woman of yours not here today, then?" had asked Gilbert, as he had swung himself from Highlander's back and down to the ground. The horse had given a weary snort as Gilbert patted his neck.

"Woman?" had asked Sam, not sure what Gilbert meant.

"You know, the one I saw at Cheltenham, Mrs Holt or something," Gilbert had continued.

"Oh, you mean Isabella Hall," Sam had reminded him, "My office manager."

"You ever get to the bottom of all that?" Gilbert had asked, as they walked together towards the weighing in area, "You got Pips' pictures all right, I suppose?"

"I did, thank you," Sam had replied, unwilling to involve Gilbert in the results of his attempts to resolve the mystery, "But they weren't really clear enough to be certain."

"That Irish chappie, though," had persisted Gilbert, "I think he's the one who used to train that Gold Cup horse you've taken on. Monaghan, or some such name, isn't it? He must have upset the owners, don't you think?"

"I couldn't say, Gil," Sam had responded, wishing Gilbert would shut up. He had been touching on a sore spot.

Why the horse had been sent to Sampfield Grange was a question that Sam still couldn't answer. Ranulph Dicks had also asked the same question when Sadie and Claire O'Dowd had boxed the horse over to Ranulph's yard, ready to work out with some of Ranulph's prospective Festival runners. Sam had floundered in his attempts to explain the owners' decision, eventually saying that he assumed that they wanted a UK mainland base for the horse.

"Still," had said Ranulph, for whom tact was not a strong point, "A horse of that ability, they could have sent him to a top yard anywhere in the country. Not short of money are they?"

"I think that is unlikely," Sam had said, shortly, "They're a bank."

"Oh well, count your lucky stars, Sam," Ranulph had said, dismissively, "I have to say he is a real picture of a horse. Saw him jump like a stag at Leopardstown. Went well on that heavy ground, too, no problem. Who bred him?"

"Eugene Foley in Gleannglas," Sam had told him, "He's by Tabloid News."

Ranulph's eyebrows had shot up.

"Is he now?" he had said, "Mallows Stud, then? But I don't know the breeder."

Sam had been spared a continuation of this unhelpful discussion by being told that the Dicks' ride was ready to leave. There had been fifteen horses in the string. Claire was still acting as Tabikat's work rider, whilst Sadie had been assigned to a horse from the Dicks' yard.

"Good girl, that head lass of yours," Ranulph had commented, as they had watched the line of horses clatter out of the yard into the neighbouring lane, where water from a recent cloudburst was running freely along the little gullies by the clogged verges. "Amelia knows her of old. Happy to have her over here if she wants a bit more experience than your place can give her."

"Well, she'll be needed to ride work on Tabikat once the Irish girl goes home," Sam had reminded him, "Claire's going back from Cheltenham with Brendan's team after Festival Trials day."

"So we'll be seeing lots more of Sadie and Tabikat here, then," Ranulph had said cheerfully, motioning Sam towards a mud covered Japanese 4WD, already occupied by a small and grubby terrier, in preparation for the ride up onto the Dicks' gallops. "Great responsibility for the girl," Ranulph had added, starting the engine.

And for me too, had thought Sam, as the vehicle had jolted along a farm track which led up to the gallops, the little terrier standing on his lap to look out of the front windscreen.

Kye had not been asked to accompany Sadie to the Dicks' yard that day and had been left to oversee the feeds and the work riders mucking out from the first lot. Isabella had been in the office, looking at that silly racing tipster kitten on the computer, as usual, so he had had plenty of time to turn things over in his increasingly unsettled mind.

Kye had described to Gray the unwelcome experience of being warned off by the woman in the car park at Cheltenham racecourse. Having reviewed their plans for the forthcoming race meeting at Taunton, at which Curlew Landings was due to run, they had decided not to try to do any business at Taunton. They had agreed that Kye should wait to see whether the aggressive woman reappeared. Although Kye had put off his customers on New Year's day by suggesting that the watcher was from the police, he was pretty sure that she was another player, and that this at least would tell them whether her, or her boss's, territory extended to Taunton racecourse. They could then decide whether to go ahead with further trading at Cuffborough point to point course, when Highlander ran there later in the month. It had seemed like a good plan in the circumstances.

Taunton races had passed without incident, at least as far as Kye was concerned. There had been no sign of the woman, nor any evidence that anyone else was dealing drugs in the vicinity. Kye had as a consequence been able to watch Curlew Landings' race and had been able once again to pay attention to the doings of Mr Sampfield, Sadie and Merlin ap Rhys. And he had not been happy with what he had seen.

Mr Sampfield had seemed on edge all day at Taunton. Kye had already seen that his boss had been distracted ever since they had brought Tabikat back to Sampfield Grange at the beginning of the month. Kye, in common with everyone else, had been greatly impressed by the beautiful chaser which had been entrusted to their care. Claire O'Dowd, he could see, was dreading the day she had to leave the horse behind, whilst Sadie could not wait for her chance to take over the work on him. By the time of the Taunton race meeting, Claire and Sadie had started to share the work riding, and the two of them had seemed to have reached an uneasy truce over Tabikat's care. Merlin ap Rhys had told Sam that he would be available and willing to ride Tabikat in the Gold Cup and had made it his business to attend Sampfield Grange whenever practical on the pretext of riding the horse.

Kye did not have to be a genius to understand Merlin's other motivation for coming to Sampfield Grange. Although Merlin himself was businesslike and circumspect around Sadie in public, Sadie was unable to conceal her open adoration of Merlin, so the development of the relationship between them was obvious to everyone, even, Kye noticed, to Mr Sampfield, who was determinedly trying to ignore it.

Kye was not sure how he felt about what had happened between Sadie and Merlin. Sadie had been a means to a selfish end for him. She had secured him his comfortable billet at Sampfield Grange. He had enjoyed getting her into his bed, but neither of them had been under any illusion that the sex they had together was opportunistic rather than indicative of anything serious between them. Kye had been hardly in a position to object when Sadie had deserted his room and moved into the spare bunk overhead Claire O'Dowd. Kye had made no comment about the change and neither had Sadie. Even so, he felt a surge of annoyance whenever Merlin's black sports car turned up at the yard.

Kye's curiosity had also been piqued by Mr Sampfield's behaviour. Kye could see that Mr Sampfield thought that he was out of his depth with the new horse. Kye privately thought that Tabikat could not have done better than to be sent to a trainer like Mr Sampfield, who, for all his stuffiness with people, was an excellent judge of horses and would move heaven and earth to ensure that those under his roof received the best care and training. Kye thought that it had taken some guts on Mr Sampfield's part to seek Mr Dicks's input to the training programme, something which other trainers might have seen as a sign of weakness.

In one respect, though, Kye thought that Mr Sampfield had made a mistake. And that had been to run Curlew Landings at Taunton that day. It was as if Mr Sampfield had lost confidence in Curlew. Curlew's quite reasonable performance at Cheltenham needed to be improved upon, not taken as a setback. But Mr Sampfield had seemed to Kye to be in danger of taking the horse backwards by presenting him with such a very much easier challenge in the Taunton race. The Taunton track was relatively flat with sharp turns at either end and was generally very much less threatening than the undulating and tough galloping track at Cheltenham. Also, the opposition Curlew would face would not be of the same standard as the horses which Curlew had met in his previous race. After all, he had come third at Cheltenham after leading most of the way, which was no disgrace, and the two horses which had passed him on the final run up the hill were trained by top trainers and had excellent pedigrees.

Kye knew that Merlin and Sadie also agreed with his view, because he had heard them discussing it when Merlin had been at Sampfield Grange a few days before the Taunton meeting.

"I don' understand Mr Sampfield at all," Merlin had said, "I'm 'appy to ride the 'orse, of course I am, but e's capable of more."

"I know that," Sadie had replied, "But I can't tell Mr Sampfield what to do."

"I don' see why not," Merlin had contradicted her, "You're not 'is servant, whatever 'e may think. You're a good 'orsewoman, you are, Sadie, and 'e should be lis'nin' to you."

At Taunton races, as Curlew Landings had been led around the paddock by Sadie, Kye had been able to see Mr Sampfield in the centre of the elongated grass area. Mr Sampfield had been in conversation with Merlin, who had shaken his head at something Mr Sampfield had said. Sadie had been looking anxiously across at them. Kye had wondered if Merlin was tackling Mr Sampfield about his decision to run Curlew here, in which case, had thought Kye, this was probably not the best moment to do it.

Merlin had picked up two other rides at the Taunton meeting, so had had plenty to occupy him, but Curlew had been clearly his best ride of the day. Merlin had proved his point by bringing Curlew home to a comfortable victory during which the horse had scarcely been off the bridle. In one respect, though, Kye thought that Mr Sampfield's decision to run the horse at Taunton had been proved right. Curlew had been much brighter after the race than he had been after his run at Cheltenham, and Kye realised that tactics designed to restore Curlew's confidence might have been beneficial. But they didn't solve the problem of getting Curlew up the Cheltenham hill.

Now Kye was sitting in the horsebox, days after the Taunton meeting, at the Cuffborough point to point course. Kye's business was done for the day, the absence of the Cheltenham woman from the race meeting at Taunton having emboldened Kye and Gray into a resumption of their usual trade. It was getting dark by the time Sadie had got Highlander Park settled in the box and swung herself up into the passenger seat.

"Guess what, Kye?" she said as she shut the heavy door, "Mr Sampfield's entered Curlew in a Novice Hurdle at Festival Trials day at Cheltenham on Saturday! Isabella did the entry last week but he told her not to mention it to anyone, in case he changed his mind. Tabikat's going there anyway for the Steeplechase trial, so that'll be both of them. Think of that, Kye! Sampfield Grange with two runners at Cheltenham and one even entered for the Gold Cup!"

"Merlin must be pleased," said Kye, putting the horsebox into gear and starting to move it across the muddy parking area towards the steep little lane beyond the exit.

"Yes, he is," said Sadie, not recognising the sarcasm in Kye's tone, "Mr Sampfield called and told his agent, Jacko, this morning."

Kye did not know what else to say, so he concentrated on manoeuvring the box out between the posts of the metal farm gate which closed the course off from the lane. The lorry started to grind steadily upwards along the hill which led out to the main road. The bulk of the racing traffic had left earlier, so their progress was unhindered. Mr Sampfield had already disappeared in his comfortable Range Rover ahead of them.

Kye's phone emitted a whistling sound. It was an incoming text. Taking advantage of an enforced stop at the junction with the main road, he quickly looked at the message. His heart lurched. The message was from Gray.

Probs. IH nos. c u 7 mine.

Kye texted back an upward-facing thumb and drove the horsebox out of the junction into a gap in the late Sunday afternoon traffic. His mind was in turmoil. IH must be Isabella Hall. But what did she know? It couldn't be the drone which had shown up the problem that Gray mentioned in the text. The drone had packed up on them three weeks ago and was still not fixed.

"You really aren't with it, are you, Kye?" Sadie was saying to him, irritated at not receiving an answer to a question she had asked about Curlew Landings' training.

"I said," Sadie repeated when Kye shrugged his shoulders, "That Mr Sampfield thinks that Curlew could use a pace setter for his training. Tabikat's the only one good enough to do that. That means you have to ride Curlew, Kye," Sadie added for emphasis, "And I'll be on Tabikat."

"That sounds great, Sadie," Kye said, genuinely pleased, his problems with Gray momentarily forgotten, "Mr Sampfield will soon see what we can do with his best horses."

But Kye's problems were soon to close in on him again when he met Gray later that evening.

"That woman at your place," Gray began, before Kye had even managed to sit down on his customary seat in the workshop, "She knows about us. Teeg heard her say so this afternoon."

"How does Teeg know Isabella?" asked Kye, mystified by Gray's reference to his sister, Tegan.

"Teeg 'as a weekend job at The Charlton Arms," Gray told him, "And your Isabella woman was there this afternoon with 'er lover boy."

"What, Mr Stanley?" asked Kye, surprised, "I thought that sex business was just a blind."

"Well, not according to Teeg," said Gray, "They was in a bedroom together all afternoon and Teeg took 'em up some tea. The bed clothes was all over the place, like, and she was in the bathroom. He was saying something to 'er about illegal drugs and racing and texts, Teeg said."

"Yez sure she heard right?" asked Kye. He had met Tegan only once and she had not struck him as the sharpest knife in the box.

"Well that's what she said," Gray went on, "And I saw the old cow myself, coming down the stairs, bold as brass. And I know he was up there with her too. Came down once she'd gone."

Kye was silent for a while. He was thinking hard. Was there a connection between the woman at Cheltenham and Isabella Hall? After all, Mr Sampfield's cousin had claimed to have seen Isabella there in October. Maybe she was connected with the aggressive woman's boss? Maybe she was the woman's boss? Or maybe Mr Stanley was. How else could the woman have known Kye's name? Or maybe, as he had always half suspected, Mr Stanley was top filth and Isabella an undercover operative. Maybe – and his heart suddenly grew cold in his chest – the police investigation in Liverpool had finally caught up with him.

"We're going to have to do something about this," he told Gray.

32

Kye and Gray decided to lie low and to try to learn more about the activities of Isabella Hall and Frank Stanley. Any plans which Kye might have had in mind for further trading at Cheltenham racecourse were, in any event, to be thwarted by the fact that Sampfield Grange had two horses to take the races that day. The larger of the yard's two horseboxes, normally used only for transporting horses to meets of the local hunt, was to be taken to Cheltenham on the final weekend in January. This horsebox had not received the same modification to its chassis as had the smaller vehicle and so provided no facility for Kye to conceal his illegal wares. His regular customers might be disappointed, but that was tough, thought Kye, who was rapidly beginning to lose his appetite for the venture.

The last Saturday in January turned out to be a cold and gusty day with flecks of rain and occasional sleet floating in the air. Kye, Sadie and Claire all shivered together as they prepared the dignified Tabikat and the more chippy Curlew Landings for their journey together to the racecourse.

As Kye drove the horsebox into the racecourse entrance amongst the earlier members of the arriving crowds, he looked warily around the parking area for the aggressive observer from his previous visit. To his relief, there was no sign of her.

Tabikat's race was the third on the card and Curlew's was the fifth. Sam had, as usual, gone to the racecourse ahead of the horsebox and was already standing in the stabling area with Brendan Meaghan when the horses were brought in. Brendan had runners of his own that day, and Claire O'Dowd greeted her colleagues from the Irish yard as though she had found several long lost relatives.

Kye had not met Brendan Meaghan before, having been otherwise occupied on the previous visit to Cheltenham, but knew that he had been one of the two Irish trainers whom Lewis said had had runners in the race at the October meeting at which Mr Peveril had said he had seen Isabella Hall. As Kye recalled, Isabella had been said to have been standing with the trainer, together with a man they had all assumed to be Mr Stanley, in the parade ring when they had nearly been knocked over by Mr Mortimer's horse. Kye wondered if today might be a good opportunity to see whether he could gain any information from Mr Meaghan about the activities of Isabella Hall. He did not know that his employer had already tried to do the same, but without success.

Making an excuse to leave the stable area for a moment, Kye quickly called Lewis on his mobile phone.

"What were the names of the two Irish horses in that first race in October?" he asked Lewis, once he had explained the plan to him.

There was a lengthy pause during which Lewis retrieved the half-forgotten information. Eventually Lewis told him,

"Mr Carter's horse was called Willow Cutter and Mr Meaghan's was called Rushside Brook," he told Kye, "Mr Meaghan's horse won the race."

"And what was Mr Mortimer's horse called?" asked Kye, "You know, the one which spooked?"

"That was Chilton Marsh," said Lewis's disembodied voice.

"Where's Isabella now?" Kye wanted to know and was told that she was out on her bike, no-one knew where.

"But she said she'd be back to watch Tabikat and Curlew on the TV with us," Lewis said.

"At least that means that she's not here," thought Kye, as he ended the call.

Merlin ap Rhys had been at the racecourse for some time that day, as he had two rides in addition to those on Tabikat and Curlew Landings. Sadie had seen him earlier in the week when he had come to Sampfield Grange to ride out, but this had provided them with no opportunity to be alone together.

"I'm going to forget what you look like," she said, when they were able to speak for a few minutes together after Merlin had come back from the first race, "And I think you look a bit muddy again," she added with a giggle.

"Now, *cariad*, stop that. I need to concentrate on ridin' the 'orses," Merlin told her, although he could not help being turned on by the memory her remark conjured up. He tried hard to think of something else, but it was difficult with Sadie standing beside him.

Whilst the second race was in progress, Tabikat was brought down to the pre-parade area by Claire and Sadie. Sadie, knowing that this would be Claire's final day with the horse had agreed that Claire could lead him up in the parade ring. Brendan Meaghan had no runner in the second race and was walking behind them, talking to Sam. Kye trailed along behind, looking for his opportunity to speak to Mr Meaghan.

There were eight runners in the third race, most of which, like Tabikat, were Gold Cup entrants. During the month in which Tabikat had been at Sampfield Grange, Sam had laboriously studied his race record, and had learned that, despite his excellent form in Ireland, the horse had never raced outside its native country until the run in the Hennessy Gold Cup at Newbury. This meant that not even Brendan Meaghan really knew how Tabikat would take to the challenging Cheltenham course. Newbury was a left handed course too, but it was flat, whilst the Cheltenham course was the very opposite.

Sam had asked Brendan outright why Tabikat had effectively been thrown in to the Cheltenham race. He could see that it was essential to see how the horse went on the track, but it seemed to Sam that this was something which could better have been assessed earlier in the season. After all, they might just find out that Tabikat was entirely unsuited to be a Gold Cup runner.

Brendan's explanation, when Sam had raised this with him, was simple.

"The owners wanted it," he said, flatly.

Sam was beginning to wonder ever more about the sanity of Tabikat's owners. The Levy Brothers appeared to be both entirely dominant in the decisions about their horse's career whilst at the same time being completely elusive and disinterested. No connections had appeared at the racecourse to watch Tabikat's race, so his supporters consisted entirely of the staff of Brendan and Sam's yards. The only person Sam had met who appeared to know the Levy family personally was Stevie Stone, who Sam could see in the parade ring talking animatedly into an iPad held in front of her. Her brightly coloured hair was down around her shoulders, but, as he watched, she quickly shut the iPad and hurriedly wound the hair into a pony tail, which she then crammed under her usual burgundy felt hat. But, before he could approach her, she ducked under the white rail and disappeared into the collecting crowd.

As usual, TV commentators were roving the parade ring, each accompanied by a camera, hoping for interviews with connections of the horses in the race. The racing press had belatedly picked up the move of Tabikat to Sampfield Grange, and Sam was soon approached and asked to give his comments on the horse's chances.

"He's been working well at home," Sam told the TV interviewer, conscious that other racing reporters were standing nearby with their hand held recorders listening to what he was saying, "But we don't yet know how he'll take to the Cheltenham course. Merlin's been working with him this week and we're hopeful of a good result today."

Tabikat's race turned out to be a hard fought affair. The field included the most recent winners of the Grand National and the Hennessy Gold Cup, who between them took first and second places in the race. Tabikat, however, was far from disgraced in running, and Merlin brought him home in fourth place. The only drawback as far as Sam was concerned was that one of the most fancied Irish contenders, called Macalantern, had, much to the horror of those

352

who had backed it, fallen at one of the jumps in the back straight, thereby creating some doubt as to whether the result was a true reflection of the relative merits of the field. The fallen horse was fortunately uninjured and was sure to be back, barring further mishaps, for the main event.

Nevertheless, Merlin came back more than pleased with Tabikat's performance.

"No problem at all, Mr Sampfield," he told Sam, with a grin, from his seat on Tabikat's back, as they walked the horse towards the fourth place spot in the Cheltenham ring, "'e was focused, 'e jumped well, and all in all 'e took to the course pretty good. Only thing is, I'm not so sure 'e's got the speed 'e'll need for a Gold Cup race, but there's nothin' wrong with 'is stamina."

Tabikat himself was made a great fuss of by Claire and Sadie, who told him repeatedly what an amazing horse he was. Tabikat accepted the praise graciously, although Sadie noticed that the horse seemed to be looking around the paddock for something, once Merlin had dismounted and gone off to weigh in.

"What're you looking for, Tabsi?" she asked him, patting his neck, although she knew that the horse could not tell her.

Whilst Tabikat was being taken back to the stables by the two women, Kye found his opportunity to speak to Brendan Meaghan who had remained in the pre-parade area in preparation for his runner in the fourth race. Mr Sampfield had disappeared after speaking to Merlin, so Kye decided to seize his chance.

"Excuse me asking, Mr Meaghan, but do yez know a man named Frank Stanley?" asked Kye, "I think he might be one of your owners."

Brendan Meaghan was surprised by the sudden question from Kye, whom he had hardly noticed amongst the various stable staff milling around the horses.

"Well, I cannot recall anyone of that name," he said, furrowing his brow.

Kye forged on, inventing what he hoped was a convincing story.

"When I was here in October at the Showcase meeting," he said, "I thought I saw Mr Stanley with yez. He used to own horses at my old yard. One of them was called Chilton Marsh. His horse was there in the first race that day and it was acting up in the parade ring."

Brendan looked at Kye suspiciously.

"I don't know what you are trying to find out, young fella," he said, "But you'll not get it from me."

"Mr Stanley once offered me a job, that's all," said Kye hurriedly, "I was just trying to find a way of contacting him."

"Thinking of leaving Mr Sampfield, are you, then?" asked Brendan.

Kye's inventiveness was being to flag and he shrugged his shoulders awkwardly.

"Look, I don't know the fella," said Brendan, taking pity on him, "Not a name I've heard before and he was not with me at any race meeting here or anywhere else."

Brendan turned away to speak to the staff who were bringing his horse towards them allowing Kye made a thankful escape, his heart beating hard in his chest. Unless Mr Meaghan was lying, it was not Mr Stanley who had been with him and Isabella Hall at the race meeting. So, who the hell was it? It was still possible, Kye conceded to himself, that the Irish trainer whom Mr Peveril had seen was actually the other trainer, Mr Carter. But somehow, he was sure that it was Mr Meaghan.

Whilst Kye was attempting without success to solve the mystery of Frank Stanley, Sam had left Tabikat in the care of Sadie, and had gone to see if he could track down Stevie Stone. He had a question to ask her. Stevie had told him that her late mother, Susan Stonehouse, had once been one of the owners of Tabikat, but, according to Isabella Hall, the paperwork had mentioned a Captain T K Stonehouse also as a co-owner.

Stevie Stone's revelation about her mother's ownership of the horse had intrigued Sam. The Stonehouse and the Levy families were clearly known to one another and Brendan Meaghan had already told him that the Levy family was related by marriage to Eoghan Foley. The sheer oddity of the way the owners were managing the training and running of their horse was something which irritated and upset Sam. All the horses he had trained to date had been his own property so he had not previously experienced the challenges of dealing with owners who might have their own ideas about what they wanted for their horses. And Tabikat's owners seemed to be a particularly perverse lot into the bargain.

Feeling unequal to the task of searching the internet himself, Sam had decided to engage the assistance of Helen Garratt. Helen had been interested in Sam's story about the ownership of his new equine charge and promised to find out what she could and to come back to him. She had called him back in some excitement to tell him the horrifying tale of the events which had led to the death not only of Susan Stonehouse but also of her husband Peter. Sam was shocked to hear for the first time of Peter's death, as Stevie had not mentioned this part of the ghastly saga when they had spoken.

"I imagine it was because he was not one of the owners of the horse," Helen had pointed out, "That is what you were asking her about, as I understand."

"And what about Captain Stonehouse?" asked Sam, "What about him? He must be a relative surely?"

But Helen had not been able to find out anything at all about Captain Stonehouse.

"And the other thing I don't understand," added Sam, "Is the connection of the Levy Brothers with the Stonehouses. Brendan told me that the Levy family was related to the Foley family by marriage, but that does not explain how the Stonehouses fit in to the picture."

"Perhaps Stevie Stone can tell you," suggested Helen.

Sam was destined to be disappointed in his effort to find Stevie Stone, as his path away from the pre-parade ring was expertly intercepted by a tall and lanky man in a tweed cap and jacket, who had clearly been waiting nearby to speak to him.

"I do apologise for detaining you, Mr Sampfield Peveril," the man said, "I am not sure whether you remember me?"

As Sam cast about in his mind to recall the name of the speaker, who did indeed seem vaguely familiar, the other man saved him the trouble.

"I am Toby Halstock," he said, "I used to own Curlew Landings. It is a great pleasure to see him run here today. I am just sorry that I no longer have the good fortune to be his owner. Do you think he might be a Festival contender?"

Sam was too courteous to do anything other than respond helpfully to the urbane and garrulous Toby Halstock's approach to him. By the time he had explained that he doubted that Curlew Landings was a Festival prospect, but that much depended on how he fared in the forthcoming race, and had then answered a whole series of further questions about alternative options for the horse, it was too late to search out Stevie Stone. Instead, he had to return directly to the pre-parade ring to join Sadie and Kye, who had brought Curlew Landings himself down to be made ready for his race. Toby Halstock said he would be watching both the preparation and the race with interest and the two men parted company at last.

Kye had a genuine and direct interest in the performance of Curlew in the upcoming race. As Sadie had predicted, he had ridden Curlew for most of the past two weeks, working alongside Tabikat with a view to improving the young horse's ability to keep something in reserve for a final assault on the Cheltenham hill. Curlew seemed to have enjoyed working alongside Tabikat, especially when they were both boxed over to Ranulph Dicks' yard one morning to work with the Dicks horses. But Kye privately wondered whether they had already found the bottom of Curlew. He was speedy enough when he was out at the front, but he did not seem to Kye to have the staying power to maintain his momentum on upward sloping ground once he was getting tired.

Merlin ap Rhys did his level best with Curlew Landings, and sent the horse powering off round the undulating contours of the racecourse with the rest of the ten strong field in hot pursuit. At the final hurdle, Curlew was still in the lead, but his advantage was being inexorably worn away until, once again, two horses passed him on the run in, and he had to be content with third place. Curlew put his head down and battled hard, trying his best to respond to Merlin's efforts to push him to stay ahead. But it was in vain. It was a truly gutsy performance, but the outcome was not what Sam had been hoping for.

"I'll be 'onest with you, Mr Sampfield," said Merlin, as they spoke after the race, with Curlew Landings looking dead on his feet beside them, Merlin having dismounted him as soon they came off the course, "I don't think this is the best place for 'im. 'e needs a flat course, like Newbury, where 'e can get up some real speed without getting too tired at the end."

Sam had to agree, and so, privately, did Kye. Sadie, for her part, did everything she could to tell Curlew how well he had done.

"I'm just glad you're back in one piece," she whispered into one of his ears.

Brendan Meaghan's runner had come second in the same race so the two trainers stood briefly together by the winner's enclosure.

"You want to watch that lad of yours," said Brendan, pointing towards Kye, who was putting a sweat sheet over Curlew's steaming back.

"Who, Kye?" asked Sam, mystified by the other man's sudden comment.

"Is that his name?" said Brendan, "Well, he tells me he has been offered another job."

"Another job? By whom?" asked Sam, surprised to hear that Kye had been sharing such information with Brendan Meaghan. He was not aware that the two of them had even spoken together.

"A fella called Frank Stanley," Brendan told Sam, "Maybe you know him?"

Sam was expecting to hear the name of another trainer, so the mention of Frank Stanley shocked him into open mouthed speechlessness. He managed only a shake of the head and a brief thanks to Brendan before the two of them parted company. Sam could not believe what he had just heard and wondered if Brendan had mistaken what Kye had apparently said to him. He was not aware that Kye had even met Frank Stanley, even on the day that Frank had turned up so unexpectedly at Sampfield Grange. Perhaps it was just a coincidence of names. But, even as Sam thought this, it did not seem at all likely.

The shock of Brendan's revelation put out of Sam's head any thought of seeking out Stevie Stone to ask his questions about the connections between the Stonehouse and Levy families. He remained standing in the parade ring, trying to calm his nerves, as the connections gathered there for the sixth race and someone he knew called over to him to join their group.

The unpleasant surprises of the afternoon were not yet over, however. In the sixth race, Merlin ap Rhys's horse was a faller at the last fence, and Merlin was taken to hospital with a dislocated shoulder and suspected fractured wrist.

And, as Kye walked back to the horsebox to make it ready for the return journey, a figure emerged from the gathering shadows and blocked his path.

"Hello, our kid," said the slick young man who stood in Kye's way.

It was Kye's brother, Bronz.

33

Sadie had taken many falls from horses during her relatively short lifetime, and had watched numerous others do the same. But the race meeting at Cheltenham was the first time that she had really cared about the consequences.

Merlin had walked from the racecourse into an ambulance and been taken to hospital to have his shoulder reset and his injured wrist X-rayed. Sadie had been in the stables with Curlew when she heard what had happened, and it was by then too late for her to speak to Merlin to discuss the impact of the accident on their plans for the weekend. The proposal had been that Merlin, having no rides booked for the following day, would follow Sadie down the M5 that evening and put himself up at The Charlton Arms for the night, where Sadie, once the two horses were settled, would join him. As it turned out, Sadie was obliged to accompany Kye home in the Sampfield Grange horsebox having been unable to contact Merlin, whose mobile phone remained in his pocket of his black leather jacket at Cheltenham racecourse.

Sadie had to be content with texting a message instead.

Gone home [sad face]. Hope you ok. Call me [heart].

She then sat in silence in the horsebox, watching the dark countryside go by, feeling cheated.

Kye was far from being in a talkative mood, so Sadie's silence did not bother him. He had hardly registered the emotional goodbye scene with Claire O'Dowd when they had parted company in the Cheltenham racecourse car park.

Bronz had been the last person he had expected to see that day.

"Christ Bronz, what's yez here for? Something bad happened?" he had asked Bronz, his first idea being that his brother had brought bad news for him.

He should have known better.

"Let's see, now," Bronz had taunted him, "How bad do yez want it?"

But Kye was having none of this from his younger brother.

"For fuck's sake, stop trying to be clever, Bronz," he had snapped, "There's going to be people here soon. Bizzies too, I shouldn't wonder, knowing this place. What's this about?"

But Bronz was not to be hassled.

"Nice set up, this," he had said, waving in the direction of the horsebox, "Sheryl tells me yez doing good trade here."

"Who's Sheryl then? What does she know about anything?" asked Kye, trying to play for time.

"Sheryl, prin! Show yesself!" called Bronz, and, as Kye had half expected, the hard faced young woman he had met on New Year's day emerged from the side of the nearby brick building to stand next to Bronz. Kye had been conscious of numerous racegoers streaming along the road behind them, talking and laughing, many of them loud and drunk, some quiet and morose, some chatty and happy. He had wished that he was one of them, either going off to a fun evening in the pub, or else to a nice home somewhere away from all these problems.

Kye did not know what would have happened next had it not been for Sadie, who had suddenly appeared at his elbow.

"Are we ready to load, Kye?" she had said, "Mr Sampfield wants to know."

"Yeah, bring the horses out," replied Kye, adding, "Bye then, nice to see yez two," in the direction of Bronz and Sheryl.

"I'll be in touch, yez can count on it, our kid," Bronz had told him, as he and Sheryl had linked arms and joined the other racegoers leaving the course. Kye had watched the two of them being ushered across the road by a helpful policeman who was stopping the traffic coming off the small roundabout in front of the course entrance so that the spectators could cross the road in safety. Kye had not known, though, that another policeman, this one not wearing a uniform and a high visibility jacket, had been watching him and his brother with interest.

Sam, as usual, drove some distance ahead of the horsebox on his way back to Sampfield Grange. The weather was dark and gloomy but the promised heavy rain had not yet materialised.

Sam had been used to a quiet and orderly life of which he was totally in control. Ever since the unannounced re-appearance of the long absent Frank Stanley last October, that control and order had been lost. After almost four months of surprises and unexpected events, Sam was becoming fed up of his life being disrupted. He was sure he was being made use of in some way that he could not fathom. As he gripped the steering wheel of the Audi, he decided that it was about time he took control of his life again. He just needed to clarify how to do it.

So, as the M5 rolled smoothly beneath the wheels of the Audi, Sam tried to assemble his muddled thoughts into some kind of order.

As far as Tabikat was concerned, Sam was confident that the horse could safely be declared to run in the Gold Cup race, so long as he remained fit and healthy over the next few weeks. Even though Merlin had doubts about his speed, Tabikat was still a realistic contender and there was no reason that Sam could see why the horse could not run into a place if things went his way on the day. The real problem with Tabikat was not the horse himself, but the owners. Sam's intention to get some information out of Stevie Stone had been undone by events that day, but Stevie could easily be tackled again the next time he encountered her. Brendan Meaghan, notwithstanding the lengthy background information he had provided about the gelding and its breeder, had been unforthcoming about the horse's present ownership. There was one additional option open to him, Sam told himself, and that was to contact Eoghan Foley himself and to ask him directly about the sale of the horse to the Levys and the Stonehouses.

Curlew Landings, for his part, had not been able to achieve what they had all hoped in the hurdle race at Cheltenham today. Again, Sam was content to go along with Merlin's suggestion that Newbury might be a better option for the novice to try to chalk up another win. There was a meeting at Newbury in two weeks' time at which a suitable race could probably be found. The difficulty now was that Merlin was injured, and, until Sam knew how serious an injury it was, he would have to consider the possibility of finding another jockey for Curlew if he ran again so soon. Sam was less worried at present about Merlin's likely availability to ride Tabikat in the Gold Cup, as the Festival was still over six weeks away.

Sam's third problem was with Kye. Sam had considered Kye to be a good young horseman with genuine potential as a jockey, but had recently been in some doubt as to Kye's commitment to his role at Sampfield Grange. This doubt had escalated to a full-blown worry by the revelation that afternoon from Brendan Meaghan.

Sam tried to sort out the elements of the information with which he had been so unexpectedly presented by Brendan. The suggestion that Kye had been offered a job by Frank Stanley defied belief. Frank had said he was with the security services, whatever that meant, and he could have nothing to offer in the way of employment to a mechanic and stable groom. Sam thought it most likely that this tale had been made up by Kye as a way of asking Brendan Meaghan about Frank Stanley. But Sam could not at first think why Kye would have any reason to think that there was a connection between the two men, until he suddenly remembered the incident in the Cheltenham parade ring in October, during which Gil had said he had seen Isabella Hall and an unknown man standing with Brendan Meaghan. Perhaps Kye had somehow found out about this and was, like Sam before him, trying to find out whether this man was Frank Stanley. But why would Kye want to know about someone who, as far as Sam knew, Kye had not even met?

Sam suddenly had a new idea. Perhaps Kye was not trying to find out about Frank himself, but about Isabella Hall. All the staff would know that Isabella had come to Sampfield Grange as a result of Frank's direct intervention with Sam. Maybe Kye had assumed, as Sam had himself earlier assumed, that the two of them were there together with Brendan Meaghan that day. To think that Kye was prying into Isabella's affairs made a little more sense to Sam, as she worked alongside him, and her rather off-putting manner, or perhaps a disagreement between them, might have sparked some kind of resentment on the part of Kye or one of the other staff.

Although he did not know it then, Sam had correctly arrived the explanation of the purpose of Kye's question to Brendan Meaghan. But, fortunately for Kye, the real reason for Kye's interest in Isabella Hall and Frank Stanley would remain a mystery to his employer.

In the meantime, as he turned the Audi into the entrance of Sampfield Grange, Sam resolved to do two things. The first was that he would call Eoghan Foley and ask him some questions about Tabikat's owners, and the second was that he would also call the number Frank Stanley had given him, and find out what the hell Frank had got him into. The making of these two decisions made him feel a lot better.

Merlin ap Rhys's dislocated shoulder had been put back into place at the Gloucestershire Royal Hospital that afternoon. The associated soft tissue damage around the affected joint was, fortunately, not serious. The suspected fractured wrist turned out to be badly sprained and swollen, but no bones showed up on the X ray as having been broken. With his left arm in a sling, and dosed up with painkillers, Merlin had ordered a taxi to take him back to Cheltenham racecourse, where he retrieved his possessions from the jockey's changing room.

Merlin found three messages on his phone. One was from Sadie, one from Jacko, and one from his sister Rhian in Chepstow. Both Jacko and Rhian had seen Merlin's fall on the TV coverage that afternoon and both separately demanded that he call them. Merlin did so before turning his attention to Sadie's message. He instructed Jacko to cancel all his bookings for the next week and accepted his sister's offer for her husband to drive to Cheltenham to bring Merlin back to his home in Chepstow.

Jacko was doubtful that a week would be anything like long enough to recover from such an injury as Merlin had sustained, but knew better than to argue with Merlin, especially when he was in pain and stuffed full of analgesics.

Whilst waiting for his brother in law to arrive, Merlin put a call through to Sadie, who was gratifyingly sympathetic about his predicament.

"I'd love to come and make you feel all warm and comfy," Sadie told him. Merlin rather liked the sound of that.

"Thomas my brother in law is comin' to drive me back to Chepstow," he told her, "Any chance you can come up and see me tomorrow or Monday? I could do with a bit of your TLC, *cariad*, I really could. I can jus' see you now, looking all sexy in a nurse's uniform."

Sadie was not sure how she could get herself to Chepstow, let alone obtain a nurse's uniform, but she promised to see what she could do. Her first action was to put a call through to Amelia Dicks.

Lewis had heard the horsebox enter the yard about twenty minutes after Mr Sampfield's arrival and was subsequently able to inform everyone that food would be ready within the hour. It was whilst Sadie was changing her clothes in the cottage that the call from Merlin came through to her. Sadie's subsequent call to Amelia Dicks received the response that Sadie had hoped for. Now she just had to tackle Mr Sampfield.

Kye was still cleaning out the horsebox in the yard as Sadie breezed into the Sampfield Grange kitchen.

"Have you got the racing all recorded from this afternoon, Kelly?" she asked her sister, who was busy cooking.

"Yes, all done. We all watched it too," replied Kelly, "It was really exciting seeing Tabikat run. The TV commentators said some really nice things about him – that he'd not been seen at Cheltenham before, that he was a picture of horse and looked really fit. He went off at 12 to 1, you know. And there was a Grand National winner in the field too. Merlin looked really smart in those blue and gold colours. We were all cheering them like mad. Even Isabella got excited. More than us even."

"That's great, Kelly," said Sadie, pleased to hear that Tabikat and Merlin had attracted such positive attention, "It's just a shame that Curlew didn't manage to do better than last time. And he tried really hard, bless him. And then Merlin got injured in the next race, you know."

"Did he?" asked Kelly, immediately concerned, "We turned the TV off after Curlew's race was over. Is it bad?"

Sadie gave her a summary of the more repeatable bits of what Merlin had said to her, and then asked her sister, "Is Mr Sampfield about, Kells? I need to ask him something."

"I think he's in his study," Kelly told her.

"I'll go and knock on the door," said Sadie, marching out of the room quickly, before she had second thoughts.

Sam's study door was open as Sadie approached it. She could hear him speaking and realised that he was on the phone. Not deliberately trying to eavesdrop, she hung about in the passageway outside, but eventually her curiosity got the better of her, and she began to listen.

Sam's unaided efforts to look up a telephone contact number for Eoghan Foley had eventually been successful and he copied the number down carefully onto the top page of a small notepad on his desk. Taking a deep breath, he pressed the numbers into the keypad of the desktop phone.

After a pause, he had the sound of an unfamiliar ring tone. The tone seemed to go on for a while, and Sam was beginning to wonder if anyone was at home, when the phone was eventually answered and a young male voice said, *"Trathnona maith. Feirm Enda."*

Sam was nonplussed. It had not occurred to him that his call would be answered by someone speaking in Irish Gaelic. At least the name Enda was clear enough.

"Good evening," he said, hazarding a guess that this was what the young Irishman had said to him. "My name is James Sampfield Peveril, calling from England. May I please speak to Eugene Foley?"

"Is it about a horse, sir?" asked the other speaker, switching at once to English.

"It is," replied Sam, "It is about Tabikat."

"Tabikat, is it?" the young man with the soft lilting voice was clearly not expecting this, "I'll get my father. Hold on there, please."

There was a pause, during which Sam noticed Sadie hovering near the study door. Rather to her surprise, he motioned her to come into the room and pointed at a nearby chair. Sadie sat down, puzzled, wondering what was going on. It was not like Mr Sampfield to invite his staff into the private rooms of his home.

Sam heard the sound of the telephone being picked up by someone at the other end.

"This is Eoghan Foley," said the new voice, which also spoke with a slow and flowing Kerry accent, "I am told that you are calling about Tabikat, Mr Sampfield. Did the horse come out of his race well this afternoon? It seemed to us here that he ran well for you at the course. What was the opinion of his jockey?"

Sam was mightily relieved to realise not only that Eoghan knew who he was but that he was clearly keeping himself informed about Tabikat's progress in England.

"He's come out of the race well, Mr Foley," he assured Eoghan, "I have his groom with me now and she is more than happy with him."

Sam looked at Sadie for confirmation and she nodded enthusiastically.

"And his jockey was pleased with his focus and his jumping but did express the view that he might not have enough speed when it comes to the Gold Cup itself," Sam added, trying to ensure that Eoghan Foley received all the information he had asked for.

Eoghan made a non-committal sound at the other end of the phone. Sam could not tell whether he agreed or not.

"The reason I'm calling, Mr Foley," Sam said carefully, "Is not so much about the horse as about the owners. I really would like to be able to talk to them about the horse, but they are very elusive. And no-one came to the race today to watch Tabikat run. I know that Mrs Susan Stonehouse is no longer with us, but I thought that the Levy family and maybe other members of the Stonehouse family might be there. I know from Brendan Meaghan your family is related to the Levys and I wondered if you might be able to put me in touch with any of them."

Fortunately, Eoghan did not seem too put out by the question, as Sam had feared he might be.

"Was Stevie not there today?" he asked, "I saw her on the television broadcast right enough."

"Yes, she was," said Sam, "But I didn't get an opportunity to speak to her."

"And Brendan?" Eoghan asked.

"Well, he has told me quite a lot about the horse and about your family, but he didn't seem to be able to put me in touch with the current owners," Sam replied, carefully.

"Look, Ephraim and Aoife are in Bahrain, and Isaac along with them," Eoghan told him, "So they'll not be turning up a race meeting in Cheltenham. But Daniel's in England I reckon and TK ought to be home surely by now. You could try talking to them. It's Daniel and TK that I wanted to have the horse."

"Daniel and TK?" Sam repeated, "Is that Daniel Levy and Captain T K Stonehouse?"

"Indeed it is," responded Eoghan, "But surely you know that the horse is in England to set things right for the family? Brendan told me that the people in England had everything in hand."

"I am not sure I understand what you mean," said Sam, puzzled, "We'll do our best with the horse for the owners when he runs in the Gold Cup, obviously."

Sam stopped, not knowing what else to say.

Eoghan was silent for a while.

"Perhaps I have said more than I should," he said, eventually, "But I cannot see the harm in you speaking to Danny and TK about the running of the horse. It would be good to see the two of them together at the races."

"How can I contact them?" asked Sam, hurriedly seizing his chance.

"Look, Danny works with an Formula 1 outfit," Eoghan told him, "Harlow something, I think Aoife said they were called. We don't see TK these days so there's nothing I can tell you. Speak to Stevie, she'll know."

Sam sensed that he was not going to get any further, so thanked Eoghan Foley and was about to end the call, when the Irishman suddenly added, "But I'll be seeing you myself soon enough. Caitlin and I will be there to watch Tabikat run for the Gold Cup."

Sam could not believe what he had just heard.

"It will indeed be a great pleasure to meet you both, Mr Foley," he said, meaning every word, "I have heard a lot about you."

Putting the phone down, Sam looked over at Sadie. He was highly pleased that his decision to take the initiative to find out more about the horse's owners had been met with a helpful response.

"That was Tabikat's breeder, Sadie," he said, "He seems really pleased with what we are doing with the horse."

"And what Merlin's doing too…." Sadie added, pointedly.

"Ah yes, and how is Merlin?" Sam asked, having momentarily forgotten about Merlin's fall in the sixth race that afternoon.

"He dislocated his shoulder, Mr Sampfield," said Sadie, "He's gone home to Chepstow and he's asked me to come over to see him there. I'd like to go, if you'll let me."

Sadie had never asked a favour of Mr Sampfield before, and was not sure how he was going to react. But she was in for a surprise. Buoyed up by the relative success of his discussion with Eoghan Foley, Sam was in a generous mood. As soon as Sadie told him that Amelia Dicks had agreed to ride out on Tabikat, he agreed to her request to go and stay with Merlin for the next two days. And when Sadie said that she was not sure how she would get there, he told her to take the Range Rover.

As Sadie was thanking Mr Sampfield for his generosity and understanding, Merlin's brother in law was carefully steering his white van along the A48 to Chepstow. Merlin was slumped in the passenger seat, his face pale.

Thomas was trying to drive as smoothly as he could, but his van was not the most comfortable of conveyances. As they approached Chepstow, Merlin's mobile phone shrilled in his pocket. It was Sadie, calling to say that she was on her way up the M5, and would see Merlin later in the evening. She didn't have a nurse's uniform, though, she said apologetically.

"I don't believe it. Sadie's comin' to look after me," Merlin told his brother in law, "I didn' think that *hen ffasiwn* boss of 'ers would let 'er."

"Is she the one that broke your bathroom basin?" asked Thomas, who was a plumber and had had the job of fixing the damage created during Sadie's previous visit.

"Yes, she is," replied Merlin, suddenly feeling a lot better.

"I'm looking forward to meeting 'er," said Thomas, suppressing a laugh.

34

As Sadie was speeding up the M5 in the Range Rover, Kye was sitting silently in the Sampfield Grange kitchen with Lewis and Kelly, watching the recording of Tabikat's and Curlew Landings' races. Gloomily, he listened to Mr Sampfield being interviewed by the TV anchor and watched Claire and Sadie leading the two Sampfield Grange horses around the parade ring in their respective races.

"Shame that Merlin got injured," commented Kelly, experimentally, wondering why Kye was so quiet, "I expect Sadie will cheer him up. Fancy Mr Sampfield letting her take the Range Rover like that."

"Yeah," said Kye, not really listening, and more preoccupied with wondering what the hell Bronz wanted. He didn't have to wait long to find out, as a message from Bronz suddenly pinged itself onto the screen of his mobile phone.

Call me

was all it said.

Kelly having failed to get a rise out of Kye with her jibe about Sadie and Merlin was prevented from resuming her attack as Kye suddenly stood up and announced that he was going back to the cottage.

Once away from Kelly's and Lewis's prying eyes and ears, Kye called Bronz, who came quickly to the point.

"Where yez get yez gear?" asked Bronz without preamble.

"Local," replied Kye, shortly.

"Yez'll be gerring from us now," Bronz told him.

"How come?" asked Kye, "Youz lot don't have anyone round here."

"Not in that poxy horse place of yours," Bronz said contemptuously, "At Cheltenham races. At the Festival. And its not just weed, it's gonna be something major going down."

"What sort of major" asked Kye, fearfully.

Bronz sneered down the phone.

"Yez'll be told," he said, "Be in touch, our kid."

Whilst Kye was staring in trepidation at the now blank screen of his mobile phone, Sam was sitting in an armchair in the Sampfield Grange drawing room looking at the plain white card which showed Col. F E Stanley's mobile phone number.

The conversation with Eoghan Foley had given him a little more information about Tabikat and his connections but the information had not provided any sort of link to Frank Stanley or Isabella Hall. In practical terms, the only connection between them was the sighting by Gilbert Peveril of Isabella Hall with Brendan Meaghan at Cheltenham racecourse. But Frank Stanley had not been there, so there was no obvious reason to suppose he had any connection with Brendan. But Frank did have a connection with Isabella. It was Frank who had asked him to give Isabella a job. And Frank had referred to the day and venue of the Cheltenham Gold Cup as the point at which he would be able to talk again to Sam. And Sam had been unexpectedly sent a horse which was entered for that very race.

There absolutely had to be a connection between Frank Stanley, Isabella Hall, and the arrival of Tabikat at Sampfield Grange.

Sam gritted his teeth, picked up his mobile phone, and dialled Frank's number. Frank answered the call almost immediately.

"Sam?" he said, tension sounding in his tone, "What's happened? Is Isabella OK?"

Sam was not expecting this question to be the first thing which Frank had to say to him, and stammered slightly as he replied.

"No, no, nothing's happened. Isabella is OK as far as I know, although I haven't seen her since this morning. But I need to speak to you, Frank. I want to know what the hell is going on. All these mysteries. It makes me feel as if I am being taken for a fool. And I don't know why and I don't much care for it, to be honest, Frank. You are making a lot of assumptions about my willingness to play along with this.. this .. charade. And about my loyalty to you. I know that Meaghan sending me that horse is something to do with you and I want to know what it is."

Frank had remained silent during this chaotic torrent of words from the usually restrained Sam. Eventually, he responded, apparently choosing his words carefully.

"I thought you would enjoy training the horse, Sam," he said.

"Well, I would, I mean, I do," Sam spluttered, enraged at the relative irrelevance of Frank's comment.

"And Isabella is doing a good job for you, is she not?" Frank went on.

"Yes, of course she is, although she's a bit of an odd type," Sam replied, becoming even more angry.

"Can you really not trust me on all this until Gold Cup day?" asked Frank.

Sam was not sure how to respond to this question. His lifelong loyalty to Frank was not in question, but he needed to know what was going on.

"It is not that I don't trust you, Frank," he said eventually, "But I really don't think that you trust me. Why can't you tell me what is going on?"

"Because you don't have security clearance," Frank stated baldly.

Sam had not expected this stark explanation for Frank's behaviour and was reduced to asking rather tamely,

"What do you mean, Frank? What security clearance? What for?"

"Look," said Frank, "You are a small part of a big operation and I really cannot talk to you about it. I brought you in precisely because I knew you could be trusted and that you of all people would not let me down. You'll be told all about it once it's finished. In the meantime, your job is to look after Isabella and make sure the horse is fit to run on Gold Cup day."

"I spoke to Eugene Foley," Sam told him, "Is he in on whatever this is? And what about Brendan Meaghan?"

"Eoghan and Brendan know as much as you do," Frank told him, "They've been asked to play their part in things too."

"Eugene said something about setting things right for the Stonehouse family," Sam persisted.

"And that is exactly why he and Brendan agreed to the horse coming to you," Frank stated, "That is their own reason for being involved. They both asked a lot of questions about you before they agreed. Neither of them had ever heard of you and it was essential that they should trust you with their precious horse."

Sam was wrong footed by this revelation and for a moment could think of nothing to say.

"For God's sake, Sam," Frank went on, emotion entering his voice for the first time, "Believe me when I say that it is because of what I know of you, and because of what happened with us, that I know I could trust you with my life. And Isabella's too. I am asking you to bear with me for just a few more weeks, and then I promise you will know everything."

"Your life?" said Sam, "And Isabella's? It is not that serious, surely?"

"Regrettably, Sam, it is," Frank told him, and was silent.

"Very well," said Sam, somewhat unnerved by this statement, "But can you at least tell me something about the owners of the horse?"

"What do you want to know?" asked Frank, "Isn't it is the paperwork? And I saw you talking to Stevie Stone, so I should have thought she would have told you. Or Eoghan. Or Brendan."

"I know that Susan Stonehouse is dead," Sam said, feeling on slightly safer ground, "But Eugene Foley mentioned Daniel Levy and Captain T K Stonehouse and said I might contact them to talk about the horse. That's not going to cause your .. er .. operation.. a problem is it?"

"I hadn't really factored them in," said Frank, slowly, "I didn't think either of them were involved with the horse any more. What did you have in mind?"

Sam felt a little flattered to be consulted about his intentions.

"I thought I might see if they would come to see him run in the Gold Cup," he said, "Or even come here to Sampfield Grange to watch him in training. Eugene Foley gave me the impression that they were the real owners of Tabikat."

"Inviting them to Sampfield Grange would probably not be the best idea," replied Frank, who appeared to be thinking on his feet, "They are not on good terms with each other, I am told."

"Why not?" asked Sam.

"Well, you realise that the horse was apparently bought by Daniel as an engagement present," said Frank, "Eoghan must have told you that?"

"No, he didn't say anything about that," replied Sam, trying to absorb this new information, "An engagement present? Engagement to whom?"

"To Tabitha, of course," Frank replied, "So, Eoghan didn't tell you?"

"Tabitha?" asked Sam, trying and failing to identify the person to whom Sam was referring, "Who is Tabitha?"

"Captain T K Stonehouse, of course," said Frank, a little impatiently, "Tabitha Katherine Stonehouse, she's an Army Officer, a Captain in the Royal Engineers. She's Stevie's sister. And Daniel Levy's one-time girlfriend. Daniel apparently thought she was meant to have the horse because of her childhood nickname. Tabby Kat. So he bought the horse from Eoghan and put it into training with Brendan Meaghan."

The family jigsaw finally made sense to Sam.

"I need to think about this," he told Frank, "Thank you for taking me into your confidence this much, at least. Since you've explained the reason, I will undertake not to press you for any more information about your operation. And what you said about Isabella is safe with me. I can see that I will have to be content that you should trust me with all this."

"And I appreciate that you trust me," responded Frank, "This is tough for everyone involved, believe me, Sam."

"I agree," said Sam, "We'll talk again in March. Thank you, Frank. Goodbye."

As Sam pressed the key to end the call, he was almost immediately alerted by a hesitant knock on the half open drawing room door. It was Lewis who stood facing him, outlined by the door frame.

"I apologise for interrupting, Mr Sampfield," he said, "But will you be wanting anything before Kelly and I turn in for the night?"

"No thank you, Lewis," replied Sam, rather shakily, "I'll get myself a drink, don't worry."

Lewis quickly wished him good night and scurried off down the corridor, anxious to speak to Kelly, who was doing the last of the clearing up in the kitchen.

"Guess what, Kells?" he said, "Mr Sampfield was just on the phone to that Mr Stanley. I only heard the last bit of what Mr Sampfield said. They were talking about an engagement and an operation," he paused significantly, "And, about keeping a secret about Isabella. And he mentioned someone called Tabitha as well."

"A secret?" repeated Kelly, "So Mr Sampfield knows about Mr Stanley and Isabella, then."

"Looks like it," said Lewis, "I wonder who this Tabitha is? Maybe she's another of Mr Stanley's girlfriends and he doesn't want Isabella to know. An operation, though…. what could that be?"

As Kelly and Lewis were excitedly speculating about what Lewis had overheard, Sadie had finally reached a dark and rain swept Chepstow. She called Merlin as she came over the stone bridge leading into the town.

"I'm here at last," she said, "But I need some directions. And I'm really sorry, but I couldn't get a nurse's uniform. I'll go out for one tomorrow."

"You really are something, *cariad*, aren't you?" Merlin felt almost cheerful again at the realisation that Sadie had thought that he was being serious about the nurse's uniform, "You can nurse me with nothing on at all, as far as I'm concerned."

"Is that OK?" asked Sadie, "That'll make things a bit easier then."

Merlin was not so sure it would make things easier, but, as he gave Sadie directions to his house, he was sure it would make them a lot more interesting. His shoulder was feeling less painful already.

35

In the two weeks leading up to the race meeting at Newbury, Kye had been in a state of gradually escalating fear and panic. On the day after the ominous conversation with Bronz, and taking advantage of having the cottage to himself, he had called Gray and told him that their trading arrangement would have to cease.

"It's that cow from your yard, isn't it?" Gray had said angrily.

"No, it isn't her," had replied Kye, "I don't know what she knows. But what's really fucked us is those people at Cheltenham. We're on their patch, Gray. They're into something heavy. Smack, base, charley … you know, serious shit. At the Festival."

"Whoah," had said Gray, "That's well out of our league, Kye, man."

Kye had been relieved that Gray had been so easily scared off. Kye had no idea what Bronz was planning, but he was quite sure that the plan would involve Kye being in the front line. The vicious characters who had run the smuggling operation in Liverpool were not going to front up their own dirty work. If anyone was going to be the fall guy, it was going to be some minnow such as Kye.

But Gray had had one last bit of fight in him.

"Look," he had said, "I still got some gear here, you know. I paid out for that stuff. We can't just trash it. Can't you shift it somewhere else where this lot aren't going to be wasting their time?"

"I guess so," Kye had conceded, "Let me have it and I'll stash it in the usual place. I'll see what I can do to move it when we next go to Cuffborough or somewhere else out in the sticks."

Gray had accepted the suggestion with relief, with the result that a consignment of weed and a few white tablets were now well hidden in the box attached to the chassis modification underneath the smaller of the two Sampfield Grange horseboxes.

Sadie had returned to Sampfield Grange two days after her departure in Sam's Range Rover, ready to ride out once again on Tabikat. Amelia had enjoyed riding the horse over the two days, saying that he was a dream ride with loads of ability.

"Merlin says he's not quick enough to win the Gold Cup," Sadie had told her.

"Well, he isn't a speed horse, I agree," had replied Amelia, thoughtfully, "But we know he can get a shift on when he puts his mind to it. He could do very well in a steadily run race. But that's Irish racehorses for you. Merlin will have to hope that the ground doesn't dry out too much and the front runners don't go off too fast."

"Have you spoken to Mr Sampfield about it?" Sadie had asked, concerned that there should be no disagreements about the running of the horse in the future.

"He agrees with Merlin," Amelia had replied, "And how is your sexy Welsh lover boy, then?"

"Making the most of his injury at home," Sadie had told her, "But he says he's going to be back to ride Curlew at Newbury next Saturday week. He's having lots of physio on his shoulder and wrist."

"You be careful, Sadie," Amelia had counselled her, "He's got a bit of a reputation, you know. And not just as a jockey."

Sadie knew that Amelia was right to warn her. During her two days in Chepstow, comments made to Merlin on a visit from Rhian and Thomas, when they had thought Sadie to be out of earshot, had injected a small dose of reality into her delicious dream world.

"She's a lovely girl," Rhian had said, "If you weren't my brother I'd say she's too good for you. I don' want you breaking 'er 'eart now."

"Or any more washbasins," Thomas had added.
Sadie had not been able to hear Merlin's reply but it had ended with

a laugh.

"I'm just going to enjoy him whilst he lasts," Sadie had told Amelia, boldly, although the thought of the relationship possibly coming to an end made her suddenly feel a bit sad. Still, there's plenty of other fish in the sea, she had told herself, not really believing it.

Sam had felt as if a burden had been lifted from his mind following the conversations with Eoghan Foley and Frank. Granted, the information about Frank and Isabella trusting him with their lives sounded rather frightening, but knowing more about what was happening around him made Sam feel more in control. And he was more pleased than he could express, even to himself, that Frank should have come to him, in however odd a way, for help.

Sam remained curious about Isabella Hall. Although he had found her strange and unforthcoming, it had not occurred to him that she might be Frank's colleague, rather than a friend of his ex-wife, as he had originally described her. Sam now wondered if the story about Mr Hall having died was true or was just another invention to maintain a cover story. But nothing he had heard had yet explained why Isabella was at Sampfield Grange or how her presence was connected with that of Tabikat.

Sampfield Grange had two runners at Newbury in mid February. Sam had found a novice hurdle race for Curlew Landings and a National Hunt Flat race for Highlander Park. This meeting would be their opportunity to test the hypothesis that Curlew would run back to his best on a flatter course as well as to give Highlander some experience at a bigger course in a race under rules. Gilbert Peveril's amateur rider's permit fortunately allowed him to ride Highlander Park in the race concerned, and Gilbert had confirmed that he was willing and available to do so. But Sam began to think that it was about time Kye was asked directly whether or not he wished to renew the conditional jockey's licence which had lapsed since he left his previous training yard. He could not continue to rely on Merlin and Gilbert to be available all the time.

Sam's new and more considerate attitude towards employees whom he had previously taken for granted, and which had been evident in his offer to Sadie of the use of the Range Rover, had continued over the two days of Sadie's absence. Kye's strange statement to Brendan Meaghan about being offered another job, untrue though it clearly was, at least in the terms in which it had been described, had made Sam realise that he could be in danger of losing Kye. Perhaps the reason Kye had spent so much time tinkering with the horsebox whilst at the race meetings was because he was not being given any opportunity at Sampfield Grange to progress his previously initiated career as a jockey.

With this in mind, Sam had asked Kye, as the two of them had followed Amelia Dicks on Tabikat back down the hillside track to Sampfield Grange, whether he would like to apply to renew his conditional jockey's licence with Sam as his sponsoring trainer. Mr Sampfield's offer had been to Kye the one ray of light in his increasingly darkening and miserable thoughts following the Cheltenham encounter with Bronz.

"That would be right great, Mr Sampfield," he had replied, enthusiastically, "I'd do a good job for yez, I promise."

"I'll ask Isabella to fill out the application for us today," Sam told him, feeling pleased, "It's too late now for anything at Newbury, but we'll have a look out for something suitable once the licence comes through."

Curlew Landings' second appearance at Newbury races, together with Highlander Park's debut race, happened on wild, wet and windy day on which spectators clutched at their hats and open umbrellas were entirely useless. Grey clouds scurried madly across the sky, blown by a gusty and noisy South-Westerly wind.

Curlew and Highlander had been loaded into the large horsebox as the wind whipped around the buildings, putting anything which was not stored away or tied down in danger of being carried up into the hills behind the yard. Fortunately, Sadie oversaw a clean and tidy operation at Sampfield Grange, so there was little opportunity for any loose item to blow away, but Highlander Park in particular did not like whistling noise made by the fast moving air as it swept across the roof of the barn. A set of earplugs was of some help in getting him loaded, but the feel of the cold air ruffling his back and mane was clearly unsettling him. The sides of the box continued to be pushed and rattled by the persistent wind as Curlew stepped up the ramp, resplendent in his travelling gear and looking disdainfully at his nervous fellow passenger.

Managing the smooth driving of the large vehicle in the blustery conditions on the journey to Newbury took all Kye's concentration, and he felt relieved when he was at last able to park the horsebox alongside those from the other yards which had runners that day. A few of his previous stable staff acquaintances made eye contact with Kye and looked at him questioningly as he jumped down from the cab, but Kye shook his head at them and drew his index finger across his throat. Sadie was too busy unfastening the ramp at the side of the lorry to notice anything unusual about Kye's behaviour.

Merlin had been passed fit to ride on the previous day, but had decided to confine himself to a single ride on Curlew Landings to test how his shoulder held up. Sadie had not seen him since the day she had left Chepstow, when the pain from the injury was still clearly evident. Jacko had arranged the retrieval of Merlin's BMW from the racecourse car park at Cheltenham and Merlin had driven it himself to Newbury racecourse, his shoulder still feeling stiff, but fairly mobile, and, for now at least, relatively pain free. To his surprise, he had genuinely missed Sadie's company once she had taken the Sampfield Grange Range Rover off into the darkness of a rainy night over a week ago. The smile on his face when he saw her approaching him with Curlew Landings in tow was not entirely attributable to his recent memory of their joint physical activities in his bedroom, which had been of necessity rather more restrained than on the occasion of her first visit.

Curlew's race was the first on the Newbury card and Highlander's bumper was the last. This was an inconvenient arrangement as far as managing the two horses was concerned, as it involved a great deal of waiting time for the Sampfield Grange party between the two races. But it could not be helped.

Standing in the parade ring before the first race, Sam found himself approached once again by the TV anchor who had interviewed him at Cheltenham. Sam kept one hand on his brown fedora hat, which the wind was threatening to remove, as the smartly dressed interviewer spoke to him.

"You're running Curlew Landings in this first race, Mr Sampfield Peveril," the smooth voiced man began, "Are you hopeful of his chances? He's won here at Newbury before."

"Today's race is a stiffer contest for him," Sam replied, wondering whether Kelly, Lewis and Isabella, perhaps even Frank, were watching their TV sets or iPads and hearing what he was saying, "But we do think he is suited by the course. Merlin knows the horse well and thinks he's in with a chance."

"This is jockey Merlin ap Rhys's first ride back after injury at Cheltenham two weeks ago," the interviewer clarified for the benefit of any viewers who might not have understood Sam's reference to Merlin, "Speaking of Cheltenham, Mr Sampfield Peveril, can you tell us anything about Tabikat? How's he come out of the race there?"

"He's come out of the race very well," Sam assured him, warmly, "We're very pleased with his work at home."

"Are you intending to get another run into him before the Gold Cup?" asked the interviewer, already knowing the answer, but wanting the viewers to hear what Sam had to say about the horse.

"No, he'll go straight to the Gold Cup now," answered Sam.

"And what do you think of his chances?" asked his questioner.

"Well, so long as we keep him fit and healthy, he's got a good a chance as any of them," Sam answered, guardedly.

At that point, Merlin came to join them in the parade ring and the interviewer thanked Sam and turned away in search of other prey before the bell rang.

Sadie was walking along the elliptical path with Curlew Landings, who, fortunately, seemed unbothered by the windy conditions. As Sam legged up Merlin, in his red and green Sampfield Grange colours, into the saddle, Sadie gave Merlin a small smile and told him to stay safe.

"And keep Curlew safe too," she added, as she led Curlew Landings and Merlin along the horse walk and sent them both out onto the course.

Merlin and Sam were proved right about Curlew's performance on the Newbury track. Merlin set Curlew off at a fast clip in front of the eight strong field, and, whilst their early lead was gradually eroded, nothing got past them throughout the entire race and Curlew came home in first place by a length. Merlin was interviewed by the same TV anchor after the race and had a grin all over his face as he expressed his satisfaction with Curlew's performance. Sadie's grin as she led a tired Curlew into the winner's enclosure was even bigger.

Sam had watched the race on the big screen in the parade ring. Whilst he was waiting for the victorious trio to return to the parade ring he noticed two things. The first was that Stevie Stone, wearing her usual burgundy hat, was standing amongst the nearby crowds, apparently interviewing some of the younger female spectators and the second was that Curlew Landings' former owner, Toby Halstock, was positioned not far away from her, leaning on the plastic rail which encircled the winner's enclosure. Sam felt a slight pang of compassion for the friendly and polite man who had spoken to him at Cheltenham. It must have been galling to see how successful the horse he no longer owned had now become.

Sam was determined, though, that on this occasion Toby Halstock would not prevent him from speaking to Stevie, so he studiously avoided catching his eye. After Sam and Merlin had accepted their prizes for Curlew's win, and Sadie was walking the horse back to the stables, Sam was pleased to discover Stevie waiting for him at the parade ring exit.

"Well done, Mr S P," Stevie congratulated him, "Jayce and Tabby Cat tipped Curlew Landings today, so lets hope all the smart girls made a killing on him. But I want to ask you a favour. Would be willing to do a piece for my vlog this week?"

Although flattered to be asked, Sam felt rather doubtful.

"I'm not sure that a traditional yard such as mine would really fit with your .. er .. style," he replied, trying his best to be diplomatic.

"Well, we're working up a piece about the Gold Cup runners," Stevie went on, smiling at Sam's comment, as they walked together towards the Owners and Trainers bar, "And you, Mr S P, have the perfect excuse to be part of that, as you train one of the runners, and he shares his name with our main star."

Sam looked blank.

"Tabby Cat," Stevie prompted him.

Sam laughed.

"Yes, all right then," he told her, "Just so long as it is you who interviews me and not that talking kitten."

"That's a promise," Stevie assured him.

As they walked in the direction of the grandstand, Sam decided to take his chance.

"I've been talking to Eugene Foley," he began, deciding not to mention Frank Stanley unless Stevie did so first, "I understand that Tabikat was once a gift to your sister, Tabitha."

Stevie did not reply for a moment and seemed to be thinking. Sam pressed on.

"The thing is," he said, "I'd very much like to talk to the owners of the horse, perhaps invite them to come and see him train. I understand from Eugene that Daniel Levy and Tabitha Stonehouse are both in the UK at the moment. But he didn't have any contact details for them. I wondered if you had?"

"I am not sure that either of them would be able to come to Sampfield Grange," Stevie said carefully, "In fact, I am not sure that TK would want to, especially not if Danny was there at the same time."

"Did they fall out?" asked Sam, curious to know the background to the change of ownership of the horse.

"In a manner of speaking," Stevie said, as Sam held open the door to the Owners and Trainers bar so that she could pass through. They sat down together at the nearest empty table.

"I expect you've been told," Stevie went on, "That Danny bought the horse for TK as an engagement present. Everyone thought it was such a coincidence that the names matched. We used to call my sister Tabby Kat when she was a little girl and Danny really wanted her to have the horse. Danny and TK had been together for years, since they were at school. The trouble was that TK wasn't ready to get engaged and she found it hard to accept such an extravagant present, even from someone as rich as Danny and his family. She had her career in the Army to think about and Danny was planning to become a motor racing engineer. Also, she's not really a follower of horse racing. So, she agreed to be an owner, so long as our mother was listed as an owner too. That way it could be seen as a gift to the family and not just to TK, and not a promise to get engaged. TK also insisted that Danny himself stayed as part owner. So that's how Tabikat ended up with three owners: Danny, as Levy Brothers International, TK, who is called Captain T K Stonehouse in the paperwork, and my mother Susan Stonehouse. The irony is that of the three of them, my mother was the only one who was actually a racing fan and she and my father would always come to watch Tabikat run in Ireland. That's another reason that TK wanted her to be one of the owners, as she knew our mother would get some real enjoyment out of the horse, whereas she and Danny wouldn't really be around. Danny travels all over the world with Harlow Motosport and TK was stationed in Afghanistan in theatre then sent somewhere classified in the Middle East. The ownership arrangement worked fine for a while, until our mother died. And after that TK didn't want to have her own name on the ownership list. It was just too painful a reminder for us all."

Sam listened without comment to this lengthy explanation from Stevie. It certainly confirmed the information which Isabella Hall had told him was contained in the ownership records for Tabikat.

"So will there be no-one at all from the owners' families to see Tabikat run in the Gold Cup?" Sam asked eventually as Stevie fell silent and seemed to be trying to prevent herself from crying, "Eugene Foley said he would come, and I am assuming you will be there, but the horse deserves all our support, so I should really like to see Daniel and Tabitha .. sorry, TK .. too, if we could persuade them. I realise that the rest of Daniel's family are in Bahrain, but I would appreciate being able to invite Daniel to join us, at least."

"You can try," Stevie told him, "There's no harm in asking, I suppose. You are quite a determined man, Mr S P," she added, trying to laugh.

Stevie rummaged in the large handbag which she had placed on the floor beside her, and took a business card out of her purse.

"These are Danny's contact details," she said.

"And TK?" persisted Sam.

"I'll speak to her," Stevie said firmly, and stood up, saying, "I need to get back to the parade ring. I'll be in touch about the interview."

As Stevie was parting company with Sam, Sadie and Merlin were sitting in Merlin's car in the jockeys' car park. Sadie had taken advantage of the lengthy gap until Highlander Park's race to leave Kye in charge of the horses for a while. For once, she thought, Kye had seemed not to want to be tinkering with the horsebox, and had raised no objection to Sadie's instruction.

"How's the shoulder?" Sadie asked Merlin as she got into the passenger seat of the black BMW.

"Stiff," replied Merlin, leaning across towards her, "Like something else will be soon with you sittin' there."

But, unusually, Sadie ignored the provocative remark and persisted with her enquiries about Merlin's health.

"So you'll be all right to ride Tabikat in the Gold Cup, then?" she asked.

"Well, so long as nothin' else 'appens to me in the next three weeks," Merlin replied, feeling that he was stating the obvious and wondering why Sadie was being so insistent.

"Well, just be careful then," Sadie told him.

"So, 'oo is it you really care about, *cariad*?" asked Merlin, "Me or the 'orse?"

"Both of you, of course," Sadie replied, as if stating a simple fact.

Merlin suddenly felt his throat tighten, and he swallowed hard. Sadie had been good fun, and a willing player in his sex games, but he didn't want things getting heavy. He soon realised that he needn't have been concerned.

"Tabikat won't win if he has a different jockey, that's all," Sadie said flatly, "So you need to make sure you're fit to ride him."

"Well, you'd better look after me, then, 'adn't you?" Merlin said, feeling relieved, and, leaning in further towards her, he pushed his hand between her thighs.

36

Highlander Park's first race under rules was a disaster.

Sam and Gilbert Peveril were waiting together in the centre of the parade ring as Kye led in the young horse to walk the circuit along with the twelve other eager participants. Although the gusty wind had died down a little, Highlander was still up on his toes and Kye needed to be vigilant to stop him from whipping round in response to every strange noise and unexpected movement. The crowd had thinned considerably since the running of the previous race but there were still plenty of chattering people lining the parade ring rails. Highlander had encountered noisy spectators before at the Cuffborough point to point meetings, but this crowd was louder and more diverse than those he had been used to seeing. Coupled with the unfamiliar surroundings, the circumstances were highly unsettling for him, and he made sure that everyone knew it.

"I saw your friend Toby Halstock earlier," Sam told Gilbert as they watched Highlander hopping and jogging along the parade ring path, Kye trying hard to keep him calm, "He must be sorry not to own Curlew Landings any longer."

"Oh, Toby's used to all that," Gilbert responded, dismissively, "Quite the pragmatist, that chap. Things always going wrong for him one way or another. Easy come, and all that. Now then, James, what about young Highlander here? Shall I put him at the front, or what?"

Sam was privately thinking that Gilbert would do well to stay on Highlander's back, given the mood the horse seemed to be in, but suggested that trying to keep him covered up would be the best policy in today's circumstances.

Gilbert noted the advice with a doubtful "Hmm" and accepted Sam's assistance in legging him up into his potentially perilous position in Highlander Park's racing saddle. Kye accompanied horse and rider as far as he could onto the course, but after that Gilbert and Highlander were on their own.

In the event, Gilbert had no opportunity to carry out Sam's instructions. As the horses milled around at the start, Highlander decided to try to get rid of some of the opposition by aiming several sharp kicks in their direction. Fortunately for all concerned, his hooves did not make contact with any of the other horses, but the result was that Gilbert was already hot and sweating before the race began as a result of the effort of trying to keep the agitated Highlander in order.

Once the race set off, Highlander immediately towed Gilbert to the front. Gilbert, who much preferred a married man's gallop to a full scale cavalry charge, was left with little option but to ride prominently, and, from then on, had no role other than that of passenger, as Highlander Park carted him forcibly along the Newbury track. With no jumps to make him concentrate, Highlander simply saw clear space ahead of him and ran into it like a thing possessed. Eventually running out of steam about half a furlong from the finish, the horse suddenly slowed down to little more than a canter and was passed by most of the field, joining the back markers as they straggled across the line.

Kye grabbed Highlander's bridle as soon as Gilbert got him back to the horse walk. Gilbert was so out of breath that he could hardly speak, his round face now matching his red hair, which was plastered to his skull beneath his riding hat.

"Bloody Hell, lad," he gasped to Kye, as Highlander Park, having now exhausted all his nervous energy, plodded obediently back towards the paddock, "What have you been feeding our young headcase here? Dynamite?"

Kye had to suppress his laughter. Mr Peveril was a good rider, but, in Kye's opinion, no longer young or fit enough to be dealing with the sort of problems Highlander had created for him in this race.

Sam was waiting for them in the paddock, along with Sadie and Merlin, who had watched the race on the big screen. Sadie and Merlin had had to keep straight faces all through the race, in deference to Mr Sampfield, whose expression had been a picture of mounting horror as the race progressed.

"Good God, James, old man," exclaimed Gilbert as he slithered gratefully down from the saddle, "If this little maniac is to be entered in any more of these races, you can count me out. You need a pro jockey to ride him, like this fellow here," he went on, pointing at Merlin with his whip.

"I don' know, Mr Peveril," replied Merlin, "I'm not sure anyone could 'ave done much with the 'orse in that kind of mood. When they get somethin' into their 'eads like that, it's very 'ard for even the best jocks to stop 'em actin' up."

Slightly mollified by Merlin's comment, Gilbert stomped off to weigh in. Although they were disappointed that Highlander had made such a mess of the race, it was difficult for the Sampfield Grange party not to feel at least a little amused by Gilbert's obvious discomfiture.

As Gilbert disappeared into the weighing room, Sam turned to Merlin and said,

"That was kind of you, Merlin. I'll need to give some thought as to what we do with Highlander after this fiasco. Now, have you the time for a brief word about coming to ride out on Tabikat?"

"Of course, Mr Sampfield," replied Merlin, "I'm not goin' anywhere just now."

Whilst Merlin was talking to Sam, Sadie and Kye prepared the two horses for their return to Sampfield Grange. Sadie told Kye to take Curlew Landings down to the box ahead of Highlander Park, who still needed to cool down. Sadie would follow with Highlander Park when he was ready to load. The arrangement also gave Sadie a useful opportunity to say goodbye to Merlin and to find out when he would be coming to Sampfield Grange.

As Kye led Curlew down towards the horsebox car park, he became aware that a tall man wearing a tweed jacket and cap was following him. It was nobody he recognised, and his heart began to beat hard. Since the encounter with Bronz and Sheryl at Cheltenham, he was very wary of anyone who appeared to be taking an unnecessary interest in him. Kye put his head down and continued to walk purposefully towards the car park, trying to behave normally and as though he had not noticed that he was under observation.

But soon Kye became aware of heavy running footsteps behind him. His whole body tensed as the sound of the footsteps came nearer. Curlew Landings, sensing something amiss with his familiar young groom, skittered sideways and lifted his head in alarm.

"Hey there, you lad!" came an authoritarian voice from behind Kye, "Just stop right there, will you? Where are you going with that horse?"

Kye let out his pent breath in a sharp gasp of relief. The voice was unrecognisably that of Mr Peveril. As Kye brought Curlew Landings to a halt and turned round, he saw Mr Peveril hurrying towards him accompanied by the tall man who had been following him. Mr Peveril seemed to have recovered somewhat from his exertions in the recent race, but his face remained flushed.

"I'm taking him back to the horse box, Mr Peveril," he said, as Gilbert and the other man came closer.

"Yes, yes," replied Gilbert impatiently, "This is Mr Halstock, a friend of mine. He used to own Curlew Landings. Just wanted a chance to see him before he went back to base."

As the two men patted Curlew Landings, who lapped up their attention gracefully, and talked optimistically about the horse's future career, Kye tried to get his emotions under control. Was he always going to have to live like this? Looking at every stranger with suspicion, wondering if he was under scrutiny? Being a conditional jockey in a safe haven with Mr Sampfield would certainly be a wonderful life compared with this constant stress and uncertainty. But was even the rural backwater of Sampfield Grange going to be a safe haven? Bronz could easily track him down wherever he tried to hide himself. And who was going to help Kye if Bronz and his crackhead cronies did find him?

When Gilbert Peveril and Toby Halstock eventually wandered off, chatting amicably, Kye continued his walk with Curlew Landings into the horsebox parking area. And there, waiting to receive him, were uniformed police.

There were three of them, two men and a woman, all standing by the Sampfield Grange horsebox. Kye had no choice but to continue towards the waiting figures, who stood in silence, watching him approach. Kye brought Curlew to a halt by the box.

"Can I help yez gents and lady?" he addressed the nearest male police officer in what he hoped was a confident tone, although his throat felt as if sandpaper had been stuffed into it.

The previously silent policeman ignored Kye's offer and merely said, pointing at the horsebox,

"Are you responsible for this vehicle, sir?"

"Yes," Kye said, "I've brought this horse down to get it loaded up."

"We have reason to believe," the policeman went on, ignoring Kye's reference to Curlew Landings, "That drugs are being sold in this car park."

He stopped speaking and looked at Kye questioningly.

"You wouldn't know anything about that, would you, sir?"

"No, nothing at all," Kye replied, in what he hoped was an honest sounding tone, although his heart was beating so hard that he felt as if it would jump out of his chest, "I've not been near the car park since we arrived this morning."

"You won't mind if we have a look inside your vehicle, then," said the police officer. It was not a question.

Kye put his hand into his jacket pocket and produced the keys for the horsebox. Curlew Landings shifted impatiently by his side, keen to get into the horsebox where he knew a haynet would be waiting for him.

"Could you unlock the vehicle for us, please, sir?" the officer asked.

"Not whilst I am holding this horse," replied Kye, "He won his race this afternoon, so he's quite a valuable animal. I can't risk him getting loose."

Kye was not really sure why he was bothering with these delaying tactics. The larger of the two Sampfield Grange horseboxes was clean. It had never been used to carry drugs and there would be absolutely nothing for the three police officers to find. But something in his bones told him that co-operation with the bizzies was fundamentally wrong. They were the enemy, end of story.

"Very well, sir," said the police officer, holding out his hand for the keys.

Kye watched as the two other police officers, searched around the cab of the horsebox. As Kye expected, they found nothing.

Kye indicated to the officers how to open the ramp to the box and watched with some satisfaction as they struggled with the unfamiliar task. Curlew tugged at his head collar and stamped his feet, wanting to go inside.

"Inside's clean too," said the female officer when she eventually came out, "Nothing here either, not even any cash."

Kye, listening carefully to what they were saying, whilst making a pretence of being preoccupied with adjusting Curlew's travelling boots and tail guard, inferred from this comment that the police officers had already searched outside and under the lorry. Someone had been telling tales, he realised angrily. And he already thought he had a pretty good idea who it was.

The first police officer handed the keys slowly back to Kye. The man's expression had not changed.

"Thank you for your co-operation, sir," he said, looking Kye full in the face, "Have a safe journey home."

Kye remained silent as the three officers walked back towards the racecourse buildings. Curlew Landings snorted crossly, wondering why things were taking so long.

"That was a serious piece of shit, Curlew," said Kye, leaning against the horse's shoulder, his heart rate beginning to slow down.

As Kye stood still, trying to get his thoughts in order, he heard Sadie's voice calling him.

"Why's Curlew not loaded, Kye? I've got Landy here now."

Kye looked up to see Sadie and Merlin approaching with the disgraced Highlander Park in tow. Highlander looked as if butter would not melt in his mouth and was walking placidly, ignoring the surroundings which had appeared so terrifying to him earlier in the afternoon.

"Sorry, Sadie, the bizzies were here, asking questions," Kye told her, thinking that it would be best to tell the truth in case she and Merlin had met the officers as they crossed the car park.

"You mean the police?" said Sadie, surprised, "What did they want, then?"

"No idea," Kye responded, "Just seemed to be nosing around. Maybe checking the horseboxes are roadworthy. Looking for bald tyres, broken lights, and that."

"Oh well, we'll be all right then," said Sadie dismissively, "With you looking after everything."

With Merlin lending an extra hand, the two horses were quickly loaded. Kye sat in the cab whilst Sadie and Merlin took what Kye could see in the wing mirror to be a highly tactile leave of each other. That bloody jockey really thought he was something, the way he had his hands all over Sadie, Kye mused gloomily, as he waited for the two of them to push themselves apart.

On the journey back to Sampfield Grange, Sadie was initially in a chatty mood. As a result, Kye learned that Mr Sampfield would be away overnight, having been invited to spend the rest of the weekend with Mr and Mrs Peveril.

"Poor Mr Peveril," Sadie giggled, "He did look a sight after that race. I expect he'll need a few drinks this evening. Perhaps you'll get to ride Landy in future, Kye."

This possibility had not occurred to Kye until now, and the thought of riding Highlander Park in a race made him feel slightly happier. He had been gratified by Sadie's enthusiasm when Mr Sampfield had informed her that an application had been submitted by Isabella Hall for the continuation of Kye's training under Mr Sampfield.

"And Merlin's coming to ride out on Tabikat this week," Sadie went on, "Maybe he can give you some useful advice too, Kye. Mr Sampfield's very good and all that, but he's never been a pro jockey like Merlin."

As the horsebox trundled with its two human and two equine passengers along the darkening road to Sampfield Grange, Sadie suddenly fell silent and spent the remainder of the journey looking pensively out of the cab window. This suited Kye, who used her silence as an opportunity to get straight in his mind what exactly had happened in the Newbury racecourse car park, and, more importantly, what he was going to do about it.

The police in the car park had said they had reason to suspect drug dealing. Kye had no way of knowing whether the Sampfield Grange horsebox was the only vehicle to be searched, or whether other horseboxes had also been investigated. Whichever it was, the police had clearly already looked around the box from the outside, which suggested, to Kye's mind at least, that they knew, or suspected, that it might have been modified in some way. The police had not, of course, specified the grounds for their belief that drugs were being sold, so they had either seen it for themselves or else someone had reported it to them. Potential informants could possibly have been found amongst those to whom he had been selling in the past, but these people would have had no knowledge of the storage arrangements for the weed and pills, as Kye had always been careful to ensure that the gear was out of the compartment before he called anyone over to the horsebox.

Kye did not need to think hard to recall that the only person who had ever seen him under the horsebox at a race meeting was Isabella Hall. And then there was that conversation which Gray's sister Tegan had overheard between Isabella and Mr Stanley in their bedroom at The Charlton Arms.

And if Isabella Hall was a bizzy herself, as Kye suspected, and was working for Mr Stanley, then she could easily have tipped off the filth at Newbury racecourse. Luckily for Kye, she had made a mistake in thinking that both horseboxes were being used for carrying the merchandise, which meant that he had got away with it this time. But if Isabella Hall had grassed him up once, then she might do it again. The quicker he acted further on his intention to find out more about her and what she was up to, the better. He was very well aware of the remaining gear currently in storage in the other horsebox, currently parked in the Sampfield Grange yard.

It was dark when the horsebox arrived back at home, and even darker when Sadie and Kye had settled the two tired horses into their stables for the night. As Sadie and Kye crossed the yard towards the big house, they both became aware of a small figure standing beside Tabikat's box. It was Isabella Hall. She was stroking the horse's nose and talking to him in a quiet voice. The horse had its head lowered towards her as if he was listening to what she was saying.

"You go on ahead, Kye," said Sadie, "I'll go and find out what she's up to over there. Weird cow."

Isabella did not seem to hear Sadie approaching, and jumped when Sadie addressed her.

"What are you doing?" Sadie asked, more harshly than she intended.

"I'm talking to Tabikat," said Isabella, sharply, "What does it look like? He's not your personal property, you know."

Sadie was astonished by Isabella's aggressive tone. Isabella had always spoken to her in a polite and distant manner, and Sadie had never suspected that the other woman had a temper.

"Suit yourself," she snapped back, and swung off towards the house, wanting suddenly to find her sister Kelly. Sadie had something important she needed to discuss with her.

The following morning was bright and calm, the blue sky and wispy clouds showing no sign of the previous day's strong wind. Kye chose his time carefully. Once the horses had been exercised, the breakfast finished, and the work riders gone for the day, and Sadie was yakking yet again to Kelly in the kitchen, Kye watched to see what Isabella Hall would do. As he went about his morning work in the sun warmed yard, he saw Isabella appear in her cycling gear at the entrance to the flat above the garage. She descended the external stone steps, fastening up her cycle helmet.

"Yez out for a ride round, then?" Kye called out to her, "Nice day for it."

"Yes," replied Isabella, pulling her bike out of the garage, "I'll be gone about an hour. I don't think anyone's going to need me just now with Mr Sampfield being away."

Kye watched his quarry cycle down the entrance lane to the road and turn off to the right. He waited until she had been out of sight for several minutes and then, checking that no-one could see what he was doing, sprinted up the steps to the chauffeur's flat. The door was locked, but Kye had no difficulty springing the worn tumbler catches with a penknife, a skill which he had learned during his teenage years in Toxteth. Slipping quickly through the green painted wooden door, he shut it behind him and looked quickly around.

Sampfield Grange's chauffeur's flat, disused until Isabella's arrival, was no better appointed than the cottage in which Kye and Sadie lived. It consisted of a single open room with a small shower cubicle and toilet partitioned off in one corner, clearly added in more recent years, when even the chauffeur would not have been expected to use a shared outside toilet. The ceiling was low, and sloped downwards along with the angle of the roof. There was a small round window over the front of the garage and a larger dormer style window overlooking the track which led up to the hills and gallops behind the building. A little window was set in the upper part of entrance door, but, notwithstanding the presence of three sources of natural light, the flat was still gloomy.

The few items of furniture were old and heavy, clearly discarded from earlier days in the big house. There was a high wooden-framed bed, a capacious chest of drawers and a wide cupboard. The floor was boarded and several rugs had been laid down on the wooden surface in an attempt to create some warmth. The heating was supplied by a propane gas heater standing against one wall. The whole place was meticulously neat and tidy.

Kye was not entirely sure what he was looking for. Seeing that Isabella was off on her bike, she could not have been carrying much in the way of personal effects, he reasoned, so there must be something in the flat which would tell him something about her. Maybe something he could use.

Opening the bottom drawer of the chest, he found what looked like Isabella's work clothes, consisting of two folded pairs of black trousers and a number of dark coloured tops. The next drawer up contained cycling clothes and underwear. But it was in the two smaller top drawers of the chest that Kye made his finds. And they gave him a massive shock.

The left hand drawer contained several small white cardboard boxes, each adorned with a typed label. On the top three boxes, Kye read names such as Paroxetine, Lorazepam, and Nefopam. The names appeared to be the names of drugs, but Kye's knowledge of legal drugs was limited and he had no idea what their purpose could be. Carefully looking at some of the other boxes, he found more familiar names such as Ibuprofen and Codeine, and one empty box labelled Prozac. Shit, he thought, no wonder she's like a zombie sometimes. She must be drugged up to the eyeballs.

But the contents of the right hand drawer were even more shocking. In that drawer was a small brown cardboard box, which, when Kye pushed back the already opened top, proved to be half full of small calibre bullets. Next to the box were two large flat knives sheathed in black cases, and a small folded hand towel. And finally, there were two objects which Kye did not recognise, but which he had a horrible suspicion might be stun grenades or something worse.

Kye stared dumbfounded at the little arsenal. What the hell was Isabella Hall doing with this lot? They weren't police issue weapons. They looked more like something a terrorist, or someone bent on going on a killing spree, would have. As he stared in bemusement at his unexpected finds, he did not hear the flat door opening behind him. But he did hear the voice of Isabella Hall saying levelly,

"Just stand very, very still, whoever you are. I've got a gun pointing right at your head. And don't even think of trying to use any of that stuff. You'll be dead before you touch it. There's back up on its way."

Kye was utterly petrified. He stood stock still. It suddenly dawned on him what must have been wrapped in the hand towel in the drawer.

"Isabella," he managed to gasp out, "It's me, Kye. I'm sorry. Please don't do anything."

"Step backwards and lie face down on the floor," Isabella ordered him, not acknowledging Kye's confession, "Keep your hands away from your pockets."

Kye did as he was told, and lay still with his face pushed against the musty carpet, his stomach churning with fear.

"What the fuck are you up to, Kye?" asked Isabella, in an angry voice, "Thieving for drugs?"

Kye could think of no answer to this, so he stayed where he was, trying to stop himself from vomiting on the smelly rug.

"Or is someone paying you to spy on me?" Isabella went on, a sharp edge entering her more usual flat and expressionless voice, "Gave you that stupid drone so you could follow me, did they? And where are you sending the pictures, you little toe rag?"

As Kye started to try to speak, he heard the sound of running footsteps coming up the stairs outside the door.

"OK, Isabella," a male voice said, "You can stand down now."

As the newcomer spoke, Kye felt someone in heavy boots crossing the wooden floor. Rough hands grasped him by the armpits and yanked him to his feet. He found himself looking into the faces of two heavily armed police officers. A third was standing next to Isabella, who was holding a handgun, which had clearly been the item missing from inside the folded towel he had found in the drawer.

"I know who this is," Isabella was saying tiredly to the man who stood next to her, "He works here. I don't know what he's doing in here. Sorry I called you out. I thought it might be …" she stopped suddenly, biting her bottom lip savagely.

"You did exactly the right thing, love," the armed man assured her, "Whoever he is, he's coming with us now."

As a terrified and uncomprehending Kye was hauled down the steps of the chauffeur's flat into a waiting black van where a driver was sitting patiently at the wheel, Sadie and Kelly, alerted by the noise of the vehicle, came running from the boot room door along the path towards the garage, followed soon after by Lewis.

On both the previous evening and again this morning, Sadie had been sobbingly confiding to her sister that she was sure she was in love with Merlin ap Rhys, but could not tell him for fear that he would end their relationship. Sadie was sure that Merlin wanted her only as a sex partner to keep him entertained in bed, in the car, on the floor, in the shower, or even on the kitchen table. Kelly had been enthralled by Sadie's semi-pornographic account of her relationship with Merlin, and had been enjoying offering all kinds of apparently well-meaning advice.

But Sadie's troubled love life did not come anywhere near in the interest stakes to the sight of Kye being thrust into a van by three armed police officers and Isabella Hall sitting at the top of the garage steps with her head buried in her hands.

37

By the first week of March, Aleksander Paloka was once again resident in his expensively decorated apartment overlooking Hyde Park in London. The last occasion on which he had favoured the city with his malign presence had been on the occasion of the conviction at the Central Criminal Court of his late father, Konstantin, for his part in the murder of Jerzy Gorecki. Then Aleksander had sat in the public gallery, an anonymous figure watching the British justice system do its laborious and relentless work, unable to prevent the inevitable consequences to his father's freedom. For once, there had been no-one that Konstantin could bribe, threaten or subvert, and the witness whose testimony had had his father sent down for life was not the usual desperate and terrified individual who could be disposed of by violence and intimidation.

Aleksander had no doubt whatever that the British authorities had played a part in his father's subsequent murder in prison. Whether it had been a contract put out on his father's life by another criminal gang, or whether it was the British police themselves, Aleksander did not know. But the fact remained that he would not have been at the mercy of whoever cut his throat if Susan Stonehouse had not given evidence against him.

Much had changed for Aleksander since the day of his father's death over a year ago. Aleksander had inherited a thriving international criminal empire, one which satisfied his every need for money and power. But two people, significant to his new life, were now dead. Susan Stonehouse, whom he had vowed to kill, had died twelve months ago by her own hand before he could reach her. And his revolting and obese brother Egzon had perished six weeks ago in that stinking basement of his in the house in Tirana, surrounded by his screens and computers, apparently shocked into heart failure after being outmanoeuvred by a cleverly set up cyber attack.

Aleksander did not miss his brother. There were plenty of techno nerds within the Paloka empire eager to take Egzon's grubby place and they did not hesitate to put themselves forward to their new boss.

Aleksander had chosen two of them. One of them was to work on the re-creation and protection of Egzon's former responsibilities for online fraud, blackmail, extortion and other associated cyber-criminal activities. The second individual had been tasked to find out exactly who had perpetrated this devastation which had brought down Egzon's carefully constructed defences and to find out how they had done it.

This second young man had had a British computer science degree and very little sense of right and wrong. He had cut his criminal teeth on cracking his way into the bank accounts of unsuspecting fellow students and cleaning them out overnight. He had been careful to avoid leaving any trails, and even the banks' experts were unable to discover how their customers' accounts had been accessed. The perpetrator had moved up in the world of cyber crime, finding ever more ingenious ways of overcoming firewalls and other barriers set up by financial institutions to protect their interests. As far as he was concerned, this had been a battle of wits between himself and the people who worked equally ingeniously to protect the hacker's targets. In this, the young man had resembled Egzon. But there the similarities stopped. This one had been young, skinny and bespectacled, with a serious cocaine habit.

The second of Egzon's replacements had been pleased by the opportunity to become a cyber detective. He had never tried anything of the sort before and had considered it an interesting challenge to his skills. His initial analysis had shown that Egzon's well protected systems had been destroyed by an online ninja bomb which had been introduced into one of the operating systems through an innocuous link to a local radio station website. This site had merely acted as a temporary host to the warrior virus, which had been carried in a news item placed on the site from a source in Italy. Carefully hacking into the site in Italy, the young man had nearly disturbed a small bomb bot, which, if triggered, would have destroyed the link to the source of the item. Working around the destructive device, the cyber detective had become interested. These people had expected someone like him to come along, and they were trying to trap him. Good on them, he had thought, but you won't win.

The young man's work had taken several days of careful experimentation with different routes and sources, during which time he had avoided a number of cling-on type devices and other viral traps which had been laid along his route. But, eventually, he had reached the now repaired Carcassonne node. At this point, there had appeared to be an impenetrable blockage which had him metaphorically scratching his head as he had snorted another line of the cocaine which had been brought to him in the cell like room from which he was working. But somehow, he was not sure quite how, a small window had opened in the firewall and he had found himself inside a computer which appeared to be full of records of sales of cases of Minervois and Corbieres wines.

The young man knew little or nothing about wine, but he had recognised financial records and tax returns when he saw them and easily deduced that this was a wine merchant of some kind. It seemed an odd place from which to launch a cyber attack on such well constructed systems as Egzon's, but it had been definitely the end of the line. After a bit of poking around, the young man with the British computer science degree had discovered the trigger which had set the ninja bomb on its way. It was a name, an English name. It was Susan Stonehouse.

When the young man had reported his findings to Aleksander, he had genuinely feared for his life. Aleksander's rage and fury had been like nothing he had ever witnessed.

"You are telling me that a dead woman has done this?" had screamed Aleksander, as the young man had cowered in fear and Aleksander's bodyguards had stepped in closer.

"No, Mr Paloka," the young man had whimpered, "It is typing the letters of the name into the French computer which has caused it. The bomb was linked to the sequence of the key strokes. Anyone could have done it. Is this name important in some way?"

"This Englishwoman is the cunt that killed my father," had snarled Aleksander, "But she is dead. Or maybe still alive but with a different name. Why should anyone dare to use her name to attack me?"

"I can find out more about how it was done, if you like," the young man had offered nervously, hoping to work his way back into Aleksander's favour, "It might lead you to the perp."

"Go ahead, then," Aleksander had told him, "And send him in more shit to keep him awake," he had added in the direction of one of the guards.

The young man had started on the next stage of his project by researching Susan Stonehouse. He read the accounts of the incident at Little Uppingham airfield and had noted with a shiver that Guy Griffin and Jack Dilley were serving time for protecting their now-dead boss. He had read about the murder of Konstantin Paloka in prison, the death of the comatose Peter Stonehouse, and the subsequent suicide of Susan Stonehouse. He had viewed with amused detachment Egzon's online intimidation of Susan Stonehouse which appeared to have driven her to take her own life. And he had looked carefully at the police archive which held the CCTV pictures of Susan Stonehouse throwing herself onto the line at Golders Green Underground station.

The young cocaine addict was familiar with the Underground from his days in London and had himself often travelled on the mighty Northern Line. There was something about the recording which had seemed odd to him. He had replayed it several times, watching the grainy image of a small woman toppling onto the line in front of an incoming train, the train coming to a sudden halt with its back two carriages still short of the station. A small group of panic stricken passengers were pointing at the track in front of the train. Then the train was evacuated and the scene of the suicide was obscured from view by an impatient crowd of people who knew they should be sorry for the person who had jumped, but who were really just annoyed at being made late for work that morning.

A uniformed ambulance crew was seen arriving up the steps onto the platform and disappearing into the milling crowd. After a further pause, during which the crew had apparently climbed down onto the now non-electrified track, they emerged carrying a stretcher on which there appeared to be a body covered with a blanket. Horrified passengers stepped aside to let them pass.

But the young man had lost interest in the body recovery proceedings. As he ran the recording further forward, he had seen the train inch its way on the restored electrical power towards the normal stopping place at the end of the platform. Out of the train had stepped the driver together with a second person also in London Underground uniform. They had walked quickly along the platform and disappeared down the station steps. A replacement driver had acknowledged them as she had made her way to the front of the train.

The young man had run the recording again, just to be sure. But he was right. There had definitely only been one person in the cab of the train when it entered the station. But two people had got out.

Perhaps, as Aleksander had hinted, Susan Stonehouse was not dead after all.

The young man had considered what to do next. After Aleksander's behaviour when he had told him the news about the trigger for the ninja bomb, he had been reluctant to provoke a similar reaction. But if he could track Susan Stonehouse down, and discover her new identity, then he was sure that Aleksander would be pleased and that maybe his own position in the Paloka empire would be enhanced as a result.

Snorting another line of cocaine to keep his mind in gear, the cyber detective had decided that he needed to get inside the mind of Susan Stonehouse, or, more accurately, those who were protecting her. Putting herself in Aleksander's firing line had been a highly foolhardy, or very brave, thing for the woman to have done, particularly as she had apparently had little to gain at a personal level from exposing herself to such risk. It followed then that she must have been offered protection by the law enforcement authorities in the UK.

Tracking down the new identity of Susan Stonehouse had been a daunting task, but the young man had been sure that some trace of what had happened to her would exist somewhere in the cyber world. He had needed to gain access to confidential police records and to those of the British security services. Even if Susan Stonehouse had been given a new identity in another country, the trail would start at home. Once he had hacked his way in, he discovered that there was a great deal of information about Susan Stonehouse, but that all of it concluded with her death on the tracks of the London Underground network. He had searched around to see if there were any encrypted records of people currently in witness protection schemes, but such files had been impossible even for him to access, try as he might. Traps had been placed against them in case anyone were foolish enough to try to break in, and he was wary of causing another cyber attack on the Paloka systems such as the one which had killed Egzon.

The young man had tried everything he could think of, but to no avail. Eventually, on the second afternoon, out of his head on coke, he had typed in fury into his search engine "Where the fuck are you Susan Stonehouse?". To his astonishment, there had been an answer. It was from a source he had never heard of, Weatherbys in the UK. Susan Stonehouse was registered as the owner of an Irish bred racehorse called Tabikat.

The cyber detective had never heard of Weatherbys. Having read its website, he had learned that its main business was to provide racing services to the British Horseracing Authority, including daily racecard production, equine pedigree research, printing, publishing, marketing and ticketing services. There were IT operations underpinning this and the other companies in the Weatherbys group. The young man had browsed the public areas of their site as well as that of the British Horseracing Authority.

The young man had not had any experience of horseracing whilst in England and was unsure where to move next in his quest for information. He was aware that the Paloka empire had large operations in online betting and a profitable line in the corruption of fading sportspeople, but the information he had located appeared to be unconnected with gambling or bookmaking.

Setting aside his search for information on Susan Stonehouse, he had decided to see what might be discovered about her horse. There had been plenty of information to be had about racehorses, he had quickly discovered, most of it highly public and fraught with a plethora of contradictory expert opinion. People had seemed to be making money out of all aspects of the horseracing industry, from honest employment as stable staff through to more dubious activities in providing racing tips. Sorting out the sources of factual information from the welter of opinion and speculation took him some time, but the young man had eventually discovered that Tabikat was an eight year old Irish bred horse which held an entry for a forthcoming major race called the Cheltenham Gold Cup. The news and other reports which he had found online overwhelmed him with detailed information about the Cheltenham Festival in general and the famous Gold Cup race in particular.

The cyber detective still had a quick mind, although the cocaine would soon begin take its eventual toll on his senses, and he had absorbed the data very efficiently. Tabikat had only recently come to Britain, it appeared, having previously raced only in Ireland. Tabikat had run only two races since his move, one at Newbury racecourse and one at Cheltenham. He had not won either of them. His trainer was a James Sampfield Peveril, a fair skinned man who spoke with an upper class English accent and was clutching a brown fedora hat on his head when interviewed on television at Newbury racecourse. The horse's most recent jockey was Welshman called Merlin ap Rhys, although a different jockey appeared to have ridden the horse when it was racing in Ireland. There was another trainer called Brendan Meaghan who had been involved with the horse then. James Sampfield Peveril's training establishment was in Somerset, a rural English county which the young man had never felt it necessary to visit.

As far as the smacked up cyber detective could tell, the horse's race record was entirely genuine and had not been altered in any way. The history of its ownership through, struck him as odd. The horse had first been owned by Eoghan Foley of Gleannglas, wherever that might be, and then by Levy Brothers International, Captain T K Stonehouse and Susan Stonehouse. Then the ownership had reverted to Levy Brothers International at about the time that Susan Stonehouse had apparently died. This at least had made sense. The most recent change of ownership to Susan Stonehouse as sole owner had been recorded only a few days before, and made no sense at all.

The young man had considered, as he set out another line of cocaine on the desk, what he could learn from all this. The first possibility was that there had been an error in the record keeping by Weatherbys and the British Horseracing Authority. Susan Stonehouse's name had always been on their records as an owner and someone could simply have made a mistake when updating the horse's record at the time it was transferred from Ireland to the Somerset training establishment. It seemed unlikely that these record keepers would necessarily know whether people who had been registered owners in the past were still alive.

The second possibility was that the information was correct. This did not prove that Susan Stonehouse was alive, merely that someone wished the horse to be registered in her name, and, he had supposed, to run in the race wearing her racing colours. This could be some kind of sentimental action on the part of her family and friends, the young man had thought, but it seemed a bit pointless, given that the owner herself could not be present to see the horse run in the race.

The third possibility, and the young man had hardly dared think it, was that this was all part of some kind of trap. If Susan Stonehouse were still alive, and wanted to attend the Cheltenham races, then this could easily have been achieved under her new identity, under the guise of which she could turn up and watch her horse unrecognised. So, it followed, the young man had thought, that she was either genuinely dead, but someone wanted it to appear as if she were alive, or else that she was alive and was deliberately putting her name in the public domain so as to attract attention. And whose attention might she, or rather than authorities protecting her, wish to attract? That of Aleksander Paloka, of course.

As the young man had turned these thoughts around in his mind, he had begun to realise, slowly and reluctantly, that he had been set up. Someone had known that a cyber detective such as himself would come along to find out what had caused the catastrophic meltdown of Egzon's systems. The trail, carefully laid for him to follow, had been sufficiently difficult to make the detection task appear realistic, but sufficiently clear to ensure that he had reached the right result – the name of Susan Stonehouse. That same name had been inserted into the British racehorse owners' records at just about the time that he had started searching for Susan Stonehouse's new identity. It had served the purpose of distracting him and had pushed his focus onto that evidently well known Gold Cup horserace in England. It was important that he get back to looking for where Susan Stonehouse was really hiding.

Did the upper class Englishman who was training the horse at this very moment know what had been done to the ownership records, he had wondered. Was he in collusion with those who had made the change of name which had so distracted his online detective work? Quickly checking into a database of British racehorse trainers, the young man had easily discovered an address and telephone number for Sampfield Grange, apparently the ancestral home of the trainer concerned, and now, he assumed, the location of the horse Tabikat too. But that did not mean that Susan Stonehouse would be there, either with her old or her new identity.

Whilst he had pondered how to use this information, the young man had become aware that someone was standing behind him. He had felt rather than seen that this was Aleksander and his bodyguards, two thickset men who stayed by their boss's side even in this ugly warehouse basement, well protected as it was from the eyes of the outside world.

"Well, my little cyber rat? What have you found out?" had asked Aleksander, unnervingly politely.

The young man would have liked more time to prepare his answer, but he had had no option but to speak.

"Susan Stonehouse did not die on the tracks of the London

Underground," he had started, hesitantly, "I believe she is alive, with a new identity."

"And what is the new identity?" asked Aleksander, his voice still quiet, as the bodyguards stood equally quietly behind him.

"That I have not yet discovered," had replied the erstwhile cyber detective, "But I have discovered the identity of someone who may be able to tell us."

"And who is that?" had asked Aleksander.

"James Sampfield Peveril, Sampfield Grange, in Somerset, a county in England," had replied the young man, fearing that he was playing his cards too quickly, "He is a racehorse trainer. He is training a horse which appears to belong to Susan Stonehouse. Training it for a big race. The Cheltenham Gold Cup."

Aleksander had sucked in his breath.

"I know this race," he said, "It is one of the best of its kind in the world. Perhaps I should attend."

"But Mr Paloka," had begun the young man, "There is something not right here. I sense a problem...."

The young man had been about to explain that there was no way in which Susan Stonehouse's handlers were ever going to lay down such a simple route to discovering her whereabouts, that is, not unless and until they wanted her to be found. If they wanted her to be found, they wanted Aleksander to find her. In which case, they would be ready for Aleksander and would have set a trap for him.

But the young man with the British computer science degree had had no chance to tell Aleksander any of this. This was because Aleksander's bodyguard had just shot him in the back of the head.

38

By the first week of March, the incident which had led to Kye's arrest on a Sunday morning two weeks earlier had already become part of history in the Sampfield Grange yard.

Sam had returned home on the afternoon of the day after the Newbury race meeting to what had seemed like uproar. As he had turned the Audi towards the garage, he had noticed that Isabella Hall was not in her usual place in the yard office, and that Sadie was running towards his car, evidently having been awaiting his arrival. Lewis and Kelly had been peering from the kitchen window, having agreed that Sadie should approach him first on his arrival in the yard.

Sam had spent a pleasant evening at the Peveril household, whilst Gilbert had regaled an aghast Philippa Peveril with the story of Highlander Park's crazy behaviour in the Newbury bumper. As the story had progressed, Sam had noted with amusement, one would have thought Highlander's deportment to have been comparable to that of a scarcely broken-in wild horse.

"Don't worry Pippa," Sam had reassured Gilbert's sweet, plump wife, who, having confined her own horse-related activities to those of a spectator, had looked increasingly alarmed throughout the narrative, "I will be putting my new conditional jockey up on Highlander Park at Listed races in future. Gil can just take him to the points, if he wants. The horse has always behaved well at those. I think he was just spooked by the wind and the noise at Newbury."

Having driven home mulling over plans as to where Highlander Park might be entered to race next, Sam had not expected to be told by Sadie on his arrival that his prospective conditional jockey had been arrested by three armed police officers that morning, and that no-one knew what was happening.

"Why was he arrested?" Sam had asked, trying to get his head around Sadie's rather garbled and dramatic account of the incident.

"None of us knows," Sadie had told him, "It was something to do with Isabella, but she won't speak to us. She's been in her flat all morning. We've knocked on the door, but there's no answer and the door's locked."

"What do you mean, it was something to do with her?" Sam had asked, his heart sinking, as he recalled the information Frank had shared with him about Isabella's role in Frank's mysterious classified operation, not to mention the apparent threat to Isabella's life.

"Well, Kye was in her flat," Sadie had replied, "That is, we think so, anyway. The police took him down the stairs from there and she was sitting at the top, looking like she was crying."

"Oh, God," Sam had said, "Is she safe?"

"Like I said, she won't answer the door, so we don't know," Sadie had informed him, turning pale, "Do you think something might have happened to her, Mr Sampfield?"

"How long is it since you last saw her, Sadie?" Sam had asked her.

"About three hours," Sadie had informed him, "We tried to get her to come down for lunch, but she didn't answer."

"I'll speak to her myself," Sam had said, advancing towards the steps at the side of the garage, "Don't worry, Sadie, please."

But Sam had been very worried himself as he had ascended the stone steps at the side of the garage, Sadie watching him from below.

"Isabella!" had called Sam, knocking on the door, "It's James Sampfield here. I need to talk to you, please. Are you all right in there?"

Rather to Sam's surprise, the door had been opened almost at once, and Isabella Hall had stood silently in front of him.

Sam's first reaction had been that Isabella looked very unwell. There had been sunken rings below her eyes, which had become large and staring, with dilated black pupils. Her breathing had been laboured, as if she had been running, and her whole demeanour had been indicative of someone defeated and utterly exhausted.

Sam had taken a deep breath.

"May I come in?" he had asked.

"Yes, of course," had replied Isabella, and she had moved backwards from the door so that he could enter, "There's not really anywhere for you to sit down, I'm afraid."

Sam, looking around the flat which he had not entered since childhood, had been shocked by the poor effort Lewis and Kelly seemed to have made to produce comfortable accommodation for Isabella. The flat had struck him as a dismal and gloomy habitation for someone who was supposed to be a skilled employee on his staff. A woman such as Isabella Hall was unlikely to be used to living in such poorly appointed accommodation and he had felt a sudden pang of guilt.

"Sadie tells me something happened which led to Kye being arrested," Sam had begun, looking round for a chair, and finding none, sitting down on the edge of the bed. Isabella had sunk down onto the floor by the ancient chest of drawers, which Sam had recognised as being from his mother's old bedroom, "Sadie's worried about you. Can you tell me what's been going on?"

"I'm very sorry, Mr Sampfield," had said Isabella, in a quiet and scarcely audible voice, "This is all my fault. I overreacted. I thought Kye was a.. a.. burglar. So I called the police."

"Why did you think Kye was a burglar?" Sam had asked.

"Because he looked as if he was searching my flat," Isabella had stated, baldly.

Sam had been saved from continuing the conversation by a knock on the door.

"Who is it?" he had shouted, testily.

"Police, sir," had come the immediate reply, "I have Mr McMahon with me. May we come in?"

Without waiting for permission, the police officer had opened the door and walked in, Kye following immediately behind him. It had been the same officer who had arrested Kye earlier. This time, though, the officer had not been carrying a firearm and he had sent a warning glance to Isabella, who had remained sitting on the floor. Sam, though, had not seen the officer before and had accepted his and Kye's arrival with some relief.

"Mr McMahon has come to apologise for frightening Mrs Hall," the police officer had said, "Is there somewhere we can sit down?" he had added, looking around the dingy flat.

Sam had felt embarrassed. He had marched across to the door and had shouted across the yard, correctly assuming that Sadie, Kelly and Lewis were all hovering about and within earshot.

"Lewis! Get some decent chairs up here at once. We need four of them. Now!"

Lewis was not used to Mr Sampfield speaking to him so sharply. He and Kelly had scurried off immediately to comply with the instruction.

As Sam had remained waiting outside at the top of the stairs for the chairs to be brought, he had been, conveniently for Kye and the police officer, temporarily out of earshot.

Kye had knelt down by Isabella on the floor. The police officer had stood between them and the door, apparently waiting to assist with the chairs.

417

"I'm sorry, Isabella," Kye had said in a low voice, "I didn't mean to scare you. I was being stupid. I thought you were spying on me."

When Isabella made no response to this comment, Kye had gone on, by now overwhelmed by his situation and almost in tears,

"I met Mr Stanley. There's people from Liverpool on my case, Isabella. Bad people. He's said he'll help me if I help yez. Yez can trust me to do this, I promise. Give me a chance. Please, Isabella."

"Thank you, Kye," Isabella had said eventually, with a heavy sigh, "You deserve better than this. We all do."

The police officer had shifted his feet beside them.

"You need to get a story straight, Isabella," he had told her, firmly, "The Lord and Master will be back in with the chairs any moment, and I'll have to take this lad away again if you can't agree something."

To Kye's relief, Isabella had taken a deep breath, and had made a visible effort to pull herself together. In something approaching her usual steady voice, she had responded,

"OK, Martin. I'll spin him a line. You keep your mouth shut for now, Kye. Just act contrite. I'll need to know what you've agreed with Frank Stanley, but we have to get Mr Sampfield sorted first."

"And you need some bloody decent furniture in this place," the police officer had added, "Jesus, I can't believe they've made you live in this dump. It's like a prison cell."

So, as Lewis and Kelly had arrived at the foot of the garage stairs with a collection of chairs, the police officer had shaken Sam's hand and told him that Mrs Hall did not wish to press charges and that Mr McMahon was apologising to her now for his behaviour. The police officer had left, Isabella had confirmed the same story, and she and Kye had sat on the newly arrived chairs for some time in the flat after Sam had left them together, at Isabella's request.

Sam's anger towards Lewis and Kelly about the poor conditions in which Isabella Hall had been living had continued for the rest of the day. It had been partly fuelled by the knowledge that he should have checked for himself that a woman whom Frank had asked him to help was being properly looked after. Sam belatedly suspected that Lewis and Kelly had deliberately made the flat uncomfortable in the hope that the new employee would leave, and Lewis's brother could be installed in the flat instead, as Lewis had originally been planning.

"When I say I want accommodation to be made ready for a new employee, I expect it to be done properly," he had told Lewis, shortly, "Make sure you speak to Isabella this week and get something better sorted out. I can't believe the poor woman hasn't even had a proper chair to sit on all these months."

Lewis had known better than to argue with Mr Sampfield, although his private view had been that, as Isabella was mostly in the office, out cycling, or in bed with Mr Stanley at The Charlton Arms and probably other places too, she wouldn't have made much use of any chairs in her flat anyway.

When Isabella and Kye had appeared at the evening meal, apparently now on friendly terms, the whole incident had been dismissed by the two of them as a misunderstanding. Kye had explained that he had been looking for Isabella, not having found her in the office and not having realised she was out on her bike. So, he had decided to go up to the flat to look for her. The flat door had been left unlocked, but it had been so dark in there that he had been looking around for a light to switch on when Isabella had come back, seen him, and called the police. Isabella herself had chipped in with a story about a friend having been attacked by an armed burglar at her home some years ago, and said that this memory had caused her to overreact when she had seen the shadowy figure of Kye in the gloom of the flat.

The story had not adequately explained a number of facts, such as why Kye had not noticed Isabella's missing bicycle, nor why the police who had attended had come so quickly and were armed, nor what was so urgent about Kye's need to see Isabella that he could not wait until later in the day. But the two of them had stuck to the story, and, although Lewis in particular, still smarting from his reprimand by Mr Sampfield, remained suspicious, nothing more could be got from either of them, and the incident gradually began to lose its significance.

By the first week of March, the Sampfield Grange yard was almost entirely focused on getting Tabikat fit for his run in the Gold Cup. Tabikat usually worked alongside Curlew Landings on the Sampfield Grange gallops and continued to be boxed over to the Dicks yard every other day by Sadie to enable him also to work with the Dicks horses. Ranulph Dicks had no runner himself in the Gold Cup so his yard had now unofficially adopted Tabikat as their own runner as the Festival began to approach.

Stevie Stone appeared at the Sampfield Grange yard to interview Sam as had been agreed between them at Newbury racecourse. Stevie arrived in an elderly green Mini Cooper, which appeared to date from the day the new Mini plant in Oxford had first gone into production. Her style of interviewing was to prove rather different than that of the smooth TV professional to whom Sam had spoken at Newbury and Cheltenham.

Isabella Hall was sitting as usual in her office as Stevie and Sam walked past the door towards Tabikat's stable. It was a bright and breezy morning with clouds travelling in fluffy chunks across a bright blue sky. The Sampfield Grange operation was, as always, tidy and clean, with yellow daffodils rising in clumps from the grassy verges by the sides of the lane leading up to the yard. Snowdrops shook and shivered in the wind whilst the crocus flowers were being encouraged to open by a warm sun which intermittently flooded the yard when not covered by the clouds.

Stevie's objective was to interview Sam standing in front of Tabikat's stable, so that the horse himself could be seen by the viewers as Sam spoke about him.

"I'll put Tabby Cat and Jayce in afterwards," Stevie explained, "So don't be put off when I start speaking to them as I ask the questions. We have to give the impression that Tabby Cat's here as well. And also that Jayce is listening in too. Don't worry, he isn't."

Tabikat inclined his head towards Stevie as she approached his stable and allowed him to fondle his nose for a while, nodding his handsome head up and down appreciatively.

"That means he remembers me," Stevie said, laughing, although Sam noticed that there was a catch in her voice as she ended the sentence.

Sam stood obediently in front of the stable, as Stevie held her iPad up towards him. Stevie asked him only four questions, apparently in conference with Tabby Cat, and then closed the iPad and put it away in her capacious handbag.

"Is that all?" asked Sam, surprised.

"Yes, that's all, as far as you are concerned, Mr S P," Stevie told him, "I've got a bit of work to do on it now and you can all have a look at it on the Racing Tips for Smart Girls app in a couple of hours time. I just need to find somewhere to sit down for half an hour."

"You can use the office, here, if you like," Sam offered, "I'm sure Isabella won't mind."

Stevie seemed to hesitate as she looked across at the office where Isabella remained sitting, apparently looking at something on the screen of the computer.

"Better not," Stevie said, "I've got to get on. Nice to see you again, Mr S P. Say goodbye to your stable staff for me. I always look out for them at the races now. Sadie and Kye, isn't it?"

"That's right," Sam told her, "You've got a good memory, Miss Stonehouse."

"Oh, you mustn't call me that," said Stevie, hurriedly, "I only answer to Stevie Stone these days. Keeps the family connection with Tabikat out of the picture. People might think I was biased otherwise."

Stevie's venerable Mini nosed its way down the lane to the road below just Merlin ap Rhys's rather newer black BMW was coming up the hill towards her. As the two drivers manoeuvred the cars to squeeze past each other, Merlin rolled down his window and signalled to Stevie to do the same.

"Hi there, *cariad*. I'm Merlin ap Rhys. You're the tipster girl, aren't you?" Merlin said to Stevie, without preamble, "The one with the talkin' cat, isn' it? My sister likes list'nin' to you. You been talkin' to Mr Sampfield about Tabikat, 'ave you?"

"Yes, I have, Mr ap Rhys," said Stevie, smiling at Merlin's forthright approach to her.

"You wan' to talk to 'is jockey too?" asked Merlin, "I'd be 'appy to make time for you, I would."

"I'm leaving now, but maybe we could talk at the Festival," Stevie replied, thoughtfully, "It would be good for the smart girls to hear from the jockeys. I'll need to know a bit about you, though, not just information about riding Tabikat. Smart girls like a bit of human interest and gossip, not just racing facts and figures. Things like where you went to school, whether you have a wife, girlfriend, children, your favourite pastimes, that sort of stuff."

"No problem at all," replied Merlin, promptly, "Maybe you an' I can go for a drink and then we can discuss all those things and a lot more too. What do you say?"

"I say that I will see you at the Festival, Mr ap Rhys," replied Stevie, with a smile, "Just make sure you don't get injured again. Maybe Sadie won't be so keen to look after you if you're not going to be fit to ride Tabikat."

Stevie rolled up the car window and drove on, leaving Merlin open-mouthed behind her.

"'ow the 'ell does she know about Sadie?" he muttered to himself, "I wonder 'oo's she's been talkin' to?"

Merlin could see Sadie herself standing in the yard ahead of him. As he stopped the car, Sadie came over to stand by the door.

"You been talking to that vlog woman?" asked Merlin, "The one with the talkin' cat. She was just goin' down the lane. Seemed to know all about us, she did."

"No, she only spoke to Mr Sampfield," said Sadie, surprised, "I didn't know she knew who I was."

"Oh well, I suppose it's 'er job to poke her nose into people's lives," said Merlin, dismissively, "Any'ow, 'ow are you, *cariad*? I've thinking about you keeping my bathroom rug warm."

But Sadie did not seem in the mood for recalling their joint exploits in Merlin's bathroom. Instead she said,

"We've got a problem, Merlin. I haven't told Mr Sampfield. I wanted to ask you what you thought, first."

"What's up?" Merlin asked, suddenly serious, "Nothin's 'appened to Tabikat, 'as it?"

"No, it's not that," said Sadie, "But someone's been watching us when we're out on the gallops. Just here, not at the Dicks's. A man in the trees with binoculars."

"Probably jus' someone trying to get an inside line on Tabikat," Merlin replied, "Sellin' on information and such to tippin' lines."

"Well that's what I thought," said Sadie, "But Kye saw him too, and he was worried about it and I don't know whether we should tell Mr Sampfield."

"Well, I'm 'ere to work with Tabikat now," said Merlin, "So let's go up onto the top jumps line and see if we can see anyone. I'll tackle 'im myself, if I 'ave to."

"OK," said Sadie, relieved, "I'll get the horses ready now. I'll ask Isabella to call Mr Sampfield back down. He went to get changed after the interview with Stevie Stone."

"'oo's Isabella?" asked Merlin, opening the boot of the BMW to get out his riding gear.

"She's Mr Sampfield's office manager," Sadie told him, "Surely you've seen her before? Come over, and I'll introduce you."

The two of them walked the few yards to the office where Isabella Hall was reading a sheet of paper with handwritten notes on it.

"Hello, Isabella," said Sadie, "This is Merlin ap Rhys, Tabikat's jockey. He said he hadn't met you when he's been here before."

Isabella looked up at Sadie, an expression of alarm briefly visible on her usually expressionless face. Merlin stepped forward.

"'ello Isabella. Pleased to meet you.." he started, but his voice tailed off, "But I do know you already," he said, slowly, "You were with Mr Meaghan that day he asked me to take the ride on Tabikat in the 'ennessy. I thought you was the 'orse's owner."

39

Sadie had been correct when she had told Merlin ap Rhys that Kye was worried by the unidentified observer on the Sampfield Grange gallops who had apparently been watching Tabikat's work through binoculars. Kye's worry had stemmed entirely from having no idea who or what the person was really watching.

If the person was a betting tipster simply trying to get inside information, then Kye was not much bothered by that, and could soon ensure, with the help of other Sampfield Grange staff, that the individual was seen off. But his fear was that the observer had something to do with Bronz and the Liverpool drugs gang. Or that the observation could have something to do with Isabella Hall, whose life, Kye now understood, was in even more danger than his own.

When Kye had been dragged down the steps of the chauffeur's flat at Sampfield Grange, he had expected to be taken to a police station. The three police officers who had arrested him had sat silently in the back of the black van as it had trundled purposefully away from Sampfield Grange. Kye had been pushed face down on the floor, and one of the police officers had placed a leather booted foot in the small of Kye's back.

"Don't try to move, sir," he had said. Kye hadn't tried.

The van had not, however, gone to a police station. After about fifteen highly uncomfortable and stressful minutes, the van had come to a halt, and Kye had been ordered to get up and get out.

Kye had found himself in the driveway of a small, whitewashed cottage. He had not recognised the building, but the whirr of a microlight overhead and persistent buzz of airborne model aircraft nearby told him that he was somewhere in the vicinity of Old Warnock airfield. It was the place where he had seen Isabella meet her pilot friend who had landed there in the small blue and white aeroplane.

The police officer nearest to Kye had pushed him towards the front door of the cottage.

"What's going on? Where's you taking me?" Kye had asked in sudden alarm, wondering whether he had been set up, and these armed men were not bizzies at all.

There had been no answer to his questions, but, as the front door of the cottage had opened, Kye had found himself face to face with the mysterious visitor who had arrived without warning to speak to Mr Sampfield almost five months ago. The man who had generated so much salacious interest from Sadie, Lewis, and Kelly as Isabella's supposed secret lover. Frank Stanley.

"Thanks Martin," Mr Stanley had said, "I'll take it from here. I'll give you a shout if I need you to take him anywhere."

At the end of the following hour with Mr Stanley, Kye had come to realise that where he went next was entirely his own decision. He had also soon learned that Mr Stanley knew a great deal about him. Mr Stanley had known about the HGV modifications at the garage in Cheshire, and about Kye's enforced move from the Cheshire yard to Sampfield Grange. Mr Stanley had known about Kye's drug dealing operation with Gray and about the attempts to follow Isabella Hall with the drone which had so mysteriously gone wrong shortly afterwards. Mr Stanley had been aware of the approach made to Kye by Bronz and Sheryl at Cheltenham racecourse. And he had also known all about Kye's family back in Toxteth and was aware of the application made for Kye to become a conditional jockey with Mr Sampfield.

Kye had stared miserably at Mr Stanley as these facts had been set out in ruthless detail. It had therefore come as a surprise to Kye to hear Mr Stanley say to him,

"So, I think you and I are in a position to help each other, Mr McMahon."

"How?" Kye had managed to croak.

"How would it be," asked Mr Stanley, "If you were able to wipe the slate clean? You never got implicated in that activity in Cheshire. No-one but Isabella and I know about the drug dealing at the racecourses. There are all your former customers, of course, but, if the supply now dries up, they're not likely to inform on you. And it is possible to ensure that no action is taken, should any of them do so. The real problem is your brother Bronz. Am I right?"

Kye had nodded, unable to speak.

"So what's the deal with Bronz?" had asked Mr Stanley, "We saw them approach you and we know he's been in touch, but we haven't seen any goods change hands yet."

"Bronz's people want to shift some serious shit at Cheltenham races," Kye had told him, "I guess I'm going to be the fall guy who fronts it up. I'm not exactly sure how it's meant to work yet. But I know I won't be able to say no. They might do something to mum or to my sister Britney or baby Taylor. Or to Mr Sampfield's horses. I don't know. They're real bad people, Mr Stanley. They've got me by the balls, I know they have."

Mr Stanley had seemed to be thinking. At length, he had said,

"Merseyside Police are keen to get their hands on these people, you know, Kye. Will you help them?"

"Me, helping the bizzies, that's a laugh," had spluttered Kye, unable to take in what had just been suggested.

"Well, I can always ask Martin to take you to the local police and have you charged with possession with intent to supply Class B drugs," had suggested Mr Stanley, "And with breaking and entering into Isabella's Hall's flat. We can supply plenty of sound evidence of both those crimes. You'll lose your job with Mr Sampfield, your chance of a career as a jockey, and probably go to prison. Is that what you want?"

Kye had stared at Frank Stanley in silence, but the stresses of the last few weeks and the hopeless situation in which he now found himself had eventually taken their toll on even Kye's tough defences, and tears had begun to form in his eyes and run down his cheeks.

"Yez fucking people have got me by the balls, too," he had said.

"I'm offering you a way out," Frank Stanley had said, bluntly, "It's up to you whether or not you take it. And by the way, I'm not a bizzy, and nor is Isabella. Isabella's got a soft spot for you. She thinks you deserve a chance, God knows why, after the way you've behaved towards her. I'll leave you to think about it for a bit. Do you want some water?"

It had not taken long for Kye to agree. Frank Stanley had told him very little other than that he should go back to Sampfield Grange prepared to apologise to Isabella Hall and be ready to follow her instructions. Kye was also to continue to co-operate with any instructions received from Bronz and to report what he did to Isabella.

"Can't yez tell me anything more?" Kye had pleaded, "Like what's Isabella doing at Sampfield Grange if she's not spying on me? Who is she to yez anyway? Lewis and that lot think she's yez mistress."

"Well she isn't," had said Frank Stanley, "She's working with me and her life's at considerable risk. Much more than yours, I might add. Just respect that, Mr McMahon. I need you to help her not to ask questions about her."

"Does Mr Sampfield know about any of this?" had persisted Kye, desperate to understand what was going on.

"Not really," said Frank Stanley, "Just that he is responsible for helping me protect Isabella. Now don't ask me anything else, or I may change my mind."

So Kye had been duly returned to Sampfield Grange, still fearful and with no choice but to hope that he could trust Mr Stanley and

Isabella Hall.

Kye was due to ride out with Merlin, Sadie and Mr Sampfield that morning. The application for the conditional jockey's licence for Kye had been accepted by the BHA and Mr Sampfield had said that they would look for a suitable race into which Highlander Park could be entered with Kye as his jockey.

As Kye tacked up Highlander Park, who had been upset not to go out with first lot as usual, and was, as a result, now raring to go, he heard Sadie and Merlin approaching from across the yard.

"That's bloody weird, that is," Merlin was saying, "I could 'ave sworn it was 'er that was the owner. But she says that the 'orse is owned by a bank. Maybe that old guy who was with 'er 'ad somethin' to do with the bank then. It was definitely 'er, even though she said she didn' know me."

"What old guy?" Sadie asked him, her mind suddenly alert. She remembered how Lewis and Kye had tried to find out more about Mr Peveril's apparent sighting of Isabella Hall at the Cheltenham Showcase meeting last October, in particular trying to identify the man who had been seen accompanying her there. Perhaps at last, she thought, they would all be able to confirm that it was Mr Stanley.

"'e was tall, grey 'air, poker face, walked with a stick, must 'ave been about 60," Merlin replied, promptly.

"That doesn't sound like Mr Stanley," Sadie commented, disappointed.

"oo's 'e, then?" asked Merlin.

"We think he's Isabella's boyfriend, don't we, Kye?" Sadie responded, attempting to draw Kye into the conversation.

Kye's recent experiences had made him wary of getting involved in local gossip about Isabella Hall, so he said, carefully,

"Well, we all thought he was, but we've not seen him around much."

"Well that doesn't mean anything, if she's keeping him a secret," said Sadie with a laugh.

Merlin, though, was still thinking.

"You could be right about the old guy bein' 'er other 'alf," he said, "She stuck to 'im like glue all the time Mr Meaghan was talkin' to me."

"Perhaps she used to work with him at the bank that owns Tabikat," suggested Kye, suddenly, "We know that she knows about accounting and suchlike. She saw that Mr Purefoy off from here, didn't she?"

Kye had no reason whatever to think that this speculative information was true, but it seemed to make sense to both Merlin and Sadie as a possible explanation of the odd situation, and they both nodded in unison.

"Mr Sampfield's coming now," Kye pointed out, seeing Sam approaching from the direction of the big house, "We'd better get a move on with the horses."

The ride consisted that morning of Sam on his usual mount, Caladesi Island, Merlin on Tabikat, Kye on Highlander Park, and Sadie riding Ranger Station for a change, having already taken out Honeymoon Causeway with first lot. The plan was to go up to the row of practice jumps at the top of the hill and allow the two competition horses a chance to work together over a few of them. Sam was interested to see how Highlander would take to jumping fences with Kye on his back and also thought that Merlin might be able to give Kye some useful advice as well as schooling Tabikat.

The bright clear weather meant that the surrounding countryside was visible for miles round once the little party reached the top of the hill.

"You've such a great place 'ere, Mr Sampfield," called out Merlin, as the horses lifted their heads to the sun and their riders took in deep breaths of cool, clean air.

Kye was determined to keep a good look out for the watcher with the binoculars. If the person concerned were trying to get inside information on Tabikat's progress, then he would have been waiting for the horse to appear, given that he had been absent from the earlier ride. But there was no sign of anyone at all on the sunny hillside, and Kye soon became immersed in the schooling work and forgot about his concerns.

Kye could see why Mr Peveril had had so much trouble with Highlander Park in the Newbury bumper. The more sedate pace and smaller fields of the Cuffborough point to point races had not really sparked the young horse's ambition. Going upsides a faster horse like Tabikat, Highlander suddenly woke himself up and went for the practice jumps with gusto. Kye revelled in the experience, and would have happily ridden all morning if Highlander's stamina could have taken it. More than ever, he hoped against hope that Mr Stanley could indeed wipe the slate clean, as he had put it, and give Kye the chance to make a career as a jump jockey. Mr Sampfield seemed pleased with everything too, and chatted amicably to Merlin as the horses made their way back to the yard along the primrose lined track spotted with slowly drying muddy puddles.

Kye was soon brought down to earth once back in the Sampfield Grange establishment by seeing a text message on his mobile phone. It was from Bronz.

Shits in. Call me.

Merlin and Sadie were too involved in making plans for their next meeting to notice Kye slipping off once the horses had been untacked and put back in their boxes. With shaking hands, Kye keyed in Bronz's number.

Bronx seemed to be in a relaxed mood for once.

"Hello, our kid," he said to Kye, "It's ready to go for us at Cheltenham."

"Yez know I'm only there on the Friday, don't you?" Kye warned Bronz, "We don't have any runners on the other days."

"No probs," Bronz responded, "This is just a trial run for next year. Gold Cup day, isn't it? There'll be plenty of people there for that."

"Fine," said Kye, "What do I do?"

The instructions from Bronz were simple. Kye was to park the horsebox at the furthest end of the parking area. Once the horse had been unloaded and was installed in the racecourse stables, Kye was to return to the vehicle, sit in the driver's seat, and someone would bring the gear to him. Buyers would be sorted and all Kye had to do was to sit there and hand over the goods to them. The stuff itself would all be ready packaged, paid for, and well disguised, courtesy of Sheryl.

"I don't understand why you need me," Kye ventured to say to Bronz, "You could be doing this yesselves."

"We ain' gorra posh horsebox," Bronx told him, "You look respectable. As if yez belongs there. We don't."

There was no answer to that, so Kye ended the call and went in search of Isabella Hall, who was in the office watching the computer screen, on which Mr Sampfield was apparently being interviewed by Tabby Cat, whilst Jayce made helpful interventions.

"Tabby Cat says to put an each way bet on Tabikat in the Gold Cup and we agree with him, don't we Jayce?" came the sound of Stevie Stone's voice from the computer speaker, "And lucky Tabby Cat will be out talking to Tabikat's jockey on the day of the race. And, just listen up to this, smart girls, magic Merlin ap Rhys is a single man, so we all need to get an eyeful of him. See you then. Jayce says bye too."

"Sadie's not going to like that," said Kye, as Isabella looked up from the screen.

Isabella gave a small shrug and did not reply to his comment. Kye tried a different approach.

"Merlin knows you were with Mr Meaghan at the Cheltenham Showcase meeting in October," he said, "We all do, Isabella. Mr Peveril saw you there and he told Mr Sampfield. We heard him."

Isabella sighed.

"Why are you lot so nosy?" she said, "Can't I go out for the day without people checking up on me?"

"It's a small place here," said Kye, "Lewis and Kelly like to be in control of everything and everyone. They only accepted me because Sadie brought me here. Anyway, Merlin was wondering if that bloke you were with was from the bank that owns Tabikat, so I said he probably was and that you likely had worked there with him."

Isabella looked surprised.

"You don't have to cover for me, Kye," she said, "But that's a good explanation, even if George has never worked in a bank in his life, and nor have I, for that matter. Let's just say he's an old friend who invited me along at the last minute. I didn't think anyone would even see us there, let alone anyone connected with Sampfield Grange. Shows that you can't be too careful."

Kye decided not to press the issue further, notwithstanding the intriguing naming of the mysterious man by Isabella as George.

"Isabella," he said, keeping his voice down, "I heard from Bronz. He's setting me up as a drug dealer on Gold Cup day. What do I do now?"

40

Aleksander Paloka had no intention repeating the mistakes which had led to the detonation of the ninja bomb via the trap set in the Frossiac wine museum computer. Sending in a drug dealing pimp, particularly one known to the police, had been an unwise decision, one for which a wretched individual in Toulouse had already paid a heavy price.

Aleksander had spent some time acquainting himself with such information as was readily available about the man he was intending should lead him to Susan Stonehouse. James Sampfield Peveril had been revealed to Aleksander to be a pillar of the English country establishment who owned land and property in both the UK and Australia. Aleksander learned that Mr Sampfield Peveril was a very rich man, who seemed to spend his time playing at being a horse racing trainer. Aleksander had checked this information by installing a covert watcher on the picturesque hillside near James Sampfield Peveril's country pile, who had reported back that he had seen the gentleman concerned riding out on his land on his horse along with other riders every day. The watcher also thought that one of Mr Sampfield Peveril's employees may have seen him, at which point Aleksander ordered that he be withdrawn. There were to be no more accidents like the one in Frossiac.

James Sampfield Peveril appeared to be unmarried and to have no mistress, children or even siblings. An old fashioned English playboy, probably a homosexual, thought Alexsander disgustedly. Aleksander, evil to the core though he was, had nothing but contempt for men who did not work hard to create their own wealth. Nor did he have any truck with male homosexuality, except when it could be used as a tool for blackmail and coercion.

As the repulsive little cokehead had told him, this James Sampfield Peveril was indeed the trainer of a racehorse called Tabikat, which was owned, according to official records, by Susan Stonehouse, and entered to run in the Cheltenham Gold Cup. It followed in Aleksander's mind that Susan Stonehouse must therefore be in regular contact with James Sampfield Peveril.

In the run up to the Cheltenham Festival in two weeks' time, the racing papers were packed with information about horses being prepared by their trainers to run in the four days of races, including those entered in the pinnacle race of the meeting, the Gold Cup. What could be more natural, Aleksander thought, than a journalist wanting to interview James Sampfield Peveril and Susan Stonehouse about the chances of their horse in the prestigious race? Naturally, the journalist would like the two individuals to be brought together for this discussion, if this could be arranged.

Aleksander needed a *bona fide* racing journalist to undertake this task for him and his deputies had no difficulty in finding one. Bribery and corruption in sport was a speciality of the Paloka empire so a name well known in equestrian reporting was easily persuaded to undertake the task in return for knowledge of his predilection for child pornography, supplied through the Paloka dark web systems, not coming into the public domain.

As a result of Aleksander's arrangements, a telephone call was received on the landline in the yard office at Sampfield Grange on the Friday before the Cheltenham Festival, exactly one week before Gold Cup day.

"Good morning," the well spoken male caller began, as Isabella lifted the receiver, "May I speak with Mr Sampfield Peveril?"

"Could I know with whom I am speaking?" Isabella responded formally.

"Good God, yes, should have said," answered the caller, attempting to laugh, but in reality feeling sick at what he was being obliged to do, "I am Gerald Gibson, freelance racing journalist. I'd like to interview Mr Sampfield Peveril, if possible. It is unusual for him to have a horse in a race such as the Cheltenham Gold Cup and it would be interesting to know the story behind it."

"Mr Sampfield is out at the moment with the horses," Isabella informed Gerald Gibson, "Perhaps I can be of some help?"

"Well, if you could, dear lady, that would be wonderful," Gerald ploughed on, "Are you acquainted with the horse's owner?"

"Which owner do you mean?" asked Isabella, "The horse has had several owners."

"I am referring to a Mrs Stonehouse," Gerald said, putting the name forward with some trepidation, "She is listed as the current owner. Does she come to Sampfield Grange to see her horse working? Do she and Mr Sampfield Peveril have a good working relationship concerning his training? These are the kinds of questions I should like to be able to ask them at a face to face interview. It is for a feature which I am compiling about owners of this year's Gold Cup horses."

"I am sorry, Mr Gibson," responded Isabella, "But I have never met Mrs Stonehouse. I don't believe she has ever come to Sampfield Grange."

"Well, Mr Sampfield Peveril must communicate with her, I imagine," Gerald pressed on, "I wonder if I could call back to speak to him when he is available?"

"Please call back in about two hours," Isabella told him, and cut the connection.

Isabella had the Sampfield Grange yard to herself at that moment. Sam and Sadie had gone over to the Dicks yard with Tabikat, whilst Kye, Lewis and Kelly, with two of the remaining work riders, were still in the kitchen finishing breakfast. It was a dull, grey day, with little or no wind, the weather appearing to have got itself stuck in a newly-worn rut.

Isabella Hall took a deep breath, and picked up her mobile phone.

AP hooked

she typed, and pressed the Send button.

The text was answered within seconds.

Time to go And GH

Isabella responded with

Kye?

Covered

came the answer.

On bike in 10

finished Isabella.

Isabella was already wearing her green and white cycling gear. Her helmet and a rucksack, which had been packed for the last three days, were by the door of her flat. The top two drawers of the ancient chest were now empty but the contents of the other drawers were largely intact. The little shower room was bereft of any personal effects.

Isabella sprinted up the steps, collected the helmet and rucksack and put them back down on the ground next to her bike, which was leaning as usual against the warm stone garage wall. Then she walked up the short path to the boot room and let herself into the kitchen.

"Morning everyone, I'm off for a bike ride," she announced to the room at large, "Kye, you'll need to come back to the yard."

"Bloody cheek…" muttered Lewis, who now harboured an increased resentment of Isabella, "Can't she just wait for him to finish his breakfast?"

But Kye had finished eating, and stood up immediately. He and

Isabella walked together down the path towards the garage, Lewis glaring sulkily after them.

"I'm not coming back from this ride," Isabella told Kye once she was sure they could not be overheard by Lewis, "Your instructions are unchanged. Just do what Bronz tells you and Frank will make sure you're all right. And don't panic when things kick off, OK?"

"What do I tell Mr Sampfield and Sadie?" asked Kye, a feeling of dread beginning to overtake him.

"Nothing," replied Isabella, "You saw me go off on my bike and haven't seen me since. Frank will deal with Mr Sampfield, don't worry."

"Will I see yez again?" asked Kye.

"I hope so," Isabella told him, "I'll be watching you riding all the top racehorses when you're a successful jockey."

Kye was about to say that that was not what he meant, but Isabella had already hoisted the rucksack onto her back and was pushing the bike off towards the lane. He watched her green and white clad back, half covered by the black rucksack, receding down the hill, and felt sick. Whatever was happening, he had no choice but to stick with it.

Kye decided to go and talk to Highlander Park and wait to see what happened when Mr Sampfield returned.

Sam's morning at the Dicks yard had been gratifyingly successful. Tabikat had worked well with Sadie on his back, Merlin being far away fulfilling jockey bookings at Sandown Park racecourse that day. Merlin planned to join them on Sunday for a final piece of work with his Gold Cup prospect.

Sam and Sadie arrived back with Tabikat in the small horsebox at about midday, just at the same time as Gerald Gibson was calling the Sampfield Grange office for a fourth time.

Sam heard the telephone ringing as he passed the office, and seeing no sign of Isabella Hall or anyone else nearby, picked it up himself.

"Oh, at last," exclaimed the affected male voice on the other end, "I thought the telephone had stopped working."

"What?" said Sam, "Who is this?"

"Good heavens, is that Mr Sampfield Peveril himself?" the caller said, "Allow me to introduce myself. My name is Gerald Gibson. I am a freelance racing correspondent. I am preparing a feature on the Gold Cup runners and their owners and trainers. I wondered if I might obtain an interview with you and Mrs Stonehouse in relation to Tabikat?"

"With whom?" asked Sam, not sure he had heard the caller correctly.

"Tabikat's owner, Mrs Susan Stonehouse, and your good self," repeated Gerald Gibson in a clear voice, wondering if Sam was a bit deaf.

"There must be a mistake," Sam responded, "Mrs Stonehouse is no longer the owner of Tabikat. She died over a year ago. The horse belongs to Levy Brothers International. I don't have any direct contact with them, and I don't think they'd be interested in being interviewed."

Gerald Gibson had been told that James Sampfield Peveril would be unlikely to be helpful concerning Susan Stonehouse, but he had not expected to be told that she was dead.

"Well, Mrs Stonehouse is listed as the owner by the BHA and Weatherbys," he stated carefully.

"That information must be out of date," Sam replied.

"Indeed not the case," replied Gerald, "This information was entered into the records only a few days ago. It is completely up to date, I can assure you."

"I'm not able to help you, Mr Gibson," Sam told him, firmly, "As far as I know Mrs Stonehouse is dead and I have certainly never met her. I will contact the BHA and find out why this has happened. Thank you for drawing it to my attention."

Sam put down the phone and stared at the blank computer screen. He'd get Isabella onto this when she came back. He had noticed that her bicycle was not by the garage wall.

But Isabella did not come back. Sam progressed through a range of emotions from being mildly annoyed at her absence, to being very annoyed, and eventually, after almost two hours, to being worried. The Sampfield Grange employees were still finishing their lunch in the warm kitchen, when Sam came in from the hall to ask them directly if any of them knew where Isabella was.

"Out on her bike, we thought," said Lewis, "But Kye was the last one to speak to her."

"Yes, she said she was off on her bike," Kye confirmed, feeling sorry for Mr Sampfield, who was clearly very concerned.

"What if she's had an accident?" Kelly interjected, voicing the fears of the others in the kitchen, apart from Kye.

"I'll check with the police," said Sam and left the little group in the kitchen buzzing with concern. But he didn't call the police. He went straight back to his study, took out the little white card, and called Col. F E Stanley.

As before, the call was answered immediately. But this time Sam had no opportunity to speak before Frank's voice said,

"Isabella's fine. We've pulled her out. You can ask your old employee back now, Sam."

"Is that the only information I get?" asked Sam, wearily, feeling, as usual, that he was fighting a losing battle against Frank's mysterious machinations.

"What other information do you want?" asked Frank, apparently helpfully.

"Well, I won't ask where Isabella is, because you won't tell me," Sam began, "But I should very much like to know why Tabikat is now registered with the BHA as being owned by a dead woman. That must have been Isabella's doing. She dealt with all that side of things."

"That's correct, Sam," replied Frank, "And I should appreciate it if you would leave things as they are and not attempt to change the information."

"But we can't just leave it," Sam objected, "The racecard for Gold Cup day, the racing papers, and so on, will all be published with Susan Stonehouse's name and colours shown for Tabikat."

"That's just what's required," Frank commented, too tritely for Sam's liking.

"Well, there's a practical problem, Frank," he replied, "We don't have a set of Susan Stonehouse's racing colours for Merlin to wear."

"You'll find them in Isabella's flat," said Frank.

41

Kye carefully manoeuvred the smaller of the two Sampfield Grange horseboxes, with its precious equine passenger, between the white barriers into the front car park of Cheltenham racecourse. The gates had not yet opened to the public, so the roads around the course were still relatively quiet, although, on the journey through the outskirts of the town, the horsebox had encountered all the usual congestion associated with the local population travelling to their usual places of work. Sadie was dozing in the passenger seat, whilst Mr Sampfield had already gone on ahead in the Range Rover, saying that he would meet them at the racecourse.

Kye had hardly slept at all the previous night. In the darkness of his sparsely furnished bedroom at the yard cottage, the full horror of his situation had presented itself to him repeatedly, in increasingly graphic detail. Kye had never worried too much about things going wrong in his life. He had always managed to stay one step ahead of any approaching problems. But now, in the end, he was trapped, trapped between his fear of Bronz and the gang for whom he worked and his fear of Mr Stanley who had the power to have him arrested at any time. It wasn't as though he could simply disappear, as he had done before, because then there would be no-one to help his mother, his sister and her baby, not to mention that he would be spending his entire life looking over his shoulder. However he looked at it, there was no doubt that trusting Mr Stanley and Isabella Hall was his best chance of a successful outcome, but Kye did not like it one little bit. Mr Stanley had said they weren't filth, but he had certainly seemed to be on their side.

As Kye carefully reversed the horsebox into a suitable position in which they could unload Tabikat, Sadie woke up and stretched.

"It's going to be a good day, today, I can feel it," she said, yawning noisily.

"Hope so," said Kye, shortly, not sharing her optimism.

"What's up with you, Mr Grumpy?" Sadie asked him, "Today's the day we've all been working for with Tabikat."

"Yeah, I know, sorry, Sadie," said Kye, "I didn't get much sleep last night, so I'm a bit knackered. Once we've got Tabikat into the stables, I'll put the box somewhere quiet and have a kip for a while. That OK with yez?"

"Sure," Sadie shrugged, "His race isn't until 3.30 anyway. It's ages away. Lots of time for me to get him ready and looking fabulous."

Tabikat stepped out of the box in his usual regal manner and a few passers-by who had congregated near the gate so as to be ready for gate opening time, stopped to look at him.

"'ello dahlin'! Which 'orse is that?" shouted a fat man who was standing by the railings holding a can of lager in his podgy, blue tattooed hand.

"It's the winner of the Gold Cup," Sadie shouted back, as Tabikat loftily walked forward, ignoring the man who had asked about him.

"Yeah, right," the man replied, as his mates looked on, "Serious now, girl. 'oo is it?"

"It's Tabikat," Sadie replied, "He's the best horse here."

"Yer not so bad yerself," one of the other men shouted, "Got a boyfriend 'ave yer?"

Sadie ignored them and led Tabikat away, whilst Kye fastened up the horsebox ramp and climbed up into the cab. As Bronz had instructed, he drove the vehicle to the far end of the parking area, and sat in the cab, waiting for Bronz to contact him. It was a cold day, but the sun was out, and it shone warmly through the window of the horsebox. Kye leaned back in the seat, suddenly weary. He thought of Highlander Park, home in his stable at Sampfield Grange, of schooling him over the practice jumps on the top gallop, of riding Highlander at Cheltenham racecourse, of winning, of being presented with a Gold Cup by Isabella Hall. He fell asleep.

*

Sadie, having made sure Tabikat was settled in his box, sent a text message to Merlin.

Here. U?

But there was no reply from Merlin.

Mr Sampfield had told her to wait for him in the stables. So she waited, turning over in her mind Kelly's advice as to how to deal with Merlin.

"Sounds as if you're a sex object to him," Kelly had said, rather liking the sound of the term she had learned from daytime TV, "You've got to make him see you as a person."

"But I like the sex," Sadie had replied, mournfully, "We have a good time."

Kelly, who in reality was a bit jealous of a love life that sounded considerably more interesting than that which she was experiencing with Lewis, had counselled,

"Well, then, play him at his own game. Make him think you're only in it for the sex, like him. Then, when he's hooked on you, you can threaten to leave him. He'll not want to lose you if you keep giving him a good time."

Sadie was not sure her sister was right. She had a strong suspicion that if she threatened to leave Merlin ap Rhys, he would simply shrug it off, and find another girlfriend to play his erotic games.

Standing in the Cheltenham stables, absentmindedly fondling Tabikat's soft nose, Sadie said quietly to the horse,

"What do I do, Tabikat? I love him."

Tabikat blew gently out through his nostrils and in that breath Sadie heard one word. *Wait.*

Her phone pinged.

*

Sam had told Sadie that he needed to spend some time with Lady Helen Garratt, to whose box that day he had an invitation. Helen, on hearing that Tabikat's breeder and his wife were planning to be present to watch their horse run for the Gold Cup, had insisted on inviting the Irish couple to join her party.

Lady Helen had done her own research on Eoghan Foley and had learned of the tragic event at Navan racecourse which had ended his career as a jockey. Sam had brought her up to date with the more recent information he had learned about the Foley family and their relationship with the Levys and the Stonehouses, although he had withheld any mention of Frank Stanley and his role in helping him uncover Tabikat's unusual history.

"Golly gosh, Sam," Helen had said when he had explained this to her during a telephone conversation earlier in the month, "This is such a romantic story. A gift of a top racehorse would be exciting enough. But we've now got Eoghan and Caitlin, childhood sweethearts; Daniel and TK, estranged and elusive; Susan and Peter, the tragic dead couple; and Stevie the racing tipster with a talking cat. And then your efficient Mrs Hall running off with no warning, just like that. Poor Sam, your quiet life has really been livened up, hasn't it?"

Sam could do nothing but agree with her, and had wondered what further new surprises were about to be visited upon him. Although he had begun to view everyone with suspicion, including Sadie, Kye and his other employees, Sam had also felt rather excited by the knowledge that he was in the middle of something interesting and unusual. Frank Stanley's return to his life, albeit in such a strange way, had begun to stir long buried memories of the good times they had enjoyed together as youngsters, times which had been the best

445

of Sam's life. He had come to realise more than ever before that he had been living only half a life, and that, whatever the outcome of the Gold Cup and all that went with it, this would have to change.

Eoghan and Caitlin were arriving at Gloucestershire airport on a private flight arranged for them by Lady Helen. Sam had insisted on meeting them there and driving them himself to the racecourse.

As Sam sat in the Range Rover in the parking area facing the main runway, he saw a smart white Cessna Citation touch down noisily on the westerly runway. Moving to the small reception area of the airport, he did not have long to wait before a man and a woman emerged from the arrivals door.

The man was in his fifties, with a strong, wiry body. He had black hair, falling down onto his forehead, and streaked with grey. His eyes were clear and blue. He looked fit and healthy, although he walked with a slight limp. The woman with him was small and slender, her dark hair drawn back into a knot behind her head. Gold hoops dangled from her ears, and she walked beside the man with a light and confident step. She reminded Sam of the statuette of a wood nymph which stood on a small table in the Sampfield Grange Music Room, staring longingly out of the window at the scene beyond.

Sam had never met Eoghan and Caitlin before that moment, but he would have recognised them anywhere.

*

Almost exactly twenty four hours earlier, George Harvey had also arrived at Gloucestershire airport. He had been the only passenger in a Beechcraft King Air twin engine turboprop aircraft, piloted by Elizabeth Baker.

Since the incident which had led to the arrest of Youssef Saad in the Frossiac wine museum, little had been seen in the village of George Harvey. Word had gone around that he had assisted Marcel Lambert in the apprehension of a young drug dealer who had been passing himself off as a respectable businessman, but the Frossiac residents had remained puzzled as to why this unpleasant criminal should have been attracted to the wine museum in the first place. Marcel Lambert and his police colleagues had evidently been expecting the man concerned, as they had been lying in wait for him, but whether the arrival of the mysterious Englishman on the premises at the same time had been coincidental, or part of Marcel's plan, had remained a matter of excited conjecture. And how this incident was connected with the recent revelations about Maurice Vacher could not be easily understood.

Claudine and Monique would have once been happy to question Monsieur 'Arvai about the incident with the drug dealer, but the Vacher family had problems of their own. The tax evasion scam operated through the museum by Maurice Vacher, in collusion with wine producer Jean Philippe Durand had been the second most popular topic for village gossip in the last few weeks, and the Vachers had had little to say in their own defence. Although there had been no reason to connect George Harvey with the charges of fraud currently being brought against Maurice and Jean Philippe by the tax authorities, Claudine was convinced that the Englishman's presence had somehow precipitated her husband's arrest.

In any event, Claudine would have had little or no opportunity to speak to George Harvey, even had she been inclined to do so, as he had been only rarely in his rented home in recent times, and, even when his car had been seen parked outside, he had remained indoors, apparently busy with his work. He had occasionally appeared in the small *supermarche* to buy a few groceries but all attempts by the inquisitive shopkeepers to engage him in conversation, whether in French or English, had been politely fended off.

On the day before the running of the Cheltenham Gold Cup, George Harvey had left the little holiday home by the reeded lake in Frossiac for the last time. Only the waterbirds had seen him go, as it was just getting light, and a heavy mist had hung over the surface of the still pool. If Jean Philippe's spies had still been operating on his behalf, they would have seen George Harvey drive to Carcassonne and return his rental car to the airport. From there he had entered the airport café, ordered a black coffee, and had sat down to wait.

The King Air had touched down at about 1000 local time with only the pilot on board and by 1130 had been refuelled and in the air again, its new passenger sitting in the co-pilot's seat.

"This is almost like the old days, Lizzie" George had said to the pilot, as the aircraft climbed to its nominated cruising height of 8500 feet.

"I wish that were true," Lizzie had replied, "But at least we can enjoy the flight. I don't get to do this much, nowadays."

After an uneventful two and a half hours, George had been rewarded by a view of the white buildings of Cheltenham, as the aircraft made its way down towards the airfield lying beyond the grey circular glass edifice which housed GCHQ on the western side of the neat Cotswold town. The racecourse had been over to the right side of the aircraft as it had slipped down the approach just as the first race of the day was about to start.

But George was not going to the races. Having said goodbye to Lizzie, who had wished him luck and said she would be thinking about him, he had ordered a taxi to take him to a small flat in the basement of a smart Regency house in Pittville Park.

And now, as Sam's Range Rover was arriving at the racecourse at the top of the hill, George was walking, leaning on his stick, also towards the racecourse along with the thousands of other racegoers who were forming a noisy procession along either side of the park. And walking with him was Isabella Hall.

*

Merlin had been in Cheltenham since Monday afternoon. He had been staying in Prestbury in a house which had been rented to a fellow jockey whose family lived in the area. The house itself belonged to one of their neighbours, a tennis coach, who, having no interest in horseracing, but no objection to making money out of it, regularly went away on holiday during Festival week and let his house out. It was a convenient arrangement for the three jockeys and the vet who shared the place between them for the week. And more often than not, there would be even more people in the house, staying overnight in the bedrooms at the express invitation of the occupants.

Merlin had taken advantage of Sadie's absence at Sampfield Grange during the first three days of the Festival to contact some old girlfriends amongst the stable staff at the racecourse, and had been looking forward to renewing his acquaintance with one or more of them in his temporary bed. Not that he didn't enjoy being with Sadie, but he had no obligations to her, he told himself, and, anyway, she was not around. If she had been, then of course he would not have looked at anyone else.

Merlin's carefully laid plans had, though, unfortunately for him, fallen victim to his earlier offer of an interview to Stevie Stone. Stevie had sought him out on the first day of the Festival and interviewed him by the side of the parade ring shortly before the first race. Merlin had had only one ride, in the third race that day, so was in no rush.

Stevie had explained to him, as she had explained to Sam before, that she would simply ask him some questions and that the vlog would then be edited to make it appear as if Tabby Cat and Jayce were involved in the discussion. Merlin had been able to see no problem with this, and had been happy to play along. He had already viewed the vlog involving Mr Sampfield and the arrangement had seemed to work well.

Again, Stevie had asked only a few questions, one about his race that afternoon, one about Tabikat's chances in the Gold Cup, and then two questions about how he had become a jockey and whether he had a girlfriend. Merlin had suggested an each way bet on his horse that afternoon, and had said that Tabikat was in with a good chance of a place in the Gold Cup, depending on the ground. With disarming frankness, he had told Stevie that he had become a jockey because his father, who spent most of his time in the local bookie's

449

shop, had seen it as a way out of the unemployment and deprivation of the dying former coal mining village where generations of his family had been born. And, finally, he had said, flippantly, that he liked having lots of girlfriends, and that any of Stevie's smart girls were welcome to apply to him personally for the job. Even as he had said it, he had felt guilty about the joking remark, and had hoped that Sadie would not watch the interview.

The vlog had appeared online within the hour. Jayce, apparently with yet another hangover, had said he had a bad feeling about the suggested each way bet on Merlin's ride that afternoon, although Tabby Cat and Stevie told him maybe it was just the banging headache that was talking. Jayce had, though, been proved right, as Merlin's horse had been outpaced from the start and had been unplaced in the race. Tabby Cat had been purringly enthusiastic about the chances of his namesake in the Gold Cup and had told the smart girls that they should support the horse, as well as taking a proper good look at his fit jockey from the Welsh valleys.

"Single man Merlin's looking for a girlfriend," Tabby Cat had squeaked, "Says he wants the smart girls to apply."

"Tell you a secret, Tabby Cat," had said Stevie's voice, "Merlin's already got a girlfriend and we're going to get see her on Friday. Keep a look out for her, smart girls. You too, Jayce."

Merlin had been unaware of the contents of the vlog until the smirks of his colleagues in the jockey's changing room had eventually caused him to look at the Racing Tips for Smart Girls app on someone else's eagerly proffered phone.

"Oh, God,' he had groaned, as a message had pinged onto his own phone from the girl he had invited to join him that night.

Piss off shitbag

it had said.

As Merlin approached the stables at Cheltenham racecourse on the morning of fourth day of the Festival, having messaged Sadie that he was on his way, he was wondering whether Sadie was about to say something similar to his face.

*

The gates of the racecourse had been open for half an hour when Aleksander Paloka arrived at the front entrance in a black Mercedes. Instructing the silent driver to go away and come back when he was called, Aleksander and his two bodyguards got out of the car in the area reserved for taxi drop offs.

To the casual onlooker, there was nothing out of the ordinary about the three men who now joined the crowds milling around in the access road to the racecourse. All three were smartly dressed in grey suits and one of them carried a copy of a racing paper.

But there were some far from casual onlookers who had their eyes on Aleksander and his companions. And these onlookers also knew that all three of the new arrivals at the racecourse were armed.

42

On the morning of day of the Gold Cup, Daniel Levy was well aware that a racehorse trainer called James Sampfield Peveril had been trying to contact him for the last three weeks. A number of messages had pursued him on the brief visits which he had made during that period of time to Barcelona, Monza, and Spa. But he had answered none of them.

Although the Formula 1 racing season was only just about to start, Danny had had a busy three months is his role as a junior engineer in the Harlow Motosport Aerodynamics unit. His usual work involved the building and testing of models in the Harlow Motoforce plant's wind tunnel. Following the successful completion of these tests, his work moved to the production of the successful designs for testing using full size cars on outdoor tracks.

Harlow Motoforce was a relatively new arrival on the Formula 1 scene. Although its factory in Wiltshire was well funded by its millionaire owner, for whom investment in Formula 1 was an alternative to the horse racing aspirations of his older brother, its aerodynamics team was small and relatively inexperienced. But its charismatic and workaholic senior engineer, Mark Harlow, after whom its owner had allowed the company to be named, shrewdly deducing that the Harlow name was likely to carry more clout in the claustrophobic and incestuous motor racing industry, had more than made up for that. Mark's entire career as an engineer had been spent in F1, and his knowledge of his rivals' production and design methods was unparalleled.

Although Danny had enjoyed working for someone as dynamic as Mark Harlow, the team were under constant pressure to deliver results. New modifications had needed to be tested before the middle of March, ready for the first races of the season in Australia. Danny could, of course, have left the company at any time and transferred his attention to the waiting business of Levy Brothers International. His father had been patient in allowing Danny to indulge himself in his favourite hobby but the need to take over the family business would eventually have to be recognised.

No one at Harlow Motosport F1 had the remotest idea that Danny was a millionaire in his own right. To the Harlow team he was a well mannered and conscientious junior engineer, with the odd combination of a Jewish name and Irish looks, who got on with his work. The car in which he drove to work was new and not inexpensive, but a standard model. It appeared to have a personalised number plate, but Danny, when asked, had simply said it had been sold to him with the car. No-one really knew, or had thought to ask, where Danny lived or how he spent his spare time. His colleagues would have been surprised to hear that he owned a flat in London as well as a pretty stone cottage near Tetbury not to mention that he was an active member of the local Territorial Army and flew helicopters in his spare time.

Danny had picked up the messages from James Sampfield Peveril which had been left at the work number printed on the card which Stevie Stone had given to Sam at Newbury races. The messages had explained that the caller was the recently appointed trainer of Levy Brothers' racehorse, Tabikat, which had been entered to run in the Cheltenham Gold Cup, and that Mr Levy's contact details had been supplied by Stevie Stone. The caller had said that he would value the opportunity to speak to Mr Levy personally and hoped that he could find time to return his call.

Daniel had been unable to decide what to do. The plan to buy the horse from Eoghan Foley, his mother's uncle in Ireland, had seemed such an excellent one at the time. The coincidence of the horse's name with TK's childhood name was something which Danny, who was unashamedly superstitious, had seen as an omen.

It had been an omen, all right, he had reflected, listening to James Sampdfield Peveril's message for the third time, but not a good one. The young woman who had been his soul mate since they were fifteen years old had reacted in a way he had not expected. Her heart set on her long planned career in the Army, she had seen the gift of the racehorse as an attempt to pressurise her into a commitment for which she was not ready. Ironically, it had been a joint interest in

Army Cadet activities at the Home Counties independent school they had both attended which had brought the two of them together. But TK's decision to become an Army officer had become the catalyst for dividing them.

In the end, they had compromised, and the ownership had been divided three ways, with TK's mother taking a third share in the horse. It had been an uneasy compromise, but it had worked well during the years that TK had been in military service overseas and Danny had pursued what he knew would be a short lived career in F1 motor racing. Both he and TK had travelled to many and different parts of the world at the behest of their respective employers and rarely saw one another now. There had been no specific agreement to break off their relationship. It had simply stopped being a relationship.

Danny had had no intention of calling Mr Sampfield Peveril unless and until he could speak to TK. As far as Danny was concerned, TK still owned a share in the horse, even though she had insisted one year ago on having her name removed from the ownership record along with that of her now dead mother.

On the morning of Gold Cup day, Daniel had opened the racing paper which he had picked up from the village shop, and had turned to the pages which listed the races to be run at Cheltenham that day. Scanning the entrants for the Gold Cup itself, he had sat up with a jolt in his stripped pine kitchen chair, his freshly made coffee slopping over the artistically distressed wooden surface of the kitchen table onto the terracotta tiled floor. Tabikat had been shown as a runner, as Danny had expected, the horse's name at the end the alphabetical list of those declared. But instead of the blue and gold colours of Levy Brothers International, Danny had found himself staring at the purple ground covered with gold stars which had once been the racing colours of Susan and Captain T K Stonehouse. Looking at the details of the horse, he had noted with shock that Susan Stonehouse was listed as the sole owner. But surely she was dead, Danny had thought, his mind racing.

Danny had been due at Kemscott Park airfield in an hour's time to work with the Harlow team on test runs of the latest production car on the runway, which had been booked for their exclusive use for most of the morning. As he was trying to decide what to do, his mobile phone had trilled. The screen had shown the number as withheld, but the voice on the other end had been as familiar to him as his own.

"Danny," the woman's voice had said, "What's going on? Have you seen the runners in the Gold Cup?"

"I have seen them, and I don't know," Danny had replied, helplessly.

"We've got to go there and find out," TK had told him, "I'm on three weeks' leave now since my last tour and I can get to your place within two hours from where I am now."

"Don't come here," Danny had told her, "Go to Kemscott Park airfield. I can hire an R22 there and we can fly into the Cheltenham racecourse heliport. We'll be in queues of car traffic and never make it in time otherwise."

"OK," said TK, "I'll be there soonest."

"Oh, and before you go, TK," Danny had said quickly, before she could end the call.

"What?" had asked TK, impatient to be on her way.

"It's good to hear your voice," Danny had told her and had rung off.

*

At the same time as Daniel Levy was negotiating the late booking of an inbound R22 to Cheltenham racecourse, Kye was woken from his slumbers by a loud bang on the window of the horsebox cab.

"What the fuck?" he said, as he tried to shake the heavy feeling of sleep from his head.

"Lemme in, Kye," came a female voice from the side of the lorry.

It was Sheryl, carrying a large wicker picnic hamper.

"Delivery for yez," Sheryl piped, lifting the basket onto the passenger seat, as Kye swung open the door.

"What's this, then?" asked Kye, mystified by the appearance of the basket, which, when he opened the lid, proved to be full of such delectables as pork pies, pots of caviar, exotic looking bread rolls, neatly packed salads, and a whole range of items in little decorated pots and tubs. And there were two bottles of champagne in ice jackets and some expensive looking French water. The lid of the hamper was filled with plates, cutlery and plastic tumblers and champagne flutes.

"It's what yez lot does," replied Sheryl, crossly, "Eating posh grub in the car park. Too mean to pay for it inside."

"What am I supposed to do with it?" asked Kye, not understanding, "Mr Sampfield's not having a party here. He's in some posh box somewhere."

Sheryl sneered.

"Oh, but there is goin' to be a party, Kye, luv," she said, "They'll all be over to join yez soon. It's all paid for. Make sure they get what they want or they won't be happy, will they?"

Kye understood.

"The shit's in the basket?" he asked.

"Right luv," said Sheryl, "See yez later."

Shit was about the right word for it, thought Kye, as he watched her walk away. He had to hand it to her, she had dressed up for the part, wearing a silver *Posh Meals for Posh Wheels* T-shirt above a pair of tight black jeans. So she and Bronz had taken the money up front and he had to sit in the limelight of the car park pretending to host a party when he was delivering the orders of Class As. And if there was something wrong with the orders, he was the one who would be on the receiving end of the punter's displeasure. Not to mention being right in the view of any passing police officer.

Kye did not know that Sheryl had been arrested the moment she had returned to the little white van in which Bronz had sat waiting for her, already in handcuffs, just over the road. So Kye sat there and sweated, the picnic hamper by his side like an unexploded bomb.

Don't panic when it all kicks off, Isabella Hall had told him. But he had no idea what sort of kicking off she had had in mind. And she was not here to tell him.

*

Not long after the delivery of the *Posh Meals for Posh Wheels* picnic hamper, George Harvey and Isabella Hall reached the racecourse. It was almost midday, and the gathering crowds were now funnelling into the racecourse entrance. Ticket touts were roaming amongst the arrivals posting themselves in every conceivable location from the town centre to each of the arrival points at the racecourse. Red jacketed stewards were in evidence around the entrance, but there appeared to be an unwritten truce between them and the touts, who carried on their business unworried by the presence of a deterrent authority.

Frank Stanley's team and the police officers supporting them were not interested in the ticket touts. They noted the expected arrival on foot of George Harvey and Isabella Hall, who, being labelled with annual members' badges and armed with barcoded entry cards, not to mention with other badges secreted in their pockets, passed through the entrance into the racecourse without attracting any attention, other than that of the scanning machine.

*

Aleksander's trusted bodyguards were not happy with his

457

instructions to them. Insofar as they ever discussed the motivations of the man who employed them, they both considered that he had become crazily obsessed in his determination to avenge himself on the woman who he had decided had caused his father's death. True, the little shit sitting at the computer had said he thought the woman was still alive, but the kid had been out of his head on coke and his brain had probably been fried long ago. Blowing a hole in it had just been doing him a favour.

Aleksander instructed one of his guards to get them three tickets from one of the touts.

"I am going in and you're staying out here," Aleksander told the two men, "You find the vehicle that belongs to the racehorse trainer. The woman may be with him. If you see her, just watch her. She will go into the racecourse before the big race. Follow her in. The security people here are searching bags so make sure they don't find you carrying. If you don't see the woman, don't come in. I'll follow her out after the race. Clear?"

"You carrying, boss?" asked one of the guards, "Need anything extra? A blade?"

"I have hardware, and they won't find it," Aleksander told him shortly and walked off towards the racecourse entrance.

The two men stood uncomfortably in the access road. They had no idea what the vehicle the boss wanted them to find looked like. They had seen pictures of the woman, and the name James Sampfield Peveril had been written down for them on a piece of paper which one of them had in his jacket pocket. They had overheard their boss's enraged conversation yesterday with some paedo who was supposed to find the racehorse trainer and the woman, and had clearly failed. They had also heard the terrified shriek of the man at the other end of the phone when Aleksander had told him that an unknown informer had just reported the man to the police as a collector of child pornography.

The two bodyguards slowly made their way towards the horsebox parking area. There were a large number of vehicles parked there, some enormous, expensive and sleek, others smaller and older. Most had the names of the owner emblazoned on the side, but many did not.

Ponderously and laboriously, they started to work their way along the lines of lorries and box vans, reading the names, noting the positions of the unnamed vehicles, looking carefully at any people who appeared to be hanging around. But there was no vehicle marked with the name of James Sampfield Peveril nor could they see any sign of anyone who looked at all like the picture of Susan Stonehouse. Most of the people they encountered in the car park were youngsters who the two men supposed were paid to look after the racehorses. As they progressed through the car park, the loud chattering and laughter of the increasing numbers of racegoers making their way from the bus stops on the road at the front of the car park accompanied them on their way.

When they had almost reached the far end of the lorry park, the two guards had a stroke of luck. A group of six garrulous people had been walking behind them, gradually catching them up.

"Sampfield Grange," one of the people was saying loudly, "That's where the party starts."

The men pricked up their ears at the name Sampfield and turned to look carefully at the people who had said it. They were a young group, four men and two women, the men dressed oddly in baggy green jackets with a pink stripe, matched incongruously with red trousers. The women looked like posh tarts, wearing little hats with feathers sticking out and tottering on stiletto heels.

The sociable group was too wrapped up in its own concerns to notice the two grey suited men standing by one of the lorries. And nor did they notice when the same two men started to follow them.

*

Sam, leading the way up one of the grandstand staircases to Helen

Garratt's box, was fortunately unaware that his horsebox had become the centre of so many people's attention.

Eoghan and Caitlin had been enthusiastically pleased to be reunited with the beautiful horse which they had bred at Enda's Farm. Tabikat had recognised them immediately, and, for the first time in Sam and Sadie's experience, had whinnied excitedly and repeatedly, pushing his nose into Caitlin's small hand and shaking his head up and down.

"He is looking well, for sure," Eoghan had said to Sam, sounding pleased.

"And you have turned him out very nicely," Caitlin added to Sadie.

Sadie had enjoyed meeting Tabikat's breeders and had told them everything she could think of about the horse's performance at home and the pleasure she had had from riding him out every day. Her excitement was infectious, and Sam, Eoghan and Caitlin all had smiles on their faces when Merlin came to join them by the stables.

Merlin had managed to avoid being recognised by any of the incoming racegoers by coming on foot to the racecourse from his lonely bedroom, wearing sunglasses and a baseball cap along with his usual black leather jacket, even though the day was grey and cool with a sharp wind blowing from the North East.

Merlin was relieved to find that Sadie was not alone, but he now had an additional concern on his mind. He had opened the racing paper that morning to discover the change of ownership of the horse that he was due to ride in the Gold Cup. Merlin wanted first and foremost to know whether it had any impact on him, such as a last minute decision by the new owner to revert to using the horse's former Irish jockey. As Sadie talked happily to Eoghan and Caitlin, Merlin managed to get Sam to one side.

"What's goin' on, Mr Sampfield?" he asked, "The 'orse seems to have changed 'ands since the last time I last rode 'im. 'oo's this Mrs Susan Stone'ouse? Is she 'ere today?"

"It's a bit of a mystery to me too, Merlin," Sam said carefully, "But I believe it is a decision made by the previous owners. I don't know the reason. And I don't think she will be here today, I regret to say."

"Oh, well," said Merlin, "As long as I'm still ridin' him, then I don't mind 'oo owns 'im. This woman's not goin' to be takin' 'im away from Sampfield Grange then?"

"Again, I don't know, Merlin," sighed Sam, "No doubt we will find out the owner's plans in due course. Now, come and meet Eugene Foley. He's Tabikat's breeder, and he used to be a jump jockey in Ireland, so he may have some comments for you about the race."

Sadie's flow of conversation stopped abruptly once Merlin joined the little group. When Sam had eventually taken his Irish guests away to meet Lady Helen in her box, Merlin found himself alone with Sadie, who appeared to have nothing to say to him.

"You OK, *cariad*?" he asked, cautiously, putting his arm round her waist, "You seem a bit quiet."

"Just getting nervous about Tabikat," was all Sadie had to say in reply.

"You seen what that racing tipster girl's talkin' cat 'ad to say about 'im?" asked Merlin, dreading the answer.

"Yes," said Sadie, "Kelly and Lewis are going to put an each way bet on him, like Tabby Cat and Jayce suggested."

"Anythin' else?" asked Merlin, carefully.

"No, we didn't watch the rest of it," Sadie told him.

As Merlin heaved a mental sign of relief, Sadie turned away from him to stroke Tabikat's dark nose, and a tear slid down her cheek.

43

Daniel Levy had been busy in the two hours leading up to TK's arrival at Kemscott Park airfield.

Cheltenham racecourse Helicopter and Aviation Services had been unhappy at the last minute booking of Danny's incoming flight, but, on hearing that he had a runner in the Gold Cup, had eventually agreed to accommodate his arrival. Danny had asked for the necessary instructions to be sent to his mobile phone. As a regular hirer of helicopters from Kemscott Park airfield, Danny had fortunately had no difficulty obtaining the use of one of little Robinson R22 craft.

"Where're you off to, then, Mr Levy?" asked the elderly Operations Manager who sat behind the desk of the little flying school, "You're looking very smart today."

"Cheltenham racecourse," replied Danny, "Just waiting for my passenger."

"Owns one of the Gold Cup horses, does he?" asked the Operations Manager, laughing.

"In a manner of speaking," Danny replied. Not wanting to get involved in a discussion about the races, he went outside to do the pre-flight checks on the helicopter, which was located in a position from which he could keep an eye on the car park. He had no idea what sort of car TK drove these days.

Danny could also see his Harlow Motosport colleagues on the other side of the airfield and the sound of the F1 test car which they were trialling on the runway carried across to him on the North Easterly breeze. Danny's immediate supervisor had been most unhappy to hear that Danny was unwell and could not join them that morning.

"Don't forget we're going out to Oz on Sunday," he had told Danny, shortly.

Danny had assured his boss that he would have recovered in time to make the flight out to Melbourne on Saturday evening. He just hoped that none of his colleagues would spot him standing by the little white and red helicopter. Fortunately, he thought, they would probably all be concentrating too hard on running the test drive to be bothered with helicopter movements at the airfield.

As Danny waited, a familiar ex-military Land Rover Defender pulled into the car park and stopped suddenly alongside the wooden fence. A young woman with shoulder length brown hair, wearing a short, dark green coat above black boots, jumped out, slammed the door shut, and ran towards him.

"Haven't been in one of these for a while," she said to Danny as she got herself into the co-pilot's seat of the little machine, "The ones I'm used to are bigger and meaner than this. Have you done the pre-flight?"

"Hello TK," replied Danny, as he strapped himself into the pilot's seat, "And yes I have. But we need to talk."

"Later," TK told him, firmly. "We need to get through the next few hours first. I called George and he arranged for the badges to be left at the bottom gate for us."

Daniel could see already that TK meant to stick rigidly to the business in hand. Handing her a headset, he reached forward and opened the engine starting checklist.

"OK," was all he said.

*

Kye could see the little tweed-clad group approaching the Sampfield Grange horsebox, followed by two girls in what looked like highly unsuitable clothing for such a chilly day. The wind carried the sound of their voices away from the horsebox, but Kye could imagine what they sounded like.

"Hooray Henrys," he thought, "Guess it had to be. They're the only ones who can afford this sort of shit."

The foremost of the four tweed-jacketed men reached the horsebox at the same time as Kye jumped down to meet them.

"Greetings, my good sir. We're here for the party," the man told Kye.

"Are these all the guests?" asked Kye, playing along with the party facade, "No-one else expected?"

The man spread his hands in a gesture of ignorance.

"No-one else that I know," he said, "Now, where are the goods? They've been paid for and they'd better be good."

"Hamper's on the seat," Kye told him, "Yez need to check it though. Wouldn't want yez to be disappointed, would we?"

"No indeed," replied the man, who had now been joined by the rest of his group.

The hamper was lifted down from the cab of the lorry, and placed on the ground. One of the men took out the bottles of champagne and handed them to the two girls. Beneath the bottles were four small packages, wrapped in gold foil and sealed with a silver star.

"Nice touch!" exclaimed one of the men, "Looks like it's my birthday again."

Kye gritted his teeth.

"Yez can open it if you want," he said, "But take some of the food too, just to make it look as if we're really eating."

"Sure thing!" said the man, rummaging in the hamper and handing out some of the pork pies to his companions.

As the little party gathered around the hamper, helping themselves to food, Kye noticed two men in grey suits standing nearby. They appeared not to be interested in the people surrounding him, but were looking at a piece of paper which one of them held in his hand. Were these Frank Stanley's filth, Kye wondered, or just local bizzies?

The events of the next few minutes happened very fast.

The tweed clad punters removed the four gold wrapped packages from the wicker hamper and took one each. The first man carefully pulled open one corner of his package and stuck his finger into the gap. Putting the end of the finger into his mouth, he ran it around his upper gum.

"Good stuff, this," he said to Kye, "Shut up the hamper for me, there's a good chap, and we'll relieve you of it. We've got another party to go to."

Kye did as he was told, and shut the lid of the picnic hamper. As he did so, there was a sudden movement behind him, and he found himself pulled suddenly backwards onto the ground and forcibly shoved by a booted foot until he was underneath the horsebox. The fall knocked the breath out of him and he lay flat on his back, stunned and afraid.

Above him, he heard running feet, shrieks and shouts, and the words "Police. Stand still. You're under arrest." spoken loudly and fiercely several times.

Eventually managing to prop himself up on his elbow and peer out from underneath the vehicle, Kye saw the four men and two women being hustled away by a group of black clad police officers towards the other end of the car park. One of the officers was carrying the picnic hamper. But it was not only the Hooray Henrys and their girlfriends who had been arrested. Kye saw that the two men in grey suits were being held face down on the ground by four armed officers, one of whom Kye recognised as the stolid Martin who had only recently meted out much the same treatment to Kye. Martin and his colleagues were removing two handguns and what looked to Kye like flick knives from their quarry. The grey suits were soon in handcuffs, after which Martin's team hauled them to their feet. The men clearly knew better than to protest at their treatment, and walked silently with their heads down, between the officers.

The little group of police officers with their prisoners marched purposefully past the Sampfield Grange horsebox, their boots passing within six feet of where Kye was lying on the ground. Not one of them even looked in his direction.

*

Sam had told Sadie that he would join her in the pre-parade area once the very large field of runners in the third race were in the parade ring.

Merlin had rides in both the second and third races, so Sadie had been left alone to prepare Tabikat for over an hour. Sadie did not recognise many of the other stable staff, apart from Claire O'Dowd, who was kept very busy with Brendan Meaghan's numerous runners, and a couple of staff from the Dicks yard whom she did not know well. Claire had come up to see Tabikat, but otherwise she had spent her time taking horses up and down the rubber surfaced path between the stables and the pre-parade ring. Everyone was busy and occupied, and no-one had time to talk. Not for the first time, Sadie thought how wonderful it would be to work for a training yard which took runners regularly to big meetings. Weighed down though she was by her personal woes, she still felt exhilarated by the excitement surrounding such a great sporting occasion. She could hear the huge cheers of the packed crowd as the first race came to an end not far from the stable yard. Perhaps she would ask Mr Sampfield about going to work for Mr Dicks for a while or even maybe Mr Meaghan, she thought.

Sadie's reverie was interrupted by the sudden arrival of Kye, who came up behind her and tapped her suddenly on the shoulder.

"Christ, Kye, you made me jump!" snapped Sadie, "You woken up at last, have you?"

"Sorry, Sadie," Kye said, brightly, "I feel a lot better now, thanks for asking."

"That's good," Sadie told him, "Because we need to think about moving Tabikat down soon. I've done my best to make him look really beautiful today. Are you going to come this time?"

"Course I am," said Kye, who was gradually beginning to feel as though a great burden had been lifted from his back, "Wouldn't miss it for anything. And Tabikat looks really great, Sadie. Those stars on his quarters will match Merlin's new jacket."

"You'd better hope Merlin doesn't get hurt in these next two races," said Sadie, "Otherwise you might have to ride Tabikat yourself."

As Kye's face became a picture of horror, Sadie laughed for the first time that day.

"Just kidding," she said.

But, Kye thought suddenly, maybe one day it wouldn't be quite such a ridiculous joke. And for the first time in weeks, he felt happy.

*

Sadie would never forget her experience of bringing Tabikat into the parade ring before the running of the Cheltenham Gold Cup. She had been in the Cheltenham parade ring before, but she had never seen such feverishly excited crowds as those which filled the viewing areas today. Every piece of concrete, every balcony and gallery seemed to be filled. People crowded around the white fences lining the parade ring, craning their necks to get a good look at the horses. Enthusiastic voices discussed the runners.

Look, there's Macalantern, the favourite. That's Tabikat, isn't he gorgeous? I'm on Stormlighter, he's the business. Stern King Richard won't like the ground. Dolly's Boyfriend, where did that name come from? Ross is my dad's name - let's go with Less Than Ross.

All these disjointed snatches of conversations floated across to Sadie as she stepped out along the parade ring path, Tabikat, turned out like a superstar, walking grandly by her side.

There were ten runners in the race. The big screen showed that Macalantern, the property of one of the major Irish owners, was the clear favourite at 4/6. Tabikat was fourth favourite at 11/1.

As Sam stood in the centre of the parade ring, watching Sadie and waiting for Merlin to join him, the usual TV commentator sidled up to him, microphone held at the ready.

"Time for a quick word on Tabikat, Sam?" the man asked, now having found out, and decided to use, Sam's familiar name.

Conscious of the many viewers, including the Sampfield Grange staff, who would be watching him at home and whose bets might depend on what he said, Sam was cautious in his response. He told his interviewer that, although Tabikat would prefer softer ground, he thought the horse had a chance of running into a place. It would entirely depend on how the race was run, particularly what sort of pace was set at the beginning. The commentator nodded sagely, asking which horse Sam thought would set the pace. Sam identified Cloudless Morning, who, the big screen informed the assembled crowd, was currently showing at 16-1 in the betting.

Sam was rescued from the discussion by the arrival by his side of Merlin, clad in the unfamiliar purple silks with gold stars. Sam and Merlin had already discussed and agreed their running tactics. They both agreed that it was important for Tabikat to get a good start. The Gold Cup would be run at a fast pace and Tabikat could not afford to get left behind on the first circuit. The going was good to soft, soft in places, but Tabikat acted better on softer ground. Some of his rivals would like the quicker ground better and would be likely to maintain a fast gallop throughout the race. Tabikat did not have the speed to catch up again if he got behind. His best chance in the relatively unfavourable conditions lay in staying up with the pace and aiming to stick on and tough it out at the end. Whether this would be enough to keep him in contention, only time would tell, but both Sam and Merlin thought this was his best chance of being in the mix at the business end of the contest.

Sam rarely got nervous before a race, but this occasion was something well outside his previous experience as a trainer. He had never before had a runner in such a prestigious event, nor one which was going to be run under the full gaze of the worldwide jump racing community. Merlin's familiarity with such levels of pressure and publicity was far greater than Sam's, and Sam was suddenly more grateful than he had expected for the presence of the talented Welsh jockey at his side.

At the sound of the bell, Sadie turned Tabikat towards them, and Sam found himself legging Merlin up into the saddle before he had even had time to realise what was happening.

"Good luck, Merlin," was all Sam said, as Sadie stood silently by the horse's head, patting his neck. Tabikat himself seemed entirely unbothered by the surroundings, and stood like a statue as Merlin got on board.

"See you back 'ere in the winner's enclosure, Mr Sampfield," Merlin said to him, flashing a quick smile.

And with Sadie leading him by the bridle, Merlin perched on his back in his showy racing colours. Tabikat walked grandly away from Sam towards the exit from the parade ring. The crowds surged alongside the horsewalk which led to the racecourse. They seemed to swallow the horse as he passed them by, until all Sam could see was the bright gold star on Merlin's hat as he passed under the stone bridge and disappeared from Sam's sight.

44

Sam found himself standing alone. The packed layers of animated spectators who had been crowded onto the steppings and galleries above and around him were beginning to drift over to the viewing areas by the racecourse, although Sam knew that many would remain in place to watch the race on the big screen and so be sure of a good place from which to welcome the Gold Cup victor home. Sam could see as he looked around the panoramic arena surrounding the parade ring that the connections of the nine other runners were now clustered into nervous little groups around the artistically mown green lawn.

Sam spotted three of the biggest Irish owners in amongst the groups, standing thoughtfully with their respective trainers, each attended by smartly dressed wives and other family members and friends. A dour looking trainer from Dorset stood with a group of besuited owners wearing what looked like football scarves produced in their colours. Yet another group consisted of an elderly British owner with her daughter and son, talking earnestly to the female trainer, who was wearing a trench coat and waxed hat, whilst, incongruously, carrying a red designer handbag. Brendan Meaghan and Ranulph Dicks were not represented amongst the trainers of the Gold Cup horses, although Sam knew that they both had other runners that day.

As he looked at the little knots of people clustered on the lawn, and watched the surrounding spectators pointing out famous faces to each other, Sam could not rid himself of the feeling that Tabikat's connections had abandoned their dignified and almost faultless horse. Surely a Gold Cup runner deserved to have his personal supporters waiting and watching in the parade ring, living every second of the demanding race with him and his jockey. Yet Sam was standing there by himself.

Sam knew that Eoghan and Caitlin would be watching every step of the race from the balcony of the Garratt box at the top of the main grandstand. They would not miss a stride or a jump. Sadie would remain down on the course to bring Tabikat and Merlin back to the paddock, maybe even to the winner's enclosure, after the race. Brendan Meaghan and his team would be somewhere around, eagerly watching the progress of their former charge. Stevie Stone would no doubt be working hard with her iPad somewhere nearby, although Sam had not been able to locate her since the end of the first race, when he had spotted her talking to a group of shivering girls in thin dresses at the side of the parade ring. Kye had remained in the pre-parade area after they had saddled Tabikat and Sam assumed that his new conditional jockey would be watching the race closely from some vantage point.

Sam fully accepted that, notwithstanding the fact that Tabikat was for some reason racing in her colours, the deceased Susan Stonehouse could not be here. His efforts to contact Daniel had come to nothing and Stevie Stone had somehow seemed to have forgotten her promise to give him TK's contact details. Even Frank had said he would see Sam on Gold Cup day, but there was no sign of him either.

So, for the moment, Tabikat effectively belonged to Sam and to Sam alone. Sam had taken on the horse at the unexpected request of the elusive owners and Sam had trained him to the best of his ability and brought him here to compete in one of the greatest horse races on earth. Sam vowed there and then that if no-one came forward to take an interest in the horse after the Festival was over, he would offer to buy him from the Levy Brothers or Susan Stonehouse, or whoever really owned him, and that henceforth Tabikat would run in the Sampfield Grange colours.

But just as Sam heard the music to accompany the parade of runners strike up, he became aware of someone approaching him from behind.

"Mr Sampfield Peveril?" queried a male voice.

Sam turned around to find himself confronted by someone who he took at first sight to be an Irish jockey. The young man was of medium height with sandy hair and blue eyes. He was dressed in a smartly cut grey suit and wearing a pink tie into which a gold pin decorated with a diamond was inserted. Standing slightly behind the man was a young woman with shoulder length brown hair and large brown eyes. She wore a neat and short green wool coat, fastened with brass buttons, and black leather boots. Sam was sure he had never seen either of them before.

"Yes?" he replied, slightly thrown to be roused from his thoughts in such an unexpected way.

The young man held out his hand.

"My name is Daniel Levy," he told Sam, "I am sorry to be so late. We had to run up from the helicopter landing area, which we weren't planning to have to do."

Whatever Sam had been expecting Daniel Levy to look and sound like, the polite young man who stood before him was nothing like he had imagined from the description of the family provided by Brendan Meaghan and Stevie Stone. Daniel spoke with a well-educated English accent and looked like an Irishman. If it had not been for his family name, Sam could not have guessed that he had any hint of a Jewish background.

Before Sam could respond, the young woman suddenly spoke up.

"I'm TK Stonehouse," she said, shortly, "Pleased to meet you. Where's everyone else?"

Shaking hands with Daniel Levy, Sam said to her,

"I'm more than pleased to meet you both at last. Who else are you expecting?"

"Stevie, of course," TK replied, "And .. well.." her words tailed off.

"Don't worry, they're here," said Daniel, pointing to a group of three people who were approaching them from the direction of the weighing room. Sam turned his head to follow the direction indicated by Daniel's arm.

Sam realised immediately that he knew every one of the three people concerned. One of them was Stevie Stone, and with her were Isabella Hall and the tall man whom Gil said he had seen with her at the Cheltenham Showcase meeting in October last year. The man was dressed in a black overcoat and was wearing a fedora hat similar to Sam's own. He was leaning on a stick as he walked unevenly towards the growing group comprising Tabikat's connections. Isabella Hall had her arm though that of the man with the stick and was dressed in her usual black work outfit, which had been supplemented with black boots and the burgundy hat usually worn by Stevie Stone. Stevie herself was now dressed in a red fox fur jacket and matching hat.

"Well, Mr S P? Will we do?" called out Stevie, as they came closer.

As she spoke, TK ran forward to meet the new arrivals, until the four of them were hugging each other in the middle of the parade ring, Daniel Levy standing awkwardly to one side, waiting for the group to break up and to include him in the greetings.

Sam was unprepared for what was happening around him. His feeling of regret that no connections had come into the parade ring was being superseded by a realisation that they had now turned up in force, every one of them sporting owners' badges. The assembly of this group at this important moment had clearly been planned.

But there was little time for Sam to try to work anything out now. The ongoing loudspeaker announcement describing each of the horses in the parade before the main grandstand was coming to an end. Tabikat's name was the last one in the alphabetical list of runners, and Sam could hear the announcer giving his details to the watching and close packed crowd,

"And finally, horse number 10 is Tabikat, ridden by Merlin ap Rhys, trained by James Sampfield Peveril. Tabikat is eight years old and has a strong chasing record in Ireland. He is running today in the purple colours and gold stars of Mrs Susan Stonehouse. This is his first run in the Gold Cup. Tabikat has also been judged by the sponsors to be the best turned-out horse, so a £200 cash prize has gone to his groom here today, Sadie Shinkins. Well done, Sadie."

Back in the parade ring, Tabikat's newly assembled connections grouped themselves carefully around Sam and watched on the big screen as the camera showed Sadie turning the horse to the left at the end of the parade line, ready to release him onto the course. Isabella Hall was the smallest person in the watching group and Sam noticed that the tall man with the stick positioned her carefully in front of him before turning his head to speak to Sam who was standing to his immediate right.

"Mr Sampfield Peveril, my name is George Harvey," he said, "Thank you for all your help with our project. I understand from Isabella here that you have looked after everything very well."

Sam looked across at Isabella Hall, who returned his gaze with a tight and nervous smile, but remained silent.

"I am glad to see Isabella here safe today," he said, politely, wondering why she did not greet him or offer any explanation of her recent absence.

"So are we all," replied George Harvey, "But there is still some way to go yet today."

Sam was unable to guess what was meant by the other man's cryptic remark, and suddenly found that he did not care. These people, apparently orchestrated by Frank Stanley, had disrupted his life for long enough and no doubt would explain themselves when they saw fit. In the meantime, his sole thought was for Tabikat, now cantering down to the extended three and a quarter mile start. He had seen Sadie release her hold on Tabikat's bridle and say something to Merlin, who had looked down at her briefly, before he sent Tabikat forward down the hill, the last of the ten horses to go down.

Sam focused on Tabikat. His action was beautiful, clean and smooth under Merlin's tough and well balanced frame as he stood poised in the irons above the horse's withers. Tabikat's deep, dark tail streamed out behind him as he moved and the horse looked completely relaxed and happy in the electrifying atmosphere of his noisy surroundings. Sam could imagine Eoghan Foley watching with anticipation from Helen's box as the officially non-pedigree horse he had bred in such odd circumstances went down to take his chance in the most prestigious race in the British jumps season calendar. Sam wondered yet again whether Tabikat's dam was really a daughter of Alakazam. That his sire was Tabloid News was not in doubt, especially as the horse himself had the sire's clear stamp in its colour and style of running. But who knew what other talents lay hidden in the horse's secret genes?

The ten equine athletes milled busily about in a close group by the start, which was positioned further down the hill from the grandstands. Every spare bit of space in the viewing areas was now occupied by people straining to get a sight of the action. Millions more were watching on televisions and computer screens in betting shops, bars and private homes around the world.

On the big screen in the parade ring, Sam could see Merlin in his purple shirt with gold stars with the distinctive large gold star on the purple silk of his hat, keeping Tabikat moving along the edge of the group, as they had discussed.

"The horses are all at the start," the course commentator told the assembled spectators, "There is less than one minute to go to post time. A few last minute checks on a couple of girths, but all seems well. Macalantern looks to be going off favourite at 4/6."

Sam checked the odds on the screen. Tabikat was still showing at 11 to 1.

"And the starter is climbing the steps," the commentator said suddenly, "The flag is up and they're walking in."

Sam could see the yellow flag held aloft by the starter as the group of bay horses, with one iron grey amongst them, shuffled forward, jockeys eyeing each other, each of them trying to manoeuvre into his chosen place.

And then the flag dropped, the orange starting tape sprang back, and the ten horses and their jockeys suddenly surged forward.

"And they're off!" cried the commentator, as a deafening roar erupted from the frenzied crowd higher up the hill, "As they set off on this extended three and a quarter mile trip over 22 fences, Cloudless Morning takes an early lead, with Tabikat, Macalantern and Harry Me Home in close attendance. Melting Snowman is in midfield and keeping company with the second favourite, Less Than Ross. Stormlighter, Champagne Cork, and Dolly's Boyfriend are racing together behind them. Stern King Richard is the back marker as they approach the first fence, which they all take safely, although Stormlighter made a slight error which has relegated him to the rear of field with Stern King Richard."

Sam had held his breath as Tabikat and Merlin sailed confidently over the first jump, a plain fence. The horse was matching the other leaders for pace and his first jump had looked good, accurate and clean. He stole a glance at his fellow connections.

Isabella Hall was standing with her hand gripped tightly in that of George Harvey. Stevie Stone was clutching George's arm. TK and Daniel stood rigid beside Stevie, TK with her hand over her mouth and Daniel looking intently at the screen. Isabella Hall's face was as white as that of a ghost, thought Sam. She seemed to be more scared than exhilarated by what she was watching.

The field was now approaching the second obstacle, located opposite the tented hospitality facilities and temporary outdoor bars. No-one needed the commentator to tell them that there were no fallers, and a massive cheer went up as the horses rounded the continuing uphill bend, the commentator confirming that their running order remained unchanged. The fence on the uphill stretch was jumped with no notable errors by any of the contenders, and the intact field pulled its way onto the far side of the course, where the ground soon began to slope downhill.

"They're going a good pace," the commentator was saying, "And the field is beginning to string out slightly as they approach the fourth fence, another plain one. And – ohh – Melting Snowman hit it very hard, which has almost stopped him in his tracks. The jockey did well to stay with him through that. It's cost them a few places though."

The error by Melting Snowman had, fortunately for Tabikat's connections, happened behind Tabikat, who was still running in the first four.

Merlin could see Cloudless Morning slightly ahead of him as they approached the water jump. Macalantern was beside him on the rails to his left and Harry Me Home's jockey was steering a course to his right. Tabikat himself seemed entirely focused on his work and was ignoring the other horses.

"Get that fucking nag out of my line," yelled Macalantern's jockey at Merlin as the next fence loomed closer.

Merlin knew perfectly well that he was nowhere near to crossing Macalantern's running line, and merely yelled back without rancour,

"*Fwcia bant*, Aidan *chi coeliwr!*"

The other jockey laughed, as the two horses took the water jump together. Merlin felt like laughing too. The feeling of the big, athletic horse beneath him was exhilarating, like fast flowing water, even and powerful and clean. He would never get tired of it.

The first open ditch lay ahead, and the talented field got over it safely enough, although the pace was beginning to tell on some of the back markers, and Sam could see that Stern King Richard and Dolly's Boyfriend were beginning to find it hard to live with. They were strong, game horses and they and their jockeys would do their best to complete the race, but neither had run at this speed over such a distance before and Sam thought they were already well beaten.

All the horses completed the first circuit without serious mishap, although it was becoming clear which of them was likely to be in the mix by the end of the race.

"As they approach the stands for the second time," the commentator said, "Cloudless Morning is keeping his lead. Tabikat and Macalantern are vying for second place but Harry Me Home is not letting them get away. Less Than Ross and Stormlighter are still in touch with the leaders. A gap is opening up between these six and the remaining four runners.

As Merlin and Tabikat approached the uphill fence after the bend for the second time, urged along by the cheering of the spectators in the stands, Aidan Scanlon on Macalantern was still needling Merlin.

"You'll be looking at my back soon, dickhead," he shouted at Merlin, once they had cleared the jump.

Merlin ignored him. Tabikat was running downhill once again, apparently still full of steam, and it was important that both of them should conserve all their energy. Macalantern was a fast finisher and would be hard to take on up the final hill. The race had still not truly taken shape and the front runners had yet to step on the gas. Harry Me Home was already breathing down Merlin's neck, his French jockey yelling encouragement in words that Merlin, probably fortunately, could not understand.

Sam watched as the ten horses all successfully cleared the line of jumps and approached the open ditch at the top of the hill at the far side of the course for the second time. The gap between the six front runners and the rest of the field had increased still further, and, barring accidents, three of these six horses would certainly take the first three places.

The leaders began to pack closer as the front horses came to the fourth fence from home. Any one of the group was still in with some chance of winning, except Cloudless Morning, the powerful iron grey which had jumped and galloped perfectly throughout the race, and was beginning to tire. At the same time Merlin heard Harry Me Home cruising up to try to pass Tabikat on his outside.

"And as they come to four out, Harry Me Home is beginning to assert himself," cried the commentator, "Cloudless Sky is dropping back through the field. Macalantern, Tabikat, Less than Ross, Harry Me Home and Stormlighter are all still in contention as they approach the third last, which they all clear well, with Macalantern landing in the lead. Harry Me Home's jockey is giving the horse reminders, and the horse is responding."

Both Sam and Merlin from their different positions could hear the gathering roar of the crowd ahead of the horses as everyone yelled and shouted the names of the horses and jockeys they were supporting. Eoghan and Caitlin up on the balcony of the grandstand box were standing as still as statues, their attention focused on the magnificent horse which had entered the world on their remote farm. Helen stood behind them, all decorum forgotten, screaming Tabikat's name. Every guest in the Garratt box was cheering for Tabikat and willing him up the hill.

Sadie, up at the end of the horsewalk, waiting for horses and jockeys to cross the finishing line, was furiously muttering Tabikat's and Merlin's names over and over again, as she jumped up and down with the other grooms, their eyes staring at the screen facing the main grandstand.

After the third last fence, there was still all to play for, with the five leaders separated by only two lengths. But Merlin, approaching the second last obstacle, the screaming of the crowd in his ears, could feel Tabikat beginning to tire.

"C'm on Tabikat *bachgen,*" he yelled, giving the horse a slap with his whip, "We can get there, we can."

Tabikat pricked his ears irritably at the slap, but knuckled down obediently, and tackled the upcoming fence with determination. Merlin felt the horse power himself over the jump, but knew already that his momentum was beginning to fade.

"And a good jump from Tabikat keeps him in contention," shouted the commentator, "They're all approaching the last fence with a chance. It's Macalantern neck and neck with Less Than Ross and Tabikat hot on their heels. Behind them Harry Me Home and Stormlighter are far from finished."

When they jumped the last fence, Merlin knew in his heart that Tabikat could not win. As they touched down with two top rated horses ahead of them, to catch these leaders was beyond even Tabikat's magic ability. Had the ground been softer, he might have done it. But it wasn't.

The howling and shrieking of the crowd filled Merlin's ears as he pressed Tabikat on up the hill. They might not win, but they were certainly going to make sure they chased the leaders home. Cloudless Morning had dropped back behind them, but Stormlighter and Harry Me Home had both taken the final fence well and were battling up the hill by Tabikat's side.

Merlin was straining every sinew to urge Tabikat forward. Stormlighter's and Harry Me Home's jockeys had no intention of giving up on a chance of third place either, and the three horses were locked together as they followed the leaders up the hill. Merlin was not sure how he managed it, but Tabikat eventually drew about half a length ahead as they approached the finishing line. Amidst the deafening noise of the crowd, he heard the commentator howl,

"And Macalantern has won the Gold Cup! Less Than Ross was hard on his heels but couldn't get there in the end. There's a battle for third and Tabikat just gets it, with Harry Me Home and Stormlighter in a photo for fourth. Cloudless Morning, who led most of the way, crosses the line in sixth place. Champagne Cork and Dolly's Boyfriend are the only other finishers."

As a gasping Merlin brought Tabikat to a hot and steaming halt, he heard the announcer confirm the result.

"First, Macalantern, the 4/6 favourite. Second, Less Than Ross at 5/1. Third, Tabikat at 11/1. And it's gone to the judge for fourth, between Harry Me Home and Stormlighter."

"Third 'ere again," thought Merlin, as he pulled the steaming Tabikat to a grateful halt, remembering Curlew Landing's last result at Cheltenham, "But this time it's the Gold Cup!"

Aidan Scanlon on the winning horse was receiving thumps on the back from the other jockeys. Merlin added his own congratulations, his earlier rude words directed at the now victorious jockey, who he knew well, not having any lasting significance to either of them.

"Told you I'd leave you behind," crowed Aidan, "That's all of you," he added waving his arm in the general direction of the other horses, as Macalantern circled around and got his breath back.

The area at the end of the run-in was in turmoil. There were no loose horses to catch, and the eight finishers were now puffing and blowing by the top end of the grandstand. But there were grooms and a TV crew with an interviewer waiting to get a word with Aidan Scanlon, who was still pumping his first and waving his whip at the screaming crowds in the stands.

Sadie came running up the horsewalk towards Tabikat and Merlin as they made their way back past the grandstand, her face beaming with pleasure. Merlin was watching the re-run of the finish on the big screen to his right, but turned towards her as she approached.

"I knew you'd do well!" Sadie cried, "You're a beautiful, lovely, clever horse and I love you to bits!"

Tabikat looked at her as if this praise were nothing more than his due, and continued his tired but regal progress down the horsewalk.

"'ere, what about me, then?" asked Merlin, "Don't I get tol' I'm lovely an' clever an' all that?"

"It's Tabikat who did it," Sadie told him firmly, "Don't you just love him?"

Merlin did indeed love the horse which had brought him so close to glory, and said cheekily to Sadie,

"Well 'e can't give me a kiss, can 'e, so I'm expecting one from you later, *cariad*."

But Sadie continued patting Tabikat's neck as they made their way past the noise of the grandstand to the bottom of the horsewalk, where the two non-finishers were just arriving.

"Ask your girlfriend," Sadie said, under her breath, her back to Merlin.

45

The Cheltenham Gold Cup race had been watched by Aleksander Paloka on the parade ring screen from his carefully selected position on the steppings facing the winners' enclosure. Once the majority of the spectators had moved away to the grandstands and the viewing areas alongside the course, he had been able to find a location which suited his needs.

Aleksander was an intelligent and quick thinking man whose brain had been used for the wrong ends in life. Brought up in a different environment, he might have been an expert chess player or a military strategist. But, instead, his father had brought him up to focus his mental agility on making money from human misery and exploitation. Aleksander's sharp mind had been channelled solely into the business of manipulating and deceiving others, as a result of which he had eventually come to despise his fellow human beings. Exploiting, then breaking and discarding, others had been easy and he had become used to his unchallenged success. So when a non-entity of a woman had succeeded in destroying his apparently invincible father, the basis of Aleksander's warped values had been severely shaken. For the first time in his life, he had identified another human as being an object to be hated and punished, rather than a thing to be used for his own ends.

The campaign to make Susan Stonehouse suffer had kept his brother Egzon amused but in the end Aleksander had always intended to kill the woman. He had just wanted her to be made truly miserable first. The death of her husband had been a fortuitous addition to the trauma under which his victim had struggled. But Aleksander had always thought that the woman was too tough to take her own life. No-one who had had the courage to stand up in a public court and condemn his terrifying father could be so weak as to throw themselves under a train when life became difficult. That was what cowards did, and even Aleksander recognised that Susan Stonehouse was no coward. He had almost admired the way she had stood up to his father in the courtroom, openly disparaging the flimsy defence he had told his lawyer to put forward and speaking to him with a level of contempt that no-one had ever dared to display to the vicious old man.

Aleksander could well believe that Susan Stonehouse had tricked them all, that she was still alive and that she was here at Cheltenham racecourse today, ready to taunt him. The cokehead kid had tried to warn Aleksander that he might be walking into a trap. Aleksander was absolutely certain that the little rat had been right. It was a trap he was happy to walk into, and he would get out of it alive. Susan Stonehouse would not.

Before and during the Gold Cup race, Aleksander had studied the various groups of people who had been standing in the grassed area in the centre of the parade ring. It had not taken long for him to identify James Sampfield Peveril, who had been standing alone on the lawn until he was joined by the jockey wearing the purple and gold colours which had been depicted in the racing paper which Aleksander had brought with him. Susan Stonehouse's horse had been led round the parade ring by an attractive blonde girl, who had then gone out onto the course with the horse and jockey, leaving James Sampfield Peveril alone once again. But very soon after, a smart young couple had joined him, unexpectedly, it seemed to Aleksander. Then three more people had arrived, a tall man wearing a hat and a dark coat, and two women, one small and sombrely dressed and the other tall and wearing showy furs. The young woman from the first couple had greeted them as if she knew them well.

Was Susan Stonehouse among the group, Aleksander asked himself. There were only three women present, and two of them were certainly too young to be her. This left the third woman, the smaller one who had arrived with the tall man. Aleksander cast his mind back to the scene in the courtroom over a year ago. He remembered a thin, ravaged and angry woman in her fifties who could barely stand up straight in the witness box. The older woman in the Sampfield Peveril man's group was certainly slightly built, like her, but she seemed younger and stronger looking. It was hard for Aleksander to see her, as his view of her was blocked by the taller figures around her.

As the horse race began, Aleksander considered other options for Susan Stonehouse's whereabouts. Owners of racehorses of this calibre were unlikely to be found amongst the general crowds of racegoers. If they were not watching from the parade ring, they would be in some expensive box or club facility up in the grandstands. But if the horse they owned were to win, then they would need to come to the winners' enclosure to collect the prize.

Aleksander recalled to his mind the betting odds which had been displayed on the screen above the parade ring. Susan Stonehouse's horse had been the fourth favourite. So it was not expected to win. But, Aleksander noted, there were places marked out for the first four horses, their respective locations shown by numbered posts spread along the external rail of the winners' enclosure. This meant that there was a good chance that Tabikat might be in that enclosure after the race. And then Susan Stonehouse might show herself.

Quickly touching the Glock pistol neatly concealed against the small of his back, Aleksander moved down the steps toward the side of the winners' enclosure which was marked with signposts showing the numbers 3 and 4. He had to hope that the bookmakers had got it right. In his experience, they were accurate more often than not.

*

As Lady Helen Garratt watched Tabikat, with Merlin working like a demon on his back, cross the finishing line, she was at last able to stop cheering and draw breath. The whole of the Garratt box was by now in a state of nervous exhaustion and many guests quickly decided that more champagne should be opened. But most of them first came up to Eoghan and Caitlin to shake them by the hand and congratulate them on Tabikat's performance.

"Tell Sam to bring him back next year, so we can see him win," said Helen's husband, John, "I am sure you are very proud of that horse."

As Merlin was joining in the back thumping being meted out to Aidan Scanlon by his fellow jockeys, Helen grabbed Eoghan by the arm.

"Come on," she said, "Let's get down to the parade ring to see Tabikat and say well done to the team."

Notwithstanding his damaged knee, Eoghan was still a quick mover, and he and Caitlin were soon hurrying down the stairs of the grandstand to emerge into the main terrace above the parade ring. Much of the crowd was still at the front of the grandstand cheering the horses returning along the horsewalk whilst waiting for Aidan Scanlon and Macalantern to finish the interview with the excited TV presenter at the top of the run in. But a good number of people also accompanied Helen and her two guests across the terrace and onto the steppings above the winners' enclosure. Helen marched boldly down the concrete structure and stopped by the wooden post with the number three attached to it. Eoghan and Caitlin, smaller and less forceful than Helen, pushed and slid their way between the gathering spectators and soon came to stand by her side. None of them noticed a small, dark man in a grey suit standing nearby, who looked at them with sudden interest.

Sam, from his position in the centre of the parade ring, could see the first of the returning horses approaching under the bridge from the horsewalk. The noise of the crowd swelled and increased as the horses moved nearer. The unplaced horses disappeared off to a paddock at the side of the parade ring, their jockeys and connections disappointed, but glad to have the horses back safe. They would have to believe that there would be other days for them.

Sam eventually spotted the gold star on the silk of Merlin's helmet as he and Tabikat entered the parade ring, Sadie walking proudly alongside Tabikat's handsome head. The horse looked tired, but surprisingly bright, thought Sam. TK and Stevie rushed forward immediately to pat Tabikat and to shout well done to Merlin, who had a broad smile on his usually unexpressive face.

"And you won Best Turned Out as well!" Stevie added excitedly to Sadie.

Sadie was not sure she was entirely pleased to see Stevie Stone after what had been said on the Racing Tips for Smart Girls vlog earlier in the week, but she felt too triumphant to be cross with anyone just now.

Tabikat's newly found connections followed him to the third place spot in the winners' enclosure, where Merlin jumped down, unfastened the girth and started to remove the saddle.

"Well done, Sam," called Helen from the other side of the white railings, "And well done Merlin and Sadie too!"

Merlin looked questioningly at Sam.

"Lady Helen Garratt," Sam told him, "She's a friend of mine. She's been looking after the Foleys today."

"Thank you, Lady 'elen," Merlin called out, cheerily, "I 'ope you enjoyed watchin' the race, Mr Foley" he added in the direction of Eoghan, "And Mrs Foley too."

"Look, you gave him a fine ride," Eoghan called back to him, "And your girlfriend there had him turned out like a lord."

Merlin was about to say that Sadie was not his girlfriend, but he was suddenly conscious of her standing behind him, holding a bucket of water under Tabikat's nose.

"Did you 'ear what Mr Foley said about your work?" he asked Sadie.

Sadie looked up, avoiding Merlin's eye.

"Yes, I heard. Thank you, Mr Foley," she said, giving him her brightest smile, before turning away to put a sweat sheet over Tabikat's steaming back and to move him around in a small circle to help the horse cool off.

Merlin suddenly felt as if the bottom had dropped out of his stomach and he swallowed hard. This girl was one in a million, he thought. Not only was she attractive and a great horsewoman, not to mention hardworking and loyal to Mr Sampfield, but she had cheerfully done everything she could to keep him, Merlin, happy in his selfish demands on her, and had never once asked anything back for herself. Even his sister had said she was too good for him. Why could he not acknowledge that she was his girlfriend? He didn't know.

Merlin became aware that Caitlin was now speaking to him,

"And the pair of you would be welcome at Enda's Farm if you ever have time for a holiday," she said, fixing her disconcertingly direct gaze on Merlin.

"Thanks, Mrs Foley," replied Merlin, "I'll speak to Sadie."

"That would be a grand idea indeed," replied Caitlin, continuing to look him full in the eye until Merlin was forced to turn his head away.

As Merlin went off to weigh in, Helen, Eoghan and Caitlin were joined by an ever growing crush of people waiting to greet the winner. Sam and his party stood back to watch as Macalantern, with Aidan Scanlon standing in the irons and punching the air, made a regal progress, accompanied by triumphant music booming from the loudspeakers, towards the winner's position in the ring. The noise of the cheering spectators and the blaring music blotted out every other sound until Tabikat's supporting party could hardly hear themselves speak.

Sam, more pleased than he could say with the result of the race and watching the excited Irish connections of Macalantern surrounding their victorious horse, was anxious not to lose the opportunity to speak to the people who had so unexpectedly arrived to support Tabikat. Their arrival so soon before the start of the race had prevented any conversation taking place between them, whilst the present deafening racket in the winners' enclosure was hardly any more conducive to starting a discussion.

George Harvey and Isabella Hall had followed Tabikat into the winners' enclosure and were standing silently nearby watching Macalantern being welcomed by his connections. Stevie Stone and

TK were fussing over Tabikat, and asking questions of Sadie, while Daniel Levy stood rather stiffly nearby, smiling but seemingly unsure what to do. Sam did not want any of them to disappear as unexpectedly as they had arrived, and tried to decide what he could do to prevent it.

*

Aleksander Paloka had studied the actions of the people associated with the horse in the third place spot in the winners' enclosure. His plan to be in the right place to observe them at close quarters had succeeded very well, and he had even been able to pick up some of what they had been saying to each other until the noise of the crowd around him had become too overpowering.

Aleksander had noted the arrival of the three additional people who had spoken to the trainer and the jockey from behind the rails. He had deduced that they had come down from the grandstand, much as he had anticipated. The pushy woman who had cleared the way down the steppings was certainly not Susan Stonehouse. She had been too tall and was clearly a friend of the over privileged trainer, whom, he noted, she had addressed as Sam. The older couple who had followed her down the steps had been speaking to each other in a language which Aleksander had not recognised, but had switched to English when speaking to the jockey who had been riding Susan Stonehouse's horse. These two new arrivals were clearly a couple and what little of the conversation between the jockey and the man Aleksander had been able to hear did not suggest that either of the couple was the horse's owner. With her greying, dark hair and dangling gold earrings, to Aleksander this woman had looked more like a Roma than an Englishwoman.

No, Aleksander decided, if Susan Stonehouse was indeed here by the parade ring, the most likely person to be her was the small woman standing behind the horse alongside the man in the dark coat. Aleksander had so far had difficulty seeing her face, but now that she was closer, he was able to get a better look. As he peered at her, the woman suddenly turned towards him and stared him full in the face. Her expression was fixed and emotionless, and the glare from her brown eyes penetrating. The eye contact lasted only a second or two before the woman turned away, apparently disinterested in him, but the expression in her eyes had sent a shock of recognition through Aleksander. He had seen those eyes looking at his father in the British courtroom.

It's her, he breathed. Susan Stonehouse. At last.

Inwardly congratulating himself on his success, and realising that the group of people would soon be moving away from him to leave the winners' enclosure, Aleksander tried to get one last look at the woman he was now sure was Susan Stonehouse, aiming to imprint her new image onto his mind.

It was then that he realised that the tall man in the black coat was staring straight at him.

*

At last, to Sam's relief, Less Than Ross, Tabikat and Harry Me Home were able to leave the winners' enclosure. Sam held up his hand in farewell to Helen, Eoghan and Caitlin, who seemed destined to be pinned against the parade ring rails by the crowd for some time to come, and gestured to his little group to follow him, Sadie walking purposefully along the path with Tabikat towards the exit. A large number of horses due to run in the next race were already being brought into the parade ring.

As soon as we can find somewhere quieter, Sam thought, determinedly, I shall see what they all have to say for themselves, especially Isabella Hall.

As Sam passed the weighing room, the same TV commentator once again stepped forward and barred his way.

"Congratulations, Sam," he said, "Are you pleased with Tabikat's run today? And will he be going to Aintree? Or Punchestown?"

The little party accompanying Sam came to a reluctant halt as Sam stood still to answer the interviewer's questions.

"Yes, we are all very pleased with the horse," he said, gesturing to the group behind him, "I will have to talk to the owners about where he goes next."

The smooth and usually well-prepared TV commentator seemed for the first time to become aware of the people standing behind Sam.

"The horse has a new owner, I understand?" he asked, glancing at the assembled group, as if hoping that one of them would step forward. He clearly recognised Stevie Stone, but the other members were unfamiliar to him. But everyone remained unhelpfully silent.

"Yes," said Sam, pointedly, more for the benefit of the accompanying party than anyone else, "The owner can't be here with us today, I regret to say."

Fortunately for Sam, the interviewer spied more interesting quarry in the form of Less Than Ross's owner approaching them along the path, thereby allowing Sam and the other connections to escape any further unanswerable questions.

Sam's half-formed plan to invite his group to the Owners and Trainers bar was unexpectedly thwarted by Danny Levy, who touched him on the arm.

"I am sorry Mr Sampfield Peveril," the young man said, "But TK and I will have to leave you now. I have to fly out to Australia tomorrow and I need to return the helicopter to Kemscott Park airfield. TK's .. er.. car is there too."

Sam had not until then grasped the implications of Daniel Levy's earlier comment about having had to run up from the helicopter landing area, and could only nod his head in response.

"I hope we can meet again soon," was all he managed to say.

TK started to protest and then suddenly stopped speaking

"You always were a bloody tyrant, Danny," she said with a little snort which sounded almost like laughter.

Stevie Stone told Sam that she had to get back to work.

"Tabby Cat's got a heart-breaking announcement to make to the smart girls," she said, somewhat to Sam's bemusement, "But Jayce told them all to put an each way bet on Tabikat, which means our lovely audience should be feeling pleased with us. Let's hope they keep watching now that Merlin's out of the boyfriend market. Next stop for Tabby Cat and Jayce, it's the Grand National."

Outmanoeuvred once again, Sam had no option but to stand by helplessly as his guests hugged and kissed one another, until he was finally left in the rapidly filling parade ring with George Harvey and Isabella Hall.

"We owe you an explanation, Mr Sampfield," said Isabella Hall. It was the first time she had spoken.

"Yes, Isabella, you do," Sam replied.

46

It was the recognition that, not only had he been observed and recognised, but openly challenged, which added a new and urgent dimension to Aleksander Paloka's thinking. Whilst he had had no illusions that he might be walking into some kind of trap set for him by Susan Stonehouse, he had not expected the trap to be sprung right into his face.

The man and woman who had been in the parade ring with Susan Stonehouse's racehorse had been looking directly at him. The woman had held his gaze quite deliberately, and for just long enough to enable him to recognise her. But the man's gaze had been different. He had been issuing Aleksander with a challenge. I know who you are, that look had said, and I am keeping you in my sights.

Aleksander's original plan had been to locate Susan Stonehouse covertly at the racecourse and to ensure that she was followed when she left. Once he had found out where she was hiding, he would decide how best to torment and dispose of her at his leisure. But it now seemed that he might not get that chance. Susan Stonehouse had clearly brought him to the Cheltenham racecourse in order to confront him. Aleksander saw now that he was as much the target as she was. But she would not waste time trying to make his life a misery before she killed him. His father had been killed within a few days of entering the prison to which he had been sent to serve his sentence. There had been no threats or intimidation. None had been necessary. The murder had simply been carried out. His father had been completely at Susan Stonehouse's mercy.

Crushed by the crowds watching the presentation of the rather understated Gold Cup to the exuberant connections of Macalantern, Aleksander quickly reviewed the events at the trial of his father. What story was it that Konstantin had told his lawyer to present as his defence? The lawyer had said that the sister of Susan Stonehouse's husband, Peter, had been killed by contaminated drugs supplied through the Paloka controlled trafficking routes; that Peter Stonehouse had not arrived by chance at the remote building in which Konstantin Paloka and his associates had been beating up the little toe rag drug dealer; and that Peter Stonehouse had come armed to the remote airfield for the specific purpose of killing Konstantin Paloka. Peter Stonehouse had not appeared at the trial because he was in a coma as a result of serious head injuries. And Susan Stonehouse had been accused of disposing of his gun.

Aleksander did not know what Peter Stonehouse looked like. He had never seen a picture of him. All he could recall from the trial was that Peter Stonehouse owned a technology company. A cold feeling suddenly began to creep through Aleksander's perverted heart. Although the little cokebrain had tracked down the source of the fatal cyber attack on Egzon's well protected IT systems, the perpetrator who had planned and executed the attack had not been identified. The name of Susan Stonehouse had emerged from Egzon's online attempts to find out what had really happened to her. The person who had put the information out there to be discovered had clearly been telling Egzon that he had challenged Ezgon on his own ground and had comprehensively defeated and destroyed everything that Egzon had built so carefully. Was that same person now coming after Aleksander? Who had access to such expertise in cyber technology? Was it Peter Stonehouse?

Aleksander understood too late that the killers of his father and his brother now had him cornered and that they were ruthless. Although he was in a public place amongst a large crowd, he was vulnerable to anyone who had a knife like the one which had been used to kill his father. The same assassin who had wielded that knife could be here at the racecourse. A knife could be pushed very easily through his ribcage by any of the people standing around him and no-one would realise what had happened until it was too late. The spectators nearby were not looking at anything other than the horse racing events. And those who were not watching the horse racing were mostly drunk. The collapse of an unknown man in the crowd would not be recognised as a stabbing until it was far too late to save him.

Aleksander needed to get himself back outside the racecourse and into the protection of his bodyguards. Then he would be considerably less exposed to the attentions of any silent assassin. He slid his mobile phone from his pocket and pressed in a number.

The phone rang and rang but there was no answer. Aleksander began to realise that he was on his own.

*

Sam led the way to the Owners and Trainers' bar, George and Isabella following behind him. Finding a small table as far away as possible from the bar itself, the three of them sat down together, George leaning his stick against the side of his uncomfortable chair and placing his hat on the table alongside Sam's.

Sam said nothing, but sat with his hands on the table, looking at them both. He had already instructed Sadie to get Tabikat prepared for the journey home and had said that he would meet her and Kye by the stables as soon as they were ready to load him up.

"If you don't mind," George Harvey began, "We will wait for Frank to join us. He should be here in a minute or two."

"I haven't much time," Sam said, firmly "I have to meet my staff at the horsebox within the next half an hour."

"If necessary, we will come with you, Mr Sampfield," Isabella told him, sensing correctly that Sam's patience with them was wearing thin.

As she spoke, the ping of an arriving text message could be heard from George's pocket. George took a phone out of his pocket and scanned the screen. His face seemed to drain of colour.

"What is it?" asked Isabella, grabbing his arm in alarm.

"Frank says they've lost him," George told her.

Isabella's hand went to her mouth and she gripped the edge of the table.

495

"Who has been lost?" asked Sam, alerted by the mention of Frank's name.

"The man who has come here to kill Isabella," George told him, flatly.

*

Aleksander had not prospered in the vile world in which he operated by not minding his back. But he had become accustomed to having protection to help him do so. Now that he had none, he had to think for himself.

Pushing his way up the steppings, head down and shielding himself from view as best he could amongst the now dispersing crowds, his first thought was that he needed to leave the racecourse unrecognised and hence unobserved. Hiding amongst a milling crowd was his best option, but no doubt any watcher would be looking for a dark haired man in a grey suit. He needed a change of clothes.

Aleksander looked around. The weird thick green fabric which seemed to be favoured by many of the racegoers was one option, particularly since the outfit appeared to include a cap which could hide his hair. But short of making an owner give up his clothing by force, it seemed unlikely that he could lay his hands on such an outfit. A second option was the red jacket worn by the racecourse staff, many of whom he had noticed outside and inside the racecourse premises, but the staff concerned no doubt knew each other and would recognise a stranger amongst their number. The best option appeared to be an overcoat and a fedora hat, which, if he could get them, could be easily put on over his existing clothing. Aleksander decided to go up into the main grandstand. Galleries ran along the back of the grandstand passing the entrances to the bars and dining areas, from which he could see that numerous individuals had spilled outside, most of them holding glasses of beer and champagne. These people were chattering, laughing, and probably drunk, thought Aleksander. Coats and hats might well have been left inside, easy pickings for someone like himself.

The first bar yielded nothing of any use, but the second bar included dining tables at which various paraphernalia appeared to have been temporarily abandoned whilst the owners socialised over drinks or puffed on cigarettes outside. Walking casually through the room, Aleksander picked up a brown hat. In the next dining area, he removed a large black coat from a peg. Moving carefully along the gallery and down a flight of blue carpeted stairs, he shrugged on the thick coat and clamped the over-large hat onto his head. Awaiting his moment, Aleksander emerged from the door at the bottom of the staircase and inserted himself into the moving press of people outside.

Slowly, and with his head down, he made his way towards the racecourse entrance. He even threw the coins he found in the pocket of the coat into a green plastic charity collection bucket, which was thrust in his way as he walked. And soon he found himself outside the racecourse's main entrance once again. Most of the spectators were still inside the racecourse, wanting to see the remaining two races, but Aleksander judged that there were enough people around him still to provide adequate cover.

At that moment, the best course of action, as Aleksander was later to discover to his cost, would have been to call his driver and to leave the racecourse straightaway. Or, if the driver, like his bodyguards, had not answered, he could have simply walked down the road with the rest of the merry spectators and have readily summoned some other employees to drive him away to safety.

But Aleksander did neither of these things. And that was because, walking towards him along the strange black track which had been laid down for use of the horses, was Susan Stonehouse. The racehorse trainer was with her, as was the man who might or might not be Peter Stonehouse who had stared at him from the winners' enclosure. There was now also a third man with them, whom Aleksander had not seen before.

Aleksander still had his familiar Glock pistol. And he was sure that none of them had seen him.

"We're pretty sure he's still in the racecourse," Frank had told George and Isabella, when he had arrived in the Owners and Trainers' bar.

"For God's sake, Frank," George had said, "How could you have lost him like that?"

"He's not a fool, George," Frank had answered, "But neither are we."

Sam had continued to sit silently through this exchange, having maintained his resolve to keep the promise he had made to himself in the parade ring. He was going to let these people get on with whatever they were doing and not try to understand it any more. He had his own life to think about.

"If you will excuse me," he said, standing up, "I have to see to the loading of Tabikat. And I have two house guests to collect and drive back to Sampfield Grange."

Frank looked at him for the first time.

"We'll go with you, Sam," he said, "We three are Isabella's best protection at the moment."

*

Aleksander turned his face aside as Susan Stonehouse and her companions passed the racecourse entrance. He watched them carefully as they approached the red brick buildings which seemed to be where the racehorses were kept before and after their races. Horseboxes were moving about in the nearby parking area, being positioned to receive the horses which were being made ready to leave the racecourse.

Susan Stonehouse and her companions were standing alongside a small fence which ran beside the access road into the racecourse. A green horsebox was being slowly reversed towards where they were standing. Aleksander lifted the side of the black coat which covered his suit and reached into the small of his back for the Glock pistol. If he could time things right, he thought, he could shoot Susan Stonehouse and duck back amongst the crowds emerging from the racecourse, his gun concealed in the deep pockets of the stolen coat, and simply walk away. It was a risk, but the position of the horsebox was such that he calculated that he could carry it off. He remained waiting by the red brick wall, watching the group, as the reversing horsebox gradually hid them from his sight. A young man jumped down from the driver's seat and walked around the front of the vehicle to join the people waiting on the passenger side.

The positioning of the horsebox created a problem for Aleksander. It prevented him from getting a clear shot at his target. On the other hand, it enabled him to approach closer without being seen. So, he crept forward, the gun in his right hand, which was covered by the coat's capacious pocket.

The base of the horse lorry was relatively high above the ground. Aleksander was a small man and it was easy for him to crouch down low beside it. Looking under the vehicle, he could see the smartly pressed trousers of the racehorse trainer, the end of the walking stick carried by the man he was now sure must be Peter Stonehouse, and the smaller black booted feet of Susan Stonehouse. The other man seemed to be standing further back, his brown brogues suggesting that he had turned away from the others.

As Aleksander watched and waited, he became aware of more people approaching the horsebox. They too appeared to be on the far side of the vehicle. He heard two voices speaking in the same unfamiliar language which he had heard on the steppings by the winners' enclosure. He pushed himself slightly further underneath the lorry in case they should see him.

A crunching sound by his left side made Aleksander start. Someone operating from the other side of the vehicle had let down the loading ramp. He heard the people on the other side speaking. They appeared to be referring to the horse, the name of which he remembered was

Tabikat. Looking to his left, Aleksander saw that the horse itself was approaching, led forward by the blonde girl he had seen in the parade ring. Aleksander expected that she was about to take the horse up the ramp into the back of the horse lorry.

Aleksander saw his chance. The horse would provide ideal cover for what he needed to do. Susan Stonehouse and her friends were moving about talking the other side of the ramp. He knew that if he raised his head and hand above the ramp he would be able to get a clean shot at her. The man would have to wait until another day, as Aleksander was now resolved to kill him too. But today was not the time. Let him suffer first by seeing his wife die before his eyes, Aleksander thought savagely.

The blonde girl was leading the horse from its left side, so the horse was moving forward in between Aleksander and her, and she would not see him. This meant that he could get a clean shot at Susan Stonehouse, who he would be able to see clearly under the horse's body. The horse would take fright at the sound of the gun, the girl would be pushed aside, the people would be running to grab the horse and attend to Susan Stonehouse lying on the ground. In the ensuing chaos, Aleksander would slip back from the horsebox and merge into the now increasing numbers of people emerging from the racecourse. He still had the disguise of the long coat and the brimmed hat to keep him safe. He fastened the buttons of the coat and watched as the horse approached the ramp and started to walk up it. As the horse came level with him, Aleksander moved out from under the side of the ramp and lifted his head above its ribbed surface. The gun was pointed directly at Susan Stonehouse's face.

The huge crash made everyone jump back. Tabikat's hooves clattered across the surface of the lorry ramp as he reared up and struck out with his front legs. A frantic whinny came from his open mouth.

Sadie tugged at the lead rope as she tried to control her equine charge.

"Tabsi, Tabsi, calm down, what's the matter with you?" she said, shocked by his sudden erratic behaviour, "You're always an angel to load. Have all these people got you upset?"

Tabikat settled down almost instantly, snorted a couple of times, and then marched into the box as though his work had been completed.

And so it had. Tabikat had kicked Aleksander Paloka in the head.

Aleksander had never known pain like this. Deep shadows gathered across his vision, as he fought to stop himself blacking out. His heart seemed to be thumping in his brain, as if blood was being pumped up through his eyes and ears. His nose felt as if it had been smashed into pieces and he could feel the taste of iron in his mouth. He slumped back onto the ground by the lorry and crawled underneath. He had not fired the gun. The horse had seen him first.

As he surged in and out of consciousness, Aleksander was aware of the sound of the horse's hooves in the vehicle above him. Some time later, he was not sure how long, he heard the ramp being lifted and fastened. He knew that he would have to get away from the lorry, otherwise he would be seen when it moved away. He tried to get onto all fours.

But Aleksander could not move. Something was holding him, as if by the scruff of the neck. He tried to move his head but the pain overwhelmed him and he blacked out once again.

The young man climbed back into the horsebox and started the engine. As he drove the lorry away, Aleksander was dragged along beneath it, his coat collar hooked firmly in Kye's chassis mod.

*

Kye had not expected to find himself in the horsebox with Mrs Foley. He had been anticipating the drive home from the races as being in the more usual company of Sadie, but it seemed that Mrs Foley and Sadie had agreed a change of plan. As he had jumped down from the cab of the lorry, and come to join Mr Sampfield's party, which he noted now included Mr Stanley, as well as Isabella

Hall and her male friend, whom he had already seen in the parade ring, a small lady with an Irish voice had been speaking to Mr Sampfield.

"I am sure that you and Genie will have a lot to discuss on the journey," the Irish lady was telling Mr Sampfield, "So I will ride with the lad in the van. Your lovely girl groom can go and spend some time with that jockey of hers, which will do both of them a power of good. I have no doubt he will bring her home to you by tomorrow morning."

Mr Sampfield had not seemed inclined to argue with the forceful Irish lady, who indeed had been very determined to have her own way. So, once Tabikat had been loaded, having misbehaved on the ramp for the first time in anyone's experience, the small lady had climbed up into the cab beside Kye as though this was something she did every day of her life. Which indeed she did, as Kye discovered when he had politely asked who she was.

Kye soon had the lorry on the access road and round the small roundabout in front of the racecourse. The last race of the day was now in progress at the course, so, whilst large numbers of people were still inside, hardly wanting to believe that the famous Festival was over for another year, many spectators and vehicles were already making their way from the course.

Although the Irish lady seemed to Kye rather eccentric, telling him that she was not in fact Mrs Foley, but happy to answer to the name if it made Kye feel more comfortable, Kye found her an entertaining companion who asked him about his plans for his career as a jockey. Kye was chatting happily to her as he manoeuvred the lorry along Princess Elizabeth Way towards the Benhall roundabout when what felt like a thunderbolt suddenly struck him in the chest.

Down underneath the lorry was the last consignment of Gray's supply of drugs. Secreted in the metal box held in the chassis mod, these drugs could still threaten his hard won freedom from his criminal past. If anyone were to find them, the chance he had been given by Mr Stanley would be gone.

Sweat trickling down his face, Kye pulled the horsebox into a lay by on the dual carriageway which led past the famous GCHQ building towards the M5. Telling Mrs Foley that he had heard a mechanical sound which had worried him and that he needed to check that the ramp was properly locked in place, Kye jumped down onto the road and reached quickly under the horsebox. Twisting the hook which held the forward end of the metal container in place, he wrenched it out of its moorings and ran around the back of the vehicle towards the hedgerow at the side. Frantically emptying the box of its contents, he tossed the little bags and packets into the undergrowth and kicked loose earth over them as best he could without drawing attention to himself. The lorry shielded him from the passing traffic and he tried his best ensure that he was too far back for Mrs Foley to see him through the cab window. If anyone spotted him, Kye hoped they would think he had been caught short and was relieving himself in the bushes.

Climbing back into the cab, he put the metal box on the floor behind his seat.

"Just something which had come loose," he said vaguely to Caitlin, as he started the lorry, "We can go home now."

*

Kye's action in twisting the hook under the lorry to remove the box of illegal merchandise had had another effect. It had also served to release the collar of the black coat which had been holding Aleksander underneath the lorry. Aleksander had known little of the journey he had undertaken beneath the vehicle, as his brain had begun to swell beneath the depressed fracture of the skull caused by the blow from Tabikat's hoof. In addition, the thick black overcoat had ridden up around his throat, pressing onto his trachea and preventing him from breathing. The back of the thick coat had slid awkwardly along the surface of the road, slowly wearing thinner as the journey progressed.

Aleksander's hat and shoes had long gone, his socks worn to nothing as his feet dragged along the road, the skin of his ankles rubbed

503

away. His suit trousers were shredded and the skin of his calves had become as raw as hammered steak. Aleksander's semi conscious state had protected him from the worst of the pain, but, as he was suddenly dropped onto the cold road, his senses slowly returned and he found that he was in agony. He screamed, but the roar of the lorry as it departed above his head blotted out the sound.

With what was left of his functioning brain, Aleksander worked out that he was on a road. He could see a hedge nearby. If he could get across to that hedge, he thought confusedly, I can call my driver and he can come for me. Edging and crawling across the small pathway, Aleksander reached the hedge and rolled down the little bramble strewn slope beyond.

Aleksander was no longer sure whether he had already called his driver. But there was no hurry, he thought. The terrible pain in his legs and feet seemed to be receding, and he felt suddenly very tired. Slowly, he fell asleep.

As Sadie watched Merlin's last ride cross the finishing line in the final race of the Cheltenham Festival, Sam was listening with keen interest to Eoghan's account of the horses he bred at Enda's Farm. Kye was telling Caitlin about his mother and sister in Liverpool, and Frank Stanley's team were futilely scanning the moving crowds of noisy spectators now starting to leave the racecourse in their thousands. And Stevie Stone and Tabby Cat were breaking the news to the smart girls about Merlin ap Rhys's new girlfriend.

Tabikat stood proudly and peacefully in the horsebox on his way back to Sampfield Grange.

Epilogue

On a breezy morning in late April, when fluffy white clouds were being torn into scarf-shaped shreds against a washed out blue sky, old schoolfriends James Sampfield Peveril and Francis Stanley were once again sitting in the Sampfield Grange Music Room. The little statuette of the wood nymph stared as usual through the leaded glass of the window, her gaze fixed on the paddock in which the new lambs had already grown plump and contented. A line of trees swished chaotically back and forth beyond the side of the puddled lane.

Frank's green four wheel drive vehicle had arrived in the yard an hour ago, although it had not on this occasion created the same amount of disruption as on its previous visit almost seven months ago. The second lot of horses had already come back in, and their work riders were devouring their welcome breakfast around the square table in the kitchen, their outer clothing and footwear discarded in the adjoining boot room. This time Frank Stanley had been expected.

Kye had seen Mr Stanley's vehicle making its way up the lane to the yard. He had sent the work riders on ahead to get their breakfast whilst he had ensured that the yard was tidy and secure. With Sadie away in Ireland, Mr Sampfield was relying on him to take charge for a while, and Kye was determined to ensure that nothing went wrong.

"No more escaping for yez," he had told the innocent looking Ranger Station, who had as usual been fiddling with the now reinforced lock on his stable door.

Kye was not sure whether or not to acknowledge Mr Stanley. The meeting between them was never to be mentioned, he knew, but he owed Mr Stanley a significant debt. Kye had already had one ride on Highlander Park in a conditional jockeys' race at Exeter racecourse, in which Highlander, although excited, had behaved much better and run into second place. So Kye had pushed his unruly dark hair away from his forehead and waited to see what Mr Stanley might say to him.

Emerging from his vehicle, which he had parked in the same place as before, Mr Stanley had treated Kye politely, but as if a stranger.

"Good morning," he had said, "Is Mr Sampfield up at the house?"

"Yes, sir," Kye had replied, "Shall I take yez up there?"

"Not necessary, thank you, I'll find my own way," Mr Stanley had replied, "I am sure you have your work to do."

Kye had followed Mr Stanley up to the big house after about five minutes to find Lewis and Kelly in a state of barely suppressed excitement.

"It's that Mr Stanley again," Kelly had told Kye conspiratorially, "Mr Sampfield's in the Music Room with him, like before, and they've asked Lewis to take in coffee for them again. I wonder if he's telling Mr Sampfield what happened to Isabella. I'm sure it was because of you scaring her that she left, you know, Kye. Maybe he's found somewhere else for her now, so he can keep on seeing her."

Kye shrugged.

"Who knows?" he said, "Anyway, I thought yez didn't like Isabella. Aren't yez pleased to see Bethany back?"

Lewis, meanwhile, was setting down the tray with the jug of coffee and cups on the Music Room table.

"Shall I pour it, Mr Sampfield?" he asked, hoping as before to prolong his stay and so pick up some strands of the conversation which he could relay back to Kelly. It was a shame that Sadie was in Ireland with that Welsh jockey, he thought, she'd have been interested too.

"We'll deal with it, thank you, Lewis," Mr Sampfield told him, to

Lewis's disappointment.

Once Sam had poured the coffee for the two of them, he returned to his chair and looked at his old school friend questioningly.

"Things didn't work out as you wanted, did they Frank?" he said.

"On the contrary," replied Frank, "They worked out better than we expected. We thought George would have to dispose of Aleksander Paloka but in the end the job was done for him."

Sam felt a shiver go through him at Frank's casual reference to the death of the vicious gangster whose mangled body had been found on the westbound carriageway of the A40 on the outskirts of Cheltenham on the day after the Festival.

"What happened there, then?" he asked, "It sounded from the reports as if someone had murdered him and dumped his body. One of his own people, maybe? A rival?"

"Best not ask, Sam," Frank counselled him, "The last of the Palokas is out of the picture now and we can get on with dismantling their vile empire. There's plenty of others waiting to move in on the territory to fill his place, so the job's far from finished yet."

"And Isabella Hall?" asked Sam, "Can you tell me anything more about her now? I assume she's safe?"

"Yes, she's safe enough," Frank told him, "And she asked me to thank you for what you did for her. She also told me to tell you that you should listen to Lady Helen Garratt's proposals."

"Helen's coming here to see me next week," Sam told him, "And I am certainly going to listen to her. Seeing how well Kye has done has made me think that there's a lot more I could do here to give youngsters like him the chance of a career with horses. I've been too insular in this place. If nothing else, this .. this .. business has made me realise that. Being handed a runner in the Gold Cup has made me start to think what we could achieve here."

"Where's Tabikat now?" asked Frank, pleased to hear such enthusiasm in Sam's voice.

"Gone to the Punchestown Festival," Sam told him, "Brendan Meaghan has him back now and Sadie's gone with the horse for a while. Brendan even let Merlin keep the ride, which was good of him. It's still not clear to me who owns that horse, you know, but that's Brendan's problem now."

"Will you be going to Ireland yourself?" asked Frank, curiously, wondering how far Sam was really going to come out of the self-created shell in which he seemed to have been living for most of his adult life.

"Not to Punchestown," replied Sam, "But I thought I'd go over to Gleannglas and take a look at some of Genie Foley's horses. Sadie and Merlin are going to come too and give me their thoughts. If we're going to take more horses, we're going to have to expand the operation at Sampfield Grange too."

Frank nodded, but before he could say anything more, Sam spoke again.

"Could I ask you two more questions, Frank?" he said, "And then I promise I will put all this behind me and not refer to it again."

"Very well," said Frank, cautiously, "What do you want to know?"

"Isabella Hall and George Harvey," said Sam, "Are they Susan and Peter Stonehouse?"

Frank drew a deep breath.

"Susan and Peter Stonehouse are dead, Sam," he said, flatly, "And we need them to stay that way. Isabella Hall and George Harvey have their own lives to lead now."

"I'm not sure that's really an answer," said Sam, slowly, "So I guess you are really telling me not to ask you about them again."

"You had a second question," Frank reminded him.

"Yes," said Sam, "I wondered – if you have the time - whether you might like to ride out with me?"

ABOUT THE AUTHOR

Harriet Redfern was born in the North of England but has spent most of her life living and working in London. Her longstanding passion for National Hunt racing was originally inspired by watching televised race meetings whilst doing the family ironing on winter Saturday afternoons. This entertaining distraction from the housework soon became a serious pastime as her children grew older, and included a brief, although rather unsuccessful, excursion into racehorse ownership. Harriet is also a qualified pilot and aircraft owner and can be found in the skies whenever the weather is good. Now retired from her career in the University world, Harriet lives and writes in Cheltenham.

Printed in Great Britain
by Amazon

58916931R00292